Praise for *A Quiet Kind of Thunder*

"A sweet romance . . . Hard to put down."
—**VOYA**

"A delightfully original love story. Recommend to readers who enjoyed John Green's *Turtles All the Way Down* or Whitney Gardner's *You're Welcome, Universe*."
—**BOOKLIST**

Praise for *Fragile Like Us*

"A shining, lyrical, and unflinching story about the bonds of friendship between young women."
—**MELINDA SALISBURY,** author of
The Sin Eater's Daughter

"Hard to put down . . . Recommended for fans of books by Morgan Matson and Sarah Dessen."
—**VOYA**

Praise for *Goodbye, Perfect*

★ "Nuanced, compelling, honest, and important."
—**KIRKUS REVIEWS,** starred review

Also by Sara Barnard

Fragile Like Us
Goodbye, Perfect

A Quiet Kind of Thunder

Sara Barnard

Simon Pulse

New York   London   Toronto   Sydney   New Delhi

SIMON PULSE

An imprint of Simon & Schuster Children's Publishing Division

1230 Avenue of the Americas, New York, New York 10020

First Simon Pulse paperback edition January 2019

Text copyright © 2018 by Sara Barnard

Cover design and illustration by Sarah Creech copyright © 2018 by Simon & Schuster, Inc.

Originally published in Great Britain in 2017 by Macmillan Children's Books

Also available in a Simon Pulse hardcover edition.

All rights reserved, including the right of reproduction in whole or in part in any form.

SIMON PULSE and colophon are registered trademarks of Simon & Schuster, Inc.

For information about special discounts for bulk purchases, please contact Simon & Schuster Special Sales at 1-866-506-1949 or business@simonandschuster.com.

The Simon & Schuster Speakers Bureau can bring authors to your live event.

For more information or to book an event contact the Simon & Schuster Speakers Bureau at 1-866-248-3049 or visit our website at www.simonspeakers.com.

Interior designed by Mike Rosamilia

The text of this book was set in Adobe Garamond Pro.

Manufactured in the United States of America

2 4 6 8 10 9 7 5 3

Library of Congress Control Number 2016961321

ISBN 978-1-5344-0241-6 (hc)

ISBN 978-1-5344-0242-3 (pbk)

ISBN 978-1-5344-0243-0 (eBook)

For the quiet ones

1

MILLIE GERDAVEY CHEATED ON HER BOYFRIEND AGAIN.

But it's okay. No one needs to know, right? And, no, she's not going to *tell* Jack (*"Obviously!"*), and she doesn't want to be with Leo ("That muppet?"). It was just a one-time thing. Again.

Imagine the scene where I found out this news. Millie is squashed up next to me on the bench, a tissue wedged in her fist, perhaps, already soaked with her tears and snot. She is all sobs and whispers.

"I'm so glad I have you to talk to," she says.

It's a nice scene, isn't it? Two friends sharing a secret on the first day of school. Kind of natural. What could be more normal than the heads of two girls bent together, whispering secrets, one in tears, one reassuring? Nothing.

But, oh. See that other girl sitting on the bench? The weedy thing whose shoulders are a little hunched? The one who has her hair in front of her face and a book in her lap that she's not actually reading?

Yeah. That's me. The two girls are nothing to do with me, and they are having this intensely private conversation in front of me as if I am entirely invisible.

At one point, the second girl, whose name is Jez, darts a look at me then says to Millie, "Um, do you think she heard?"

"Oh, her." Millie tosses her hair dismissively. "It's okay. She won't say anything."

"How do you know?" Jez asks, a little nervously.

"Watch this," Millie says, and my heart seizes. I grip the sides of my book a little harder. "Hey! Hey, Steffi!"

Go away. Go away go away go away.

"Steffiiiiii." Millie's voice has gone singsongy. "Steffi Bro-o-o-ns!" She elongates my last name so it somehow takes up four syllables. "See?" Her voice has suddenly returned to normal. "She's as dumb as a pane of glass."

At least I didn't cheat on my boyfriend, I would say, if I could. But it's probably a good thing that I can't at that moment, because it would be a pretty terrible retort. In order to be cheating on my boyfriend, I'd have to actually have one in the first place. And I very much do not.

"She could put it on the internet," Jez ventures.

Millie is suddenly leaning forward, her head looming closer to mine. "Brons, you won't put any of this on the internet, right?"

I have a sudden vision of myself sitting at my laptop, sending a tweet out into the ether, "**MILLIE GERDAVEY CHEATED ON JACK COLE #again #lol**" while I laugh maniacally.

"Brons." There is a poke at my shoulder and I jump. "Oh my God." I can hear the sneer in her voice. "Why are you so weird? It's literally me. Millie. Like, known you since we were both five?" It's true she's known me since I was five, but still she persists, so she clearly doesn't know me very well. "Remember? You peed in my paddling pool?"

That does it. My head snaps up and I glare at her. Words fizz up on my tongue, then dissolve into nothing.

She grins at me. "There you are! I know you won't say anything." She winks, and I want to smack her. She throws her head back to look at Jez again. "Steffi is a pal." As she stands up, she gives my shoulder a faux-friendly nudge. "See you later, pal."

When they've gone, I am finally, blissfully alone. I allow myself the quietest of mutters: "You peed in *my* pool, Millie."

And then I feel slightly better.

I'm in the common area outside Mr. Stafford's office because he's asked to see me before the first assembly of the new school year. I am expecting the usual start-of-school pep talk/introductions I've had to endure at Windham High for the last five years. I still haven't figured out whether they're meant to be for my benefit or theirs.

A few minutes after Millie and Jez leave, the door to Mr. Stafford's office opens and he strides through it, already beaming. I can only assume he practices the Stride & Beam in front of the mirror.

"Stefanie!" he says, his hand coming toward me. For one horrifying second I think he is going to use it to pull me chummily to my feet, but—thank God—he just wants to shake hands. *Thank God.* Calm down, Steffi.

I try to smile back. I start to say, "Good morning, sir," but the words die in my mouth halfway through "morning" when I realize Mr. Stafford isn't alone. Dammit. I was so proud of myself for mustering actual words in front of a teacher, already thinking it was a good sign for this year, the year I turn seventeen, the year I'm meant to show I can do basic things like talk in front of teachers. I want to go to university one day, and—according to my parents—I won't ever be able to do that if I can't even talk in school.

Mr. Stafford is still beaming. "Stefanie, this is Rhys." He gestures to the boy at his side, who is smiling at me.

What fresh hell is this? Now they're parading strangers in front of me to mock my inability to speak in front of them? I can feel a familiar choking panic start somewhere in my stomach. My cheeks are starting to flame.

I look at Mr. Stafford, knowing my expression is hovering somewhere between kicked puppy and Bambi.

"Oh," he says hastily. "Oh, it's okay. Rhys is deaf."

My eyebrows shoot up.

"Oh!" he says again, looking mortified. "I didn't mean . . . I meant it's okay for you to . . . I didn't mean it's okay to be . . . though of course there's nothing wrong with being . . ."

Rhys, standing slightly to the left of Mr. Stafford, is waiting patiently. He is still looking at me, but his smile has faded slightly and he looks a little confused. Who is this gormless girl? he is clearly thinking.

"Gosh," Mr. Stafford mutters. "What a start to the year. Let me try again. Rhys—" He claps a hand on Rhys's shoulder, then gestures to me. As he does so, he turns his head so he is looking directly into Rhys's face. "This is Stefanie," he says, loudly. "STEF-AN-EEE."

Oh dear Lord.

Rhys's face breaks into a warm, if slightly amused, grin. He looks at me, then raises his hand into a wave. **Hello.**

I wave back, automatically. **Hello.** I let my hands fall into the familiar patterns. **My name is Steffi.**

Nice to meet you. Rhys taps two fingers to his right ear. **Deaf?**

I shake my head, touching the tip of my finger first to my own ear and then to my mouth. **Hearing.** I hesitate, trying to figure out how to explain myself. I could fingerspell "selective mute," but he probably doesn't know what that means, and it's not really even accurate anymore. **I can't**— I begin, meaning to say that I can't talk, but that's not accurate either, because I *can*

5

talk, physically speaking. Oh God, both Rhys and Mr. Stafford are staring at me. I can feel my face flaming. I finally sign, a bit weakly, **I don't talk.** Which is the worst response ever.

But Rhys smiles, raising his eyebrows a little as if in appraisal, then nods, and I'm so relieved, I smile back.

"Wonderful," Mr. Stafford says, looking like he wants to pass out with relief. "Wonderful. Steffi, Rhys is starting at Windham today. I thought it would be a good idea to introduce the two of you. Rhys will have a communication support worker helping him out, of course, but I thought it would be nice for him to meet a fellow student who knows sign language. So he can feel more at home."

Oh, he looks *so* pleased with himself. It makes me want to both hug and slap him. I want to tell him that I only know the really basic stuff, but the ability to speak has completely deserted me right now, so I just lick my lips nervously and nod along. The whole this-is-the-year-I'll-speak-at-school thing is really not going very well so far.

"I suppose I'll have to learn some sign language too, won't I, Mr. Gold?" Mr. Stafford turns his head to Rhys only as he says the final bit of this sentence, clearly oblivious to the fact that Rhys will have completely missed all that came before it.

But still Rhys nods cheerfully, and I feel a sudden fondness for him. He must be all right if he lets Mr. Stafford act like such a well-meaning buffoon without making things awkward for him. I wish I could be more like that, but I make things

6

awkward for everyone. People just don't know what to do with someone who doesn't speak.

I'm curious about this new boy and my mind floods with questions. What brings you to Windham? What are you studying? Do you like green grapes or red grapes? Would you rather have hair that won't grow or a beard you can't shave? What's your favorite sign? But the thought of speaking these words out loud makes my stomach clench, and my BSL skills were always rudimentary at best. Apparently, with Rhys, I can be useless in two languages.

So I just carry on smiling nervously and wait for Mr. Stafford to fill the inevitable silence. He does, bless him. "Well, on to assembly, then, the two of you. Steffi, what's the sign for assembly?"

I'm about to obediently make the sign when a spark of mischief lights from nowhere in my mind. I turn to Rhys, keep my expression completely deadpan, then sign **Welcome to the hellmouth**. Rhys's whole face lights up into a surprised grin. Oh yeah, strange new boy. The silent girl is *funny*. Who knew?

"Excellent, excellent," Mr. Stafford says, oblivious. "Let's go, then." He Strides & Beams off down the corridor and I follow, perhaps slightly reluctantly, with Rhys at my side. We walk all the way to the hall in silence, but for once it's not because of me, silent, awkward Steffi. It's an expected silence. Comfortable. It's nice.

The hall is full of students sprawled on the floor and chairs, talking loudly and easily, as naturally as breathing. *Do they know how lucky they are?* I catch myself wondering. *Do they?* Of course not. It's probably the same thing someone with cystic fibrosis thinks about me. I guess taking normal for granted is part of being human.

"People, people," Mr. Stafford says, jovial. "This isn't your living room."

No one moves.

"Sit on the chairs!" Mr. Stafford orders, more sharply and with more than a little frustration in his voice. "That's what they're there for."

He walks to the front of the collection of chairs, gesturing to Rhys to follow him. I stand there for a second, dithering, then slide into a vacant seat and slouch down a little.

"Well, now that you're all settled," Mr. Stafford says pointedly, "let's begin the new year. Welcome to sixth form, everyone. And a particular welcome to the new faces joining Windham this year."

My stomach gives a little flip. Sixth form. The big change. I'd thought I was prepared, but it still feels so weird to be sitting here in this hall, on my own, without my best friend. It's the first time I've ever sat in a first-day-back assembly without her, and I feel a sudden pang, so sharp it almost makes me gasp. It's part panic, part loneliness.

"Come up to the front if you're one of those new faces," Mr. Stafford is saying.

I ease my phone out of my pocket and peek at the screen. Sure enough, there's a message waiting for me from Tem.

Tem:
How's it going?!
I almost miss those crappy halls ;) xxxxx

I grin down at the screen, flooded with affection and relief. Okay, so Tem isn't here with me. She's left Windham to go to further education college because she can do the sports therapy vocational course there that isn't available here, and that's fine. It's good. I'm happy for her, that's she's doing what she wants. It's going to be hard, though.

Steffi:
Crap. I miss you.
COME BACK!!!! xxxx

"Twelve new students!"

I glance up, taking in the slouching, affectedly disinterested teenagers now standing beside Mr Stafford. It's common for students to move around for the start of Year 12, so it's not a surprise that there are plenty of new students to replace the ones like Tem who've left to go down the more vocational road. Windham is one of the best schools in the county, and the sixth form has an especially good reputation. Still, twelve new students sounds like a lot to me. A lot of strangers, and not one that could replace Tem. That's because there's no one like Tem in the world.

Tem:
Just SAY THE WORD, Brons!
Go on. SAY IT. xxx

My eyes slide along the line of students until they snag at the face of the one person who is looking back at me. Rhys. When our eyes meet, he grins. I can't help it; I grin back.

Steffi:
DON'T MAKE MUTE JOKES
ON MY FIRST DAY ALONE AT
SCHOOL! You MONSTER! xxxx

Tem:
You are awesome. Your voice is like a flowing stream on a warm spring day. No one in the world is youer than you. Etc. SPEAK YOUR TRUTH, EVEN IF YOUR VOICE SHAKES!!!

Tem:
Actually, scrap that. Your voice is so awesome I just want to keep it to myself. DO NOT TALK, Steffi. That's an order.

I'm bent over my phone, smiling at the screen as if Tem is looking right back at me, when my skin starts to prickle. I look up slowly, preemptive dread already sliding down my back, and *everyone is looking at me*. Horror of horrors . . . *everyone*.

Panic explodes in my chest, sending sparks through my bloodstream, down my veins, into the tips of my fingers, electrifying my hair. I try very, very hard not to vomit.

"So just speak to Stefanie if you'd like to learn any BSL," Mr. Stafford, devil incarnate, is saying. And then he *points at me*. As if he expects me to stand up and give a speech. Shockingly, I do not.

Someone mutters, "*Speak* to Steffi?" and a low laugh ripples across the room.

"Or you could just talk to me," Rhys says. His voice is a surprise, thick and slightly drawled, like he's speaking with his mouth full. The volume is slightly off, a little too loud at the beginning and then fading toward the end. He grins. "I don't bite."

The faces that had been turned to me all jerk toward him, meerkatlike, when he speaks.

"This is hello," Rhys adds. He lifts his hand into the BSL wave of greeting. He puts a hand to his chest. "Rhys."

And to my total surprise almost everyone in the room lifts their hand in response. He has the whole hall saying hello to him and I am simultaneously impressed and jealous. And also, weirdly, a bit betrayed. *He* can talk? That's just not fair, is it?

"Wonderful," Mr. Stafford says. He looks thrilled. "Now that we have the introductions out of the way, let's get on to housekeeping matters." He claps his hands in a way that makes me think that's how he thinks heads of sixth form are supposed to behave. "The common room is open to you at all hours of the day, though we ask that you work to keep it clean and tidy. Any breakages will be paid for." He waits for a laugh, which doesn't come. "Your free periods are yours to spend as you please, though we do advise that you use them for studying."

I stop listening, my eyes sliding back to Rhys, who is watching Mr. Stafford's face intently as he speaks. Every time Mr. Stafford turns his head or moves out of Rhys's eyeline, I see him tense. It makes me want to run up to the front of the crowd and grab Mr. Stafford so I can yell, "Just keep your head still! Can't you see he's trying to *read*?"

But my name is Steffi Brons and I don't speak, let alone yell. I move slowly so people won't notice I'm there, because running in public is as loud as a shout. I like to wear jumpers with long sleeves that go right down over my wrists and hands and fingers. Meekness is my camouflage; silence is my force field.

So I don't.

The ten stupidest things people say to you
when you don't talk:

10) What if you were, like, dying or something?

9) What if *I* was dying?

8) Can you talk if you close your eyes?

7) Okay, but what if I close *my* eyes?

6) Cat got your tongue?

5) Just say something. Really, just anything, I don't care.

4) Is your voice really weird or something?

3) You should just have a glass of wine.

2) Just *relax*.

1) You're quiet!

2

HERE ARE THREE SEPARATE BUT SIMILAR THINGS:
shyness, introversion, and social anxiety. You can have one, two, or all three of these things simultaneously. A lot of the time people think they're all the same thing, but that's just not true. Extroverts can be shy, introverts can be bold, and a condition like anxiety can strike whatever kind of social animal you are.

Lots of people are shy. Shy is normal. A bit of anxiety is normal. Throw the two together, add some kind of brain-signal error—a NO ENTRY sign on the neural highway from my brain to my mouth, perhaps, though no one really knows—and you have me. Silent Steffi.

So what am I? I'm a natural introvert with severe social anxiety and a shyness that is basically pathological. When I was a kid, this manifested as a form of mutism, known as selective mutism. The "selective" part sometimes confuses people, because it makes it sound as if I had the control over when to "select" my speech, but that's not the case. Selective means it's out of my control. Progressive mutism is when your childhood mutism gets worse as you get older.

I don't have progressive mutism, for the record. I've been able to talk—with difficulty—in places like school for a few years now, though the difficulty is more to do with social anxiety and shyness than mutism. This is incredibly hard to explain to people, which is why I usually don't. "I couldn't talk but now I can, sometimes, but sometimes I can't. No, I don't know why, sorry" isn't really that illuminating, as far as explanations go. And people *really* like explanations.

They like explanations and recovery stories. They like watching *House* and knowing a solution is coming. They like to hear that people get uncomplicatedly better. They love the stories of childhood mutes who meet an incredible speech therapist and recover their voice by the end of an hour-long documentary. Kids like me, who struggle through their childhood years, juggling various diagnoses that try to explain their silence to their frustrated parents, who graduate from "mute" to "severe anxiety" but still can't speak to shop assistants or call anyone on the phone, just confuse things. Forever in the gray area, in the question you see behind the eyes of teachers and family friends: "Is she just putting it on?" "It's not a real thing, is it?" They say, "It's all in your head." They say, "It's not real." And I think, *What is more real than that?* I think, therefore I am, right?

15

So, no, I'm not putting it on and, yes, it is a real thing. It just happens to be a real thing that a lot of people haven't even heard of, let alone understand.

What are you thinking, Steffi? What are you thinking? Everything, all the time.

You're so quiet, Steffi. Why are you so quiet? But in my head it's so loud.

I'm sure everyone has an inner monologue, but I doubt many are as wordy as mine.

So here I am, sixteen and silent on my first day of sixth form. I make it to lunchtime without speaking to anyone, which makes me feel weak with relief at the time but then, sitting by myself at a picnic table, horribly depressed. It is clearly not normal to go four hours surrounded by peers without talking to any of them—and then feel happy about it.

Plus, there's the whole year-I-prove-myself thing. So far, I haven't.

I miss Tem.

No, don't blame this on missing Tem. If she was around, you still wouldn't have spoken to anyone else.

But—

I'm interrupted by the sudden appearance of a boy, who slides himself casually down onto the bench opposite me and throws me a lazy grin. **Hello.**

I stare at him. Rhys squints. There's a pause.

Hello?

I pull myself together, regain my sense of movement, and answer him. **Hi.** I resist the urge to ask him what he's doing sitting with me, because that seems a bit rude even though it's what I really want to know, and sign instead, **How's it going?**

Rhys beams at me, looking far more happy than my delayed reaction deserves. **Great, thanks. I think . . . school . . . bald teacher . . . computers . . . BSL . . . tennis.**

Oh God, this is hideous. I can feel a flush working its horrible way up my neck and across my face. I can't follow what he's signing. He's too fast; too good; too relaxed. I have no idea what he's saying to me. Why would he be talking about tennis, for God's sake? Come *on*, Steffi. You can do this.

Rhys's hands still and he smiles at me, expectant. The happy, hopeful expression on his face makes me feel awful. That's why he wanted to sit with me—because he could have a conversation without reading anyone's lips or worrying he was going to miss something vital. And I've ruined it for him.

I swallow down the bubble of panic that the expectation of conversation always produces in me—even, apparently, silent ones—and force myself to smile. He is not inside your head, I remind myself. He doesn't know you're such a mess. **Little slower?** I ask. I roll my eyes, gesturing to myself. **I'm rusty.**

He grins. **Hello, rusty.**

I laugh, so spontaneously and easily it surprises me. **Dad joke.** Rhys shrugs, still grinning, looking absurdly pleased that

17

he's made me laugh. His hands start to move again, careful and slower this time. I watch, trying to follow what he's saying. This time, I at least catch more of it, but it's still not anywhere near enough to carry a proper conversation.

Sorry. I feel tight with frustration. **It's been a long time.**

He flicks his hand in the universal "no worries" gesture, then digs into his bag and retrieves a notepad. Flipping it open, he scribbles for a few seconds, then spins it around to me. He writes in quick, brisk capital letters. It is the clearest boy hand-writing I've ever seen.

I THINK ALL SCHOOLS ARE THE SAME REALLY. DO YOU KNOW THE COMPUTING TEACHER? THE BALD ONE. HE'S MY FORM TUTOR TOO—HE KNOWS BSL! SO THAT'S ANOTHER PERSON I CAN TALK TO ☺

Nothing about tennis. I must be even rustier at BSL than I thought if I invented "tennis" and missed "person." I hesitate, trying to formulate a proper reply. It feels like when I had to sit my French oral exam last year and I had to just throw the right individual words together and hope they made some kind of sense as a sentence.

Here is what I mean: What school did you go to before? Yes, Mr. Green was my IT teacher for years. He's probably easier to talk to than me!

Here is what I sign. Probably. **School earlier? Yes, Mr. Green**

teacher computer ages. He signs better. Pause. **Sorry, I am crap.** Rhys is patient, and if he's amused or frustrated by me he doesn't show it. He signs slowly, returning to his notepad when it is clear I can't understand him. The two of us make a patchwork conversation, knitting together sentences with our hands and his pen. I am concentrating so hard I don't even notice the silence, usually so heavy around me. At no point does he say, This would be easier if you would just speak.

We establish the basics. Rhys wants to be a games developer and so plans to go to university to study computer science. You don't have to have a degree to be a games developer, he tells me—practical experience is more important—but his parents are insisting. **They don't think I'll actually make it in the games industry**, he explains, and though he rolls his eyes I can see that he's too fond of them to be irritated. **They want me to have a degree as a backup.**

We have just one subject in common—math—and I tell him that I want to study animal behavior. *If* I make it to university.

Why wouldn't you? he asks, confused.

I hesitate, then attempt to explain with my limited skills. **My parents don't want me to go. They don't think I can . . . manage.**

Manage what?

Thankfully, that's when the bell rings. Even if I could talk normally or we were communicating at the same ability, I'm still not

19

sure I could explain the whole thing about my parents and university and me. How it seems like they disagree about everything except my future, which, I'm sorry, shouldn't really be anything to do with them. How they seem to think that because I don't talk much, I won't be able to deal with university. How this is the year I have to prove to them I'll be able to handle it.

Rhys stands, gathering his books and crumpling up his empty sandwich wrapper. With one hand, he waves a good-bye.

I smile and mouth, *bye*, and it makes me feel nice to think that, as far as he knows, I said the word out loud.

"Bye, Stefanie," he says out loud, his voice husky, the words like confetti, light and soft in the wind between us.

"It's Steffi," I say, surprising myself.

He pretends to doff an imaginary cap at me, which makes me laugh. "Steffi," he repeats. He has the friendliest smile I've ever seen. He waves again, then turns to jog away.

My favorite sound in the world is the bell ringing at the end of the school day. That's as true now at sixteen as it was when I was eleven. I am out of my seat and heading to the door before the bell has even finished ringing.

"Did you get the chapters, Steffi?" Mrs. Baxter calls to me. She's been my teacher three times throughout my years at Windham, so I give her a thumbs-up rather than reply, knowing she won't mind.

As soon as I walk out of the school gates, I feel my shoulders untense, my muscles loosen, my bones relax. Oh, hello, freedom. Sweet, sweet, freedom.

And, best of all, "Hello there!"

Tem. My favorite person in the world, standing just outside the gates, balancing two Starbucks cups in one hand and holding a paper bag in the other. September Samatar, best of the best.

I open my mouth, but nothing comes out. The stress of the day has taken my voice away, and I know that there's nothing I can do but wait for it to come back right now. Tem grins at me, understanding, and gestures with her head down the road. I nod and we turn to start walking together.

"Nice outfit choice," she says, eyeing me sideways as we go. I am wearing dark jeans, a plain black T-shirt, and ankle boots. "I can see you're channelling the Background look. That's very on trend, I hear. A wonderful choice for the Don't-Look-At-Me crowd."

I can't help smiling, even as I reach out and flick one of her black curls. This is what Tem does. She fills my silences.

"I brought sweet treats," Tem continues as we approach the corner. A crowd of younger boys runs past us, jostling us both as we go.

"Oi oi, sexy!" one of them yells at Tem, thrusting his crotch at her. She bursts out laughing. The boy, momentarily devastated, rights himself, swaggers his shoulders, and runs off, flicking us both the finger as he goes.

"What a catch," Tem says, deadpan. "He's going to make

some girl very happy. For thirty seconds." She is wearing a black cotton dress with short sleeves and some kind of gold patchwork at the hem, beaded sandals on her feet, bangles on her wrist. I can see why a boy would call her sexy. I'd call her Temmish.

We cross the road and head right down one of the avenues, away from the school uniforms and noise, into the quiet.

"Oh my God," I say, and it feels so good. The sound of the words coming out of my mouth, the way my jaw moves, like it's getting exercise for the first time all day. I let out a breath and grin. "Hi, Tem."

She grins back, leans over, and kisses me on the cheek. "Hi, Steffi!"

Tem and I have been best friends since we were toddlers. This was basically decided for us by my mother, which is pretty much the best decision she's ever made, especially when it comes to me. Mum was working for the Refugee Council at the time, which is how she met Ebla, Tem's mother. When she found out that Ebla had a daughter the same age as me, she suggested we meet. And that was that.

Over the next few years—which included my parents' divorce and respective remarriages; my sudden, total silence; Clark's death; and so much else—we bonded so tightly we are like part of each other. Steftember, my dad used to call us. Through so much confusion and turmoil in our lives, we have always had each other.

"So tell me everything," Tem says, leading me into the children's playground—deserted as always—and taking her usual seat in the middle of the merry-go-round. She arranges the two Starbucks cups in front of her and opens the paper bag, pulling out some kind of cake and splitting it in two with her hands. She looks up and throws me a quick grin.

"Millie Gerdavey cheated on Jack Cole again," I say, taking a sip from my cup and smiling. She's delivered me a caramel mocha. Extra sugar, extra caffeine. She *must* be worried about me.

"Good for her," Tem says, shrugging. "Anything actually interesting?"

I laugh. Tem is basically immune to gossip, which is one of her best and worst traits.

"Okay, well, not really."

"Oh, no way!" Her face drops. "All these years waiting for the freedom of sixth form, and now you're telling me it's not actually interesting?"

"It's not. It's like the rest of school, except we don't have to wear uniforms. Which is a bonus, obviously. But still. Today was mainly intro stuff, anyway. Like, getting reading lists and schedules and stuff."

"How many words did you say today?"

I think about it. "Less than twenty, more than ten."

"Hmmm." Tem makes a face. "I guess that's okay for your first day without me. I thought it might be less. Or, like, none."

"I met a boy," I say.

She is instantly alert. I swear her whole body snaps to attention. "What?"

"I met a boy," I repeat, just to annoy her.

"Stefanie!" She flaps her hands at me. "Tell me everything. And I mean everything. Immediately. And—God—I hope some of those less-than-twenty-more-than-ten words were said to him."

"Actually, they weren't," I say, enjoying the opportunity to wind her up for once. "I was entirely silent. So was he." I consider, then add, "Almost."

She squints her face into a frown, like she's trying to see inside my head. Finally, suspiciously, she says, "But you *met* him?"

"He's deaf," I say, and her face unfolds.

"Oh." Understanding lights in her eyes. "Cool! So you were signing? That's so great, Steffi. I always thought you should've carried that on."

I ignore this, because the whole should-Steffi-sign-or-not issue was bad enough the first time round, and take a bite of the cake she's brought. It's some odd mix of doughnut and apple turnover, and it tastes like joy. "His name's Rhys," I say. "Mr. Stafford introduced us because I know some BSL."

"That makes sense. So? What's he like? You know I want the details."

"Nice," I say. "Friendly. Really friendly, actually."

"I meant visually," Tem says, waving her hand. "Obviously."

24

I smile. "Also nice to look at."

"Give me something to go on! Eyes? Hair? Teeth?"

"Brown eyes. Short hair. Very nice teeth." I think of Rhys, smiling at me from across the table. "And he's biracial, I think. His skin is like a light brown?"

"I like the sound of him," Tem says, nodding. "I approve."

I smile. "You don't need to approve anything. He's just a new guy at school."

"*Sure* he is," Tem says, drawling the words. "And you 'just' wanted to tell me about him. And describe him. And make those doe eyes."

"I wasn't making doe eyes!"

She raises one perfect eyebrow at me and takes a sip from her cup, a smirk on her face. "I think it should be your mission to kiss him. I'll give you until . . . your birthday."

I laugh, half amused, half panicked. "Tem, I literally just met him today. We're not even friends yet. Slow down."

"Why should I?" she asks, shaking her head. "Why wouldn't a handsome young fellow want to kiss you? That's the question you need to be asking yourself."

I open my mouth and her hand shoots out to cover it. "That was a rhetorical question, Brons. I wasn't asking for a list."

I wait till she removes her hand and answer her anyway. "Guys like to kiss girls who can talk."

"Um, so clearly not true. You've seen *The Little Mermaid*. There's a whole song about it."

I roll my eyes. "That song is about trying to *get* them to kiss, but they don't."

"Whatever." She waves her hand. "My point is you're obsessing way too much over a tiny little detail. So you don't talk much—who cares? You can talk with your hands." Her face lights up with a mischievous grin. "*Talk*. With your *hands*." She splays out her hands around her face and mimes kissing, eyes closed, mouth agape. This is presumably meant to represent some kind of kissing-related sign language from someone who has never spoken any sign language in their life.

"Oh, stop it," I say, laughing despite myself.

"Fine, fine. Hey, do you want to come for a run with me tonight?" she asks. She grins. "I promise I'll go slow."

"How slow?" I ask, suspicious.

Tem is a runner. Technically long distance, but she has a habit of lulling me into a false sense of security by jogging for thirty seconds and then sprinting off into the distance, just because she can.

"A jog," Tem promises. "You'll barely even sweat."

"As tempting as *that* is," I say (I am not a runner), "I can't. I'm at Dad's."

"Oh," she says. "That came around fast."

I smile. "The summer's over for me. I moved my stuff in last night."

Even though they are divorced and have both remarried since, my parents live in the same town, for my sake. This was an agreement they made years back so I could alternate living with them both but also not have to do anything annoying like move schools or get three buses in the morning. They live on opposite sides of town—Windham is pretty much in the middle, which is useful—and I move between them. In term time, I stay with Dad, and Mum gets me during the holidays.

The main downside to all this, at least during term time, is that Tem lives a two-minute walk from my mother and a ten-minute *drive* from my dad, so it's less easy for us to see each other.

"I can still come over to you," Tem suggests. "I don't mind."

I shake my head. "Maybe this weekend, but not tonight. I'm pretty tired and I promised Dad I'd make dinner."

She sighs. "*Fine*. But you're just missing out on my company."

"Call me tonight, okay?" I say. "It'll be just like I'm there."

She smirks. "Hearing your voice is weird enough, let alone if I can't see you at the same time."

I glare at her. "No mute jokes on my first day back! You promised!"

"No, I didn't. You asked and I made a joke about penguins."

I roll my eyes. "You're impossible."

"I'm *wonderful*." Tem throws open her arms and beams at me. She looks so ridiculous I have to laugh.

What I mean to say through all this is that however hard it is to be the girl who doesn't talk, the girl who dithers in the corner then shrugs a reply, I have Tem. And if there's only one person in the world I can talk to, I'll choose her every time.

The five worst times to be mute:

5) When you need the toilet.

I am six years old and Tem is off school with suspected mumps (it will turn out to be the flu). I navigate my silent day alone, without my trusty interpreter, who pays as much attention to my needs as she does her own. Everything is fine until I realize I need to pee. I cannot say so. I can't even lift my hand to gesture at the door. I sit, rigid, staring at my worksheet. I wet myself. "Ewwwwww!" the class screams in delight.

4) When you're bleeding.

I'm eight years old. We're on a school trip at a family farm. We've been divided into smaller groups—I'm a Giggly Goat, Tem is a Happy Hen. I catch my hand on a barbed-wire fence and rip an impressive hole from the pad of my thumb all the way across my palm. I try to figure out how to tell the staff member looking after us—Julie—without making too much of a fuss, and end up cradling my hand to my chest for the next twenty minutes until Julie cheerfully asks me what I'm hiding. I show her my hand—now a bloody, fleshy mess—and she screams, backs away, and faints.

3) When you need a new pencil.

Eleven years old. SATs. We are ten minutes into math Paper 1 and the end of my pencil snaps clean off and goes skittering across the floor. I know I am supposed to put my hand up and ask for a spare; I know my teacher, Miss Kapsalis, will give me another if I just ask. But it is not only my mouth that has frozen shut—my limbs have gone rigid, my wrists scratching the splintered ridge of my exam desk, the pencil in my clenched fist. I can't even move. I sit, panicking, for twenty minutes until Miss Kapsalis, who is walking up and down the aisles of our desks to check for cheating, finally notices. She lets out a noise that is groan, gasp, and horror all in one and drops to my side.

"Steffi!" she whispers, even though she's not supposed to talk to us during the exam. "You need to answer the questions."

I uncurl my fingers and the broken pencil drops onto the table. I'm given a new pencil with fifteen minutes to go. Needless to say, I don't exactly come top of the class.

2) When you look a bit suspicious.

Twelve years old. Tem and I are spending a Saturday afternoon together mooching around town. We're in one of those bit-of-everything shops that sells clothes, twee gifts, and cushions. Tem is trying on a vintage prom dress, and I am standing in the corner, gazing at a shelf full of candles. The woman who owns the shop is suddenly at my side, asking me in a threateningly gentle voice what I think I am doing. I stare at her, confused and panicked in equal measure. What could have been a polite "I'm just browsing, thanks" exchange turns into her getting increasingly irate and me getting more and more frozen. No amount of ardent head-shaking is enough for me to convince her I'm not stealing anything. She is threatening to call the police when Tem comes parading out of the changing room wearing a black-and-white polka dot dress, announcing, "Just *tell* me how beautiful I am!" before she sees us both, clocks the situation in less than a second, and hurries across the shop floor to smooth things over.

1) When your best friend needs you.

Thirteen years old. I am in a stadium, watching Tem run the 800-meter final of the County Championships. She wins the race and is crackling with electricity and endorphins, leaping all over the track, hugging me, letting go, bouncing, cartwheeling. It's the first county race she's ever won. She's just collected her medal and is standing in the crowd, beaming down at it. And that's when a woman, the mother of one of Tem's competitors, says to someone—to this day I don't know who exactly she was talking to—"They shouldn't let those ones compete; everyone knows their bodies make them faster. It's not fair on our girls."

For one clueless moment I don't even understand what she means, but something about the sudden slackness in Tem's face makes it clear. There's no hidden meaning, no nice liberal understanding or context. The woman is being just plain racist about my beloved Tem, right in front of her. And this is it: the most shameful moment of my life. Because I don't say a word. I just stand there, even as I see the light leave Tem's eyes, even as she looks at me for just a second, even though she spends most of her days looking after me. No one else says anything either, but I know it is my silence that is the worst. My silence that is unforgivable.

Later, when I try to apologize—awkward and tongue-tied— she waves me away, tells me she understands that sometimes my words just don't come, that she knows I would have spoken if I could have.

So here's the thing: this was the worst time to be mute, but in a way it also saved us both. Because she didn't have to find out whether I would have been brave enough to stand up for her. And neither did I.

3

HERE'S SOMETHING PRETTY IMPORTANT YOU SHOULD know. Over the summer, I started taking DRUGS. Not Bad Drugs. Good Drugs. Prescription drugs.

This is partly to do with this being my make-it-or-break-it year, but to be honest it's been a long time coming. Ever since I was very young my parents and my doctor have been discussing whether or not I should take medication to help with my anxiety and, by extension, my mutism. (Why wasn't I involved in the discussions, you may ask? What an excellent question. Let me know if you get an answer.) The thing with SSRIs—Selective Serotonin Reuptake Inhibitors, which is what I'm taking—is that they're not supposed to be taken by "children," and that basically means anyone under the age of eighteen.

In my case, we agreed that sixteen was the right age, and on my birthday last year I had a series of sessions with a new therapist where we worked out a med plan for me, as well as Cognitive Behavior Therapy (CBT) sessions every other week. As I said, I started my first round of fluoxetine over the summer—three weeks ago, in fact. So far, all I've got to show for it is some pain in my teeth (a rare side effect, so trust me to be the one who gets it) and a whole load of trepidation. It can take up to six weeks before you really start to see its effects. Six weeks! So I'm about halfway there.

It's a weird thing. For some people, SSRIs change their life—like a fog lifting, they say. Others say it doesn't actually make much of a difference, that their anxiety remains, or in some cases it actually worsens. Which group I will fall into remains to be seen. I hope I'm one of the lucky ones. God, I hope so.

"They're not magic pills," Dad cautioned. "It's not going to be a miracle cure. You know that, Stef-Stef?"

Of course I know that. But I can still hope.

I imagine going to the supermarket and buying a bottle of milk without thinking twice. I dream of speaking to the assistant at the bank. I hope of getting through a Saturday in town without a panic attack. These are such small things to most people, but the fear of them takes up my whole world.

When I get home, I find my dad still wearing his suit from work, though he's loosened his tie and taken off his jacket, eating a nectarine over the kitchen sink. My dad is a civil servant, which means he deals with politicians all day but isn't allowed to be political. He is diplomatic, soft-spoken, and the kindest person in the world.

"Stef-Stef," he says, dropping the nectarine pit into the compost caddy and wiping his hands on a piece of kitchen paper. "How was your first day?"

"Pretty good," I say, kneeling to greet my five-year-old German shepherd, Rita, who has padded into the kitchen to greet me. She sits, tail thwacking against the floor. "I missed Tem, though."

He smiles. "Understandable. Did you make any friends?"

"Not really. They're pretty much all the same kids I've been at school with for years, Dad."

"I know, but now that Tem's moved on it's a good time for you to reconsider old friendships." He reaches down and strokes Rita's smooth head. "I'd worry very much if you were planning to spend the whole year by yourself. Especially after what we discussed."

"I did meet someone," I say quickly, hoping to avoid where I know he's going and offering a silent apology to Rhys Gold for using him as a distraction. "My head of year introduced me to a new kid who's deaf, because I know some sign language."

Dad's whole face lights up. "Wonderful!" he says, sounding just like Mr. Stafford in a way that makes me smile. "You must be a bit rusty after all these years. I'll have a look in the attic for the books we used to use. I knew I'd be glad one day that I didn't throw them away."

"It's fine," I start to say, but he's already off.

"There are probably some really great online learning platforms for BSL nowadays. I remember they all seemed a little rudimentary back then. Have a look and let me know if you need to sign up for anything or if you need to pay; it'll definitely be worth it. Maybe I could do a little refresher course too."

"Dad—"

"Lucy will be pleased! Maybe the four of us could all learn together, like we did last time."

"Three."

"What?" He's still all smiles, and I hate to do this to him.

"Three, Dad. The three of us."

There's a silence. We both look at each other. I see his smile fade and pain sweep across his face.

Dad clears his throat. "Right. Yes. Three of us. Maybe the three of us could learn together." He turns away from me and picks up an envelope from the pile of mail. "I ordered pizza for us. It should be here in twenty minutes. I got you the Garden Supreme."

"Great," I say. "Call me when it arrives, okay?"

It's been three years since my stepbrother died, but somehow this still happens. It's been three years, but I still don't know how to make it okay.

At dinnertime, Dad and I eat and talk as if nothing happened. He doesn't ask me any more questions about making new friends and I feel guilty, but also relieved. My stepmother, Lucy, comes downstairs to sit with us and talk about school, but she doesn't ask me whether I spoke or not. She isn't wearing any makeup and she looks tired.

I mentally run through any possible Clark-related anniversaries that I may have forgotten, but I don't land on any. It won't be four years since he died until next June, and his birthday was in January. I decide this is just A Bad Day. We all get them, because grief doesn't care how many years it's been. Before Clark died, Lucy was the kind of well-kept, together person who wore makeup just to sit at the dinner table with her family, but that poise is gone now, maybe even forever. It's like when death took Clark he took a big part of Lucy, too.

In my dad's family—just the three of us now, a tiny, slightly wobbly unit—we talk about mental health, which is why I know that Lucy is depressed, that it's a particular kind of depression they call "complicated grief disorder." It's strange; for all the focus there is on understanding the "cause" of a mental-health issue (people always seemed to talk as if my selective mutism could be totally cured if only they knew what *caused* it), in Lucy's case, when the cause is so clear, knowing what it is doesn't actually help. Lucy's sadness was so total, and she was so lost in it, that it didn't matter that we all knew why it had happened. Knowing the cause didn't give us a cure. Lucy had to rely on what she calls the three Ts: tears, time, and talk. ("The only things that really help, in the end.")

The irony is that people I meet now always think that my anxiety and communication difficulties were caused by Clark's death, as if I were diagnosed at fourteen instead of five. And part of me always wants to say, Would that make it better? Would that make it easier, if I could point to something as obvious as that to explain myself? Would you be more sympathetic if it was tied to something as seismic as death?

Clark's death was the worst thing that ever happened to me, but I was a selective mute long before it. It may have changed some of the specifics of my anxiety—I worry a lot more about cars now, and death in general—but it didn't create it. Sometimes things, like car accidents and the weather, just happen. And maybe that's the scariest thing of all.

/

4

ON WEDNESDAY I GET MY FIRST GLIMPSE OF WHAT
math is like in the sixth form, which is basically that emoji that
looks like *The Scream*, and also my first class with Rhys. He sits
next to me without asking, smiling at me as he does so.

Good morning, he says on arrival.

A woman I've never seen before stands at the front of the
room, just to the side of the teacher, Mr. Al-Hafi. I realize that
she is Rhys's communication support worker as soon as Mr.
Al-Hafi begins to speak and her hands and face spring into
action, turning his words into signs. Everyone around me
gawps at her until Mr. Al-Hafi loses his patience and tells them
to "at least not be so obvious about it."

The downside of all this interesting stuff going on is that I
get to the end of the lesson and realize I've only taken in about
thirty percent of it, and have made even fewer notes.

As everyone starts gathering up their stuff at the sound of the bell, Rhys touches my shoulder. **Not many notes?** he signs when I look at him. He smiles. **You must have a good memory.**

He has definitely simplified his BSL for me since we last spoke, which I love, because last night I spent a good hour or so with one of my old BSL books, sitting in front of my mirror, signing to myself.

Before I can think of how to reply, the communication support worker comes to stand beside us, and I take a step back so she can speak to Rhys. They have a quick conversation that is too fast for me to follow before she hands him a couple of sheets of paper that I assume must be notes of some kind about the lesson. Then, to my surprise, she turns to me. "Hello," she says. "You must be Steffi." Both her voice and her hands speak.

I smile back, surprised. Who told her who I am? Mr. Stafford? Rhys?

"I'm Clare," the woman continues. "I'll be popping in and out to give a bit of assistance to Rhys here at Windham. It's good to know there's another student who knows a bit of BSL."

I wiggle my hand in a so-so gesture, hoping she won't get carried away and think I can be anything like as helpful as her.

"Oh, don't be so modest," Clare chides, not even acknowledging the fact that I haven't spoken out loud. I decide I like her. "Every little bit helps. I'll see you after lunch, Rhys. Nice to meet you, Steffi."

What's your next class? I ask Rhys after she leaves.

Free period, he replies. He smiles and waves the sheets

39

Clare had given him. **I need to go over these. You?**

Also free period, I say, then quickly add, just in case he thinks I'm hinting at anything, **I'm going to the library**.

Cool. Can I come? He hoists his backpack up over his shoulder and smiles expectantly.

I have to say yes. It's only polite. **Sure.** I keep my expression relaxed, like this is a normal day for me. **This way.**

Steffi Brons-English, notes on Atonement
Chps 1-3 Sept 7th

Briony is a

Can you write instead of signing?
SORRY!

SURE ☺ WHERE IS YOUR LAST NAME FROM?

My dad's dad was German.
What about you? Where's Gold from?

WHO KNOWS? IT'S AN OLD
WELSH NAME I THINK.

Ian McEwan is

HAVE YOU READ THE WHOLE BOOK?

No, just first 3 chaps. Have you?

NO. SEEN THE FILM THOUGH.
IT'S GREAT.

Is it on Netflix?

PROBS NOT. I'VE GOT THE DVD.
YOU CAN BORROW IT IF YOU WANT.

Book opens with play-what does this
say about construction of narrati-

CAN YOU NOT TALK AT ALL?

I can talk sometimes.

WHAT MAKES THE DIFFERENCE?

No idea. Sometimes it just goes away
and sometimes it's fine.
I'm much better with people I know.
Strangers are harder.

IT MUST BE REALLY HARD.

~~Yeah. Sometimes. I guess it~~

41

Not as hard as math! ☺

Briony is a writer
What is REAL, etc.
How does

I SAID I LIKE YOUR HANDWRITING.

oh . . . thanks ☺

My email is steffi@bronsmail.com
No seriously that is my email address.
We have a family account, bronsmail.
I promise! My dad thinks it's funny.
He's really proud of it. What's yours?

RHYSESPIECES@GMAIL.COM

~~cute~~ funny address!

DO YOU USE JACKBYTES?
IT'S AN APP. LIKE A CROSS BETWEEN
WHATSAPP AND A CHAT ROOM.
MY USERNAME IS RHYSESPIECES.
SET UP AN ACCOUNT AND ADD ME!
OH AND FACEBOOK TOO ☺

42

Briony is

oh bugger this.

I play it cool and force myself not to add Rhys on Facebook until the end of the school day, when I head to the kennel where I work for my weeknight shift. I click "Add Friend," then turn my phone off and put it in my locker. Done.

I've worked at the St. Francis Kennels and Boarding since I turned sixteen. People are often surprised that I have a job, what with the whole not-speaking-much thing, to which I say—selective mutes have the right to earn money too. And I'm not even *that* mute anymore.

St. Francis is the only kennels and cattery in the county that operates a day "crèche" as well as overnight boarding, so it's always busy, even during term time. Now that school has started up again—in the summer I do a lot more hours—I work two days a week: Wednesday from 4 p.m. to 8 p.m., when I sign out dogs back to the care of their owners, and either Saturday or Sunday for the full day. At the kennels, I am happy. I am my best self. It is one of the places where I can talk almost as much as normal people, and it's one of the reasons I can believe I'll be properly okay one day.

"Hello, Steffi!" Ivan calls to me as I come through the door. He's grinning, leaning against the reception desk. Ivan has known me for years, back from when I used to visit as a silent, unhappy child. He was the one who suggested I volunteer and then, later, become a paid employee. It is an understatement to say I owe a *lot* to Ivan.

"Hi," I say, smiling back. "How's everyone today?"

"Oh fine, fine." Ivan's dog, Sia, who has free rein across the kennels and loves everyone like they're perpetually about to feed him raw steak, trots over to me and pushes his giant Labrador head against my hip. "One of the cats got out—not sure how—but we caught him in the end."

I spend a happy four hours with the dogs, running across the acre with the boarders, handing over day-dogs to their owners, whose tired eyes always light up at the point of reunion. When I get home, the smell of strange dogs on me makes Rita eye me suspiciously until I lie down on the floor with her, reminding her that she is my doggish one and only.

And then, when it's almost nine o'clock, I let myself go on Facebook.

Rhys has accepted my friend request, which was to be expected but still makes me smile with relief. I go immediately to his profile page, ignoring the two notifications I have waiting for me.

It's not stalking—it's exhibiting interest in a new friend. That's what Facebook is for. It's completely normal to—

Oh. *Oh.* Hmmm.

My heart, previously on board with my brain in the just-interested-as-a-friend department, deflates, sinks, twinges at the sight of one of Rhys's profile pictures: him and a dark-haired girl wearing sunglasses. A friend? Or a girlfriend? There is no corresponding relationship status on his profile page, which is maddening. Why can't people just be clear?

I click on to his photos and have a quick sweep through them, trying to decide. There are lots of photos of him and this girl, some with other people too and others just the two of them. I'm none the wiser. On one hand, there are no photos of them being particularly close physically—no kissing, no gazing into each other's eyes, no matching Christmas jumpers—but, on the other, maybe they just don't like PDAs.

The maybe-girlfriend's name, I learn, is Meg Callifryn, and my heart sinks further. Rhys and Meg. Goddamit. Their names are perfect together. And Callifryn? What kind of an unfairly pretty last name is that? Not like Brons, which would be okay if it was spelled Bronze, but it's not. It's German and it's Brons.

I mean, it's not like I *care*. Obviously I wasn't thinking of actually trying anything with Rhys, but . . . well. Still.

I sit back against my chair and let out a ridiculous but nonetheless satisfying huff. That's that, then. I'll just have a *tiny* look at Meg's profile. She has minimal privacy settings, so I learn that she is seventeen, was recently a bridesmaid at her sister's wedding, and can play the flute. Her own profile picture, for what it's worth, is of her and a girl. Her relationship status says she's in a relationship, but that's as far as the information goes. I wonder if she can talk.

I close the window, pause, then reopen it. I go to my own

profile page, wanting to see what Rhys will see if he looks. Which is a big if, let's face it.

My profile picture is of Rita and me—she's poking her nose into my face and I'm laughing. I close my eyes and then open them suddenly, hoping to trick my brain into thinking I'm seeing the picture for the first time. It makes me look relaxed and fun, right? And everyone likes a girl who loves animals. So far so good.

I scroll down a little. Most of the updates on my wall are photos I've been tagged in over the summer. Tem put up her annual summer album last week and I'm in about half of them. Keir also finally got round to putting up pictures from Bell's fifth birthday party in July. The mix makes me look fun-loving and happy and that's the nice thing about Facebook; it's moldable. This is me! Sort of.

Interspersed among the photos are the usual random comments and links. Most of them are from Tem, who is a prolific and loyal Facebooker. The most recent is a link to some kind of half marathon, which is her unsubtle way of trying to cajole me into running it with her, even though that is clearly never going to happen. Our conversation underneath (begun with me simply saying, "No, September.") had descended into a pun-off. *Is this not a-track-tive for you, Steffi? No, too many hurdles,* etc.

I think of Rhys reading the conversation. I hope he likes puns. Of course he likes puns—who doesn't like puns?

I click on my notifications. One is an invitation for Farmville from my cousin, which makes me want to ask her if she knows what century it is, and the other is a surprise. Rhys Gold liked your profile picture.

My heart flips. Oh. Well. That's . . .

I realize I'm smiling at my laptop. Not just smiling, full-on beaming. Six little words, so much potential. He liked my profile picture. That's something, right?

jackbytes
Sign Up

We don't ask for much!

Email: steffi@bronsmail.com
First name*: Steffi
Last name*: Brons
Desired username**: stefstef
Password***: ********

* Don't worry—this info will be kept private!
** Just letters and numbers, please!
*** Mix it up! Use numbers, letters, and different cases!

That's it! You're set up!
Welcome to jackbytes!

Now add your friends!

Import from Facebook
Import from email
Import from Twitter

Add by username: [rhysespieces] [currently online]

rhysespieces: hey!

stefstef: hiya

stefstef: so how does this work then?

rhysespieces: its like whatsapp or facebook messenger, but it doesnt store messages

rhysespieces: like a chat room, but with people you know ☺

stefstef: oh . . . why not just use whatsapp?

rhysespieces: some people dont like the whole read receipts thing. plus it's different, right?

stefstef: yeah, interesting

rhysespieces: haha, give it a go.

rhysespieces: this is cool, we're having a conversation at normal speed!

stefstef: wow, it's true! we're like normal people!

rhysespieces: i could ask you any question i wanted, straight away

stefstef: go easy.

rhysespieces: the power. the sheer power.

stefstef: you can ask, doesn't mean i'll answer

rhysespieces: that wouldn't be any fun.

stefstef: i dont think my deep dark secrets are much fun!

rhysespieces: oh, i dont mean like deep dark secrets. just like normal stuff. hey i have an idea. let's make a pact. TOTAL HONESTY. and EVERY QUESTION has to be answered.

rhysespieces: cool, huh?

rhysespieces: stef?

rhysespieces: remember i know you're still there! that's the thing about jackbytes

stefstef: i know i know. i was asking my dog if she thinks it's a good idea.

rhysespieces: . . . . . . really?

stefstef: my first question will be, why do you want to start such a potentially embarrassing/dangerous pact with a complete stranger?

rhysespieces: and my answer will be, precisely because we're strangers. i've never got to know anyone like that before. worth a go, right?

stefstef: how do you know i won't lie anyway?

rhysespieces: dunno. just do.

stefstef: okay. i accept your pact. with caution.

rhysespieces: total honesty?

stefstef: total honesty.

rhysespieces: ☺

rhysespieces: do you really talk to your dog?

stefstef: wait, are we starting already?

rhysespieces: yes!

stefstef: okay. then yes.

rhysespieces: what's her name? breed?

stefstef: rita. german shepherd.

rhysespieces: as in . . . skeeter? or . . . erm . . . ora?

stefstef: no!

stefstef: as in LOVELY rita.

rhysespieces: i dont know wtf that means

stefstef: can you send links through this thing?

rhysespieces: yeah, tap the icon that looks like an arrow in
a box and put the link in

stefstef: one sec

stefstef: [YOUTUBE–LOVELY RITA–THE BEATLES 1967]

rhysespieces: erm. stef . . .

stefstef: doesnt the link work?

rhysespieces: sure it does. my ears don't.

stefstef: FUCK. OH MY GOD.

rhysespieces: its okay, dont worry

stefstef: i'm so sorry. i cant believe i did that.

rhysespieces: seriously its fine. happens all the time with
new people. the ones who can hear anyway

stefstef: i want to die.

rhysespieces: i get the reference now. lovely rita. that's cool.

stefstef: i'm dead. this is my ghost, repenting past sins.

rhysespieces: hahahaha

stefstef: this is going to be the kind of thing i remember in
the middle of a normal day in like five years time

stefstef: hey, steffi, remember when you made a complete twat of yourself?

rhysespieces: tell me about the song

stefstef: what do you mean?

rhysespieces: i can see the lyrics, but they don't tell me much. what's it like? slow? cheerful? why do you like it?

stefstef: oh! well

stefstef: it's like, upbeat. the kind of song that makes you smile. my grandad used to sing it around the house

rhysespieces: where would you listen to it? at a wedding? a funeral where you like really loved the person so it was like happysad smiling?

stefstef: it's the kind of song you listen to in the car, on the way to somewhere you want to go, but you don't have to hurry there

rhysespieces: that's a good description.

rhysespieces: i like this song too. good choice.

stefstef: i'm really sorry

rhysespieces: petition to add new clause to the pact.

stefstef: ?

rhysespieces: we can only apologize once at a time. no repeated apologies.

stefstef: i accept that clause

rhysespieces: i have to go now. see you tomorrow?

stefstef: sure. bye!

[rhysespieces is offline]

5

I MEET TEM AT THE RUNNING TRACK AFTER SCHOOL
the next day. She is already there, bent over, her fingers stretched
toward her toes.

"Hey," I say when I get close enough.

She unfolds, a grin already on her face when our eyes
meet. "Hey!" she says. She takes in my outfit—leggings, oversize hoodie, ankle boots—and mock-pouts. "Aw, I said come
dressed for running."

"And I said, no way," I say patiently. "You can't turn me into
a runner. Give it up."

"Fine, fine." Tem tosses her hair, battled into a ponytail, and
leans over to pick up her bag. "Timer duty?"

"Naturally." I reach out a hand and she passes me one of her
stopwatches. "Can we talk first? I want to hear about college."

"In a bit," Tem says. She seems distracted, stretching up and then down again on her toes. "I need to work it off first. You ready to go?" She gestures at the stopwatch.

I nod, and she leans over to kiss my cheek. "Hi, Steffi!" She drops her bag on the floor and bounces away from me—"Bye, Steffi!"—and takes off.

I make myself comfortable on the grass beside the track and watch her run, her movements smooth and agile. Tem was made for running, I think. Like airplanes never look as comfortable on the ground as they do in the air, she comes to life when she runs. She'll run for Team Great Britain in the Olympics one day. I know it.

I let her run several laps before I get bored and flag her down. "Can we talk now?"

Tem holds up two fingers and carries on. Two minutes? Two laps? Peace? I sigh-groan and pull out my phone. I open jackbytes but Rhys is offline, so I turn it off again and play vegetable Tetris until Tem finally comes panting over.

"Something wrong?" I ask, watching her unscrew the cap from her bottle of water and take a long, slow swallow.

She shakes her head. "No, why?"

I don't push, even though I know her well enough to be able to determine her emotional state by how many laps she runs on an otherwise ordinary afternoon. "Tell me about college, then."

"It's good," she says vaguely. She begins to run through her cooldown stretches, electricity fizzing from her joints and fingertips.

"Just good?" I prompt.

Tem twists her lip, then shrugs. "It's very different from Windham. Louder. You'd hate it." She takes another sip from her water bottle. "There are so many people, which is kind of weird. Like, I used to think Windham was a pretty big school, but it turns out it's not. And because everyone's new it's like this big battle to make friends."

"You won't have any trouble making friends," I say. Everyone loves Tem.

"Maybe not, but it feels kind of fake. Maybe it's just because it's new . . . I don't know. I miss you a lot more than I thought I would." Her eyes widen. "That came out completely wrong. I just meant, I'm always—"

"I know what you meant," I say, half smiling. Tem is always the one who takes the lead, who makes the friends. The needed one. I am the one who needs, the one who misses. "How are the classes?" Tem is studying sports therapy, which she's been excited about ever since she found out it existed.

"Well, that's the other thing." Tem's brow has crinkled. "The work seems really hard. I wasn't expecting that."

"Too hard?"

Tem pauses, the water bottle to her lips, her eyes looking away from me. "I hope not." She takes a breath and then smiles at me. "But!" she says brightly. "I did meet a boy of my own."

"Ooh," I say. "Tell."

Tem pulls out her phone and opens Facebook. "Look," she begins, and I laugh.

"You got him on Facebook already?"

"Of course, that's what Facebook is for," she says, which is true. She hands her phone over to me and I look obediently.

Karam Homsi, the name reads. He looks like a model. Long-ish wild, dark hair. Brown eyes. A jokey half-smile on his face.

"He's amazing," Tem says, looking with pure adoration at her phone. "He's taking two extra A-levels at the college because his school—St. Sebastian's—will only let him do four. He wants to be a doctor."

"Wow," I say, because there's really no other response to that kind of information, particularly when it goes with that kind of face.

"And he's so nice, Stef. And not fake nice, or trying-too-hard nice. Just, like, friendly, you know? He came here from Syria when he was nine, and now his life goal is to become a doctor so he can go back and help people."

"What's wrong with him?" I ask.

She startles. "Huh?"

"What's wrong with him?" I repeat. I smile to let her know I'm teasing. "No one is that perfect."

"Oh." She lets out a laugh of relief. "Nothing's wrong with him. He's just perfect. Honestly, Steffi. I've never met anyone like him."

Tem is my best friend, and I won't hear a word against her, but this is not the first time I've heard these kinds of words come out of her mouth. Tem has what my mother calls "an open heart," which means she falls in love quickly and easily with pretty much anyone, and not just in a romantic way. When she loves, she loves completely—that's what I'm saying.

When we were kids, she went through a phase where she hero-worshipped firemen. For her seventh birthday she got to visit the fire station and have her photo taken at the wheel of a fire engine, a huge helmet resting over her curls, a gigantic grin on her face. There's a photo of the two of us, actually: her gap-toothed and grinning under her helmet, me next to her with a serious frown, holding the edge of my helmet so it would stay on my head, my hair too flat and lifeless to hold it up.

What I mean by this is that Tem fell in love with every single fireman she met that day, to the point where she still remembers all their names, even years later—"Remember when Sanjay let me try on his coat?"—and that's just how she is. Now that we're older, it's moved on from hero worship to outright please-marry-me love. She got her first boyfriend at fourteen—AJ, fifteen, swaggering jerk—and that lasted for about two months. Her relationships were pretty regular after that: a parade of new boyfriends every few months or so. Each one "different." Each one "special." Each one "not like anyone else."

In the interests of full disclosure, I should say that I have never had a boyfriend. At least, not one that existed outside of the internet. Not one I could touch or kiss or hold hands with. Making the leap from crush to conversation is just too much for me. I blame my brain.

"How did you meet him?" I ask. If Karam is taking six A-levels in the hope of becoming a doctor, it's unlikely he and Tem will share any classes.

"He's the year above us and he runs a volunteer group at the college raising money for refugees and asylum seekers. I went along because I thought I might meet some, you know, like-minded people, or whatever. Seeing as there didn't seem to be many in my actual classes."

"And you did?"

She grins, showing all her teeth. "I did."

6

OVER THE NEXT COUPLE OF WEEKS, RHYS AND I
move past the sort-of-maybe stage of potential friendship and
become actual friends. We spend most of our lunch breaks
and free periods together, sharing notes and getting to know
each other. I find out that he used to run a YouTube channel
on video games with his older brother, Aled, before Aled went
to university, and that he designed his first game when he
was eight—"a total Super Mario rip-off." He teaches me more
advanced BSL by signing song lyrics to my favorite songs. He
tells me that his dad was born in Guyana, and when I admit
that I don't even know where that is he shows me on Google
Maps. I tell him my grandad is from Germany, and he asks
me—completely deadpan—if I can point it out to him on
the map.

I don't ever ask him if he has a girlfriend, because I come

to realize that I don't really want to know, mainly because the increasing likelihood that the answer might not be yes, and where the conversation could then go, is just plain terrifying. He's turning out to be a good friend to have: smart and friendly, with a dry sense of humor and an unflappable nature I can't help but envy. To be honest, it's actually kind of a relief not to have to worry about scary things like how to flirt or what I'm wearing or how to arrange my face when I see him. We're just friends.

By late September, I'm comfortable in our friendship and definitely getting better at BSL. It's Wednesday and I'm sitting with Rhys in our math class. I try to watch Clare, his communication support worker, as much as possible, trying to keep up with her signs instead of following Mr. Al-Hafi's voice. In fact, I'm so focused on doing this that when Mr. Al-Hafi points to the equation he's written on the board, I say the answer out loud without thinking about it.

Everyone swings to look at me, wide-eyed, and my whole body goes hot. They are honestly looking at me like I just pulled out a gun and fired it.

"That's right," Mr. Al-Hafi says smoothly, God love him. "Nice work, Stefanie."

My heart is still pounding as I shrink down against my seat, scribbling furious notes across the page that don't actually make any sense. I can feel Rhys watching me, his gaze curious. He hasn't known me for years, like most of my classmates. He doesn't know just how unusual it is for me to answer a question out loud, let alone unbidden.

What *was* that? Was my mind sufficiently distracted by Clare that it forgot about its self-enforced rule to not speak in public? Or was it the medication? Was it *Rhys*? And, if so, is that thought comforting or frightening? I don't want a boy to be the reason I get better. What would that say about me if it is?

And is this what getting better is? Obviously being able to talk normally in public is what I want, but now that it seems to be happening I feel strangely unsettled. I suddenly understand a lot better what my doctor meant when he talked about my sense of self being entwined with my silence. Who *am* I if I can talk? Will that mean I say all the things I usually keep in my head? But so many of them are snide, or bitter, or just plain *dull*.

My brain battles with these thoughts until the bell rings. I blink out of the turmoil of my head and realize I haven't taken in anything that happened in the last twenty minutes of the lesson. My notepad is a mess of barely legible scribbles. I can just about make out the words math math math this is math.

Oh God, I'm losing it.

There's a tap at my wrist and I look up. **Are you okay?**

Yes, I sign automatically, then pause. I consider.

Seeing my face, Rhys puts his head to one side—like Rita does when she's confused by something—and smiles. **The pact.**

I don't know what to say. My mouth is closed, my hands are still.

Want to talk about it?
No. Yes. No.
Okay.

A conversation in fragments

A table in the common room. Rhys sits sprawled over a chair, his limbs too long and languid to fit into it properly, and I am cross-legged on the table, facing him. Our hands are in constant motion, flitting up and down from the space in front of our faces and chests to the piece of paper we have between us. He is patient, prompting me with a gentle swing of his hand. And we begin.

So.

                                          So . . .

You can go ahead. I'm "listening."

                           I don't know where to start.

Shall I ask questions?

                                                Yes.

Okay. HOW COME YOU DON'T SPEAK MUCH?

**I was a childhood mute. I stopped talking when
I was four,** which was when I went to nursery.
I just . . . didn't speak. No one knew why.
Big fuss.

You stopped speaking COMPLETELY?

Oh no. At first it was just in the nursery. I just
clammed up. **I've seen the notes my teacher made
at the time. She says it was like I was a** statue **all
day—no expressions, no voice. Like I was scared to do
anything at all. I could still talk at home and to my
family and friends.** But then it started getting
worse. First I stopped talking to anyone I
didn't know, **like people in shops and restaurants,**
and then it was friends, and then it was anyone
who wasn't my immediate family. For a while I
could only talk to my mum and dad when I was
certain there was no one else around.

That must have been hard.

I don't remember it in any detail. Most of
what I know is what people have told me over

62

the years. All I remember from the time is this kind of numbness.

So what happened?

I had to see doctors and speech therapists. I saw them for years, actually. We got loads of written materials about selective mutism. What my parents should expect. They had to get two copies of everything because they weren't exactly on great terms at the time. They divorced **when I was three.**

Maybe you were trying to bring them together by not talking?

Look, I'll answer any question you ask but don't try and psychoanaylze me, okay? I've heard it all a hundred times.

Sorry.

It makes me really mad.

Sorry.

People always want to have the answer. Even now,

after all these years. It's like, don't you think that we've all thought of every possible option already? We stopped waiting for a light-bulb moment a long time ago. It's never going to come. Sometimes things just happen.

I won't do it again.

So anyway. I was meant to be getting help but it was all a bit patchy, to be honest. I lived mostly with Mum at the time and I saw Dad at weekends. They didn't agree how to "handle me," or whatever. Dad wanted to follow what the guides said, like, to the letter, but Mum didn't really have much patience for it.

What do you mean?

I don't think she really believed that it was something that was happening to me instead of something I was doing. She thought I was doing it on purpose. Trying to make things difficult. I know it must have been frustrating, but she used to shout at me. She couldn't take it when I wouldn't talk to the rest of our family. Like my gran. Mum would be, like, "Are you trying to punish me?" and then she'd cry.

What about in school?

I was meant to get one-on-one help, but my school was quite understaffed and underfunded—it's actually been closed down since I left—and so I was just included in the SEN group.

SEN?

Special Educational Needs.

Oh. Did it help?

Well, it's not like anyone was UNhelpful, but none of it helped. I just didn't talk, but because I did all the work I think they decided it was easier to let me get on with it. They did try some of the things the guides suggested—there's this technique called "sliding in"—but it wasn't getting results fast enough so they kind of gave up. I don't want to make them sound bad,

because everyone was so nice to me, and they really tried to make me feel like it was okay to just be, you know?
And I had Tem.

Your best friend?

Yeah. We've been best friends since we were tiny. There was a time when I couldn't talk to her either, but that only lasted a few months. Literally. **But Tem doesn't care whether I talk or not, so there was never any pressure. And she NEVER looked surprised if I did talk. Everyone else used to watch me so closely . . . and if I did say anything they'd always make this shocked face that made me feel so** . . . exposed. But with Tem it always felt normal. After a while she could read me so well she used to talk for me at school, like she was my interpreter. **And that made things easier for everyone. By Year 2, I could whisper to Tem in school, and then over the next few years I could talk to her, then whisper to other kids, and then by the time I got to Year 6, I was almost normal.**
Very shy, but I could talk.

Where does BSL come in?

Oh that . . .

I've been dying to ask. I assumed it was school.

No, it actually wasn't. My uncle—my dad's brother-in-law after he married my stepmother when I was five (stop me if this gets confusing)**—is a teacher in a Deaf school. He suggested that I learn BSL when it started to look like I wouldn't be able to communicate at all. He said it might help with my confidence.**

Not SSE?

Sign-supported English?

Yeah. Wouldn't that have made more sense?

It would have made more sense, yeah, but I think Geoff loved the idea of being able to teach me this whole new language so much that he just went right for the big guns. He doesn't do things by halves. **And Dad thought it was brilliant, like a family project. He loved this idea of his new family having their own**

way of communicating. We all learned together—
me, my stepmother, him, and Clark.

Who's Clark?
?

He was my stepbrother. He's dead.

Oh shit. Sorry.

I can't talk about him right now.

That's okay. We can stick with the speech thing.
Did you use BSL at school?

Not really. My teachers knew what the basic stuff
meant—like can I go to the toilet and yes and no,
please and thank you, whatever—but no one could
hold a conversation in it. It was just a way to get by.

What happened when you got to
secondary school?

Everything went to shit.

Oh.

Yeah. The thing is, everyone at my primary school knew me, and they were used to the problems I had. So they stopped being surprised if I talked or not, and a lot of them could actually talk for me by the end—not even just Tem.

So you were comfortable there.

Yeah, exactly. It was so safe. But then secondary school was this new environment, and it was big and loud and full of strangers. I couldn't deal with it.

You went mute again?

Basically, yeah. But it was so much worse this time because I understood so much more, like what's expected of you not just by teachers but other kids, as well. I was the weird kid who didn't speak. The teachers knew about it-they must have been briefed or something- so it was okay from that side of things, but you know that secondary school is about twenty percent learning and eighty percent social. You have to talk to other kids. You just have to. And I couldn't.

So what happened?

I was bullied for a while. I was such an easy target. There were these kids who thought it was funny to grab me and do stuff like draw on me, and they'd tell me they'd stop if I just said "stop." It was horrible but it didn't really last long because Tem was there, and people liked her, so eventually they just left me alone. The school was a lot more interested in helping me than my primary school, so I spent a lot of time with the counseling team and working with tutors outside of the main class time. It all helped. I'd got a lot better by about Year 8.

So you're not mute anymore?

Oh no, I haven't been actually mute for a long time. I'm just really shy. Like, clinically shy. Socially anxious. I have some diagnoses. A whole bunch.

You don't usually talk in class?

Not if I can help it.

Is that why everyone looked so shocked today?

Yeah.

What's changed?

If I tell you, don't tell anyone.

You know I won't.

Tem doesn't even know.

Okay, now I feel bad. You don't have
to tell me if you don't want to.

I started taking medication
at the end of the summer.

Oh right.

It might be kicking in. I don't know.

That's a good thing, right?

Yeah. Bit of an adjustment, though.
I'm so used to being the quiet one.

I know what you mean.
I don't know who I'd be if I could hear.

Would you choose that, if you could?

I don't know. I really don't. I like my life.
I like being me. I feel like I'd kind of
be letting myself down—and the whole
community, which I really love—if I said I
wished I could hear. It would be like giving
up a big part of myself. So much of what I
have wouldn't have happened if I could hear.
Like, even meeting you.

Me?

Yeah. If I'd started here as just another boy
would you even have noticed me?
Why are you laughing?

Would YOU have noticed ME?

That's exactly what I'm saying.
I like the way things are. I like that I've met
you and we're getting to know each other.

Why?

What kind of a question is that?

I just don't really get it.

Get what?

Is it because I can speak some BSL?

Is what because of that?

You didn't answer my question. The pact.

You need to answer mine for me to be able
to answer yours.

Why you talk to me.

I like talking to you.

No one likes talking to me.

Isn't it more that no one usually gets the chance?

I have to go to class.

It's almost lunchtime?

Then I have to go to get food.

Okay cool. Where do you want to go?

By myself.

How have I upset you?
Don't walk away from me,
you know I can't shout after you.

"Stef."

1

I DECIDE TO TAKE THE REST OF THE DAY OFF, EVEN though I'm supposed to go to English in the afternoon. I have *Atonement* with me, so I go to Starbucks, buy a vanilla hot chocolate, and spend the next couple of hours reading in the corner. I am completely alone and it is blissful.

I don't even bother making notes; I just read until the pages run out and then I sit, slightly dazed, forced back into the real world. A couple at a table near me are trying to name all seven dwarves, but have stalled at five. A girl on my other side is scowling at her laptop and jabbing at the keys with angry fingers. When did these people come in? What time is it?

I put the book down and pick up my phone. It's almost 3 p.m. and Tem has sent me four messages escalating from a casual "Hey, I have news, message me!" to a final, desperate

"STEFFFFFFFFIIIIIIIIIIIIIIIIIIIIIIIIIIIIIIIIIIIIIIIIIIIIIIIIIIIIIIIIIII."

I finish scrolling and smile at the string of messages, then type out a reply.

Steffi:
I'm in Starbucks. What's up?

Tem:
THERE YOU ARE.

Steffi:
Here I am!

Tem:
I KISSED KARAM.

I hesitate, waiting for the jolt of surprise to pass so I can work out what I'm feeling. Obviously I know she likes Karam, but as of yesterday she was still playing it cool. And it's the middle of the day!

Steffi:
???
Wow! I think I need to hear the details?

Tem:

I can see your disapproval in nine words, Brons.

Steffi:

I'm not disapproving!

Tem:

SURE. Well I'm coming over tonight,
so you can practice being excited, okay??

Steffi:

Okay!

Tem:

Awsum. Right after school, k?

Steffi:

Was it a good kiss?

Tem:

Yes.

Steffi:

☺

I'm really not disapproving. Just . . . cautious. Protective. That's the best friend prerogative, right?

I'm still holding my phone and I look at it, nibbling on my lip, then tap the jackbytes icon. The screen loads.

[stefstef is online]
[rhysespieces is offline and cannot receive messages]
stefstef: Sorry.
[rhysespieces is online]
[stefstef has gone offline]

Tem is giddy with happiness when she arrives at my house after dinner. She throws out a cursory "How are you?" on the way to my room, but I know it's not the time to start telling her about my sort-of argument with Rhys—*was* it an argument?—so I just smile and reply that I'm fine. She is too excited to notice my sort-of lie—*is* it a lie?—and does a running leap onto my bed, bouncing a little like a child before settling down onto crossed legs.

"Go on, then," I say. Her happiness is infectious. "Share."

She does, in frankly unnecessary detail. I learn more than I could ever need to know about Karam's kissing technique—"Just enough tongue! More each time, like a taste test."—and how his hair feels under her fingers.

"He calls me Tember," she says, beaming. "Isn't that the cutest? *Tember*."

"So is he going to be your boyfriend?"

Her smile blooms ever wider. "I don't know. I hope so . . . but it's early days, obviously. And it was just a kiss."

"Just the *first* kiss," I correct, because this is the kind of thing we do for our friends.

Tem beams. "Just the first kiss," she repeats. "The first of many."

"Do you want him to be your boyfriend?"

She nods. "Of course! Stef, it's all I want. He's just . . . everything."

"That sounds dangerous," I say.

"In a good way," she replies.

"Is there a good kind of dangerous?"

She laughs. "Just you wait, Stef. Just wait."

stefstef: hey

rhysespieces: hi

stefstef: so I finished Atonement

rhysespieces: oh yeah?

stefstef: yeah

rhysespieces: did you like?

stefstef: yeah.

rhysespieces: cool.

stefstef: is it still okay for me to borrow the DVD?

rhysespieces: sure, if you want. or you could come over and watch it at my place?

rhysespieces: . . . if you don't mind having to put up with subtitles.

rhysespieces: or my cat.

stefstef: would that be okay?

rhysespieces: sure. i haven't seen it for a while.

stefstef: okay . . . when?

rhysespieces: you got plans after school weds?

stefstef: sorry yeah, I have to work.

rhysespieces: Thurs?

stefstef: yeah, could do that

rhysespieces: cool. let's say thurs after school then

stefstef: okay

rhysespieces: okay

stefstef: rhys?

rhysespieces: stef?

stefstef: i'm sorry.

rhysespieces: i know.

Here is how you say sorry in BSL:

Close your dominant hand into a fist. Hold your fist to your chest and move it in a circular motion. Make eye contact while you do it.

I practice my apology in front of the mirror, mouthing "sorry" to my reflection and circling my fist over and over again. One of the things I both hate and love about BSL is how it forces you to be genuine. Half-hearted apologies just don't work when you're communicating with your eyes and your hands. You have to mean it, or it is meaningless.

And I do want to be genuine with Rhys. I don't even really understand why I got as defensive as I did, and so quickly. He was being so sweet with me, so patient with my faltering BSL, so encouraging of my clumsy attempts to communicate in his language. And then I flew off the handle for really no reason at all. What will he think of me now?

8

THE FIRST SURPRISE IS THAT RHYS CAN DRIVE.

Seeing the expression on my face, Rhys laughs. **You didn't know I could drive?**

No! We are facing each other on either side of his car. He is leaning over the roof, elbows on the metal, a light grin on his face.

I passed my test in the summer.

How old are you? If we were talking, I would have worried about trying to ask this question in a way that wouldn't come out rude—in fact, I would probably have worked myself up into a panic attack about it—but the constraints of my limited BSL take the choice away, so I just ask.

He holds up his thumb and forefinger, like a gun, and moves his hand up and down. **Seventeen.**

I think about this, my hands waiting in front of me, but I can't think what to say. Finally, **I have many questions.**

He laughs. **Let's go. You can ask me them later.**

I get into the car, which is a battered green Skoda with an air freshener shaped like a jelly bean bouncing from the rearview mirror, and wait while Rhys wriggles in his seat and checks the mirrors. He seems a little nervous, though he's trying to hide it, and he smiles overconfidently at me as he reverses out of his space before quickly looking back at the windshield.

Rhys's house is on the other side of town from our school, not closer to my mum's or dad's house but making a kind of triangle between them. It's smaller than Mum's house but bigger than Dad's, with a slightly overgrown front garden and a very overgrown cat lying on its back in the center of it.

Rhys turns off the engine and holds his hands out in front of him. **Home!** he says, exaggerating the sign in the same way a hearing person would put on a jovial voice.

We get out of the car and head up the driveway. The cat ignores us until Rhys pushes his key into the lock, at which point he jumps to his feet and waddles up to the door, pushing me out of the way to walk in first.

Rhys rolls his eyes, points to the cat and then signs to me, **King of the castle.**

What's his name?

Javert.

I hesitate. **Like, from the . . . musical?** I have seen the stage version of *Les Misérables* once and the film about six times—overwrought and depressingly tragic musicals are my favorite—but it surprises me that Rhys's family would name a cat after a character in it. I'd always considered hearing kind of important when it came to musicals, so wouldn't Rhys feel left out?

He nods. **Mum is a big musical buff.** As if on cue, a white woman with silver-streaked brown hair comes out of the kitchen, beaming. **And here she is**, he adds. **Hi.**

"Hello," the woman says. "You must be Steffi." Like Rhys's interpreter at school, she talks with her hands and her mouth. "I'm Sandra."

Hi, I sign.

We're going to watch a film, Rhys says. **So, we'll see you later, okay?**

"Come and have a cup of tea first," Sandra says. She is still smiling at me. "I want to find out more about the famous Steffi."

I feel my face flame and I turn, horrified, to Rhys, who has reacted in exactly the same way.

"It's so wonderful that he's been able to meet someone who speaks BSL," Sandra adds. "You're a gift, Steffi."

I seriously consider running away.

Okay, bye. Rhys takes my elbow and starts steering me toward the stairs.

"Um, excuse me," Sandra says, eyebrows raised. "Where do you think you're going?"

Rhys gives her a look. **My bedroom.**

"Not today, mister." Sandra looks torn between stern and amused. "The living room is right through there."

Rhys lets out a loud huff of frustration through his nose. He makes a sign I don't recognize, following it with **always go in my bedroom**.

"Steffi is not Meg," Sandra says patiently, and though her hands are fingerspelling like an expert they may as well be punching me in the stomach with four simple words. "Living room."

Rhys sighs loudly, but obeys. **Sorry**, he says to me and I blink at him, unsure how to reply. Should I express sadness that we can't watch a film together in the privacy of his bedroom? On the comfort of his . . . um, bed? And should I do this in front of his *mother*?

"Steffi," Sandra says to me when Rhys's back is turned. "Cup of tea?"

I freeze. I can feel the old familiar fight happening inside of me. What will win? Politeness or social anxiety? Or will this be the moment my muteness rears its ugly head and shouts (silently) HI STEFFI, DID YOU THINK I'D—

"Okay," I say. I imagine pushing against a straining cupboard door and locking the beast inside. Gotcha. This time.

I touch Rhys's wrist and he turns back to me, halfway through the living room door. **I'm going to have tea with your mum.**

He spins round and throws his mother another glare, before turning back to me. **You really don't have to do that.**

"It's okay," I say. "You set up the DVD."

Rhys hesitates, looks at his mother again, and shrugs reluctantly. I go into the kitchen to find his mother already pouring out water from the kettle. Either she has a super-speedy kettle or she'd been planning this.

"How do you take your tea?" Sandra asks me with a smile.

"Just milk," I say, hovering over a kitchen stool then forcing myself to sit on it.

Sandra busies herself making the tea without speaking, and the silence hangs over us, awkward and loud.

"Thanks," I say finally when she rests the cup in front of me.

"I'm so pleased you've been able to help Rhys settle in," Sandra says, sitting on a seat opposite me. "It's such a relief for me that he's been able to make such a good friend."

Did she emphasize *good friend*, or am I just being paranoid? I try to smile, but it doesn't feel very convincing so I take a scalding gulp of tea instead.

"Rhys says you'd like to work with animals," she says.

I'm so surprised I can't even nod. They really must have talked about me if they got to the level of detail that includes my wish to work with animals.

"I've been thinking about getting a dog," Sandra continues gamely. "I'd quite like a bit of company."

"You should adopt," I blurt, thrilled to have something to say. "I work at the kennels in town, and there are some really sweet dogs that need homes."

"I'll bear that in mind," Sandra says. "Well . . ." She stands up, and I understand that I am now allowed to leave the kitchen. What was *that* all about? Weird. "I wanted to let you know that you're welcome here any time," she adds.

"Thanks," I say. I swallow my tea in three sickening swallows and plonk the cup down onto the table. I inch out of the kitchen, throwing out another "Thank you!" as I go.

When I go through to the living room, I see that Rhys has created a tiny fort out of cushions and blankets, closer to the screen than I'd usually sit and with a careful amount of space between what is obviously his main cushion and mine. The sofa, which takes up the length of the back of the room, has been stripped bare.

Rhys's back is to me and he is playing with the remote, scrolling through subtitle options. I walk over to him and settle onto my side of the faux fort. He glances at me and smiles. **Hi. Sorry about my mother.**

That's okay. She just wanted to say hello. I gesture around me. **What's this?**

He pauses and I see anxiety sweep across his face. **I thought it would be better to watch it like this. That way we can watch and talk. Is that okay?**

I smile, understanding. Our cushions and TV make a kind of triangle, making it possible for us to communicate while we watch. On the sofa, it would have been more awkward, bunched up on either side. Here we have space. **Great idea.**

He relaxes, the familiar beam reappearing. **Great. Ready to start? Oh!** He raises his finger and then jumps up. **Popcorn. Be right back.**

Popcorn. The way he put up his finger as his face pinged like a microwave. He's so adorable. Oh God, I think I love him.

I stand up to look around the room, stepping toward a family portrait above the fireplace. Rhys, who must be about ten or eleven in the picture, is standing between two other boys—one older, one younger—and in front of his parents. They look like the perfect family, standing all proud together. I find family portraits of nuclear families fascinating.

I decide that Rhys doesn't look much like either his mother or his father, though he is almost identical to his older brother. They have the same grin and the same warm, slightly mischievous eyes.

I hear the sound of Rhys returning and I glance behind me to smile, hoping it won't look weird that I'm just standing here staring at a photo of his family. **You look a lot like your brother**, I say.

Rhys is holding a giant bowl of popcorn, so he shrugs and smiles rather than reply, putting the bowl on the floor between our cushions and then coming to stand beside me.

Aled's at university, he explains now that his hands are free. I nod, remembering that he told me that a couple of weeks ago. **Edinburgh. Pharmacy, like my dad.**

Your dad's a pharmacist?

He nods. **Mum is too. That's how they met.**

Your dad is from Guyana, right? I have to fingerspell Guyana and I get it wrong, adding in at least one extra A, feeling my face warm.

But he smiles, patient, and fingerspells it correctly for me. **Yes.**

Have you ever been there?

Just once a couple of years ago. We visited my grandparents. I want to go back one day, though. He grins. **Shall we watch the film?**

I nod quickly, hoping I haven't asked too many annoying questions. We sit together on our little cushion fort and I reach for a handful of popcorn so I have something to do with my hands. Rhys presses the remote and the film starts with the sound of typewriter keys click-clacking, staccato and tense. I worry then that *Atonement* isn't the best film to watch with a deaf friend. For one thing, it's the atmospheric kind of film that uses the score like dialogue, filling in the long silences between characters with explanatory mood music. Is the closed captioning enough? I watch Rhys's face, trying to read him from my peripheral vision. Does he know what he's missing? I wonder. Does he mind? But then I turn back to the screen and realize *I've* missed a whole chunk of the opening because I'd been worrying about *Rhys* missing something. There's irony for you.

I try to settle myself into the film, but I'm so aware of Rhys beside me that I don't do a very good job of it. He is calm and still, his shoulders relaxed and his head slightly tilted. Every time he reaches for some popcorn, my heart goes *zip*, because maybe this is the time he reaches for my hand, maybe . . .

But of course he doesn't, because I am Steffi. I am not Meg.

We don't talk during the whole film. When the library sex scene happens—which I had completely forgotten about until the moment the library door opens on-screen and my entire body heats up twenty degrees—we both studiously avoid even looking at each other. When the horses are shot on the beach, I have to hold in tears, and I turn my head slightly away from Rhys so he won't see. Maybe this wasn't the best choice of film for us to watch together—so heavy and intense—but it's too late now.

When the credits roll, Rhys turns to me, his expression open and expectant. **Did you like it?**

Yes. Actually, I feel emotionally drained. I'm working hard not to act as grief-stricken as I actually feel.

How did it compare to the book?

I hesitate, trying to articulate my thoughts in my own head before I even think of translating them into the language we share. **It's a very good** . . . I flail, stopping mid-sentence. I have no idea what "adaptation" is in BSL. **Film**, I finish helplessly.

Better than the book?

No, as good. Different.

Are you okay?

Yes! Why?

I can read faces. It's what I do. Sad?

90

I think carefully, hands poised. The thing with having limited BSL skills is that it forces you to condense complex emotions into their simplest form in order to communicate them. **It made my heart hurt.**

He smiles. For a crazy moment I think he's going to take my hand, but instead he uses his own to tell me that he knows what I mean, that he feels the same.

"DINNER!" an unexpected voice bellows from behind me, and I pretty much jump out of my skin.

Rhys scowls, groans, then rolls his eyes. **Sorry**, he says to me.

"Hi!" the voice comes again and I turn reluctantly. The voice belongs to a teenage boy who must be Rhys's brother Alfie. Small for a thirteen-year-old and skinny, with a crop of messy dark hair, he is balancing on the ends of his toes and absently hopping from foot to foot, like there is too much of him to contain. "Are you Rhys's girlfriend?"

Rhys, who has got to his feet, takes a swipe at him and Alfie dodges, grinning. Ducking his head under Rhys's aloft arm, he crosses his eyes at me. "Are you?"

"No," I say.

"Aw." He looks disappointed. He turns to Rhys and they begin a blisteringly fast conversation, hands and faces in constant motion. It's both impressive and impenetrable. I realize just how slow Rhys has to be when we're talking, and it makes me feel a little embarrassed and a lot inadequate. Why is he even putting up with me?

Rhys grabs hold of Alfie's hood and pulls him in for an affectionate headlock. "Dinner?" he says out loud to me, his hands occupied.

"Um." I hadn't planned to stay for dinner.

"Dad cooked," Alfie pipes up. "And Mum set you a place at the table. *And* she put out the nice place mats."

"Sure," I say to Rhys, trying to smile. "Why not?"

When I head home a couple of hours later, I am feeling very pleased with myself. For one thing, I'm so stuffed with food—metemgee, which is a type of stew from Guyana and which I'm pretty sure has changed my life—I'm practically rolling down the street. For another, I managed to get through the entire meal without a) saying anything stupid or b) failing to say anything at all. This is, frankly, *huge* for me.

One of the times I find speaking hardest is when there are more than two people in the room. I'm mostly fine when it's one on one, but if there's a group I find it almost impossible to say anything out loud. A lot of that is because I can't insert myself into conversations; I literally don't know *how*. (What if I speak at the same time as someone else? What if no one hears me and I have to repeat myself? What if I say something stupid and they all look at me weirdly? Why would anyone care what I have to say anyway?) My brain and my mouth freeze and I just stand there, dumb, until I'm rescued (usually by Tem). Even if it's a group of friends or family, I am almost always the person watching from the side, smiling gamely, nodding, laughing at jokes, but contributing absolutely nothing.

So that's why I was so nervous about agreeing to dinner with the Gold family. All I could hope was that they would be kind enough to let me sit there and eat without doing what people usually do, which is ask me loud, patronizing questions in a bid to get me to "open up." I told myself that Rhys was there, and if all else failed I could always sign to him.

But the dinner turned out to be a revelation. I talked! I answered questions! I made a joke about fish! And they *laughed*!

I love the Gold family.

From the moment I sat down, it was different from any other dinner. They all talked with their hands, faces, and bodies as well as just with their mouths, so casually and easily that it didn't seem to matter which method any of us chose at any one time. When Rhys's mother asked me what I wanted to drink, I signed **Water, please** and no one acted like it was strange I hadn't also spoken. And then, a few minutes later, when I signed **The film was great**, I said it out loud as well, and, again, no one acted like it was strange that this time I had spoken.

This might sound like nothing to most people, but it made my heart swell three sizes. It made me beam. Druglike, it made me want more. So I talked more. I told them I wanted to study Zoology with Animal Behavior at Bangor University. I told them about Rita and how her ears had to be pinned up when she was a puppy because one kept flopping over.

It felt so normal. *I* felt so normal.

For the first time, I think I understand what my Uncle Geoff had wanted for me when he took it upon himself to teach me BSL all those years ago. It wasn't about the language itself—it was about giving me a choice. It was showing me an alternative to speech, showing me that I could express myself how I wanted, and that that was okay.

I wish it hadn't taken me so long to learn this lesson, but at least I got to learn it eventually.

I'm in such a good mood I decide to take a detour on the way back to Dad's so I can drop in on Mum. It's been a week or so since I last saw her and I want to share my good news with someone. It's after 8 p.m., so I'll have missed Bell, but at least I can see Mum.

My key to their house is in my bag at Dad's house, so I knock. It's Keir who opens the door.

"Hi!" I say, and the look of surprise on his face—at my presence, my greeting, or both—pleases me.

"Hi, Steffi," he says. He steps back so I can walk past him and turns slightly. "Joanne, Stefanie's here."

Mum comes out of the kitchen, her brow furrowed. She opens her mouth to say something, but it's at that moment that Bell, my tiny, excitable half-sister, comes flying down the stairs, wearing a Tinkerbell nightie. "Steffi!" she shrieks, then launches herself at me.

Bell is at the age where everything and everyone is exciting. As her big sister, I am basically goddess incarnate.

"Hello, Belly," I say, hoisting her into the air. She shrieks again, then throws her little arms round my neck. Bell is five, but she's very small for her age. "Shouldn't you be in bed?"

"Yes," Keir says meaningfully, raising his eyebrows at her. "Belinda *should* be in bed."

Bell rests her chin on my shoulder and nuzzles my neck. "Can you tuck me in?" she asks me.

"That's why I'm here," I say.

"See?" Bell says to her father. "I was waiting."

Keir rolls his eyes, but he smiles. "Go on, then—off with you." He turns to me. "Cup of tea?"

"Yes, please."

Keir tried to do the chummy stepfather routine for years, but we never really got along. For one thing, it always felt like he was trying too hard, especially in the days when I couldn't speak to him. Things changed around the time Clark died, when I was thirteen. I came and stayed with him and Mum for a while to give Dad and Lucy time to grieve on their own, and he was so patient and kind to me it was pretty hard to stay antagonistic toward him. He doesn't try to act like my dad anymore, but I let him be a friend.

I carry Bell back up the stairs to her bedroom and sit with her for a few minutes as she tells me about the fight her toy elephants are having (one ate all the peanuts) and her recent decision to become a world-class ballerina. Bell is a chatterbox, and it's one of the things I most love about her.

By the time I get downstairs my tea has cooled to the perfect temperature and I sit with Mum and Keir, sipping it.

"So you were actually talking?" Mum asks. "To Rhys's parents?"

I nod, beaming. "We had conversations."

"Oh, Steffi." I don't think she's ever looked at me with such happiness. There are actual tears in her eyes. "I'm so pleased. I knew it would happen one day."

"I think it really helped that I was signing at the same time," I say. "It was like a life jacket. Does that make sense?"

Mum's smile falters. "Are Rhys's parents deaf?"

"No, just Rhys."

"So why were you signing to them?"

"Because that's how they all speak," I say. "It's totally normal to them."

"It sounds like an important step," Keir says, and I notice the look he gives Mum. "That's such good news, Steffi."

"It is," I say, a little defensive now.

"But do you think . . ." Mum pauses, then persists. "Do you think you'd have felt the same if it wasn't a deaf household?"

"It's not a deaf household," I say, frowning. My happy glow has started to tarnish. "And, no, I wouldn't. I told you that. The BSL really helped."

"But, Steffi . . ." Another annoying pause. "It's great that you talked to people you didn't know, but I don't want to think you're . . . *hiding* behind BSL. You won't always have that . . . life jacket."

"Why won't I?" Frustration is building in my throat and chest. "It's not 'hiding' behind it. Would you say Rhys is hiding behind it because he uses it?"

"But Rhys *is* deaf," Mum says, almost triumphantly. "He's who BSL is for."

I push my mug away from me. "I thought you'd be happy."

"I am happy!" She reaches for my hand. "I just worry, love."

"Well, stop worrying!" I snap, snatching back my hand. "Just be supportive. For God's *sake*."

"Stefanie," Mum says warningly. "Don't use that tone, please."

I bite down hard on my tongue to stop myself responding. Nothing's changed. And, now that I'm sitting at this table, I'm wondering why I had thought it would have. Mum still feels the same way about BSL as she did when I was six years old and Uncle Geoff first suggested it. She still thinks it's like admitting defeat, like accepting a disability.

Except, to be honest, she'd probably be fine with me having a disability. So long as it was one she could point at, one she could explain.

"I should go back to Dad's," I say.

"Oh, Steffi." Mum sighs, like I'm being difficult or

something. "I'm just trying to be realistic. I don't want you to get your hopes up."

God forbid.

Mum has had an anxious daughter for sixteen years, and she still doesn't seem to get the concept of little victories. That spending an evening where I wasn't feeling sick every time someone asked me a question is actually a really big deal, and the fact that it might just be a one-off is the kind of thing I'm already worried about. There's no such thing as getting your hopes up if you're anxious. Little victories are everything in a world where worst-case scenarios are on an endless loop in your head.

But Mum has never been okay with my "issues." When I was a child who couldn't speak, my dad tried to be patient and understanding, but Mum got frustrated and angry. She was basically ready to try anything to get me to talk. She tried both the carrot and the stick, offering treats if I spoke and then threatening punishment when I didn't. She tried reverse psychology, telling me that she was really enjoying the quiet. She guilt-tripped me to tears by telling me I was making her life so hard—didn't I see how much I was upsetting her?

Once, when I was eight, she lost me on purpose at the supermarket. I went to get apples, confident that she would remain in the same place, and returned to find her gone. I wandered the aisles with increasing panic until I was rescued by a couple of shop assistants, at which point I burst into tears. I can still remember the looks of bafflement on their faces as they tried to talk to me only to be faced with my tear-stained, rigid face. I remember how they started talking to each other as if I couldn't hear them—"She must be deaf. Or maybe she's got . . . you know, special needs? What! She might have!"—before making an announcement over the loudspeaker, asking for the parent of the "quiet girl" to come to customer services.

"For Christ's sake, Steffi," Mum hissed at me as she led me—sobbing all over again—away. "You have to be able to talk in an emergency. What if you really did get lost? Do I need to put a label round your neck with our address on it? How do you think you're ever going to grow up if you can't talk?" She gave my arm a shake. "Well?"

I was such a wreck by then I couldn't even talk to *her*. It took me hours to get my voice back after that particular incident, and I refused to return to the supermarket for months.

"I won't do it again," she promised. "It was just an experiment, and it didn't work, so it won't happen again."

She never said sorry, though.

Keir eventually drives me back to Dad's house, where I grab Rita and take her for a walk in the dark. I tell her about the Golds and my mother and metemgee and *Atonement*. I ask her if she thinks I'm hiding behind BSL and she cocks her head at me, then pokes her wet nose into my hand.

I smile. "I love you too," I say.

Steffi's list of diagnoses–age five to present:

Selective mutism
Anxiety disorder (various)
Situational anxiety (school)

Then updated to:
Generalized anxiety disorder (severe)
Social anxiety (severe)
Panic disorder (moderate)
Glossophobia (fear of public speaking)

9

I MEET JANE, MY CBT THERAPIST, THE FOLLOWING
Tuesday afternoon after school. I see her once every two weeks for an hour that's usually filled with going through my worksheets from the last session and making plans for the next lot. I used to think CBT was a transformative kind of experience, something you learned once and then had forever, as if the T stood for Training instead of Therapy, as if my mind can learn commands as easily and permanently as a dog learning to sit and stay. But CBT is a process, like pretty much anything, and it takes work. A lot of work.

And a lot of worksheets.

"How did you get on with the experiment?" Jane asks, flipping over one of the sheets and scanning it quickly. She gives me one of her therapy smiles.

"Well, I did it," I say. "So . . ."

"Well done," she says. "And how did it feel?"

Part of my CBT is to do behavioral experiments, and this time it had been to go into town by myself on Saturday morning and buy any three items in three different shops. It didn't matter what the shops were, so long as one of them was the supermarket. Jane and I had filled in the preparation sheet at our previous meeting. I had to write down things like what I worried would happen and how likely I thought a particular scenario was. Like, "I think if I go to the deli section of the supermarket I will have a panic attack and die."

Okay, so the point of the exercise is not to exaggerate, so Jane wouldn't actually let me write "and die." But the panic attack bit—that's a real worry. Do you know how horrible it is to have a panic attack in a public place? Very. That's how horrible it is. Very horrible.

Anyway, after I got back from town I had to fill in my review sheet, which is basically comparing the reality with my original expectations. I hadn't had a panic attack, for example. In fact, I'd made it to the drugstore (new mascara), stationer's (a set of new pens), and supermarket (milk) and back home again without freaking out once.

"This is excellent progress," Jane says, smiling. I study that smile carefully, looking for cues. It actually looks like it might be a real smile. "Really excellent, Steffi."

"This is stuff ten-year-olds can do," I point out. As weird as this might sound, I don't like getting credit for stuff that my rational mind understands is really simple. It just reminds me how pathetic I am.

"Could *you* have done it at ten?" she asks.

"Well, no, but—"

"Well, then," Jane says. Her smile is definitely real now. "How are you getting on at school?"

I shrug. "Okay, I guess. I answered a question in my math class."

"That's fantastic!" Her whole face actually lights up. "Out loud?"

I nod. "It was a bit of surprise, actually. I didn't realize I was going to."

"And how did you feel?"

"Awful," I say. "Like I wanted to throw up."

"That's understandable," Jane says smoothly. Nothing ever seems to throw Jane. "This is all an adjustment period, like we've talked about. It's not a small thing, taking medication. And that's what I'm here for, to talk it all through."

"Why is the solution to everything talking it through?" I ask. "Why's there such an emphasis on talking? It's not fair."

"Because being part of society involves living with other people," Jane says. "And we're not a telepathic species. Talking is an essential part of understanding each other."

"I can understand people just fine," I grumble, flicking my fingernail against the skin of my thumb.

"But can *they* understand *you*?" Jane asks gently. "Remember, life is about dialogues, not monologues."

I look up at her. "Do you want to write that down so you can use it with your other clients?"

Jane laughs. "That's not the first time I've used that phrase." I laugh despite myself and she grins. "How would you feel about working on talking out loud in class over the next couple of weeks? Maybe answering some more questions? Or even asking them yourself?"

My stomach twists. "Um."

"Let's start a new sheet," Jane says enthusiastically, reaching for one. "It may help if you think about it in advance—what questions you could ask, that kind of thing."

"I'm not sure . . ." I trail off. The words just run out.

Jane, attuned to my vocal patterns, looks up and puts her pencil down. "Go ahead," she says encouragingly.

I take a breath. "I'm not sure that will help me right now."

She nods. "What makes you say that?"

"Well, I think if I feel like I have to do it, it'll worry me more. When I spoke in math, it was totally unplanned, and even though it made me feel bad, that was only afterward, not before. You know?" My voice picks up speed and comes out a little garbled, but I manage.

"That's a good point," Jane says. "And it's really good that you picked up on that. What would you like to work on instead?" She points to the sheet and smiles. "You know I like to use my sheets."

"The going-into-town one was good because it was, like, active?" I say carefully. "So . . . I don't know what that means. But . . . you know?"

Jane nods again. "I do know. It's more helpful for you to be doing something that *could* involve talking, rather than simply knowing you have to talk."

"Yeah . . . I think so."

She thinks for a moment. "How are you getting on outside of your classes when you're at school?"

"Okay . . ." I say cautiously.

"Where do you go during your break times?"

She's caught me. Dammit. "Um." I actually consider lying, but give in. "The library. Or, like, a bench outside."

"That's not ideal now that it's getting colder," Jane says, as if that's the problem. "Have you tried to go back into the common room?"

"Yes," I say triumphantly. "I've gone in with Rhys. Twice."

"Well, that's certainly a good start. How would you feel about working on that? Try to go into the common room at least once a day over the next week or two. It doesn't have to be by yourself, but that would be an even bigger step."

"Okay," I say. The thought makes me feel ill, but not as ill as having to call out in class. And I can take Rhys with me.

"Excellent," Jane says, looking pleased. She slides the worksheet and pencil across the table to me. "Shall we get started?"

It takes me the whole of the next morning to work myself up into walking into the common room. At first I intend to just pop in during the first break time, but when the time comes

I can't even bear to walk into the block, let alone the room. I dawdle outside, find a bench, and pretend to text for the entire twenty minutes.

But then as soon as I get to English the self-hatred begins. It starts quietly—*all you had to do was walk in. You didn't even have to stay there*—but I find myself spiralling rapidly until I'm basically attacking myself inside my own head. *Pathetic, Steffi. You are pathetic, pathetic, pathetic.*

"Steffi?" I look up, dazed, to see Mrs. Baxter looking at me. I blink at her. "You haven't turned a page in five minutes," she says. "Are you here with us?"

There's a soft laugh from my classmates and I swallow down a guttural sob that's building from nowhere and turn a page of the book.

"Page fifty-seven," Mrs. Baxter says. Her voice is kind, and my rational side knows that the laugh from my classmates wasn't meant to be mean, but I'm not feeling very rational right now.

Look at everyone else being normal, Steffi. And look at you. You can't even keep up with everyone reading a book. You can't even say "Yes" to a simple question. Why are you even here? Why do you even bother?

When the lunch bell rings, I don't even give myself time to think. I bolt out of the classroom, down the corridor, shortcut through the science block, and finally find myself outside the common-room door. Even though lunchtime has barely started, I can already hear the noise from inside.

"Hey, Steffi," a voice says from behind me. It's Cassidy King, one of the clever but nice bunch. She's walking past me, swinging the door open and holding it behind her for me to walk through.

"Hey," I reply. She smiles at me and heads off toward her friends, who are clustered together in the corner. I'm already imagining how I will write this down on my worksheet.

Walked into the room. Said hello—out loud!—to Cassidy King.

Right. What next? I should do something before I leave again. I can't just stand here awkwardly. I walk casually—oh so casually—over to the noticeboard and start scanning it thoughtfully.

LIKE NETBALL? MS. ILLOVIC IS LOOKING FOR VOLUNTEERS TO HELP WITH THE YEAR 7 AND 8 NETBALL TEAMS! EMAIL E.ILLOVIC@WINDHAM.SCH.UK

FOR SALE—THIRD GENERATION IPAD £500
£500?! Fuck off you joker!

FEMINIST SOCIETY—MEET IN COMMON ROOM WEDNESDAYS AT 6 P.M.! NO MEN ALLOWED!
Isn't that sexist to men?

REVERSE SEXISM IS NOT A THING
Yeah but what about male feminists?
FUCK OFF ETHAN I KNOW THAT'S YOU

So this is what I'm missing. I stand there for a full minute, trying to psych myself up to making a lap of the common room before escaping, when there's a tap on my shoulder. I turn to see Rhys's smiling face.

Hi! he says.

I'm so happy to see him I almost hug him. **Hi!** I reply. I gesture to the noticeboard. **I'm thinking of joining the Feminist Society.**

Rhys looks at the notice and his grin widens. **Cool**, he signs. He thinks for a second, then signs, **Up the women!** with an awkward little thumbs-up at the end.

I almost die with how adorable it is. **Exactly**, I sign, somehow managing not to show my complete adoration on my face. (I think.)

Want to get some lunch? he asks. **I'm on my way to the canteen.**

Sure, I sign casually. I hike my backpack further up my shoulder and smile at him. **Lead the way.**

10

ON FRIDAY, I GIVE IN TO TEM'S CONSTANT BEGGING
and agree to go running with her. It's a cool evening and the air
feels fresh because it rained earlier. Even the pavement smells
good. I bring Rita for moral support and meet Tem at the park
near my school.

"Hello!" Tem shouts happily, throwing both her arms in the
air before dropping into a squat to give Rita a hug.

"You're in a good mood," I observe.

"I am!" Tem jumps to her feet and bounces on the spot. "It's
perfect running weather. My best friend is running with me.
Rita's here. And . . ." She wiggles her eyebrows at me. "I spent
the afternoon with Karam."

We take a long, lazy route around the residential part of
town, alternating left and right turns for a while and then dou-
bling back on ourselves. Tem lets me set the pace and doesn't

complain when I have to stop and wheeze. I'm not really up to talking and running, which is fine because she talks enough for both of us.

I hear all about Karam, who seems to have become even more perfect since the last time she'd told me about him. They'd apparently spent a couple of hours writing and printing leaflets for a march that's happening in London in a few weeks' time—Karam is arranging a coach to take people into the city—and then gone for a drink after.

"An alcoholic drink?" I ask.

"For him, yes. For me, no. I wanted one, but he said no, so I had a Coke." She beams at me. "He's really mature."

They'd "talked and talked and talked," had two more drinks ("He let me have a gin and tonic after the first two Cokes!"), and then gone for a walk.

"Is 'walk' code for kissing?" I ask.

Tem grins. "Yes."

"So are you happier at college?"

"Stef, I just told you I was kissing Karam Homsi. Ask me about that. College is boring."

I roll my eyes. "How much can you really say about kissing?"

She chokes out a laugh. "I'll remind you that you said that when you finally kiss someone."

I stop running and put my hands on my waist, squeezing out a breath. "Thanks for that."

"Oh, I'm teasing," she says easily. "I just mean obviously

there's loads to say about kissing. And he's such a good kisser, Stef. Like, a kissing god."

"Are you going out now?"

"You're asking all the wrong questions!" she says in frustration. "Can't you be excited for me?"

"For kissing a guy?" I'm not sure why I'm feeling so irritated.

"For getting noticed by Karam. He's so amazing, honestly. And he wants to be with me."

"So you are going out?"

"For God's sake, Steffi!" she snaps.

"So no, then?"

Tem lets out a growl of annoyance and then turns away from me, sprinting off down the street. I watch her go, still waiting for my heart rate to return to normal. I lean against the garden wall behind me and pull out my phone. I'm not sure how long it will take Tem to make her way back to me—she always does eventually— so I open jackbytes, hoping to see Rhys's name on the online list.

rhysespieces: howdy

stefstef: ☺

rhysespieces: what's up?

stefstef: i'm RUNNING

rhysespieces: what really? right now?

rhysespieces: don't run and text, stef. that's how broken
   ankles happen.

stefstef: okay, i'm taking a break right now. how are you?

rhysespieces: i'm good. playing gran turismo with alfie. he says hi.

stefstef: hi alfie!

rhysespieces: are you running by yourself?

stefstef: no, i'm with Tem. did I tell you she's a runner?

rhysespieces: no, that's cool. i run sometimes too.

stefstef: you should come along some time.

rhysespieces: cool! it's not as fun running alone.

stefstef: are you a good runner, though? bcoz i am not.

rhysespieces: ha! i can do it without falling over, but i won't win any medals iykwim.

stefstef: still sounds better than me.

rhysespieces: well, if you fall over, i'll carry you home!

stefstef: um. okay!

rhysespieces: jk.

stefstef: so you WON'T carry me home if I fell?

rhysespieces: well obvs i would

rhysespieces: i just mean that

rhysespieces: like not in a weird way

rhysespieces: oh my god

rhysespieces: so how's Tem?

stefstef: she's good. telling me all about this guy she's madly in love with.

rhysespieces: what's his name?

stefstef: karam

rhysespieces: oh an actual guy

stefstef: huh?

rhysespieces: oh shit alfie's getting annoyed, i better get back to the game

stefstef: okay! see you next week

rhysespieces: have a good run. don't trip ☺

[rhysespieces has logged off]

I wait for five more minutes before Tem reappears at the end of the road. When she reaches me she is panting and contrite.

"Sorry," she says.

"Sorry yourself," I say. "Thanks for the breathing time."

She grins. "Everything I do, I do it for you."

"I just had a weird conversation with Rhys."

Her eyes widen. "Oh my God. Show me."

"I can't, it was on jackbytes. It doesn't save the conversations."

"Well, that's a bit bloody useless. What's the point if you can't reread the conversations afterward? Tell me, then. We can walk back, if you want."

We meander back toward my house and I recount what Rhys said as best I can. She listens, a grin broadening on her face. When I tell her how he went back to playing video games with Alfie, she outright laughs.

"Stef, you know he's in love with you, right?"

I flush. "No he isn't."

"Oh my God, he clearly is. He wanted you to say that *you* were madly in love with someone, and that someone was him."

"That doesn't make *any* sense. Why would I say you were talking about a guy if I really meant me?"

"Because people are weird."

"Oh great. That helps. And people wonder why I get anxious about talking to people? Why can't people just say what they mean?"

"Because people are weird," she says again.

"But he has a girlfriend," I add. My throat is getting tight with a confused sort of panic. "How can he be in love with me if he has a girlfriend?"

Tem looks at me, a slight frown on her face. "You don't actually *know* if he has a girlfriend or not, right? That's all in your head. Remember?"

"I'm pretty sure he does."

"Based on what? The fact that he had a girl in his Facebook picture a few weeks ago? God, Steffi. I thought you were smart."

"I . . ." I'm suddenly so confused I don't know what to say. "I'm sure he does. He . . ." What *am* I basing it on? "He must have."

"Incorrect. Besides!" Tem continues triumphantly—she is clearly enjoying this. "He could have a girlfriend *and* be in love with you. That's totally possible. More than possible. It's *probable*. You are Steffi Brons, complete knockout."

"Oh, shut up," I say, shoving her.

"You could be a knockout if you stopped hiding."

"Tem," I almost whimper, completely pathetically, and she stops walking, turning to face me.

"Steffi," she says, very seriously. "It is my duty as your best friend to explain these things to you. *One*: this Rhys guy clearly likes you a lot, whether that's with or without an existing girlfriend. And *two*: he has good taste, because you're awesome. You can be a knockout without being some kind of supernaturally beautiful extrovert, you know."

"I don't think you can," I say. "That's what 'knockout' *means*. Like, you knock them out with how gorgeous and cool you are."

"Oh, spare me." She rolls her eyes again. "*I* think you're a knockout, in a special Steffi kind of way. And I bet that's what he sees too. Can I meet him? I like him already."

I try to imagine Tem and Rhys meeting. Him, cool and calm and sweet. Her, bubbling over with warmth and fire. There's no question over whether they'll get along, because they're both the kind of people who get along with everyone. I'm the awkward one: the mutual, the hanger-on. I've never had people to introduce before.

"Do you really think he likes me?"

"Yes." Tem cocks her head, Rita-style, and gives me one of her piercing looks. Her black curls are bound tightly into her running-bun, and her makeup-free face is open and gentle. "Do you like him?"

I open my mouth, close it, nibble on my lip. This is a far more multilayered question than it may first appear to be. It is "Do I like him?" and "Can I admit to myself that I like him?" and "Can I admit out loud that I like him?" all in one.

"Maybe?" I say eventually.

Tem grins. "I knew it," she says.

On Wednesday, Rhys surprises me by turning up at the kennels during my shift. I come to reception with Anaïs—a whip-smart Frenchwoman who always looks immaculate but owns the scruffiest, dopiest terrier cross you've ever seen—so she can sign some forms, and there he is. Standing by the desk, holding a Labrador puppy in his arms.

"Hi!" I say out loud, startled into speech.

He grins at me but doesn't reply, his arms otherwise occupied with the weight of the puppy, whose name, incidentally, is Sally. **Just a second**, I sign to him, gesturing to Anaïs. I'm so flustered I mess it up and have to repeat myself. I'm suddenly very aware of my uniform—gray, long-sleeved T-shirt under green overalls. Not exactly high fashion.

"It's not a problem to move from three to four days a week," I say to Anaïs, reaching under the reception desk and pulling out the right file. I flip through it and pull out the Day Request form. "But it'll be a notice period of two weeks to make the change, and an increase of thirty pounds per month."

Anaïs nods. "I know. I read the forms when I first registered Toulouse."

"Here you go, then," I say brightly, sliding the form across the desk.

"Thank you," she says delicately, taking a pen from her bag.

What are you doing here? I ask Rhys.

I don't get an answer until I get rid of Anaïs, who manages to take her time over the form she apparently already knew all about.

Hi, I say again to Rhys, unable to keep the smile off my face. Not that I'm supposed to notice these things, but he looks extra adorable when holding a Labrador puppy.

"Hi," he says out loud. "I made a friend!"

I can see that! Shall I take her?

He nods and I lift Sally out of his arms, cuddling her warm body close. **I came by to ask you something, and when I got here the bald guy**—I assume he means Ivan here—**said that you'd probably come through here soon, and in the meantime I should look after the puppy**.

I have a sneaking suspicion that Ivan did this on purpose. That man misses *nothing*.

"Thanks for holding her," I say. Sally wriggles in my arms and tries to lick my face.

No problem. She's cute.

"What did you want to ask me?" My mind has already spun through the options. Will you help me with my math homework? Will you eat this cake I brought? Will you go on a date with me? Will you marry me?

It's my birthday on Friday.

"Oh!"

Yeah. He rolls his eyes, but he's smiling. **I know. I wanted to keep it quiet, but my parents want to take me out for a birthday dinner on Saturday. And . . . do you want to come?**

I stare at him over Sally's fuzzy yellow head. What does this mean? Is this a math-homework-buddy invite, or a go-on-a-date invite?

My parents suggested it, he says. Oh. Well that's my answer, isn't it? **I want you there too!** he adds, looking mortified. But it's too late.

"Sure, I'll come," I say. "Are you seeing your friends as well?"

Yeah, on Friday night. None of them are eighteen yet, so we can't go out drinking or anything. He smiles. **Maybe next year. But on Saturday, Meg is coming. My friend Meg. You can meet her—I think you'll get along.**

Friend Meg? Did he actually sign girlfriend but I saw friend because it's what I wanted to see? The signs aren't similar. I didn't just hallucinate that, did I? Should I ask? No. No, Steffi.

"Sure," I say again.

Great! He looks relieved. **They're booking a table tonight so I'll let you know what time and where and stuff.**

I give him a thumbs-up. "I should get back to my shift."

He nods quickly. **Of course. Sorry. I'll see you tomorrow?**

"Yeah."

Rhys gives me a little wave before he leaves. I wait until he's gone before I groan into Sally's soft fur.

"Come on," I whisper to her. "Let's get you back to your mum."

Sally yawns, stretches her head against my arm, and pees all down my overalls.

Things I worried about on the bus: a snapshot of an anxious brain . . .

Is that car slowing down? Is someone going to get out and kidnap me? It is slowing down. What if someone asks for directions? What if—Oh. They're just dropping someone off. The bus is late. What if it doesn't arrive? What if I'm late getting to school? Did I turn my straighteners off? What if the bus isn't running today and no one told me? Where's the—oh. There's the bus. Oh crap is that Rowan from Biology? What if he sees me? What if he wants to chat? Hide. Okay, he hasn't seen me. He hasn't seen me. What if he did see me and now he thinks I'm weird for not saying hi? Did I remember to clean out Rita's bowl properly? What if she gets sick? One day Rita will die. One day I'll die. One day everyone will die. What if I die today and everyone sees that my bra has a hole in it? What if the bus crashes? Where are the exits? Why is there an exit on the ceiling? What if that headache Dad has is a brain tumor? Would I live with Mum all the time if Dad died? Why am I thinking about my living arrangements instead of how horrible it would be if Dad died? What's wrong with me? What if Rhys doesn't like me? What if he does? What if we get together and we split up? What if we get together and don't split up and then we're together forever until we die? One day I'll die. Did I remember to turn my straighteners off? Yes. Yes. Did I? Okay my stop's coming up. I need to get off in about two minutes. Should I get up now? Will the guy next to me get that I have to get off or will I have to ask him to move? But what if he's getting off too and I look like a twat? What if worrying kills brain cells? What if I never get to go to university? What if I do and it's awful? Should I say thank you to the driver on the way off? Okay, get up, move toward the front of the bus. Go, step. Don't trip over that old man's stick. Watch out for the stick. Watch out for the—shit. Did anyone notice that? No, no one's looking at me. But what if they are? Okay, doors are opening, GO! I didn't say thank you to the driver. What if he's having a bad day and that would have made it better? Am I a bad person?

Yeah but did I actually turn my straighteners off?

120

11

BY SATURDAY, I HAVE NO IDEA WHY I SAID YES TO
something as terrifying as a birthday dinner. In a restaurant.
With a family I barely know. And the possibly-girlfriend-but-
maybe-probably-not of the boy I'm trying not to like.

Excellent decision-making, Steffi. You genius.

But I can't back out now, mainly because I can't think of
a way to do it without being rude or, at the very least, trans-
parent.

"I bet he tells you he loves you," Tem says, which is both
helpful and incredibly unhelpful.

"Please don't be disappointed if he doesn't," I say.

"I won't if you won't," she replies.

Dad drives me to the Italian restaurant and doesn't even get
annoyed with me when I sit motionless in the front seat for five
minutes.

"Shall we talk through what's worrying you?" he asks, patient as a saint.

"People."

"The Gold family, or the staff at the restaurant?"

"Both."

"Because you'll need to talk to them?"

I nod.

"The Gold family invited you," Dad says. "They've spent an evening with you before, and they enjoyed your company. They've invited you to share an evening with them again. Because they know they will enjoy your company again. And why wouldn't they? You are a sweet, kind, interesting girl."

I can't help thinking that my mother would have kicked me out of the car by now and told me to stop being such a self-obsessed drama queen.

"I thought that taking medication would stop me feeling like this," I confess. My throat is both tight and thick, like a tennis ball has gotten caught inside it.

Dad is quiet for a moment. "Before the medication, I'm not sure you would have even agreed to go, love," he says softly. His words surprise me; I hadn't even thought of that, but he's right. I probably would have just said no straight off the bat. "Think of the staff at the restaurant. They see and speak to hundreds of people every day. To them, you're just another customer. They won't even notice you."

I let out a long, slow breath. "They won't even notice me."

"Not even a little bit."

"Thanks, Daddy."

Dad smiles and ruffles my hair. "Have a good time, kid. Just call me when you need me to pick you up."

I get out of the car and wave through the window before he drives off. For a moment I think I see my own anxiety mirrored on his face, but he's driving away before I can look twice. I can't imagine Dad getting anxious. He has the quiet confidence I have always depended on. He is solid as a rock.

I head toward the restaurant, walking fast so my brain can't convince my feet to head in the other direction, and walk into the restaurant behind another family. I scan the tables quickly, hoping to spot the Golds before attracting the attention of a friendly waitress and, *thank God*, there they are.

I dart round a waiter and scurry over to them, my heart kicking up a storm in my chest. As soon as I lock eyes with Rhys I will be okay. As soon as I sit down I will be okay.

Rhys sees me just as I reach the back of his father's chair, and his face breaks into a beam that sweeps my oncoming panic away. He *is* happy to see me. It *is* a good thing that I'm here. He stands as I approach and pulls out a chair for me. **Hi!**

Hi. I let him hug me, wondering if he can feel the pounding of my recovering heart. I smile at the table and actually manage an only slightly garbled "Hi!" before throwing myself into the chair and reaching for the nearest menu.

"Hi!" The unfamiliar voice comes from my left, and I look over. "I'm Meg."

Meg is pretty in a natural, elfin kind of way; her hair falls in long auburn waves and her face is a mass of freckles. She doesn't seem to be wearing any makeup, and her smile when our eyes meet is warm and immediate.

"Hi," I say.

"It's so nice to meet you," she says. Like Rhys's family, she signs as well as speaking. I realize that my determination to not ask about Meg means I know nothing about their history or their friendship. How did they meet? How come she can speak such perfect BSL?

It doesn't seem the time to ask these questions, though, so I smile back and sign that it's nice to meet her too (I'm not entirely sure whether this is a lie) and then busy myself with the menu. Sandra, Rhys's mother, asks me about the kennels, and it's a topic I am so comfortable with that I talk freely. She is still thinking about adopting a dog, so I tell her about Lily, the three-legged beagle who arrived this week, and Scout, the collie cross who was left tied to the kennels' front gate overnight, in the rain.

How's Sally getting on? Rhys signs.

She's good, I reply. **She misses you.**

See! Rhys swings round to make a face at his mother. **I told you! Adopt Sally. She's so cute.**

"The dog is for me, not you," Sandra says, laughing. "And I

want to adopt a needy dog. I'm sure there'll be plenty of people willing to take on a cute Labrador puppy." She smiles at me. "Maybe I could come and visit the kennels and meet Lily."

"I work on Wednesdays and Saturdays," I offer. "If you visit on those days, I can show you around."

As Sandra nods and the waiter arrives to take our order, I make a mental note to tell my therapist about this when I next see her. I made plans! I offered to show an almost-stranger around the kennels! How's that for progress?

Meg turns out to be friendly and chatty—basically my total opposite—which is both a blessing and a curse. Chatty people are great to have a conversation with if you're shy, because they fill your silences without making you feel awkward about it—it's one of the reasons Tem and I gel so well. But the flipside is that it means Rhys is at the very least very close to a girl who is my total opposite in the most important way. Not only can she talk, she talks A LOT. And she speaks word-perfect BSL. What hope is there for me?

Not that I want there to be hope. Or do I? To be honest, I'm losing track a little.

We've just finished eating the main course when Meg stands up, pushing her chair back. "I'm going to the bathroom," she announces. "Can you come with me, Steffi?"

I freeze. This is it. The friendliness is all an act and she's going to murder me in the bathroom for encroaching on her turf.

Why? Rhys asks, looking baffled.

"Girls always go in pairs," Meg explains. She eyes me significantly. "Steffi?"

Unfortunately, I can't think of a single reason why I would refuse to go with her, so I inch back my chair and follow her silently through the restaurant and through the door marked LADIES.

"So I wanted to talk to you," Meg says, the moment the door closes. She hops up onto the counter and grins at me. "And this seemed like the best place." She clasps her hands together and brings them up to her chin. There's something endearingly childlike about her, I think.

"Okay," I say. The two syllables are about all I can manage at that moment, trapped in a small space with this sunny chatterbox, but she doesn't seem to mind or even notice.

"Rhys," she says emphatically, pointing at me. "Specifically, you and Rhys. And Rhys and me. You and Rhys and me." This girl doesn't just talk, she talks *fast*, yet still with conviction, as if she's totally convinced by every word she says, and you should be too.

I just nod. She doesn't *seem* like she's about to start yelling at me for encroaching on her boyfriend, but then again you never know.

"You know we're not together, right? Me and Rhys? Totally not a thing."

I don't know what my face does when she says these words, but, whatever it is, it must be obvious that this is really something I *don't* know, because she makes a noise that is half delight, half frustration.

"Ohmygod, I knew it!" She slaps her hand against the countertop. "He is such a muppet. I *told* him, Steffi. Like, so many freaking times."

Told him what? I want to ask. Come on, words.

"He *likes* you, okay? Like, really likes you. He thinks you're . . . you know. Sunshine."

Sunshine.

"And I said to him—*ages* ago, Steffi!—that he should tell you straight off that him and me aren't together, in case you thought we were. Because we've been friends for freaking donkey's years and so if you didn't know us you might look at his Facebook and think we were together or something, even though, ew, he's like my brother, seriously *never*. But he was all, oh, I can't just tell her that, it'll make it so obvious that I like her, and what if she doesn't like me, blah blah blah. I mean, as if. Who wouldn't like Rhys, right? He's freaking awesome."

Obvious that I like her.

"He wanted *you* to ask *him*, like the little wuss he is, and I said to him, this is on you, dude, but he never listens to me. Boys, you know?"

I nod.

"So obviously you never asked him, and he never told you, so all this time you've just been thinking that— Wait." She stops herself abruptly, and actually puts her hand up as if she's interrupting me. She looks at me. "You *do* like him, right?"

My face flames with the fire of a thousand suns.

"Ohmygod, please say you do, otherwise I've made a gigantic fool of myself." Her eyes are wide and anxious, but more in an excitable way than a Steffi kind of way. She softens a little, her voice quieting. "I was so sure that you did, from what he's told me. Do you?"

I want to say, *Ohmygod, yes. I like him so much. I might even love him. Does he really like me back? Does he does he? Really?*

I nod.

Meg lets out a happy shriek that makes me literally jump, but she barely notices as she's already sliding off the counter and throwing her arms around me.

"I knew it!" she practically yells, right into my ear. "Yay!" She actually says "yay." I kind of love *her* too. Especially when she lets me go and apologizes immediately. "Sorry, that was over-the-line touching. I get huggy when I'm excited."

I smile. "That's okay." Words! Actual words! Out of my mouth!

"Oh good! Rhys tells me I'm like an octopus when it comes to hugs. Like I've got too many arms. Where was I? Oh yeah! Boys being wusses. So Rhys has been a big wimp, but that's 'cause he likes you, I swear. He's not usually like that. Like, he's very protective of people he cares about. I'd trust him with my whole life. So. You see?" She beams at me, slightly breathless from all her talking. "I'm definitely, definitely not with Rhys."

* * *

Meg is not with Rhys. Rhys is not with Meg. My head spins. I am giddy and terrified and excited and sick.

Rhys likes me. *Me!*

When I get back to the table, I find I can't look Rhys in the eye, but from my very careful sideways glances I see him sending panicked looks Meg's way. She is smiling serenely, refusing to meet his gaze.

"You're just in time," Sandra says to me, smiling. I stop trying to not look at Rhys and see the group of waiters approaching with a candlelit birthday cake. They start to sing when they get within a couple of feet of the table and everyone in the restaurant turns to watch and smile.

If this was happening to me on my birthday, I'd be horrified, but because it's Rhys, I find myself grinning along with everyone else when he pretends to sink in his seat and put his hands over his face. While the waiters sing, his family sign the words and I join in.

Rhys cuts the cake and begins dividing it carefully into equal pieces. The waiter sets a stack of small plates next to him. "Eighteen!" he says. "Welcome to adulthood." But he's standing slightly behind Rhys, so he doesn't get a response.

"Thank you," Rhys's mother says smoothly, smiling. "I can't quite believe he's a man."

Rhys's dad claps him on the shoulder, beaming, and Rhys looks up with the smile of someone who knows he's missed the conversation but doesn't mind. He lifts the first plate of cake and passes it across the table to me. When our eyes meet, his smile broadens, just slightly; his nose crinkles, a dimple appears. My heart fizzes.

He likes me, I think. I smile back. *He likes me.*

Can I walk you home?

Rhys and I are standing outside the restaurant and I am still in the act of pulling my arms through my coat sleeves. Meg has already gone home so it is just us and his family left. I hesitate, thinking about my plan to call Dad so he could pick me up. **Are you sure? It's about half an hour.**

I don't mind. Unless . . . unless you mind?

I shake my head quickly.

For a second we both look at each other. **Okay**, he says eventually, smiling a little nervously. He does a little hop-step over to his mother, has a quick conversation, and comes back over to me, smiling. **Lead the way.** He makes a sign I don't recognize.

What was that?

Rhys pauses, looking caught. Is he blushing? **It's your name.**

My name?

He makes the sign again, his hands coming together like owl eyes then springing apart, his hands separating. His eyes meet mine and he smiles, then fingerspells the word. B—R—O—N—Z—E. Bronze.

A balloon swells in my chest. It lifts me right off the ground.

You chose a BSL name for me?

Is that okay?

Before I can think about what I'm doing, I reach over and take his hand. *I take his hand.* **It's great.**

He beams, relieved and pleased and shy, and gives my hand a little squeeze before releasing it so we can carry on talking. **How was your food?**

Good. You?

It was good.

It's hard to talk while we're walking, particularly as it's already getting darker. I feel a kick of frustration—there's so much I want to say to him. So much I want to hear. But we are who we are.

How does it feel being eighteen?

He shrugs. **The same so far. Thanks for coming tonight.**

Thanks for inviting me!

My parents are so happy I've made a friend like you. They're really pleased you came.

Friend.

I look at him, trying to read his face in the dark. One of the things with BSL is that it's pretty hard to say something you didn't mean to say. There are no slips of the tongue when you talk with your hands. So did he mean "friend" to tell me something? Was Meg wrong?

I'm pleased we're friends too, I sign carefully. His eyes flick from my hands to my face, a slight crinkle in his forehead.

Can I ask you something?

Of course. I try to cover my terror with a smile. **The pact.**

What did you and Meg talk about? When you went to the bathroom? You were gone a while.

How can I answer that? How? I decide to be playful. **Girl stuff.**

Girl stuff?

I nod. We walk in silence for a while. I slide my hands into my pockets to keep them warm and try not to breathe too loudly. This is the loudest silence in the world. I can hear our footsteps.

After a while, Rhys makes a noise I can't translate and signs something I can't read. I squint at him. **What?**

He tries again. This time, I can just make out **you** and **like** and **tonight.** Well, that sounds promising.

One more time?

He lets out a half-laugh of frustration and takes my arm, pulling me a few steps down the road until we are both standing directly under a streetlight.

Did you like meeting Meg tonight?

Really?!

I look at him directly for a few seconds, letting him register the expression on my face. Then I sign, slowly and deliberately,

Do you really want to talk about Meg?

Another long pause. He shakes his head. **But . . .**

But?

Did she tell you?

Tell me what?

Rhys raises his hands to his head and tugs on the ends of his hair, his face agonized. And then, finally, he says it. **Meg isn't my girlfriend.**

I feel a ridiculous, inappropriate beam break out across my face. **Isn't she?**

No.

That's interesting.

He looks torn between laughter and panic. For a moment we just stare at each other. The glare from the streetlight makes his face look orange. **She told you that, didn't she?**

Yes.

Did she tell you anything else?

God, this boy. He's just as much of a wuss as I am. So you know what? I decide to just go for it. Let me be the bold one for once in my tiny, scared little life. **She told me you like me.**

He hesitates. He looks like a little boy. **I do.**

Not as a friend, I amend. **As . . . more.**

He nods. **Yes.**

I'm still beaming. My face is starting to hurt. Rhys is looking at me with such hopeful fear on his face it's making me want to leap into the air and punch the stars. Cartwheel down the street. Burst into song. Say "hello!" to everyone I see.

I see him bite his lip. **Do you.** Pause. **Maybe.** Pause. **Like me too?**

I nod. My smile might break my face.

We stand there under the streetlight beaming at each other. This is the part where we kiss, right? We're going to kiss. I am going to kiss this boy. He is going to kiss me.

I wanted to tell you for so long, he says. His signing is looser and quicker now. **But I didn't know how. What if you didn't like me too? What if I ruined things? I liked getting to know you.**

I want to ask, *why?* But I also don't.

I liked getting to know you, too. I thought you might have a girlfriend the whole time, though.

His face falls. **I'm sorry.**

I didn't think I was allowed to like you.

What an inadequate word "like" is, I think. Such a small word to carry so much hope.

You are. You definitely are.

I know that now!

Rhys gives me a bashful, sheepish smile—my God he is completely, ridiculously beautiful—and then launches into a long, handy monologue about making a friend who he could talk to and not spoiling a friendship and how he tried to drop hints and—

And I take hold of his hands, move a step closer, and crane my neck. My heart is buzzing. It's making my whole body vibrate, a dizzy hum of joyjoyjoyjoyjoy.

And he hesitates, leans down, and kisses me.

He kisses me! He kisses *me!*

We are face to face and his lips are warm and gentle. They are small kisses at first, tentative, and then we are both tilting our heads; the kisses get longer. His hands—his talkative, expressive hands—curl at my waist and at my back, pulling me toward him and bridging the gap between us. He feels so warm and solid. When his tongue touches mine, I swear fireworks start going off inside of me. I can *feel* them ricocheting through my veins. He doesn't taste like strawberries or breath-mints or Prosecco—he tastes like boy. Like Rhys.

If we were talkers, maybe we'd exchange whispers between kisses. Maybe he'd put his lips beside my ear and tell me I'm beautiful. But we speak with our bodies and our faces, and so it's like we're still having a conversation. I know what it means when he takes my hand and squeezes it; when he breaks the kiss to touch his nose to mine and smile. He touches my face like it's something delicate. He doesn't need to tell me that I'm beautiful or special or wanted. I can feel it in his touch.

How long do we kiss? I don't even know. It is just me and Rhys under the streetlight (or spotlight, as I begin to think of it), KISSING. It's possible people walk past us, but I honestly don't even notice. If there's a world outside the two of us, I don't care.

What I learn about kissing: It's fun. It's hot. It's brilliant. I could carry on doing it forever.

We finally break apart when it becomes impossible to ignore my phone ringing obnoxiously in my pocket. My breathing is all over the place, my chin feels like it's been exfoliated, and I'm not sure my heartbeat will ever return to normal.

I'm the happiest I've ever been.

"Hi, Dad," I say breezily. **My dad**, I sign to Rhys, who nods, all smiles.

"Hi, Stef-Stef," Dad says. "Glad to know you're alive."

"I'm just on my way home," I say.

"I thought I was going to come and pick you up."

"Oh, well . . . that's okay. Rhys is walking me home."

There's a long silence. "Is he?" Dad's voice is the oddest mix of jokey, nonchalant, and horrified, as if I'm twelve years old instead of coming on seventeen.

We're just kissing, I half want to say. No need to freak out just yet.

But of course I don't. "Yeah, we're almost back, actually. So I'll see you soon, okay?"

"Okay, love," Dad says slowly. "Don't make it too late?"

"I won't."

When I hang up, Rhys smiles sheepishly at me. **Do you need to get home?**

I nod. **Sorry.**

Don't be sorry! That's my job. He gestures to himself, exaggeratedly gallant. **I'm a gentleman.**

I grin—*sure*—and lean forward for another kiss. I almost get lost in it again, but he guides me back, taking hold of my hand and pressing a final kiss on the side of my head.

Tem:

So, how did it go?

Steffi:

SEPTEMBER.

Tem:

Ooh this sounds promising.

Tem:

. . . or a disaster?

Tem:

SHIT BRONS. REPLY TO ME.

Steffi:

HE LIKES ME

Tem:

Woohoo!!!

Tem:

(Also, OBVS he does, you plank.)

Steffi:

HE KISSED ME

Tem:

!!!!!!!!!!!!!

Steffi:

☺☺☺

Tem:

TELL ME EVERYTHING.

How did it happen?

Is he a good kisser?

HOW FAR DID YOU GO?

Tem:

Oh screw this, I'm calling you.

YOU BETTER ANSWER.

Steffi:

[stefstef is online]

rhysespieces: ☺ ☺ ☺

stefstef: hi ☺

rhysespieces: just wanted to say good night

stefstef: good night xxxx

rhysespieces: good night xxxx

rhysespieces: ☺

stefstef: ☺

[rhysespieces has logged off]

12

TEM IS EVEN MORE EXCITED THAN I AM. SHE COMES TEAR-
ing round to see me the following morning, her whole face alight.

"Okay, tell me everything," she commands, sitting cross-
legged beside me on the bed. The bed I am still *in*, by the way.
There are very few boundaries between me and Tem. *"Everything."*

So I do. No detail is too small for her, no description too
rambling. When I describe the expression on his face as I told
him I liked him too, she almost combusts. I finally realize why
she was so frustrated by my comparatively lackluster response
to her Karam-related excitement. *This* is what she wanted.

"So are you together?" she asks. "How did you leave things?
This is very important."

"Define together," I say.

"Together is not having to say 'define together,'" she says.

"Together is 'He asked me to be his girlfriend!' or 'He declared undying love!' and so on."

I laugh. "I'm quite glad he didn't declare undying love, to be honest."

"You know what I mean. I say again—how did you leave things?"

"He walked me home. Well, to the end of my road, so my dad couldn't ambush him—my suggestion—and he kissed me good-bye. We said we'd see each other on Monday. And we had another good-night kiss thing on jackbytes."

She listens carefully and when I get to my final sentence she glows. "That's like the equivalent of a good-night phone call for the two of you, right?"

I smile. "Pretty much."

"Oh, Steffi!" Tem actually claps her hands together, then drums her fists on my covers. "I'm so happy right now."

"Do you think he *should* have asked me to be his girlfriend?"

She shakes her head. "No, this is all fine. Better than fine. Perfect. You can take things all cute and slow."

"Like you and Karam?" I say this because I think it'll make her happy, but her face falls a little.

"Maybe," she says.

I'm about to ask her to elaborate—where's her bouncy, Karam-induced happiness?—but my phone dings beside me and I grab it. Rhys.

Rhys:

Good morning, beautiful ☺ xx

"Oh my God," Tem sings, beaming. "He's got it *bad*."

I shove her away, grinning, drinking in the words on the screen. *Beautiful.* He thinks I'm beautiful?

"I thought you guys used jackbytes," Tem says, peering over my shoulder.

"We do," I say. "We text too. Jackbytes is like a phone call. The conversation isn't recorded, but texts we can keep. Now, help. What should I reply?"

"Whatever you want," Tem replies. "He likes *you*, Stef. Not me. Say whatever *you* want to say." I reach over impulsively to hug her and she yelps in surprise, then hugs me back. "My little Steffi," she says, pressing her head against mine. "Kissing a *boy*."

I twirl my phone in my fingers, smiling against the familiar scrunch of her curls against my face. "Am I all grown up?"

"Almost," she says. I feel rather than see her grin. "Almost."

At school, Rhys and I are shy and tentative with each other. When we first see each other, he does a kind of awkward two-step where he starts to lean in to kiss me and then changes his mind. He takes my hand instead, but then realizes almost immediately that we can't talk if we're holding hands, so he drops it again.

Hi, he says, his smile embarrassed.

Hi, I say, grinning. I reach up on tiptoe and kiss his cheek.

But, for the most part, things are the same. We still talk and laugh in a language that feels like it belongs just to us. We sit together in math and chat to his interpreter after class. We go to the library during a free period we both share and carry on talking across the table, my BSL improving with every passing hour we spend together. We talk every night on jackbytes. On Thursday we go to Caffè Nero and kiss in the corner until his coffee goes cold.

I think we're both too shy to bring up the possibility of using big words like "girlfriend" and "boyfriend," because we don't, though I have dreamily practiced the signs to myself so I can be ready for when we do. The thing is that it doesn't feel like we need to; everything is so soft and sweet and perfect. I'm in no rush to risk losing it with The Conversation.

On Sunday, Tem and I take our little siblings to the park to feed the ducks. Bell is dressed as a fairy, complete with wings and a wand, and she sings to herself as we walk along, holding my hand tight. Davey, Tem's five-year-old brother, takes one look at her and bursts into tears.

"What's wrong?" Tem demands, horrified. "It's Bell. You've seen Bell before."

Bell, still clutching my hand, stares at him with distant interest. She gives her wand a swish and flick in his direction, and Davey wails even louder.

Tem rolls her eyes at me, hoists her brother into her arms, and carries him a little way off the path.

"What a baby," Bell says primly, heaving a loud sigh.

"Come on, Belly," I say, grinning. "Let's get a head start on the ducks, shall we?"

We sit on the bench nearest the side of the lake and I pull out the bag of stale bread I'd brought, already ripped into pieces perfect for small hands. I hold it open for Bell and she reaches in. Tem approaches, still holding Davey in her arms. She walks round the back of the bench and leans over so she's hissing directly into my ear. "Davey wants to be a fairy."

I turn my head so I can see them both. Davey is staring at me, his cheeks still wet, his dark eyes wide and woeful.

"He's sad because Bell gets to dress like a fairy," she adds. "Isn't that right, Davey-do?" Davey nods mournfully.

"Hey, Belly," I say, brightening my voice. She swings her head toward me, already beaming. "Can Davey be a fairy too?"

Bell looks appraisingly at Davey. She shrugs. "Maybe."

"Do you want to lend him your wand?" I ask. "So he can be a fairy?"

"Not my wand," Bell says seriously. "But he can have my wings if he wants." She wiggles out of the wings that are attached to her back and holds them out to Davey.

"Go on," Tem coaxes, jiggling her brother in her arms. "Fairy it up." As Davey reaches a tentative hand out to take the wings—purple and sparkly—she grins at me over the top of his little fuzzy head. Tem and I are determined that Davey and Bell will grow up as best friends who fall in love. It has to happen. It'll be the cutest thing ever.

Tem sets Davey—bewinged, all smiles—onto the ground and sits next to me. "Go on, you two," she says encouragingly, pointing the kids toward the lake. "Go and give the ducks their treats."

Bell hops off the bench and trots the few steps down the bank to where the ducks are clustered. Davey follows, shaking his back as he goes so his wings flap.

"So," Tem says as soon as they're out of earshot, "how's it going with your beau?" She grins at me. "Full details, please."

"I've told you everything," I say, laughing. "Nothing new has happened since yesterday, I promise."

"You told me the basics," Tem says. "I want the *details*. How do you feel about everything? Do you like him more now that you're kissing, or less? How many times does he message you in a day? Do you think you'll get together properly soon?"

I try to answer her questions as best I can—more, lots, I hope so—even though no level of detail seems like it'll be enough for her. She is still giddy on my behalf, happier than I can quite allow myself to be yet, while it's all still in the possible stage. I tell her about sitting with Rhys in Caffè Nero, how he'd walked me home and we'd argued the whole way about whether the best Pixar film is *Toy Story* or *WALL-E* ("Clearly *Finding Nemo*—you're both idiots"), how we'd had to keep stopping in the middle of the street if we became entangled in a particularly long sentence.

And then Tem says it.

"Aren't you worried about people looking?"

I pause. I realize that I'm still holding a piece of stale bread between my fingers. "What do you mean?"

"Well, like, you don't talk because it makes people notice you, right? But doesn't talking with your hands in public make people notice you more?"

My heart stills. That's what it feels like—not a thundering panic or a twist of pain; it goes quiet, like it's bracing itself. I can feel something building in my head. Something coming that will ruin everything, that will take me back to where I used to be, that will spoil what I have with Rhys. Six small words that can root in my head and never leave. *Aren't you worried about people looking?*

Tem looks at me, expectant. Her expression is open but placid, like she doesn't realize the potential avalanche she's created in my addled brain. Doesn't she know? Doesn't she get it? That in anxious heads like mine all it takes is a few words to bring a careful foundation tumbling down? All I can think is, *Oh please. Please don't take this away from me, please. Please let me have this.*

I gather myself. "It's . . . different."

"Why?" It's a genuine question and I know she's not trying to destroy me. But my head is going, *Yeah, Steffi, why? It makes no sense. Of course people will look.*

"Because . . ." I try really, really hard to come up with a

reason why it's different. For my own sake as much as hers. I hit on, "Because it's still just ours. No one knows what we're saying. What I'm saying. Just Rhys. So . . . it's different."

"Oh, okay." She nods, considering this. "So it's not the sound of your voice that's the problem, but the words you actually say? What makes you not talk, I mean."

Here's the thing about anxiety: it's not rational. It's not *rational*, but it's still *real*, and it's still scary, and that's okay. That's one of the things my therapist used to tell me. It doesn't make it any less difficult because it doesn't make sense. But that's pretty hard to explain to people like Tem, who are too pragmatic to worry about much of anything.

"Mmmm," I say. "Look, I'm just crazy, okay? Can we talk about something else?"

Tem's brow furrows. "You're not crazy, Stef."

"Whatever." My entire body is fizzing with anxiety. My fingers are twitching. "Belly," I call, desperate for a distraction. My sister spins on the spot. "Don't put your feet in the water, okay?"

"Okay!" she calls back sunnily.

Tem changes the subject. "Hey, can I ask you a favor?"

"Sure," I say, my eyes on my little sister, who is adjusting Davey's wings with an expression of absolute concentration.

"Karam is having a Halloween party next Saturday and . . . I really, really want you to come."

"Okay . . . ," I say slowly, waiting for more. Tem knows

how I feel about crowds, noise, and alcohol, which is why she'd never usually ask if I'd come to a party with her. She has other friends for crazy-fun-party-time.

She turns slightly on the bench to face me. "His mum is going to be away so it's just his dad, but his dad will be there, so it's not going to get really crazy, or anything. He says his dad is really, like, chilled out, you know? I know you don't usually like this kind of thing, I get that, honestly, but this will be different. I've thought it all through. See, it's Halloween, so you can come in costume, and you can get something that covers your face if you want, so no one will even know it's you." Her voice is starting to speed up, words falling over each other. "Or we can go as pandas! Pandas, Stef! Remember how we used to dress up as pandas together?"

We have literally not done this since we were eight years old.

"Karam wants me there, so obviously I'm going to go, but I think it would be really great if you came too. Then you can meet Karam, and you can tell me what you think. And—this is the best bit, Stef—you can invite Rhys. That way it'll be like a social occasion that's not school or anything to hang out together, plus I can meet him—and I really want to meet him—and you know you can always be with me or him, so you won't ever be on your own, and you won't have to talk if you don't want to." She stops abruptly, practically breathless. She looks at me, her lip slightly dented from where she is clearly biting it from inside her mouth. Quietly, she adds, "I know it's a big ask,

Stef. But it would really mean a lot to me if you came."

The thing is, that's all she really needed to say. There are some people you will do anything for if they really need you. And this is Tem.

"Sure," I say. "Of course I'll come."

stefstef: hello!

rhysespieces: hello there ☺

stefstef: how are you? what are you up to?

rhysespieces: okay, you? just playing minecraft.

stefstef: haha

stefstef: wait, really?

rhysespieces: !! ☹

stefstef: sorry!!! i honestly thought that was a game for kids

rhysespieces: ☹☹☹☹☹

stefstef: AGH can i start again?

rhysespieces: go for it

[rhysespieces has logged off]

[rhysespieces has logged in]

stefstef: hello!

rhysespieces: hello there ☺

stefstef: so I have a question for you

rhysespieces: cool. i'm listening.

rhysespieces: hahaha "listening"

stefstef: are you doing anything next saturday?

rhysespieces: i hope so

stefstef: oh, okay. Have you already made plans or something?

rhysespieces: what? no, i mean i hope that i'll be doing something with you

rhysespieces: like seeing you, not DOING something

rhysespieces: oh fuck

stefstef: ☺

rhysespieces: i am so much smoother in my head

stefstef: i hope for your sake that's true

rhysespieces: ask me again

stefstef: are you doing anything next saturday?

rhysespieces: no plans yet. why?

stefstef: my best friend is going to a halloween party and she's invited us both. interested?

rhysespieces: stefanie brons, are you inviting me on a date?

stefstef: yes.

rhysespieces: interesting

stefstef: HEY, you know how I have massive anxiety?

rhysespieces: haha sorry sorry. of course. sounds great. costumes?

stefstef: ☺ yes

rhysespieces: MATCHING costumes?

stefstef: hold your horses, i don't think we're there yet

rhysespieces: damn, i bet you'd be cute as hell as one half of a horse

stefstef: i'm going as a panda

rhysespieces: okay i take it back. THAT sounds cute as hell.

stefstef: ☺

rhysespieces: i am definitely in. let me know location and times and stuff?

stefstef: i will. i don't know them yet, but i'll tell you when i do.

rhysespieces: cool, and let me know what alcohol to bring

stefstef: oh. you don't need to worry about that for me.

stefstef: i mean, just bring whatever you want

rhysespieces: you don't drink?

stefstef: not party drinking, iykwim?

rhysespieces: okay, gotcha. i won't either, if you want?

stefstef: aw ☺ it's fine.

rhysespieces: sure?

stefstef: yes. i have to go to bed, see you tomorrow?

rhysespieces: yep. sweet dreams xx

stefstef: ☺ xxx

[stefstef has logged off]

13

ON SATURDAY, I SPEND THE AFTERNOON AT TEM'S house so we can get ready together. And by "get ready," I mean she gets dressed and then talks me down from a panic attack. While she sips a pre-mixed vodka and Coke from a can, I hold a glass of ice water to my forehead and try to calm myself.

"Which heels do you think I should wear?" Tem holds up two different shoes, both sporting heels higher than I have ever even attempted.

"Those," I say, pointing at the shorter of the two. "They'll be easier to walk in if you get drunk."

"I'm taking flats in my bag," Tem says, peering into the mirror and putting a speculative hand on her curls. "So that's not an issue." She throws a grin over her shoulder at me. "Or Karam could be carrying me."

I can't help grinning back, because her mischievous enthusiasm is infectious. "What kind of panda wears heels, anyway?"

"A teenage one trying to impress a boy," Tem says promptly. Her head is bent and she's rooting through her makeup bag, lining up lipsticks on her dressing table.

"Does it matter that I'm wearing Converse?" I ask, my brain seizing on something new to panic about.

"Of course not." Tem leans in to the mirror, carefully running the lipstick over her bottom lip. "You can be a grunge panda." She presses her lips together and pouts at her reflection. "Do you know what Rhys will be wearing?"

"No, he wants it to be a surprise. How about Karam?"

She shrugs. "Zombie doctor. Okay!" She claps her hands and steps away from the mirror, turning in a circle so I can admire the full package. "What do you think?"

"Pandarific," I say, smiling. She looks fantastic. "Karam will love it. Everyone will."

When we were kids, Tem and I went through a phase where we were both obsessed with pandas. Tem decided they were like us in animal form—black and white; cheeky and shy; lovers of food, sleep, and play—and that was all it took. I got a panda dressing gown for Christmas; she got the pajamas. For three Halloweens in a row, we dressed in matching panda onesies.

Unfortunately, we've both outgrown those particular onesies— both in size and maturity level—so we've had to make our own costumes this year. Tem has pulled out all the stops. She's wearing black skinny jeans, a tight white vest under a black leather jacket, and a panda-ear headband. I, on the other hand, am wearing leggings, white high-top Converse, and an oversize panda hoodie that I bought on eBay. It has a hood with ears on it.

"I like it," Tem insists when I make worried-face at her. "You look adorable."

Staring at the two of us in the mirror—her beaming, me with a slightly more wobbly smile—it occurs to me that we don't look like a matching set at all anymore. Once we were the same height, but now in her heels she towers over me. She has managed to make her panda outfit sexy; I still look like a child playing dress-up.

And yet we're both going to this party to meet our maybe-one-day-could-be boyfriends, I remind myself. In this, we're still the same.

At five o'clock the two of us take Davey trick-or-treating. He's wearing a full fairy outfit, complete with a curly blue wig and silver glitter on his cheeks, and he looks so brilliant I pick him up to cuddle him close.

"Panda!" he shouts happily, pulling on my hood.

"Fairy!" I shout back, jiggling him so his wings flap.

We're only outside with him for about half an hour, but that's enough for all three of us. Davey gets tired, I get stressed, and Tem is just impatient to get to the party. Still, we have to wait until 8 p.m. before we can actually go, so we end up being stressed and impatient in her kitchen instead. We eat fajitas straight out of the pan, take selfies with the pumpkins we carved earlier that day, and try to tell ghost stories that tail off midway. Tem redoes her makeup three times. I eat an apple.

"So this is what a social life feels like," I say.

She throws a chocolate at me and it bounces off my face.

We get the bus to Karam's house at quarter to eight. Tem plays with the zip of her jacket and drums her fingernails against the window. She keeps pulling out her phone to check it, then sighing.

"Does Karam know I'm coming?" I ask.

"Oh yeah," she says. "He's looking forward to meeting you." She smiles at me, a flash of normal Tem on her face, before she returns a furrowed forehead to her phone.

When my phone beeps, her head jerks instinctively and I roll my eyes, waving it at her to show that it's mine. It's Rhys.

Rhys:
I think I'm here. Are you inside yet?

"Rhys is there already," I say, anxious. I look out the window, as if that will somehow let me know how close we are to a complete stranger's house. "Are we almost there?"

"Five minutes," Tem says. "Tell him to go in and wait for us."

"He literally knows no one," I say, swallowing a shot of irritation. "Not everyone can just make friends like you can."

"He made friends with you," Tem points out. "But fine. Whatever. Tell him to wait *outside* for us."

When we get to Karam's house, Rhys is leaning against the front wall, doing the whole fake-reading-a-text-message thing that I'm pretty sure has fooled no one since 2003.

"Oh my God," Tem says, thrilled. Her voice is light with joy. "That is the best costume I've ever seen in my life. That's him, right? Oh, please tell me that's him. It'll make my life if it's him."

Rhys is dressed like a mime. An actual French mime, complete with a painted white face, white gloves, and a bowler hat.

"That's him," I say, grinning. What I want to say is, *He's mine.*

When I reach his side, I poke his arm to get his attention and his head jerks up. A huge grin breaks across his face when he sees me, his eyes flicking from my face to my feet, taking in my costume. He takes hold of one of my panda ears and tugs it playfully.

Hello.

Hi!

He kisses my painted black nose, softly so it won't smudge.

You look amazing.

Thanks! I take a step back and gesture to Tem, who is watching us in the same kind of way a bird would after its chicks had managed to fly for the first time. "This is Tem." I say the words out loud and sign them.

"Hi!" Tem says, bounding forward.

Rhys grins. "Hi," he says out loud. To me, he adds, **Panda number two?**

I laugh. "I'm Panda number two. Tem is number one."

He shakes his head. **Not to me.**

It's cheesy. It's silly. But I beam as if my whole body has been filled with happy juice.

"Shall we go in?" I suggest.

Tem looks at me as if I've just sprouted wings right in front of her. "Since when are you so keen?"

Rhys takes my hand and smiles at me, nodding his head in the direction of the house. *Yes*, he is saying without words. *Let's go in.*

"Come on," I say to Tem. My bubbling happiness comes out as laughter. "We don't want to miss the party."

My bravado fades as soon as I get through the front door. The house is almost humming it's so loud, with music pumping from somewhere further inside. There are people everywhere, all of them total strangers, drinking, smoking, and talking. Talking loudly.

I pull my hood up right over my head and peek out under it. My heart is pounding inside my throat.

"Holy shit!" someone shouts, and for a second I think they're talking to me. But of course they're directing the words at Tem. "That is some fucking costume."

Tem grins. "Oh, this old thing?" She reaches out both her arms and the guy who spoke—he's dressed as Elsa from *Frozen*—lifts her into an elaborate hug.

"Damn," he says, putting his hands on her hips and surveying the whole outfit. "When you said panda, I thought you meant, like . . ." He searches for the word, spots me, and clicks his fingers. "Like that!"

I want to raise my eyebrows and say sarcastically, *Thanks, dude.* But I can't. The words just aren't there; that's what it feels like. As if the words I form in my brain have gotten stuck there instead of zipping down the neural superhighway to my mouth.

"That's what I was going to wear," Tem says, filling my silence as always, so naturally no one who wasn't me would notice anything unusual. "But Steffi got there first, so I had to make do. Max, this is Steffi."

"Ah, the famous Steffi," Max says, beaming at me. "You make a very fine panda."

I give him a thumbs-up to cover the fact that I can't reply and he grins, amiable.

"And this is Rhys," Tem adds, gesturing.

"Awesome costume." Max nods.

"Thanks," Rhys says. I feel his hand take hold of mine and give it a quick squeeze before letting go.

"Where are the drinks?" Tem asks.

"Kitchen," Max says. "Follow me, my lady."

"I can't believe you're wearing that," Tem says as she starts to follow him. Rhys and I glance at each other, then fall into step behind her.

"Elsa is queen," Max says. He throws a grin over his shoulder. "And so am I."

The kitchen seems to have more people in it than the rest of the house combined and it's suddenly hard to breathe. I wonder if I can pour myself a glass of water without attracting any attention, but when I turn I find Rhys standing next to me, carefully pouring a can of Coke into a cup for me. He presents it, smiling.

Thank you. I make the sign as pronounced as I can for emphasis.

He puts his bottle of cider on the counter to free his hands, then quickly asks, **Shall we go outside?**

I nod, then reach out a finger to poke Tem. "Want to come outside with us?"

"Sure," she says gamely. "See you later, Max."

"Where's Karam?" I ask her as we go.

She shrugs. "I'm sure we'll find him soon."

We do, eventually. After about half an hour of the three of us sitting on a blanket laid out on the grass and making a three-way conversation about mimes and pandas, her whole posture suddenly changes and she stops mid-sentence.

The boy she's looking at has appeared on the patio with a couple of other guys, a beer in hand. He has the easy command of everyone around him, the way some people seem to be able to do effortlessly. His dark hair is messy, but in a constructed way, and the stubble on his chin makes him look older than the eighteen years Tem described. Even though he's smiling there's a seriousness to his face, a perma-crease in his forehead. As he walks in our direction, flanked by friends, I see a thin silver chain round his neck, falling beneath his plain T-shirt.

He doesn't look like a boy, is what I mean. He looks like a man.

"Oh, hey," he says, pausing as he passes us, spotting Tem. "You made it."

"Hi," Tem says, her voice higher than usual. She jumps to her feet to stand beside him, but neither makes a move to kiss hello. "Come meet my friends?" There's a hopefulness in her voice that surprises me, as if she is steeling herself for a no.

"Of course," he says, smiling as he turns to us. He drops casually to his knees on the blanket. "Hiya. I'm Karam."

"This is Steffi," Tem says, pointing at me.

"Hi," I say, and she beams at me as Karam nods and shakes my hand. See what I mean? Like a man.

"And this is Rhys," she adds, gesturing to Rhys.

"All right, mate," Karam says, shaking Rhys's hand. "Awesome costume."

"Thanks," Rhys says. He coughs a little, and I realize suddenly that he's nervous, maybe even more nervous than I am. "What's your costume?"

His volume is all off and my stomach twists on his behalf, but Karam just looks down at himself and grins. "I'm one hundred percent Karam Homsi. Accept no substitutes."

"Not a zombie doctor?" I ask. Wasn't that what Tem had said?

"Nah, couldn't get the gear," Karam says casually. "So these are the panda costumes, then?" He appraises me, smiling, as I hunch down under the hood for effect. "That's cute."

"That's what I was going for," I say dryly. Something about Karam's easy manner has relaxed me, and my voice has returned.

"And you," Karam says, turning to Tem, his smile widening into a sharp grin. "Wow."

Tem's whole face lights up. "That's what *I* was going for," she says.

"How are you guys doing for drinks?" Karam asks, looking back at Rhys and me.

"We're good," I say, looking at Rhys for confirmation.

"Tem?" Karam prompts.

"I'm empty," Tem says, holding up a glass that I swear was half full just thirty seconds ago. "I think I need a refill."

I expect Karam to go and get drinks for them both, but she disappears off with him, leaving Rhys and me on the blanket. Before she does this she glances at me, her whole face a hopeful question, and I nod a little so she knows it's okay.

There's a slight pause as Rhys and I look at each other, suddenly a little awkward alone in the dark at a party where there's alcohol and dancing and expectation. But then he shuffles a little closer to me, his mouth bumps up against mine and we're kissing.

Kissing, I'm discovering, has its own time zone. I have no idea how long Rhys and I spend on the blanket, lip-locked, before we're interrupted by an amused-sounding "Hello" from above us.

I break away from Rhys, blinking. Tem is back already and she's standing above us, hanging on to Karam's arm, a roguish grin on her face.

I cough. "Uh. Hi."

"Oh, don't let us disturb you," Tem says grandly. "Please continue your disgraceful PDA."

Rhys glances at me, a clear request for a translation on his face. I roll my eyes at him. **Tem just thinks she's being funny.**

"What did she tell you?" Tem asks immediately. She settles down, cross-legged, on the blanket. I notice that the glass she's holding has been filled to the brim.

"She said you're very funny," Rhys says, straight-faced.

"Oh." Tem is pleased, oblivious to the joke. "Well, that's true."

I turn my head just slightly away from Rhys so he can't see my mouth. "Make sure you look directly at Rhys when you talk, so he can read what you're saying," I say quickly to Tem. Even though I've turned away, I still lower my voice instinctively.

Tem turns obediently toward him. "What are you drinking?" she asks, enunciating.

"Magners," Rhys replies, turning the bottle so she can see the label.

Tem makes a face. "Ugh."

Rhys points at her, eyebrows raising. *You?* he is asking.

"Vodka and lemonade," she says. "Drink of champions."

I look at Karam, who has sat down beside Tem. "So how's the party going so far?" Ask open questions, my CBT has taught me. Invite people to talk about themselves. It's a bit of a non-question, but it'll do.

"It's cool," Karam says, nodding. "Some people really made an effort with the costumes. Did you see the C-3PO?"

I shake my head.

"Keep a lookout. And Gay Max came as Elsa."

I hesitate. "Gay Max?"

"There are two Maxes," Tem puts in. "Gay Max and Short Max."

"Right," I say. "So you call the gay one . . . Gay Max?"

"He came up with it after watching *Big Hero 6*," Karam says. "So if it's offensive, it's on him."

Rhys is watching us, looking baffled. When I meet his eye he fingerspells, **M-A-X?** and I smile and shake my head. **Costumes. I'll tell you later.**

"Tem told me you're studying six subjects," I say. "Wow."

Karam laughs and gives a modest shrug. "Yeah. I want to be a doctor. Taking more subjects gives me the best chance of getting into the best medical schools."

"He's basically a genius," Tem puts in.

"I just work hard," Karam says. "But it'll be worth it." He takes a sip of beer. "I came here when I was nine years old. Did Tem tell you that? From Syria. I'm going to become a doctor and go back. Help everyone who didn't get all the opportunities I had."

I squash the uncharitable thought that he sounds like he's given this speech more than once and smile. "That's very noble."

He frowns. "It's just luck that I'm here and so many aren't. I want to pay it back."

"Well, maybe by the time you're qualified they won't need so many doctors," I say.

I realize what a stupid thing this is to say the second after I've spoken, partly because I hear the words come out of my mouth and partly because Karam makes a face like I just vomited into his lap.

"Rhys wants to be a games developer," I say, my voice coming out a little shrill. I look at Rhys. "Tell them about wanting to be a games developer."

Rhys blinks at me, then turns obediently to Karam and Tem. "I want to be a games developer."

"Cool," Karam says, nodding. "Want kind of games?"

"Video games," Rhys says.

"Cool," Karam says again. "I wish I had more time for games. I used to play them more when I was a kid. All the Mario games, you know?"

Rhys has a genial, placid smile on his face, so I have no idea if he's offended by the implication that video games are for kids.

"Me too," he says. "They're great."

"What kind of games should I look out for?" Karam asks.

I leave them to it and scoot closer to Tem, who is making quick work of her vodka and lemonade.

"Hi," she whispers, giving one of my panda ears a friendly tug. "How's it going, Panda Two?"

I look over at Rhys, who's leaning onto his right knee, watching Karam's face intently as he talks. With his mime makeup on, he looks like he's taking part in some kind of screwball comedy sketch.

"Great," I say. "It's going great."

After a while, Tem and Karam excuse themselves to "go and check the alcohol situation" and leave Rhys and me alone together on the blanket again. The garden lamps that had been shining since we'd first sat down must be solar-powered, because they've dimmed so much now it's getting harder to see Rhys's face. We've given up trying to have a conversation as we normally would and have arranged ourselves so I am sitting between his legs, my back against his stomach, my head leaning back against his warm chest. Rhys is holding his phone out between us.

Rhys:
Yours is the best costume

Steffi:
No, yours is

Rhys:

Yours! Mine's barely a costume.
I'm a mime every day.

Steffi:

A cute mime

Rhys:

Just cute?

Steffi:

Very cute.

Rhys:

Anything else?

Steffi:

Handsome?

Rhys:

Getting warmer

I laugh, wrestle the phone from him, and start to reply, but he yanks it back and we end up sprawled over the blanket, all lips and tongues and hands.

I'm so distracted by all of this that he manages to grab hold of the phone, scuttle away from me, and write a new message. When he turns to show it to me, the glow of the phone lights up his face. He seems suddenly shy and unsure. The message says: Will you be my girlfriend?

My whole body goes *ZING!* but I frown thoughtfully, as if I'm considering. I take the phone from his nervous fingers and pretend to type back a long message. The longer I pretend, the more alarmed he looks.

When I finally turn the phone around, it takes him less than a second to read the three letters on screen. Y.E.S. His eyes lift to meet mine and I'm ready for him. **Obviously**, I sign.

Rhys leans forward and cups my chin in his hand. It's a movement I've seen in films, read in books, imagined so many thousands of times you'd think it wouldn't be a surprise. But it is. It feels unique even though I know it isn't. It feels special even though a gesture like this is surely a cliché. It still feels like it belongs to us.

We kiss for a while and then head back into the house together, hand in hand, to get fresh drinks. The kitchen has emptied since we were last here, and from the sounds coming from the living room, it seems like most people have moved in there. Karam is leaning against the counter talking to a boy wearing a hockey jersey and a mask pulled up to rest on the top of his head. He catches my eye and smiles in the automatic way friendly people smile at people they recognize, and lifts his hand in an acknowledging wave. His smile is warm and easy, and I realize I understand why Tem likes him so much.

This thought makes me wonder where Tem is, then remember how she once told me that her strategy was never to be "too clingy" at parties with boys she likes. But still, I'm sure it won't be long before she's back by his side, wherever she is.

Are you having a good time? Rhys asks me.

I nod, an uncontrollable smile spreading over my face. **Are you?**

He touches my hand. **Definitely.**

I don't add what I'm thinking, which is that this is the first time I've gone to a party (or really anything remotely social) where I haven't gone off to hide in the bathroom and cry. There's being open and honest with your boyfriend, and then there's just overshare. **Yours is the best costume here**, I say instead.

He laughs. **You're just saying that because you're my girl-friend.**

"Hey!" Karam has come to stand beside us. "How's it going?" Rhys gives him a thumbs-up and smiles. Karam glances at me, and I nod enthusiastically. The silent duo.

"It's cool watching you speak to each other," Karam says, settling himself against the kitchen counter. I watch him, taking in how easily he fits himself into any space and any conversation, hoping to pick up some tips. He probably doesn't even realize he's doing it. Maybe I'd be the same, if it had never occurred to me that I might be unwelcome. "Maybe I should learn sign language," he muses. "It'd be a good skill for a doctor to have, right?"

Rhys nods. "Definitely."

"Do many doctors speak it?"

Rhys shrugs. "Not really." Something about the way he says this makes me think it's not a topic he's comfortable discussing. "There are interpreters, sometimes."

"I guess it's the kind of thing you learn if you need to," Karam says. "It's not like learning French. I mean, we'll all go to France at some point, right? But you only need BSL if you . . . need BSL."

I worry that he's talking too much for Rhys to follow, but when I look at my boyfriend—*my boyfriend*—he is moving his head in a bit-of-yes/bit-of-no motion.

"I think more people should learn it," he says.

"Me too," I pipe up.

"It must be quite isolating," Karam says. He talks with the ease of someone who has never been made to think what he has to say is unimportant. "Being so cut off from the world."

I see a frown pass over Rhys's face, but he covers it with another smile. "The hearing world," he says. "But there's a Deaf world, too."

"And Rhys can talk and read lips," I say. "So he's not isolated."

"How come you can speak it?" Karam asks me. "Sign language, I mean. You can hear just fine, right?"

"I was a selective mute," I say, going for the simplest explanation.

"Oh right, yeah," Karam nods. "Tem said." He smiles at Rhys, friendly but slightly patronizing. It's the classic doctor look you get before they tell you to be more careful roller skating next time. "Lucky for you, right?"

"What's that?" Rhys asks. I'm not sure if he's asking Karam to repeat himself because he didn't catch it, or if he's saying he doesn't understand what he means. It occurs to me that this is probably deliberate, and it makes me fall a little bit in love with him even more.

"Finding a girl who speaks your language," Karam says. He grins. "So to speak. It must make things easier." He glances back to me. "And you too, actually. Not having to talk out loud so much?"

I'm saved from having to reply to this by Ron Weasley, Indiana Jones, and my very own Panda Tem, who walk into the kitchen arguing about gnomes.

"Hello!" Tem yells, throwing her arms around me.

"Oh, hi," I say. I stretch carefully round her and take the cup from her hand, sliding it out of her reach on the kitchen table. "Want some water?"

"Water? Ew, no. I'm totally fine." She lets me go and moves beside Karam. "Hi."

"Hi," Karam says, an amused smile flickering on his face. He reaches up and twists one of her curls around his finger. "You doing okay?"

She nods happily.

"Want to go see what's going on outside?" he asks.

Tem glances at me. Even in her drunk state she thinks of

me, and this is exactly why I am so lucky to have her as my friend. I nod a little at her and she beams.

"Okay!" she says to Karam, taking his hand. "Let's go."

When they've gone, I turn back to Rhys. I'm not quite sure what to say.

People say stupid things all the time, Rhys says, as if he can read my mind. **Don't worry about it.**

But I worry about everything.

Is he right, though?

Right about what?

Is that why you like me? Why we like each other? Because we can communicate easier?

Rhys smiles, his mouth widening and curving, his teeth flashing white. **That's how we met. It's not why we like each other.**

What's the difference?

I realize after I've asked it that it's probably not the best, nor the most flattering, question for a girlfriend to ask her new boyfriend, but anxiety has twisted my thoughts in that way it does, making me phrase things differently and inappropriately. It's a self-fulfilling prophecy, anxiety. You worry so much about being wrong in a certain way that you screw it up anyway.

But Rhys just laughs a little, his constant smile affectionate, and touches his fingers lightly to my cheek. **I don't feel like this about everyone I "communicate" with. It's got nothing to do with why I like you.**

Why *do* you like me, then? My need for reassurance has overtaken everything.

Rhys holds one hand in the air and circles the other beside it, then leans the second hand back sharply. It's like he's reeling something in. I blink at him. He grins. **Someone's fishing.**

I can't help it; I laugh, and the horrible swirling feeling in my stomach eases, just slightly.

There are lots of reasons, he adds. He takes a strand of my hair in between his fingers and rubs it gently. **Too many to mention.** I take a step forward and lean my head against his chest. He puts his arms obligingly round my shoulders and squeezes gently, rocking us a little from side to side like we're dancing to music that—because we are us—doesn't need to exist. I let out my breath slowly through my mouth, counting the beats, feeling my heart calm.

How to look after your very drunk friend:

Step 1: Find her in the bathroom, slumped against the towel rack.

Step 2: Ask her if she needs to be sick. Try not to get offended when she yells that she's NOT DRUNK, GOD, STEFFI!

Step 3: Tell her it's fine when she apologizes, bursts into tears, and then falls asleep on your shoulder.

Step 4: Accept gratefully when your boyfriend offers to get his dad to give you both a lift home.

Step 5: Coax Tem out of the car, across her driveway, and to her front door. Wave at your boyfriend through the window. Try not to beam like a five-year-old at the circus.

Step 6: Root around in her front pocket for her keys. Make a joke about inappropriate touching. Laugh when she earnestly tells you that you could touch her anywhere, because nothing's inappropriate when you're best friends.

Step 7: Write it down so you can mock her with it tomorrow, and for the rest of time.

Step 8: Tell her mother that yes, you both had a great time. Pour two glasses of water, carry them both up the stairs. (Make her go first, so you can catch her if she trips.)

Step 9: Help her take off her makeup and convince her to brush her teeth. Put her to bed. Tell her it's not a good time to start singing "My Name Is Panda."

Step 10: Wait until she's snoring away, just in case. All is well. Go to sleep.

14

I'M SOMEONE'S GIRLFRIEND.

I, Stefanie Elizabeth Brons, silent and not-at-all deadly, am someone's *girlfriend*. How did this happen? I actually don't know. A boy I could talk to walked into my life and now I get to touch him whenever I want and when he talks to me he says nice things and looks at me like I'm special. Last night we talked on jackbytes for two hours. He told me that he loved my voice.

My voice? I asked.
Yeah, your voice. The way you talk. The words you use. The way you put them together. Your voice.

He told me how when he was a kid he formed a band with his brothers. Rhys on the drums, Aled on guitar, Alfie taking lead vocals.

You can play the drums?

Yeah!

You never told me.

You never asked.

It's not the most obvious question to ask a deaf person—Can you play a musical instrument?—but I learn my lesson. I try not to assume anything about him. Or, at least, assume less.

He tells me his family is very musical and so it was always a part of his life. His parents encouraged him to try playing different instruments to see if he felt drawn to any of them, and with drums he could feel the music. It's all about the beat, and you don't need to hear to feel that.

I had thought I'd gotten to know Rhys pretty well over the last few weeks, but I'd barely scratched the surface. Every little piece of information makes me like him even more.

It's a Thursday, just a few days after we officially got together, and I've gone to Rhys's house after school. Unlike last time, it's empty. Rhys explains that his mother and Alfie are at the orthodontist and his dad is still at work.

Want to see my room? he asks.

I follow him up the stairs, keeping my eyes on a small hole at the ankle of his sock. Javert the cat is licking himself at the top of the stairs, one leg straight in the air. "Very glamorous," I say softly, reaching down to rub his head.

Rhys pauses in the doorway of his room, his smile a little shy. **Here**, he says, gesturing. **My little corner of the world.**

The room is smaller than my own and I try to take in as much of it as I can as quickly as I can, sketching it into my mind so I can return to it later rather than stand there and gawp, which is what I really want to do. It's neat—far neater than I'd expect a boy's room to be—with navy-blue walls and an off-white carpet. In the corner is an entertainment unit complete with TV, Xbox, and some kind of LEGO tower. Over the radiator hangs a kind of woolen shelf, and I'm about to ask what it's for when Javert ambles in and hops up onto it. Ah. Cat seat.

I turn to grin at him. **Did you tidy up for me?**

He laughs. **No, I just like to keep things nice.**

In the corner of the room I see what must be his drum set, though it has a dustcover over it so I can't say for sure. I consider asking him to play for me, but I'm too worried that I won't be able to successfully feign enthusiasm, so I don't. Instead, I bridge the small gap between us and tilt my face toward him. Kissing Rhys in his bedroom is different from kissing him anywhere else, even though his door is open and we stay standing several paces away from his bed. There's an intimacy to it that makes my heart fizz in a whole new way.

Seeing inside his room feels like a step, so I offer another.

The following Monday, the first big meeting of our relationship takes place: Rhys meets Rita.

And my dad. But mostly Rita.

175

Rhys walks me home from school and I stop in to grab my dog, who scrambles all around my legs, whining in delirious excitement at the sight of both me and the leash. When we get outside, she spots Rhys. Her tail goes rigid and her ears twitch.

"Rita," I say, squatting to her level and putting my hand at the furry scruff of her neck. "This is Rhys. He's very important. So be nice." I look up at Rhys and grin hopefully. **This is Rita**, I sign.

Rhys hesitates, then kneels down in front of us. **Hello, Rita**, he signs. **My name is Rhys. It is excellent to meet you.**

Rita cocks her head.

"Paw," I murmur into her ear.

Rita lifts a paw to Rhys and his whole face lights up. He takes it, beaming at me, and gives it a little shake.

See, she likes you! I say, getting to my feet and curling my fingers through the coil of Rita's leash. **Come on. Let's go for a walk.**

Later, he meets my dad and Lucy. Dad is guarded but polite, squinting at Rhys under his glasses at every opportunity. Lucy seems pleased to have someone to host and has made a beef Wellington in honor of the occasion. Both of them, adorably, try to use sign language to talk to Rhys. It's not the greatest success ever, but I can tell Rhys doesn't mind.

A few hours later, Mum calls. "So when am I going to meet this new boyfriend of yours?" I love how she says "new," as if he's the latest in a long line instead of the first boy I've ever even kissed.

I turn my phone away from my mouth so I can sigh, then

return it to speak. "How did you know about that?"

"Your father told me. It's just the kind of information every mother loves to hear from her ex-husband. Her teenage daughter's milestones."

Is she teasing or berating me? I really can't tell.

"I was going to tell you," I say. "When I saw you."

"Steffi, any news that makes you happy I want to hear immediately," she says. "Even small things. But especially big things, like first boyfriends."

"I'll tell you about the next one," I say. I'm joking, but even the thought makes me feel disloyal to Rhys.

"Can I meet him?" she prompts. "How about the two of you come over for dinner on Friday?"

"I'll see if he's free," I say. I can decide if I'll tell him about this phone call later.

Sunday evening

rhysespieces: do you believe in god?

stefstef: no. do you?

rhysespieces: i don't know. i think so.

stefstef: is your family religious?

rhysespieces: we go to church, but not massively.

rhysespieces: i definitely believe in life after death

stefstef: really?

rhysespieces: yeah. you don't?

stefstef: i'd like to. i wish i could believe i'd see clark again.

stefstef: or that he's somewhere good, still keeping an eye on me

rhysespieces: he might be

stefstef: mmm.

rhysespieces: you surprise me. i didn't have you pegged as a skeptic ☺

stefstef: just too realistic, maybe?

rhysespieces: energy doesn't disappear. it changes. and we're energy, right? ☺

stefstef: ☺ that's a nice idea

rhysespieces: can i ask you about clark?

stefstef: no need, i can guess the questions. he was my stepbrother. he died in a car accident on the way home from his first year at university.

rhysespieces: shit ☹

stefstef: the guy in the other car had a heart attack at the wheel and rammed him head on. clark didn't have a chance. but it wasn't the other guy's fault.

rhysespieces: did he die too?

stefstef: yeah.

rhysespieces: that must have been awful

stefstef: it was.

rhysespieces: were you guys close?

stefstef: no one could have had a better stepbrother. can we talk about something else?

rhysespieces: of course. i'm sorry xxx

stefstef: how's alfie?

rhysespieces: he's good. how's rita?

stefstef: she's sulking because i haven't taken her for a walk yet.

rhysespieces: poor rita. you should do that.

stefstef: yeah, i guess i should. at least it's stopped raining.

rhysespieces: want some company?

stefstef: is the company you?

rhysespieces: yes.

stefstef: then yes ☺

rhysespieces: on my way.

stefstef: xxxx

rhysespieces: xxxx

Monday

rhysespieces: can i ask you something?

stefstef: of course! we still have the pact, right? ☺

rhysespieces: yeah! okay so, you know how when you're with my family you sign while you talk out loud?

stefstef: yeah . . .

rhysespieces: how come you don't do that with your friends?

stefstef: um, god, i don't know . . . is that really bad? have i done something wrong?

rhysespieces: no! i'm just asking, honestly

stefstef: i havent even thought about it

stefstef: should i sign as well? it's just because they don't know BSL, so i guess i just didn't think i needed to?

rhysespieces: i know, but the BSL would be for me . . . you know?

stefstef: i'm sorry ☹☹☹ i thought you read lips when you're in the hearing world

rhysespieces: i do, but because i have to, not 'cause i want to

stefstef: oh

rhysespieces: like, i miss so much of what's going on in a group if people are talking. you know at karam's halloween party? you guys were talking away and i basically had no idea what was going on

stefstef: i feel awful

rhysespieces: i'm not trying to make you feel bad. i just wanted to check that it wasn't me.

stefstef: ??

rhysespieces: that you weren't . . . you know. ashamed of it. of me.

stefstef: WHAT?! NO.

stefstef: do you really think that??

rhysespieces: not now that i've spoken to you. but you wouldn't be the first hearing person who gets embarrassed about signing in public

stefstef: why would anyone be embarrassed?

rhysespieces: well, communicating with BSL is so different from what hearing people are used to. it's so visual, you have to be expressive. you know what i mean?

stefstef: yeah . . . but why would that be embarrassing?

rhysespieces: some people get self-conscious. i had a friend once say they felt like they were performing every time we were out together in public

stefstef: a friend said that to you?

rhysespieces: he wasn't trying to be mean. besides, i'm used to it. its just another thing that comes with being Deaf in a hearing world. people take speech communication for granted and they think anyone who communicates differently is weird or different. some people don't like having to face that

stefstef: i don't think of talking like that, though

rhysespieces: but, stef, of course you do—you spent most of your childhood trying to learn how to talk in public, didn't you? because not talking somehow wasn't acceptable to society?

stefstef: well . . .

stefstef: wow

rhysespieces: mind blown?

stefstef: yeah. i never though of it like that before

rhysespieces: anyway, i just wanted to check. that it wasn't a problem for you, i mean

stefstef: it's not. at all. i'm really sorry i made you think i might be ashamed. i'm really not. i promise

rhysespieces: <3

stefstef: are we okay?

rhysespieces: of course

stefstef: are you upset with me?

rhysespieces: not even a tiny bit

stefstef: i'm still learning how to be a girlfriend

rhysespieces: MY girlfriend. that's what's important to me ☺

stefstef: xxxxx

rhysespieces: are you okay?

stefstef: yes. are you?

rhysespieces: yes xx

stefstef: xxx

Tuesday

rhysespieces: you looked extra pretty today ☺

stefstef: ☺☺

Wednesday

stefstef: Sally the puppy has been adopted!

rhysespieces: NOOOO!

rhysespieces: i didn't even get to say goodbye ☹

stefstef: oh, she's not going yet. they don't go till about 12 weeks.

rhysespieces: is the new owner nice? they better be nice

stefstef: i don't know, i didn't meet them! Ivan just told me about it during my shift

rhysespieces: i'm already bereft

stefstef: there'll be other puppies!

rhysespieces: BEREFT.

stefstef: try harder to convince your mum. get a puppy of your own.

rhysespieces: i'll try.

stefstef: i'm going to send you some pics of Rita from when she was a puppy

rhysespieces: can you send some of you too?

stefstef: ☺

Thursday

stefstef: do you have any plans tomorrow night?

rhysespieces: yes, I'd like to spend some time kissing my girlfriend

stefstef: ☺☺

rhysespieces: want to come over to my place?

stefstef: yes, but I can't. my mum's invited you over for dinner.

rhysespieces: ah! the mother!

stefstef: yeah . . .

rhysespieces: sure.

stefstef: she'll be nice

rhysespieces: i know! i'm not worried.

stefstef: i am a bit.

rhysespieces: why? mothers love me. i'm adorable.

stefstef: you are adorable.

rhysespieces: you'll see. i'll make you proud.

stefstef: xxxxx

rhysespieces: xxxx

Rhys turns up at my mother's house on Friday wearing a shirt and tie, which is the most perfect thing that has ever happened in my life, second to kissing him. He smiles a bashful, nervous little smile when I open the door.

"Hi!" I say, unable to stop the word spilling from my mouth. **You look great.**

He beams. **It's my brother's tie.** He takes hold of the tip and looks down at it, then back at me. **Is it too much?**

I shake my head, grinning. **No way.**

"Hi!" Bell comes steaming down the stairs wearing her favorite purple-and-silver fairy costume. "Hi!" She launches herself at Rhys, waving her wand up to his face.

"Belly," I say, reaching for her shoulders and pulling her gently back from him.

"Hi!" she shouts, spinning around and hugging me.

I pick her up, rolling my eyes and smiling at Rhys, who

looks slightly alarmed. **Come in**, I say with one hand.

"Hiiiiiiii!" Bell chirrups insistently.

"Hi," Rhys says obediently. He smiles at her. "I'm Rhys."

"Your voice is funny," Bell says.

"Bell," I say disapprovingly, squeezing her hip. "Don't be rude."

"My voice sounds different because I'm deaf," Rhys says to her.

"Deaf?" Bell repeats slowly, questioningly. I hear footsteps behind me and glance round to see Mum coming out of the kitchen.

"That means I can't hear like you can," Rhys explains, tapping his left ear and then hers. "My ears don't work like yours."

"I hope you're not being rude, Belly," Mum says, coming to my side and squeezing Bell's cheek. She turns to Rhys and smiles. "Hello, Rhys. I'm Joanne."

"Hello," Rhys says robustly, sticking out his hand for Mum to shake. He's a bit too robust, actually, and he kind of knocks into her hand in an unintentional one-sided fist bump and they both let out awkward little laughs.

"He can't hear," Bell reports, jumping down from my arms and standing beside Mum, swinging her arms from side to side. "His ears don't work."

"Belinda!" Mum says sharply, and Bell's eyes go wide. She only gets "Belinda-d" when she's done something really bad.

"It's okay," Rhys says. "She's right; they don't." He clears his throat. "Your home is really lovely."

"Well, thank you," Mum says. "Are you hungry?" She turns to start to go into the kitchen, angling her face away from him in the process. "I've made a beef stew, so I hope you are!"

Rhys looks at me and I sign a quick translation.

"Sounds delicious!" he says, and we share a smile that is just for us. I take his hand and we head into the kitchen together.

By the end of the meal, I'm pretty sure I'm not the only one falling in love with Rhys. Keir was won over as soon as he found out that Rhys likes video games, and we lost both of them for ten minutes while they compared stats on various games I'd never heard of. Bell learned how to fingerspell her name and sign **Can I have some ice cream, please?** and Rhys, in turn, learned the names of all the fish in the tank.

Mum, as ever, is harder to read.

"Did you like him?" I press. "Tell me that." Rhys has gone home, Bell is in bed, and Keir is watching the football game in the living room. Mum and I are sitting together in the kitchen, eating the remains of an apple tart straight out of the tray it was cooked in.

She smiles. "Of course I liked him, Steffi. He's lovely. Very polite, very sweet. And I can tell he cares about you very much."

"Oh," I say. To be honest, I'm surprised she's being so positive. "Well, good."

"You are going to be . . . sensible about this, aren't you, love?" Mum says.

I look at her suspiciously, parsing her words for trouble. "Sensible how?"

"I know how exciting it is, being in love for the first time," she begins.

"Oh God," I interrupt. "Let's not. Please." I cast around the room for a distraction. "How's Bell getting on at school?"

"And Rhys is a very handsome, sweet young man," she continues.

"Oh *God*."

"But you're still very young. Try not to get carried away."

"Okay, great, thanks. Got it. How's work?"

"Make sure you use protection."

"Mum!"

"And remember there's no shame in waiting if you're not sure you're ready. Waiting is good. I know how your generation is about sex—"

"Oh, do you? How's that, then?"

"—But the first time is going to be a big deal for you. Even on a purely physical level."

"Mum!" I'm in agony. "Stop."

"Make sure you get some practice in," she adds. Oh God, is that a *smirk* on her face? Is she enjoying this? "Your aunt Louise gave me a vibrator for my sixteenth birthday—did I ever tell you that? Told me the same thing. And she was right."

"Are you trying to traumatize me?" I'm trying to keep the level of shock and disgust in my voice down, but the matter-of-fact way she's said "vibrator" has cracked me up.

Mum, her face uncharacteristically open and flushed, grins

at me. She seems pleased to have made me laugh. "Should I have gotten you one for your sixteenth?"

That does it. I'm laughing so hard I choke on a piece of pastry and have to spit it out into the sink.

"Yes," I manage. "You should have. You failed the motherhood test."

"I'm so ashamed," Mum says, deadpan. She digs her spoon back into the tray. "Well, you've picked a nice boyfriend. So I can't have done that badly."

I smile at her. "He is a nice one, isn't he?"

She nods. "Very nice."

I sit back down and pick up my spoon again. I don't think I've ever liked my mother quite this much.

rhysespieces: what are you doing this saturday?

stefstef: working!

rhysespieces: when till when?

stefstef: 10–4

rhysespieces: cool! want to come meet my friends? ☺

stefstef: !! really?

rhysespieces: yeah!

rhysespieces: only if you want to?

stefstef: of course!

rhysespieces: it's my group of friends from my old school

rhysespieces: just hanging out at owen's house. pizza.

he's got a pool table.

stefstef: cool ☺

rhysespieces: are you in?

stefstef: yeah!

rhysespieces: great! i'll pick you up after your shift?

stefstef: are they Deaf?

rhysespieces: yes, steffi, they are Deaf.

stefstef: was that a bad question? are you offended?

rhysespieces: haha no!

stefstef: i'm nervous

rhysespieces: don't be. they all want to meet you

rhysespieces: and you speak BSL! nothing to worry about ☺

stefstef: will meg be there?

rhysespieces: no—different crowd

stefstef: oh, okay

rhysespieces: they're good guys. you'll like them.

stefstef: will you prep me before?

rhysespieces: i'll prep you anytime ☺

stefstef: rhhhhhhhhhhhhhys

rhysespieces: yes. i will prep you.

stefstef: i'm going to be nervous about this all week.

rhysespieces: i guess i'll have to try to find a way to
    distract you then ☺

stefstef: ☺

rhysespieces: ☺

stefstef: xxx

rhysespieces: xxxx

15

IT IS, UNFORTUNATELY, NOT AN EXAGGERATION TO say I spend the next week worrying. My head has an ongoing conversation that goes something like this:

Bad brain: You know that thing on Saturday? It's going to be a disaster.

Good brain: No, it won't. It'll be fine.

Bad brain: You'll say something stupid.

Good brain: No you won't.

Bad brain: Yeah. You will.

Good brain: Okay, yeah, you will. But that's not a disaster.

Bad brain: Yeah it is. Rhys will be like, damn, I've made a mistake here.

Good brain: No, he won't.

Bad brain: Yeah. He will.

Good brain: That might happen, actually.

And so on.

By the time Saturday actually comes around, I'm sure I've been through every possible scenario. Twice. It's like the multiverse theory playing out in real time in my head. All the potential outcomes I've already lived through. It's almost enough to persuade me not to go.

But I have to go, because I'm someone's girlfriend now, and with that moniker come certain responsibilities. Responsibilities like meeting his friends and not flaking out of plans at the last minute.

Rhys turns up to meet me at the end of my shift at the kennels, all smiles, holding a single daisy between his finger and his thumb.

For you, he signs gallantly, tucking it into the front pocket of my overalls. It immediately falls out. "Oh," he says, instantly mournful.

We go back to my house so we can spend some time together and I can change. After an awkward few seconds, we agree that I will change clothes in my room while he waits in the kitchen with Rita. I can't help but think about how one day I might undress in front of him and the thought alone makes me simultaneously terrified and giddy.

After I've changed he comes into my bedroom and we talk

for a while. I'm sitting on the bed and he's on the floor, Rita curled up in his lap, her head on his knee.

So what do I need to know? I ask.

He laughs. **What do you mean? Nothing.**

Your friends. Tell me your history and stuff. How did you meet? How long have you been friends?

Rhys considers, his fingers rubbing the scruff of Rita's neck. **A long time. Do you know about how my old school worked?**

I shake my head. **I know you must have gone to Ives. Right?**

He nods. **I guess that was obvious.**

Ives Academy is the integrated school in our county that is known for accepting students of all abilities and needs. People call it a special school, but the whole point is that it's not. You've got your deaf kids and your hearing kids, autistic kids and non-autistic kids, kids in wheelchairs and kids who have full mobility. And all of these kids take classes together, socialize together, share the same canteen. "A microcosm of society," the head teacher said in an interview once.

The reasonable question at this point would be, "So, Steffi, how come you didn't go to this amazing school?" and the answer is that you have to be either located within a strict radius of the school or able to demonstrate that you will "genuinely benefit" from the "resources available." To cut a long story short, I could not demonstrate this, and that is because I was coming to the end of primary school when I met the admissions team and was in a good place, mutism-wise. I thought I was doing just fine, and so did everyone else. And then secondary school happened and it was too late.

My parents actually considered moving me to Ives after the first disastrous year, but I refused, because I couldn't bear the thought of not being with Tem. Swings and roundabouts, you see? Everything is a choice.

My close group of friends are all Deaf, Rhys begins. **The Deaf kids kind of stuck together at Ives—just made things easier, you know? And most of us knew each other through our local NDCS.**

NDCS?

National Deaf Children's Society. There's a strong local group here.

What about Meg?

Meg's different. He pauses, then gives a rueful grin. **Do you want to hear the Ives story or the Meg story?**

Both!

Okay, fine. Meg can hear just fine, but her parents and her sister are all deaf. So she is the only hearing person in her family, and I am the only deaf person in mine. We bonded! We're like opposites of each other. We met at an NDCS event when we were kids and our families both thought we'd be really good for each other. And we have been. She's great.

I bet your parents wanted you both to fall in love.

He laughs, and I know immediately that I'm right. **No way. Just friends.**

Does she go to Ives?

Yeah, but even though we're best friends we didn't hang out much at school. She has her own friends, and like I said I have mine. Ives is like its own little world. It has its own rules.

Sounds weird.

He shrugs. **Most things sound weird from the outside.** The corners of his eyes crinkle. **Like you and me.**

I grin. **You think we sound weird?**

Yeah! The deaf boy and the mute girl.

"Hey," I say, pointing a finger at him. "Look, this is me talking. Hear me roar."

I can't, he replies, deadpan. **That's the point.**

We both start to laugh and Rita jumps to her feet, alert.

"Sorry, sorry," I say quickly, reaching out to her. "Sit, it's okay." I look at Rhys, grinning. **She's not used to so much *noise*.**

Rhys bounds toward me and tackles me onto the bed, tickling me until I shriek. He kisses me, and goose bumps prickle all over my skin. His hand strokes the side of my face, his thumb on my neck. *Oh my freaking God*, I am thinking. And also, *There is a boy on my bed*. No, *There is a boy on top of me*.

And then there's a cough in the doorway and I leap away from Rhys as if he's electrocuted me. He looks confused for a second until I smooth my hair back and smile nonchalantly. "Hi, Dad."

"Hi," Dad says, looking like he can't decide whether to be amused or horrified. He attempts a smile that looks more like a suspicious grimace. "Hello, Rhys."

"Hi, Mr. Brons," Rhys says, scrambling off the bed and then hovering awkwardly right beside it, Rita skittering at his feet.

Dad gives an odd little nod, then looks at me. "Keep the door open, okay?"

I flush scarlet and he hurries away before I can reply.

Rhys coughs. I look at him to see that he's just as red as I am. **Sorry.** I swear my heart swells to three times its size.

Don't be. I move across the bed on my knees and put my head against his chest, closing my eyes for a moment so I can appreciate his steadiness, his smell, the Rhysness of him. After a second I feel him set his hand gently on my hair.

When I lean back and sit up properly, we're both smiling. He drops a kiss onto my forehead and I have to resist the urge to tell him I love him. It's too early for that. (Right? Right.)

We don't pick up the conversation about Ives and his friends until we're getting into his car to drive to Owen's house, and by then it's too late to properly get into it.

Give me the basics, I beg as he parks outside a row of houses and turns off the engine. **What do I need to know?**

Rhys holds up three fingers. **Lewis, Owen, and Mete. All good guys. They like football. Lewis is the Mario Kart master. Plus Alyce—Owen's girlfriend.**

Are they all deaf?

195

Mete is completely deaf. Owen and Alyce both have cochlear implants. Lewis has some hearing in his left ear. But we use BSL together all the time. Ready? He puts his hand on the door handle and smiles expectantly.

I can't think of a reason to delay him any longer, so I nod. I'm trying to remind myself that this isn't like all the other times I've gone to some kind of social event. This isn't me trying to hang out with Tem's other friends. It's not like that time I went to my cousin's birthday party and ended up crying in the bathroom. This is different. This is Rhys's friends. We all speak the same language.

We head up the driveway together and then wait on the doorstep as Rhys presses the doorbell. It makes the usual noise but through the front windows I see a blue light flash three times.

The door opens and a gangly, curly-haired boy with glasses and a huge grin is standing there. **Hi!** He claps Rhys on the arm and steps back so we can come in. **I'm Owen**, he says to me. **Good to meet you!** He puts a hand to his chest and beams. **I'm the good-looking one.**

Yeah right, Rhys replies, giving him a shove.

I'm Steffi, I say. I can feel how static my signs are compared to the two of them. They move so loosely, their whole bodies a seamless part of the conversation, while I move from sign to sign carefully, thinking through each one as I go. **Nice to meet you too.**

Rhys is grinning from Owen to me, unmistakable pride on

his face. I smile back but my skin feels prickly. *I can do this*, I think. *I can I can I can.*

We go downstairs to the basement, which is clearly the designated Owen Space of the house. There's a big TV and at least three games consoles, a raggedy sofa with sagging seats, and a mini fridge in the corner. Two boys are sitting on the sofa, having a rapid-fire argument about . . . I squint, trying to catch some words.

Owen leans over the sofa and cuts through their conversation with an arm swung lazily between them both. He points at us. **Look! It's the girlfriend!**

The two boys turn to stare. Two heads poke over the ridge of the sofa back, eyes wide. I glance at Rhys and realize he's looking at me too. In fact, everyone in the room is looking at me, waiting for me to say something.

Oh, hello, nightmare come to life.

Hi, I manage, and then my mind goes blank.

Before this can get any worse, there's a clattering on the stairs and a girl is suddenly beside us. She's small and round, with a mass of frizzy curls and a lanyard round her neck that reads ALYCE BREENE—CATERING (SS).

Hi! Sorry I'm late. Traffic was a bitch. As she signs she is unwinding her bag from where it has tangled at her waist and throwing it onto the carpet. **Oh my God! Are you the girlfriend?** She points at me, beaming, then swings around to Rhys. **Okay, she's real. I'm sorry I doubted you, Gold.**

197

Rhys takes a step toward me and I feel his hand curl at my elbow. It's meant to be reassuring, I know, but in reality all it does is make me realize that the anxiety that's building inside me must be clear in my face.

Want a drink? one of the boys on the sofa asks me.

Shit. Does he mean alcohol? Can I handle alcohol right now? Should I ask for water?

Coke? the boy prompts. He leans over to the fridge and pulls out a can.

I nod in relief and he throws it at me. Miraculously, I manage to catch it, but I'm so flustered by the throw and surprised by my catch that I fumble and drop it anyway. It bounces on the carpet and rolls under the sofa.

Nice. The second boy gives me a thumbs-up.

Rhys drops to his knees, retrieves the can, and opens it for me, tapping the top first so it won't fizz up and make this moment even more embarrassing.

After this display, they very kindly let me be for a while. Rhys takes my hand and leads me over to one of the large beanbag chairs, letting me sit between his legs so I feel guarded and secure. I sip my Coke and watch them all talk, trying to keep up but mostly failing miserably.

Here's what I learn: That thing I told myself about us speaking the same language? Yeah, that was bullshit. Total, hearing-person oblivious bullshit. *They* speak this language, and I know *some* of it. I can understand it and even communicate using it if everyone goes a bit more slowly than usual and is willing to repeat themselves at the sight of my flummoxed face. But I speak it in the same way that someone who gets a B in French can speak French when they go to Paris on holiday. As in, can speak it to other people who also got a B in French. Actual French people? Not. So. Much.

BSL is, at best, my second language. My stuttering, earnest second language, where I am trying my hardest but will need several more months—if not years—to be properly fluent. I thought I knew what that meant, given that I've been getting to know Rhys for a while now and have spent two evenings to date with his BSL-speaking family.

But now I understand what the difference is. All of those occasions were in the hearing world. It was BSL as subtitles; BSL as an extra tool. This is the Deaf world, something I'd never really given much thought to even existing until now, when I can see it in front of me. Five BSL speakers having two different conversations across a living room at once, laughing at jokes, getting each other's attention with taps on the table and clicks in the air. It's seamless and intuitive and fun to watch.

It's terrifying.

Is this how Rhys feels at school every day? In it, but not part of it? How have I not even thought about this before? I'd thought I was attuned to him. I'd thought I understood what his life was like.

Between signs he always returns his hands to me. He touches

my shoulder with his chin, squeezes my fingers, kisses my hair. Every time he does this, my heart calms, just a little. It reminds me that I am with him, that we have a tiny island of our own, whatever world we're in. That this is about an us, not a them.

After the first hour, I've relaxed a little. I manage to have a conversation with Alyce about Ives and what sixth form is like there. She signs carefully for me, clearly used to having to go slow, going on to tell me that she and Owen have been together for three years and are planning to open a cat café one day. I tell her about the kennels where I work and she lights up, asking if she can visit.

Owen sets up Guitar Hero on his Xbox after we order pizza and I watch as the boys argue over what songs to play. I tap Rhys's hand and lean round so we can talk. **Can I ask a really bad question?**

He grins. **Yes, we can play Guitar Hero even though we can't all hear very well.**

Is it as fun?

He shrugs. **I don't know any different. I think it's fun. You don't need to hear the music to be able to play. You follow the notes on screen.** He hesitates. **I love Guitar Hero. Being able to play rock music with my friends. Feeling the rhythm.**

When they start playing, Rhys squeezing my shoulder as he gets up to stand with one of the guitars as I settle back against the beanbag, I eat pizza and watch. They're all much better at this game than I was expecting, making me think that being able to hear the music is perhaps the least important part of playing guitar, and Rhys is the best of them all.

Three slices down, they all start gesturing to get me to play.

No way, I say, alarmed, holding up my arms in front of my chest like a shield.

Come on, Rhys cajoles. He holds out the second guitar to me.

I want to carry on refusing, but I remind myself that I'm here for Rhys, not me, so I force myself to stand up and take the plastic guitar from him. It's light in my hands. He chooses a song on the easiest setting—"Heart-Shaped Box"—but I still fumble with the buttons, laughing with embarrassment, missing at least half the notes.

You just need a bit more practice, Rhys tells me when we finish. He's clearly tried to go easy on me, but he still beats me by miles. He leans over and kisses me, right in front of all of his friends. **We can play at my house.**

For a second I think it's just me who's read an innuendo into these words, but then his grin widens, and he shows all his teeth. He winks at me.

My entire body explodes in a shower of all-singing, all-dancing sparks.

By the time we leave Owen's house it's 10:30 p.m. and it's started to rain. Neither of us has an umbrella so we hurry to the car, me holding my arms over my head and Rhys ambling along behind me as if the rain doesn't bother him at all. At the car I bounce on my feet by the locked door, pulling fruitlessly at the handle.

He grins at me from the driver-side door, taking his time with his keys.

"You suck," I say.

He finally unlocks the door and I scramble in, shivering, shaking my wet hair so the droplets fly all over his car. I'm about to start complaining when his hand takes a hold of my chin, his lips open against mine and—*oh hello*—we're kissing.

It's just brief, but it's enough for my body to heat up, my heart to start thundering, a soppy grin to appear over my face. As Rhys starts the engine and cranks up the heating, I slide my hair behind my ears and settle back against my seat.

I like your friends, I tell him.

He looks pleased. **Really?**

Yeah. They're very friendly.

I told them to be nice. You'll know they really like you when they start giving you a hard time. He rests the side of his forehead against the headrest, his eyes on me. **Was it okay? I could tell you were a bit nervous.**

I pause, trying to decide how best to respond. **I thought I'd find it easier. The BSL.**

He nods. **Did we go a bit too fast? Sorry.**

No, you were at normal speed. I'm just slower than I realized. You're brilliant.

I roll my eyes. **No, seriously.**

You are. You hear perfectly. Why would you need to speak BSL as well as us? They all think it's awesome that you know as much as you do.

I want to say, I want to be part of your "us," but how can I? Won't it sound ridiculous? **Do you think I'll be as good as you one day?**

He smiles at me, reaching out a finger and wiping a drop of water from my cheekbone. **Depends how long you stick with me.**

This time, I kiss him. And this time, it lasts a little longer. His hand travels down my back, curls around my waist, hesitates. His thumb eases under my shirt and touches bare skin. Electrical tendrils jolt into my bloodstream and dance through my veins.

The engine is still running and eventually we break apart so Rhys can drive me home. We spend the journey in silence, him paying extra careful attention to the dark, wet roads, me watching the rain running down the windows.

I wait until he's pulled up outside my house to begin talking again. **Do you miss Ives?**

I can tell by the time he takes to respond that his answer is more complicated than a simple yes or no. Finally, he gives a slow half-nod. **I miss my friends, but I'm not sad I left.**

Why did you leave?

The rain drums down on the roof, steady and comforting. I wonder what sense of it Rhys gets, whether he can feel the drumming, or if it's all dependent on sound.

I wanted a challenge. Rhys makes a face. **No, not a challenge. I needed to push myself. I want to go to university but I worried that I'd gotten so used to Ives that I'd find it too hard. They make everything as easy as they can at Ives—which is great, of course. But they won't do that at university. At least, not in the same way. So I decided to move to a totally hearing school when I had the chance, to see how I dealt with it.**

I wait, but he doesn't say anything. I prompt, **And?**

And it's been hard. He looks away from me, his face twisting slightly. His usual cheer has gone. **I thought I'd handle it so much better.**

I'm surprised. **But you are handling it**, I say. **You're handling it amazingly.**

He shakes his head. **No. I'm just really good at not showing when I'm not keeping up.**

I'm sure they'd help if they knew you were struggling. . . .

His head shakes again. **No, I'm not struggling. It's just harder than I thought. I think I took it for granted how Deaf-aware everyone was at Ives. The staff and the students. It's about more than just having someone interpreting the teacher during lessons.**

Could you ask for more support?

They're already doing as much as they can. They've run Deaf-awareness training for the teachers and it's helped a bit, but a lot of the time they just forget. It's habit, you know? I can't blame them. I wish . . . He stops himself, frowns, and then shakes his head, looking away from me and out of the window at the rain.

I touch his hand so his gaze returns to me. **What do you wish?**

I wish I could do this on my own. That I didn't need anything extra. I wish I could do it all by myself.

You are doing it yourself.

But even as I say this I know what he means, at least in a way. Maybe for me the equivalent is medication; I still can't quite get over the feeling that it's some kind of leg up to get me where I want to be. A kick start that I should feel lucky to have. It feels like a kind of cheating, almost, despite what my therapist says, which is that there is no such thing as cheating when you are trying to navigate a difficult world with the body and the tools we've been given. That we all have our methods, and life isn't a video game. There are no cheats. "If there were," she added once, "I'd be out of a job, for one thing."

I think you're amazing, I say finally. Because I do, and also because everything I've just thought feels far too complicated to translate into sign language at this time of the evening.

He smiles. **I think *you're* amazing.**

The rain continues to drum down. He takes my hand and kisses my fingers, his eyes on mine. I think about how him holding my hand like this is the BSL equivalent of putting a hand over someone's mouth, but because we are us we are still communicating. It's in the crinkle at the corner of his eyes, the softness of his touch. The question in the parting of his lips.

We kiss between the two front seats and it's like a whole conversation of its own. His hands on my face and my back ask questions; I reply with the way I nod my head as we kiss. I feel so safe in this car, hidden from the world under the blanket of rain, Rhys in my head and my hands and my mouth. At one point his hand slides up under my shirt and I find myself arching my back in response. His fingers feel warm and perfect against my skin.

Some time later—who knows exactly how long—I walk into my house in a bubble of heat and joy. I barely notice Dad's jocular attempts to ask me how my evening went. I just wave happily at him, pour myself a glass of water, and go to my room. When I climb into bed, I think about everything that comes after kissing, all the places we have to go together. I wonder if he's thinking about this too. I think about him thinking about me until my cheeks burn and my toes curl.

Before I fall asleep I check my phone and see a message waiting for me. The first two words make my heart leap into my throat.

Rhys:

I love kissing you. You taste like stars. xxx

I hug my phone to my chest, roll onto my back, and beam at the ceiling.

The ten best things about having a boyfriend:

1) Kissing. (It's pretty great.)
2) Getting to learn sign language. (Note: may only apply to Rhys Gold.)
3) Sharing private jokes.
4) Coming up with your ship name together. (Rheffi ☺)
5) . . . And your superhero/outlaws/explorers/pop duo name (Bronze & Gold, natch).
6) Learning silly little things about him that most people will never know. (Rhys still sometimes has nightmares about the Groke from the Moomins trying to eat him. Adorable.)
7) Frequent compliments, usually accompanied by 1)—Kissing.
8) Holding hands.
9) Having someone duty-bound to listen to your complaints/rants/rambling stories.
10) Kissing.

16

AT WORK THE FOLLOWING SATURDAY, RHYS'S MOTHER, Sandra, arrives at the kennels near the end of my shift. I'm on litter-tray duty in the cattery—my least favorite job—and so it's Ivan who comes to find me to tell me she's there.

"There's a woman here to see you," he says. "She says she'd like to have a look at the rescue dogs? Sandra Gold."

"Oh!" I say. I pause, looking down at the pile of litter trays I still have to clean.

"It's fine," Ivan says. "You're off the hook this time. I've asked Michael to take over." As he speaks, Michael appears behind him, looking sulky.

"Thanks!" I say, peeling off my gloves, beaming at Michael. "I owe you."

Michael mutters something that I ignore as I leave the cattery and follow the path round to the front office. Sandra is standing in the reception area, reading a leaflet.

"Hi, Sandra," I say, pausing by the desk and then hovering a little awkwardly.

"Hello, Steffi!" she says, her smile warm. She puts the leaflet back on the pile and taps her hands together. "I've come to meet Lily."

"Who?" I ask stupidly, then remember. "Oh!" She means Lily the three-legged beagle that I'd mentioned way back at Rhys's birthday dinner. "Lily's already been adopted." Lily got scooped up within about a week of her arriving at St. Francis. She was *adorable*.

Her face falls. "Oh. Oh dear."

"We have others," I say quickly. I try to gesture grandly with my hands, but it doesn't quite work. "Let me give you the tour."

We have twenty-five rescue dogs currently staying at St. Francis, and I already know which of them will eventually be adopted and which won't. It's the kind of thing you pick up quite quickly if you work at a rescue center like this, whether a dog is adoptable or not. It's a combination of breed, age, and temperament. An old, quiet Labrador is almost guaranteed a new family. A boisterous Staffie is not, much as it breaks my heart.

I lead Sandra down through the kennels, stopping at each run to introduce the dog within. I leave the biters and the growlers behind their gates, but for the friendlier ones I unlock the door for a proper greeting. Sandra is hesitant around the dogs, standing slightly behind me and only reaching a hand to the dogs when I assure her they're safe.

"What kind of dog were you thinking of?" I ask after a while. When I'm in my St. Francis uniform, my voice comes easy.

"A gentle one," Sandra says with a little laugh. "Not too much energy."

"Maybe an older dog would suit you," I say. "In fact . . ." I skip the next couple of kennels and come to a stop. "You know what? I think this is the perfect dog for you."

Petal is an eight-year-old spaniel who was brought to St. Francis a couple of months ago after her elderly owner died. She's the sweetest dog, but incredibly mopey—even getting her out for her daily walks is a trial sometimes.

I rattle through the basics, squatting onto the floor next to Petal, who shuffles over to me and rests her head on my knee. "She's got a lovely temperament," I say, stroking her ears. "And she's very low-maintenance."

"Hello," Sandra says softly, awkwardly sinking down beside me. "Hello, Petal. Oh, you're very beautiful."

"Shall we take her out for a run?" I suggest cheerfully. "To help you visualize her being your dog?"

Two hours later, I'm back at reception with Sandra, this time accompanied by Ivan and Petal. Sandra, looking a little shell-shocked but happy, is filling in a pile of forms, and Petal is sitting at her feet.

"We'd usually arrange a home visit first," Ivan is saying. "But as Steffi knows you and I trust her judgment, I'm willing to waive that this time. So long as you don't mind her checking up on you quite a bit in the first couple of months." He gives me a small, understanding smile. I smile back happily.

"Oh, I think I'll be very grateful for Steffi's visits," Sandra says, and my smile grows into a beam.

Petal is an extra excuse, if I ever needed one, to spend more time at the Gold house. She's so well trained there's not really much need to worry, but Rhys's mother has never owned a dog so I go through all the basics, explaining about feeding times and regular walks. This is a topic I'm most comfortable with, and that, plus the fact that I love the entire Gold family, builds my confidence in everything from my abilities to my speech.

"You're spending a lot of time over there," Dad says to me, about a week after Petal's adoption. "If you and Rhys want to come over here instead sometimes, that's fine with us."

"I know, Dad."

"Okay, good. Just wanted to be sure."

"It's only because of the dog," I remind him. "People need training just as much as dogs do, you know."

He smiles. "Yes, I'm sure. This kind of thing . . . helping people learn how to look after new animals . . . is this what you'd like to do for a career?"

I nod. "Something like this, yeah. Working with animals, anyway."

"Maybe you should think about expanding," he says. He comes into my room—where I'm sitting on my bed doing homework—and leans slightly, anchoring his hands in his pockets. "Maybe turning some of the people you know from the kennels into clients. You could build up a client list before you've even left school. One day it could be your own business."

"Maybe," I say. "But I don't think I'll start doing anything like that until after university. I'll be more prepared then."

A slight frown passes over Dad's face. "I meant as an alternative to university."

"Oh, Dad," I snap, instantly irritated. "Will you stop? I get enough of this from Mum. I want to go to university, okay?"

"I know that, love." His careful calmness gets my back up even more. "But I'm a little concerned that you haven't made as much progress as we'd hoped. With your communication, I mean."

"Well, I don't know where you're getting that from," I say, beginning to type more ferociously than necessary on my keyboard, not even looking at whatever nonsense is appearing on screen. "I'm doing a lot better, actually. I can talk at school now."

"A word or two, every now and then," Dad says. "That's not really what we had in mind. By now I'd hoped that you'd be talking to more of your peers. But I don't hear you mention anyone at school except Rhys."

"God, what do you want from me?" I demand. "You're meant to encourage me to push myself."

"That's what I'm trying to do," he says, his forehead scrunching. "But I also want to protect you, Stef-Stef. There's no shame in not going to university. It's a good thing to consider alternatives."

As far as I'm concerned, there is no alternative. I gave up on my dream of being a vet because of my stupid chronic anxiety when I started secondary school, which was when I realized that a job that requires so much interaction with people was not exactly made for me. In its place I put a new dream, smaller, but more achievable. I would be an animal trainer, ideally working with guide dogs or other service animals. You don't necessarily need a degree or anything like that to be an animal trainer, but my academic heart was set on university. I researched until I had formulated my new plan: Zoology with Animal Behavior. I'd learn all about animals in beautiful North Wales. It would be perfect.

When I first brought this up, aged fourteen, I quickly discovered that my mother didn't agree. "But, Steffi," she said, frowning. "Steffi, you don't need to go to university."

"I do," I said. As far as I was concerned, this comment made no sense. I had the online prospectus right in front of me. I was literally pointing to the course I wanted to take. "See? Eighty-five percent of students are in full-time work after graduation. That's pretty good, right?"

"Anyone can work with animals," Mum said. "What I mean is, why put yourself through all of that if it's not necessary?

Work at the kennels, get some experience. Maybe you can work there full-time one day."

I shook my head. "I don't want to work in the kennels—I want to actually train the animals."

"I'm sure you can get experience doing that too, love. Isn't it fairly simple to get a job in a zoo, or something?"

"Firstly, no," I said, irritated. "And, secondly, I want to go to university. I want to learn all that stuff. It sounds amazing. Look, Animal Ethics and Welfare. Herpetology!"

"What's herpetology?"

"I don't know, but if I do this course I can find out."

"Steffi," Mum said again. It was both annoying and worrying how she kept using my name. "Do you realize how difficult university would be for you? You can barely talk to your classmates, and you've known a lot of them since you were very young. There are thousands of students at universities, of all ages and from all over the world. Not to mention lecturers and professors. Do you think they'd be as accommodating of your problems as Windham has been?"

Talk about a kick in the teeth. Mum and I have been having variations of this same argument ever since.

Last summer, after I took my end-of-year exams, the whole parental troupe and I sat down over dinner to discuss it "calmly and rationally" (Keir) without any "sulking or slamming of doors" (Dad). The five of us went to the nearest Italian restaurant and talked it all over for the first time.

"I'm just worried it might be too much for you," Mum said. "Why not work for a few years and then see if you still want to go when you're a bit older?"

"Because I want to go now," I said, already annoyed. We'd been in the restaurant for fifteen minutes. "With everyone else."

"Everyone else can talk," Mum said.

"Joanne," Dad said.

"I'm talking right now!" I snapped.

"Stefanie," Dad said.

"Are you sure it's what you really want?" Lucy asked me gently. "University can be a very overwhelming experience, even for people who don't have any kind of social anxiety. I think what your mother is trying to say is that the benefits might not balance out the risks."

"Yes," Mum said. "That is what I was trying to say. Thank you, Lucy."

I can never quite figure out if Mum and Lucy actually like each other.

"It's also a lot of money," Dad said. "I know you don't want to think about it like that, Steffi, but it is the reality. It's very expensive nowadays. You'll be repaying the loans for decades. It's not a cheap experiment."

"It's not an experiment at all," I said. "It's my life."

"It's one small part of your life," Dad corrected. "Don't go thinking it's the be all and end all. Plenty of people don't go. The majority, in fact."

"Why is it so important for you to go?" Keir asked. This is a very Keir question. He teaches Philosophy at A-level and likes to feel like he's asking the deeper questions.

"Because I want to," I said. Which was a shorter way of saying that I wanted to prove to myself that I could, that I didn't want my anxiety to be the reason I didn't do something so huge, even if it terrified me.

"Do you understand why we're concerned?" Mum asked. She was using her overly reasonable voice.

"No," I said flatly.

"We care about you," Lucy said. "That's why we're concerned." We were having this conversation only a few weeks after the third anniversary of Clark's death. I wanted to say, "I don't even drive. It won't happen to me." But what would have been the point of that?

Instead, I said, "I thought you wanted me to be independent."

"We do," Dad said. "When you're ready. I'm not sure you *are* ready yet, love."

"Why not?" I demanded. Frustration was starting to spill over. "How can I prove it?"

And that's when they all came up with my Two Year Plan. That's what they called it, like they were economists deciding the fate of a nation, or something. The first year would be the most crucial. I would need to try harder at school, talk to people I didn't know, receive positive feedback regarding my voice from my teachers at parents' evening. I'd work with my therapist to learn more coping strategies and to overcome more of my anxiety—they'd also have meetings with her so they could be updated on my progress.

If I'd proven myself by the end of the year, I could go on to begin the application process for university as normal with everyone else in my year. Over the course of the next year, I would jump through some more hoops to prove my gung-ho talky-talkiness. By the time my final exams came round and I'd received my acceptance (providing I was accepted, of course, though this had always been taken as a given), I'd be all ready to go. No one would try to stop me.

When I try to explain all this to Rhys, he's confused. **But why don't they want you to go?** he asks. **I don't get it. Isn't it exactly what they want?**

They're worried, I say. **Mum thinks I'll have some kind of breakdown if I go away by myself. To be honest, I don't know if there's anything I could do that will stop her worrying about that.**

Why is she worried about that?

I shrug. **Because it's a possibility. But I'd rather do it anyway, and she thinks it's not worth the risk.**

He looks suddenly worried. **What do you mean? Why is it a possibility?**

I tap the side of my forehead with one finger. **Not so good in the head. She said once that if I had bad legs she wouldn't encourage me to run a marathon.**

He makes a face. **That doesn't even make sense.**

I shrug again. **Mothers.**

What about your dad? He seems so reasonable.

That's more complicated. I think of Clark packing up boxes on his last day at home before moving to Bristol University. *Will you miss me, Steffi?* Grief, sudden and acute, seizes my heart, then lets go. **Dad's worried too. But for different reasons.**

What reasons?

I could tell him about Clark. I could explain how Clark didn't even really want to go to university, but Dad and Lucy convinced him. They had what was basically the opposite argument with Clark than they now have with me. With him, it was, *You should go, it'll be so good for you.* And Clark eventually gave in and went, and then, just as he was on his way back to us for the summer, he died. His death was an accident—we all know this—but grief has a way of twisting sadness into guilt, remorse into regret, until it becomes irrational. Now they want to keep me extra close, extra safe, from somewhere in their heads that has morphed into something dangerous. University.

I could tell Rhys that in all the times my parents and I have spoken about me going to university we never mention this, never even mention Clark's name, but he's there. Every time. **Dad stuff**, I reply, which is meaningless but at least isn't a lie. **If I could just prove to them both that I can do it**, I say. **I think they still think of me as the mute kid, you know? But I'm not.** I hesitate. **Or am I?**

218

He smiles and touches my face. **You're not.**

But I think, to my parents—all four of them—I still am, and that's why they act like the great university decision is theirs, not mine. The difficulty is mine; the dream is mine; the medication is mine; the therapist is mine. But the decision? All theirs.

But now I have Rhys. My very own spanner in the works. No one saw someone like Rhys coming—especially not me.

Reasons I want to go to university:

To learn stuff.

To challenge myself. Everyone thinks I can't.

Tem's not going to university, and at least one of us should go so the other can visit.

The university has a Dog-walking Society. Really.

Student discounts.

I don't want to be stuck selectively mute in Bedfordshire forever.

Clark never got to finish university, and when I graduate I can tell myself it's for both of us.

17

THREE WEEKS AFTER RHYS AND I BECOME A COUPLE, I turn seventeen. It's a Thursday, the same day as the American Thanksgiving, and so my dad and I host Bronsgiving in my honor. I invite Tem and Rhys, because they're the only guests I need, and Mum comes along too, leaving Keir at home to look after Bell. Lucy goes all out, making traditional American dishes like pumpkin pie and green-bean casserole as well as the giant turkey and trimmings.

We sit in the dining room together with the lights dimmed low and candles lit all around the room. We drink champagne and I feel cozy and happy and special. Instead of the American tradition of everyone saying something they're thankful for, everyone toasts me, one by one. If I were anywhere else, it would be awful, but I'm here at home with my best people, so I blush with happiness instead of shame.

It's all pretty perfect, is what I'm saying.

Tem has bought me a panda charm for my bracelet, plus seventeen individually wrapped Lindor truffles. Her card features a black Labrador puppy and a white cat cuddling on a cushion. Inside she's written,

They're almost as cute as us!
Happy birthday, bestie.
Love, The Tempest xxx

"The Tem-best," I say, because some things never change, and hug her.

My first ever present from my boyfriend—from a boyfriend generally, in fact—is a couple of Pop! figures: one WALL-E, one EVE. They are adorable and perfect. **I thought about getting you** *Toy Story* **ones**, Rhys says. **But it's not a love story.**

I reach over and hug him. When we break apart, I see every single person in the room beaming at me.

If this whole thing were a film, this is where it would end. Me, bubbly happy, surrounded by people I love and who love me. Secure in myself and my place at the table. Talking freely. This would be the final shot: me sitting back after hugging Rhys, taking in the smiles of my family, smiling back as Rhys's hand finds mine under the table and squeezes.

But this isn't a film. He lets go of my hand, we eat cake, and then he leaves, followed half an hour later by Tem and my mother. There are dishes to wash and leftovers to wrap in foil and plastic wrap. Lucy drinks a glass of wine and sits on the sofa, her fingers on her forehead, eyes closed. I take Rita for a late-night walk, and it rains.

When I get home, I shower and go straight to bed, still feeling the warmth of the day, and I snuggle under my covers, replaying the moments in my head. How good it all felt. How lucky I am.

And then it happens. The panic. It's slow at first, creeping through the cracks in my thoughts until everything starts to feel heavy. It builds; it becomes something physical that clutches at my insides and squeezes out the air and the blood.

Who am I to be this lucky?

It won't last.

It won't last.

Rhys will get bored of me.

Tem will find better friends.

I make Lucy miserable because I remind her that her son's dead and all she's got is me.

Of course you're happy with people who love you. What about everyone that doesn't? They're all still around.

I can't breathe.

You don't even have any real problems and look at you.

I sit up in bed and rake my fingers through my hair, trying to steady myself. Breathe, breathe, breathe.

Imagine if you had real problems.

This is pathetic.

You're pathetic.

My breath is wheezy. A tiny whimper escapes.

You thought getting a boyfriend would solve everything?

Rita has jumped onto my bed. She's nuzzling my face with her wet nose. I try to inhale through my nose, smelling her fur.

You're taking medication and it's still not enough.

Nothing will ever be enough.

There's just you. Never enough.

Not even close.

It takes me a long time to calm down and when I do I realize I'm crying, clutching the ruff of Rita's neck. I've drowned out my own cruel thoughts by reciting the lyrics to "American Pie"—my dad's favorite song—half in my head, half in a whisper.

I breathe in a deep, shuddering breath and let go of Rita. She lets out a whiny huff, then licks my face.

"Sorry," I whisper, touching my cheek to hers. "I'm sorry."

I wait until my hands have stopped shaking, then lean over to my bedside cabinet to pick up the notepad my therapist gave me when I first started taking medication. I glance at the clock and write 2:11 a.m. Panic attack. I hesitate, the words blurring through a film of tears, and add, Help.

Panic attacks are a lot like being drunk in some ways: You lose self-control. You cry for seemingly no reason. You deal with the hangover long into the next day.

So that's me the following Friday, walking as if there's

cement in my shoes, a weight round my shoulders. On the way to school I email the doctor's office and ask for an emergency appointment with Jane, my therapist, for that afternoon. They try to call me back and I watch my screen light up, then fade. They leave a voicemail, and when I listen it's Jane's voice, calm and steady, saying she has time at 2:30 p.m. I spend the next few hours watching the clock.

What's wrong? Rhys asks me for the fourth time that day. It's lunchtime and I am still holding the sandwich I've been ignoring for ten minutes.

Nothing, I sign automatically, not even looking at him properly. I haven't told anyone about my middle-of-the-night breakdown. Not even Tem. *Especially* not Rhys.

You're all—he makes a sign I can't read, and in my tense state it winds me up.

I don't know what—I make some kind of approximation of the sign—**means**. I can feel that my movements are sharp and irritated, but knowing it doesn't help. I'm basically snapping at him with my hands.

His eyebrows raise a little. **I said**—he fingerspells slowly—**J-I-T-T-E-R-Y**.

I swallow down whatever mean retort is gathering and shake my head instead, pressing my lips together.

He puts his hand on my wrist. "Stef," he says. That whisper of a way he says my name. Still as soft as confetti.

I cram my sandwich into my mouth to avoid answering,

but my hands are still free and he's still looking at me patiently, waiting for an answer. For God's sake.

I'm fine, I say. **I'm fine.**

"I'm falling apart," I blurt out, walking into the room ahead of Jane and dumping my bag on the table.

"I can see that," Jane says, smiling a little. She closes the door behind us and comes to sit down opposite me. I'm already in the chair, drumming my fingers on the pine table. "Do you want some water?"

I consider, then nod. "Yes, please."

I watch Jane walk over to the water cooler, taking her time as always. Jane never rushes or hesitates. She's like calm in the shape of a person.

"Thanks for fitting me in today," I say. I try to remember that this is Jane's job, that she doesn't actually owe me anything beyond me being a client. Remembering that also helps me frame my anxiety as part of her job too. Something she deals with every day. To her, it's normal. I'm a client, not a problem.

"I had a cancellation," Jane says, coming back to the table with a paper cup of water. "So you were lucky in that sense." She sits down. "Now. Where do you want to start?"

"Well." I take a sip from the cup. "It was my birthday yesterday."

"Oh yes. That's right. Happy birthday."

"Thanks," I say automatically.

"Did something go wrong?" she prompts.

"No. That's the thing. It was perfect. I was so happy."

Jane watches me, nodding, a soft expression on her face that I can't quite read. It's almost a smile, but there's a sadness to it that I don't understand. She knows what I'm going to say, I realize. She *gets* this.

"It was the best day. We had, like, a Thanksgiving thing. And then I went to bed and . . ." I pause, remembering how it had come on so suddenly, manageable at first and then unstoppable. "I had a massive panic attack. A really bad one. The worst for months. It wasn't even . . ." I take a deep breath. "It wasn't even triggered by anything. I was *happy*." I can feel frustration, thick and cloying, in my throat. I hope I don't start crying. "It's not *fair*."

"What isn't fair?" Jane asks gently.

"That I still get like this even when I'm happy." I am digging my fingers into the cotton of the skirt I'm wearing, twisting and tugging. "That I can still get anxious when I'm . . . not."

"You know that your anxiety isn't about happiness and sadness," Jane says. "It isn't a cause and effect. Sometimes—often, even—there'll be very clear triggers, but not always. Chronic anxiety is a form of illness, Steffi. It's not something you bring on yourself by how you feel on any given day."

"But this wasn't just anxiety," I say. "This was a massive panic attack. Like, about-to-get-murdered panic attack. And I was as safe as anyone can be. I was as *happy* as anyone can be."

I can almost see her decide to change tack before she starts speaking again. "Do you want to talk me through your thought process before, during, and after?"

I shake my head. "These aren't supposed to happen," I say. "I'm on medication. I'm happy. It's meant to go away now."

"Steffi," Jane says, still gentle, still calm. "You know that's not how it works."

"Why *not*?"

"Because anxiety doesn't care if you're happy or not," she says patiently. "Just like cancer doesn't care if you're happy. Or a broken leg. Or diabetes."

"That's not the same."

"Blaming yourself for your illness will hinder your recovery process," Jane says. "It won't help. If you tell yourself you're not allowed to have panic attacks because you're 'meant to be happy,' it will make you feel worse. It will feed the negative emotions."

"I'm not blaming myself."

"Good, then talk me through your thought process."

I take another sip from my cup, trying to remember. "I was in bed," I say finally. "Thinking about how nice it had been that day, how lucky I was to have Rhys and Tem and my family. And then . . ." I swallow. "And then I got scared."

Jane nods. "Scared of what?"

"Scared that . . . it wouldn't last. That it would go away."

Jane is silent for a while, letting us both digest these words. Her, hearing them for the first time. Me, hearing them aloud.

I try to smile. "Isn't that stupid?"

"No, Steffi," Jane says quietly. "It's not stupid at all."

18

SOMETIMES, I JUST GET SO TIRED OF BEING ME.

It takes a few days for me to pull myself out of the post-birthday post-panic-attack funk, but I manage it eventually, as I always do. I don't see Tem or Rhys that weekend. Instead, I go to work on Saturday and spend most of Sunday with Rita at Dunstable Downs. December is just over the hill and it's starting to get properly cold. Rita flies over the grass, as perfectly happy as only dogs seem to be. As I watch her run, I think about how I wish I didn't think so much. How everything would be simpler if it were just . . . simpler.

I take Monday off school—Jane's suggestion, and therefore valid—so I don't see Rhys until Tuesday, which is also the beginning of Advent. I had thought I would tell him what had happened, or at least give him some kind of an insight into what a mess my head can be, but as soon as I see him I know I can't. How could I ever explain the tangles my anxiety ties me into? I'd sound ridiculous. *Yeah, I got scared after my birthday, so I had to not see anyone. . . . Sorry . . .* A proper explanation is beyond my BSL skills, so that's that. When Rhys says, **Are you okay?** I nod yes, and don't elaborate.

We make a vague plan to do something after school, but it rains so we end up driving to the park and just staying in the car. I'm not complaining, mind you. It's nice in his car. Being with him, just the two of us, in the dry, cozy car, makes me feel safe and happy, warm and fuzzy. We kiss for a while across the front seats, then move to the back seat where we can talk with more room. We each lean against one side of the car and have a long, sprawling conversation about pretzels (soft versus crisp, sweet versus savory) and then sports (he can just about tolerate football) and finally what the cutest animal is. He is showing me a picture of a quokka on his phone when I take it from him, put it on the seat beside us, and climb into his lap.

I can be assertive, see. I can be bold. I can be the kisser instead of the kissed. I'm not shy all the time.

We kiss until the rain stops. The fisherman jumper I'm wearing ends up on the floor of the car. Rhys's hands are steaming hot against my bare skin—my *bare skin!*—but I can feel the hesitation in his movements and his breath. *Are you sure?* he is asking me. *Is this okay?* It's more than okay. It's a fucking revelation.

This is as far as we go: his fingers under the strap of my bra, a shudder of a breath against my neck, a tentative thumb on my nipple. And then when he slides his hand away he takes mine and squeezes it. We kiss with closed lips and smile at each other. It's dark now, which is why Rhys leans round me to switch on the roof light.

I'm still on his lap and my heart thumps as he looks at me, his whole face slightly tense, as if he's trying to hold this moment in place.

"Okay," I say out loud, half laughing with embarrassment, reaching for my jumper.

Sorry, he says immediately. He's blushing. **You're beautiful.**

I shove my head into my jumper so he can't see me beaming and pull it slowly over me so I have time to rearrange my face. **Thanks.**

Are you . . . he hesitates and bites his lip. I suddenly know what he's going to say, and I'm struck by a crazy urge to laugh. Isn't the answer obvious?

Am I what? I ask innocently.

He swallows. **Are you a virgin?**

I smile. **Yes. Are you?**

He nods. **Yes.**

My heart starts thumping again. He kisses me, more gently this time, then pulls me in for a tight hug. I wrap my arms round his neck, rest my head against his, and we stay like that for a while, in this moment, in this place.

* * *

If I had an older sister, this would be when I'd go flying up the stairs to speak to her. That's what older sisters are for, right? To do your makeup and tell you about sex.

But, anyway, I don't have an older sister. So, naturally, I go to Tem.

"God, Steffi," is her first response. "You've gone from nought to nipple in one month. That's impressive."

I'm so hyper on oxytocin and Pepsi Max that I crack up. I laugh so hard tears brim around my eyes. When I wipe them, trying to get myself under control, I see that she's grinning at me.

"It's so great seeing you this happy," she says.

I screw the cap back on my Pepsi Max, hold it between my knees, and rest my chin on it. "It's great *being* this happy," I say. A sense memory of my panic attack just a few days ago flickers in my head but I think, *No*. I imagine a door in my head and close it firmly.

"So long as you're not rushing," she cautions. "There's no hurry, right?"

"Sure," I agree. "I don't think we will. But . . . I mean, if things carry on like they are now, we definitely will. Someday. Fairly soon. Ish."

"Have you said 'I love you' yet?"

"Oh God, no!" I shake my head, horrified. "It's way too early."

Tem shrugs. "Feelings are feelings. They don't care about things like timing. Hey, you'll tell me when you do have sex, right? Like, immediately. Roll off the bed and text me."

I laugh. "I can't promise it will be immediately. But yes. Obviously." I make a face at her. "So long as you promise not to preach."

She puts a solemn hand to her chest and bows her head. "I do so swear."

Like I said earlier, Tem likes boys. She likes flirting and kissing and falling in love. But sex, she insists, is not an option until marriage. Most people don't believe her when she says this—"People still do that?" is a common response—but the mix of Christian commitment and Tem stubbornness is potent. So though she's ahead of me in experience—she's certainly done *other* things—one day I'll overtake her. When I want to, I will, and the only thing that will stop me is if I don't want to. That's a kind of power, I think.

When Tem looks up again, she's beaming. She reaches over to hug me, squeezing my head between her arms. "Ohhhh, Steffi!" she crows. "You're all grown up!"

"Get off!"

My head is squashed right between her boobs. "Talking about *sex* with a *boy*. Having *nipple touches!*"

"Get off, September!" When she doesn't release me, I try a different tack. "How's Karam?"

It works. She releases me with a happy, Karam-induced sigh. "He's great," she says. "As usual. It's the march this weekend. You know, the one I told you about a while back?"

I nod. "You're still going?"

"Oh yeah. Karam's running it and I'm like his second in command. We've been spending a lot of time after college making plans."

"Is that a euphemism?"

She scrunches her nose at me. "*You're* a euphemism." Which means yes. "It's great to spend so much time with him . . ."

I wait, but she doesn't pick up the sentence, so I prompt, "But?"

There's a pause, then she shakes her head. "No but. It's great to spend so much time with him. We have such a laugh, Stef. And I know he likes me."

"Do you think you'll get together properly?"

"I don't think we need labels," she says airily. "We just have fun together. Every time I see him, it's like . . ." She hesitates, her eyes darting up to the ceiling. "Like lightning. That bolt of lightning that people talk about. That's how I know it's real. I felt it the very first time I saw him, and it was like my heart was going, *Yep, that's him. Zing!*"

"Lightning?" I echo, thinking of Rhys. The first time I saw him, I didn't think anything beyond, *There is a person I don't know*, probably with a hint of *I hope I don't have to speak to him*. And, even now, seeing him doesn't induce a jolt of electricity. Touching him and kissing him does a lot of the time—is that the same? Is that what she means?

"Yeah, didn't you get that with Rhys?" She looks at me expectantly. "Like . . ." She illustrates her thoughts by making

233

a fist with her right hand and swinging it dramatically toward her heart. "Zing!"

I could lie, but this is Tem. What would be the point? "Not really," I say. "It's more like . . ." I try frantically to find an analogy that sounds as good as lightning. "Like thunder!" I say, a little too triumphantly.

Tem blinks. "Loud and scary?"

"Well, no." I frown. *Too late to backtrack, go with it, Steffi.* "It's the bit after the jolt. You know how you *feel* thunder? Like that low rumbling, deep in your stomach and your chest? So I get the little jolts, like when we're kissing, but then for a while after, while I'm with him, I get that happy, lasting kind of feeling. Like thunder." I'm warming to my theme. "With lightning, you're never really sure if that's what it was; it's just a flash. Thunder, you *know*. You feel it."

Tem is quiet, her expression bordering on sulky. "Well. I *feel* the lightning with Karam."

"Great," I say robustly. "And I *feel* the thunder."

We look at each other, and I can tell she's waiting for me to relent in the face of her disagreement, but I don't. I wrinkle my nose and cross my eyes until she laughs and shrugs.

"Okay, fine," she says. "You can have your quiet thunder. I'll keep the exciting lightning."

I roll my eyes, smiling. "You do that."

19

THE FOLLOWING WEEKEND, RHYS AND I GO CHRISTMAS shopping together. It's mostly for his benefit rather than mine—I'm the super-organized kind of anxious person, meaning I'd bought all the presents I needed online at the beginning of December. I'd got Rhys a remote-controlled robotic raptor.

But Rhys, being of boykind, hasn't got any of his presents yet. He hasn't even got a list.

The best thing to do is start with your family members, I say. We're in the line at Starbucks, which extends all the way through the shop, planning the day. Well, *I'm* planning the day. Rhys is trying to decide whether to go for the Christmas spice blend coffee or a vanilla latte. **Hey.** I give him a poke. **Concentrate. Shall we start with your mum?**

Rhys shrugs. **Mum likes candles. I always get her a candle.** I frown. **Bit obvious.**

He wiggles his nose at me. **So?**

I bet you get your dad a tie every year, I say, rolling my eyes.

What's wrong with a tie? All dads love ties.

Basic, I sign, grinning at him. **You're basic.**

We reach the front of the line and Rhys orders for us, choosing the Christmas blend for himself and my usual vanilla hot chocolate for me. We head out into the cold, still no clearer on what shop we're going to first or even who we're buying a present for, but it doesn't seem to matter.

Signing is a bit more difficult with a cup in one hand, but we manage. Rhys is laughing as he signs; he's telling me a story about the Christmas he and his brother got their mother the same bath set. We're surrounded by people but I'm looking at no one but Rhys, the two of us completely in our own bubble—a warm, happy bubble. I'm having an entire conversation and I'm not saying a word. Is anyone looking at us? Probably. I don't even care.

We're walking at an angle to each other so we can walk and talk, navigating our surroundings with glances. Rhys is slightly in front of me, walking backward, and it is this fact, plus the aforementioned bubble, that causes Rhys to walk right out into the road, straight into the path of an oncoming Royal Mail van. The van is far enough away that most people would be able to get out of the way at the first sound of a horn, but Rhys doesn't hear the horn.

I lunge out into the road and grab hold of Rhys, pulling

him out of the way with seconds to spare before the blur of red, the blare of a horn being pounded in fury, and a fist waving out of an open window. I take all of this in for less than a second before the bicycle hits us both.

Firstly—*ow*. The front wheel careens into Rhys's leg and then over my left foot, the handlebars hitting the space just below my ribs.

Secondly—*shit*. We manage not to fall, Rhys's hands grabbing on to my forearms, righting us both. His cup of coffee has gone flying into the road, spraying us, the road, and the bike with lukewarm liquid.

"What the fuck?!" the cyclist roars. He's managed to stop his bike with his feet and I don't think he or his bike are even slightly dented, but still he is reaching up and ripping off his cycling goggles—yes, really—to yell at us. "What do you think you're doing? Watch where you're going!"

Everyone is staring at us. I am definitely not in a bubble anymore. But near-death-experience adrenaline apparently beats anxiety, because I have my voice and I use it to yell right back. "He's *deaf*!"

"That's why you should fucking *look*!" The cyclist climbs back onto his bike and presses his feet into the pedals. "Fucking kids," he throws over his shoulder as he begins to ride away. "Fucking deaf fucking kids."

Rhys steps back up onto the pavement and I follow silently. The shock of the last minute has made my hands start tingling.

I let out a breath. Rhys isn't looking at me; he's examining his hands, taking his time over them, studying the streak of wheel mud across his fingers.

I touch his shoulder and he looks up slowly. **You okay?**

He shrugs.

I attempt a shaky grin. **You're welcome.**

He frowns. **What?**

I just saved your life, I point out. **Better a bicycle than a van, right?**

He looks at me for a long moment, his expression unusually unreadable. He pushes his fingers into his pockets and shrugs again.

Are you okay? I ask again.

A flash of irritation crosses his face, so alien I almost don't recognize it for what it is. He clenches his hand into a fist and moves it up and down, which is the sign for yes. But the way he's making the motion, it's more like he's saying YES, for God's sake, shut up.

I bite my lip, wrong-footed, unsure what to do or say. I hesitate, then reach up and sweep my fingers across his cheek, wiping off droplets of coffee. He closes his eyes, takes a hold of my fingers, and kisses them. Before he lets go he sighs slowly, opening his eyes, then smiles.

Sorry.

You don't need to be sorry, I reply, surprised. **It was an accident.**

He shakes his head. **My fault. Wasn't looking.**

Neither was I. We're both stupid. I smile, hoping the tension in his face will ease.

You—he begins, then stops.

Go on.

You wouldn't have been in the road. That was me not looking. I always look.

"Rhys," I say, because it's one of those moments where I need to say his name and I haven't yet learned how to fill the same impulse with BSL. **We were both not looking.**

He presses his lips together. **No. I always look. If you weren't here, I would have been looking.** He suddenly squeezes both his hands into fists, as if he's keeping the words in, stopping something else coming out.

I feel my eyes widen. **What does *that* mean?** The words have kick-started my heart—it's cantering in panic in my chest.

He shakes his head again. **Nothing. I'm sorry. I want to keep you safe.**

The words are so confusing. Do they even go together? What does keeping me safe have to do with anything? It was so clearly just an accident.

"Rhys," I say again, but he stops me, putting a finger to my lips. When he removes it he leans down to kiss me, his lips pressing against mine. I open my mouth and feel the familiar, fizzy jolt at the touch of his tongue. His arm curls around the back of my neck.

When we break apart he pushes the tip of his nose to my cheek, smiling now. He kisses me again, reaches down, and takes my hand. **Let's go**, he signs.

We carry on with the day we'd planned—buying presents for the whole Gold family, pausing to kiss on a bench, sharing a crêpe from the Christmas market—but it doesn't feel the same after the collision. Rhys is a little distant, a slight frown in his eyes, and I'm fluttery with anxiety, jumping at every noise and checking all around me before I cross the street. Still, we don't talk about it, skating around it like a crack in the road, as if it didn't happen.

I don't mention it to anyone else, either. Even Tem, though I'm not sure why not. Maybe I just don't want to take the shine off the perfection of our relationship, but when she asks how our trip was I tell her it was magical. "He got Beats headphones for his older brother," I say. "Red ones."

"Generous," she says. "I hope he gets you something just as good." He does. We don't exchange Christmas presents until Christmas Eve, which is the compromise both our parents force us into instead of allowing us to see each other on Christmas Day. I work at the kennels until mid-afternoon, and then Rhys picks me up and drives me to his house. He's bought me a handmade quokka figurine, almost too beautiful to be real, and small enough to fit in my hand. When I pull back the tissue paper to reveal the intricate carvings, I almost cry.

After the presents, we sink into each other and kiss for a while. Let me take this opportunity to say that "kiss" is one of the most inadequate words in the English language. It sounds so innocent and sweet. But we are lying on his bed. His stubble is scraping my chin. My bra is unclasped. His hand is under my shirt, stroking circles on my stomach and sliding, oh so hesitantly, up . . .

Anyway. So we kiss.

I spend the two weeks of the Christmas holidays at Mum's house. Even though I miss Rita, there's no better place to spend the season than in a house with an excitable five-year-old. Especially a five-year-old who insists on being called Sleigh Bell all the way through December and who likes to dress up in sparkly costumes.

Tem comes over at 9 a.m. on Christmas Day for hugs, presents, and hot apple juice. We huddle together in the garden, watching our breath frost in the air in front of us, until she has to leave to go to Mass.

"Have fun," I say, hugging myself for warmth on my front step as she heads off down the driveway. "Say hi to Jesus for me."

"I will!" she sings, spinning on the spot but somehow not breaking her stride.

I wait until she's out of sight, then head back into the house. Bell has changed into her Cinderella outfit and is singing Christmas songs at the top of her voice. Keir is on the phone to his sister, who is coming over with her family, giving directions. I take the opportunity to go to my bedroom and open up jackbytes, hoping to talk to Rhys, but he's not online, so I text him instead.

Steffi:

Merry Christmas, Boyfriend.

I like you a lot. xxx

His reply comes about an hour later. I'm sitting in the living room with my family and Keir's, watching Bell and her cousins open presents.

Rhys:

Merry Christmas, Girlfriend. I like you even
more xxxx

My heart fills and I curl up even tighter in my armchair, hugging myself. I take a quick selfie of my bashful, beaming face and send it to him. When I look up, Mum is smiling at me. I'm so full of happy I smile back.

We eat a lot of food and then go through Christmas traditions like we're ticking them off a list: a flaming Christmas pudding only the adults eat; charades; an argument over what to watch on TV; Trivial Pursuit; a walk round the block; more arguments about TV; and then, finally, the elongated good-byes, sleeping children carried to the car, and Mum's gentle sigh of relief as the door closes.

And that's Christmas over for another year. I take a box of chocolate mints to my room and snuggle up in bed with my phone, talking to Rhys until everyone else in the house has gone to bed and it's all quiet and still.

I work at the kennels for the next few days and then spend New Year with Mum, Keir, and Bell. Rhys and his family are visiting his grandparents in Wales and Tem is at a house party with Karam and his friends. Though she'd invited me, I didn't seriously consider going, and I don't think she expected me to. Instead, I sit on the sofa with a drooping Bell on my lap as the hours pass, waking her with a squeeze when the countdown starts.

"I stayed up!" she yells, blinking. "Happy New Year!" And then falls asleep again.

I'm in bed by half past midnight, and asleep by one.

"You wild child," Tem teases me the next day, the two of us lolling on the swings as Davey and Bell run around the playground.

"I've never claimed to be a party animal," I retort. "And at least *I*"—I gesture to myself as obnoxiously as possible—"am not hungover."

Tem scowls. "Yeah, yeah. Don't rub it in." She stretches, her feet dipping into the woodchips below the swing. "I shouldn't have had so much prosecco."

"Did you have fun, though?"

She nods, but there's not much fun in her face, to be honest, though I put this down to the hangover rather than a lie. "It was great."

"Who did you kiss at midnight?" I'm teasing. It's obvious who she kissed at midnight.

A wolfish grin streaks across her face. "Not just at midnight, my friend."

"How late did you stay up?"

"Until about four."

"Really?" I make a face. "What's there to do once the countdown's over?"

She laughs. "Oh my dear, sweet Steffi."

I reach over, pick up a handful of woodchips, and toss them at her. They scatter over her jacket, fall into her curls. "It's a totally fair question."

Tem twists her fingers into her curls and pulls them in front of her eyes, digging through for woodchip dust. "We carried on drinking. Bit of dancing, bit of kissing. You know. Normal stuff." The slight edge in her voice surprises me. Is that a dig? Tem never makes digs at me.

"Normal is in the eye of the beholder," I say.

She doesn't laugh. "Is it?"

I try not to sound offended. "Since when do you care about doing what's normal?"

"For God's sake," she mutters under her breath, but of course I hear her anyway, as I was probably meant to. "Stop being so judgmental, Steffi. It's weirder to be the seventeen-year-old who doesn't go out drinking on New Year's."

"Ouch," I say quietly.

I wait for her to apologize, but she looks away from me instead, pushing her feet against the ground so she swings back and then forward again. In just a few seconds she is zipping past me, a blur of black curls and denim.

I'm more confused than hurt. I don't understand why she's being so defensive with me, when she knows I'm the last person in the world she'd ever need to be defensive with.

"Steffi!"

I look up. Bell is running over the grass toward me, breathless and excited, holding something between two cupped hands. Davey is trotting along behind her, hopping after every second step.

"Watch out, Bell—" I start to say, but it's too late, and of course the inevitable happens. Bell bounds across the woodchips, trips over her dangling shoelace, and falls forward, directly into the path of Tem's oncoming feet.

"Bell!" Tem yells, trying to twist herself out of the way. She goes flying off the swing, avoiding my little sister's head by mere millimeters. I can tell that she intends to land on her feet, but the momentum and the twist of the swing ruins this and she lands heavily on the grass instead, cursing on impact.

Bell, splayed at my feet, immediately begins to wail. I'm already off my own swing, which was practically stationary anyway—an anxious person is a safe person—and kneeling in front of her, carefully easing her into a sitting position. Her face is a blotchy mess of blood, tears, and woodchips. Davey takes one look at her and bursts into tears too.

"Shit," I say, breaking my formerly unbroken promise to my mother to never swear in front of Bell. "Oh, Belly-Bell. Where does it hurt?"

She doesn't actually need to answer me, because it's clear what the problem is when she opens her mouth to let out another ear-splitting bawl. There's a gaping hole where her two front teeth should be, and her top lip looks like it's almost ripped in half.

"Jesus, Bell," Tem is starting to say as she limps over to us, but she stops herself when she gets a good look at her. "Oh shit."

My hands are shaking. "Bell, stop crying, darling." I never say "darling," and the word sounds strange coming out of my mouth. I try to wipe her face, but she just howls and jerks away from me.

I have no idea what I'm doing. Shit. "Bell," I say again, my volume escalating, "why didn't you stop your fall?"

My beautiful idiot little sister still has her scraped and bleeding hands cupped together, still clutching whatever it was she was coming over to show me. I try to open them, but she's too frazzled to notice, clenching her fingers even tighter together instead.

"Bell!" I snap. I know this won't help anything, but I can't help it. My nerves have clocked on to the situation and are sending "PANIC!" signals across my whole body. I wrench open her fingers and a bright yellow bottle cap falls out. "Oh, Bell, for God's sake!"

There's a hand on my back, and then Tem is squatting beside us both. She keeps one hand on me as she touches her other to Bell's face, gentle and calm. "You're all right, Bell," she says softly. "You've just had a bit of a bang, that's all. Steffi's going to give your mum a ring so she can come and give you a cuddle. Okay?"

Bell lets out a wrenching, hiccupy sob, then nods.

"Don't we need to go to the hospital?" I ask. "Look at her lip. Won't it need stitches?"

This is the wrong thing to say, because Bell's face scrunches in fresh horror. "Stitches?!" she wails, her voice distorted by the shock and the blood. And the mutilated lip.

Tem gives me a look and I balk. "Steffi's going to give your mum a ring," she repeats to Bell, her voice even more deliberate this time.

"Yes," I say, scrabbling for my phone. "Yes, she is. See, Belly? I'm calling Mum."

Bell looks at me, tears dribbling down her face. She looks so sad and pathetic I almost start crying myself, but Tem gives me a surreptitious shove and I leap to my feet, tapping my phone to unlock the screen and make the call every older sibling dreads.

"Mum? It's me. Look, don't panic, but something's happened to Bell. . . ."

20

IN THE END, BELL ONLY NEEDS A COUPLE OF BUTTER-
fly stitches, but the way Mum goes on you'd think she's going to be scarred for life.

"She might be *traumatized*," she frets.

"She's clearly not traumatized," I say impatiently. If anything, Bell just seems thrilled that she's allowed to eat ice cream for dinner. The only person really bothered about the hole where her teeth should be is Mum.

I end up going back to Dad's house earlier than usual, blaming it on coursework but mainly wanting to get away from all Mum's fussing. Rita is beside herself, leaping all over me as I drag my suitcase through the hall.

"Happy New Year," Dad says, giving me a huge hug. "And welcome home."

I grin, hugging him back. Dad isn't really supposed to say

things like that to me, but I don't mind. His house always feels more like home to me than Mum's, anyway, and I've missed him and Lucy over Christmas.

The three of us celebrate my homecoming with a curry made from leftover Christmas turkey and vegetables and then have a quiet evening in watching Pixar films. We don't talk about Clark, but he's all I can think about, and I can tell he's on their minds too. It's like the polar opposite of how the last few days have been with Mum, Keir, and Bell. Midway through *Cars*, I fall asleep.

By the time I see Rhys again, we've been apart for over an entire week and I've missed him more than I ever thought I could miss someone. He comes over to pick me up and I'm giddy just waiting in the hallway, listening for his car. When I open the door I actually leap at him, throwing my arms round his neck like some kind of period-drama damsel. He hugs me back just as tight, his grin is just as wide, and it feels like something has changed. The word "love" hovers. It waits.

But not yet. Not quite yet.

School starts up again and with it normality. It's Friday and I'm sitting in English, the last lesson of the day before we're all released back into freedom and the weekend. Everyone is a little bit restless, watching the clock and letting out audible, periodic sighs that Mrs. Baxter studiously ignores.

"I want us to think about women and girls," she says, her back to us as she writes on the board. I think, as I always do now, about Rhys and his lip-reading. If he was here, he'd be lost right now. "How are women represented in *Atonement*?"

I knit my fingers together over my copy of the book and rest my chin on the ridges, listening as Cassidy King starts in on a rant about passive women in books written by men. If I were a talker, I might challenge her on this, but I'm not, so I don't.

"Are they passive?" Mrs. Baxter asks in a voice that gives away nothing of her own opinion. "Wouldn't you say they are the impetus for the narrative?"

"That doesn't make them active participants in it," Cassidy says. "The story happens to the men."

"Only if by 'story' you mean 'war,'" Anthony Mitchell says. I write "passive?" on my notepad, then add a few more question marks for good measure. Anthony and Cassidy—who have been on-again off-again for the last three years—start arguing about strong female characters, so I doodle a caterpillar wearing fluffy slippers from one end of my page to the other.

"Let's bring in some more people on this," Mrs. Baxter says, her voice cutting through Cassidy's increasingly shrill tone. Something tells me she and Anthony are off again. Again. "Kasia, what do you think makes a strong female character?"

"Not needing a man," Kasia suggests. "Like, fighting her own battles."

"Literal battles?" Mrs. Baxter asks.

"Those too."

"How about you, Steffi?" Mrs. Baxter's voice is casual. "What makes a girl strong?"

250

"Agency," I say. One word. Three syllables. I haven't looked up from my notepad; my caterpillar looks great in his slippers.

"Nice word," Mrs. Baxter says. "What do you think Steffi means by agency, George? And does Briony have it?"

I can feel eyes on me, but I still don't look up. My cheeks feel red but my heart isn't hammering; my palms aren't sweating. Under the caterpillar I write "agency" and then add a smiley face.

Do *I* have agency? I give my caterpillar a hat with a fluffy bauble on top. Okay, yes, I have it. But do I use it? Or do I just let things happen to me?

I feel like I'm hovering on the edge of some kind of epiphany, but it's just out of reach. I carry on drawing, sketching out a beetle friend for my caterpillar, letting my mind whir as the pencil moves. If I really did have agency, wouldn't I be the one choosing about going to university, not my parents? Why am I letting them act like it's their choice to make?

And Rhys. Being with him is my choice—my choice and his—and maybe that's part of the reason my parents are so angsty about the whole thing. Maybe they're used to making decisions for me, and I've just let them for so long they don't know what to do with this new, agency-having Steffi.

I should do something, I think. Make a choice that is so definitively mine they'll realize that I really am my own person, and it's fine to let me be that. That they can trust me not to fall apart. (*Can* they trust me not to fall apart?) (Yes. Yes they can,

Steffi, and so can you.) Then I can go to university. And then my life will really begin.

The bell rings and I close my notepad, already standing up and reaching for my bag. Across the room, Anthony leans on to the corner of Cassidy's desk and starts talking in a low voice while she makes a show of ignoring him.

I leave the classroom and head down the hall, pulling out my phone as I go. There's a message from Rhys telling me to meet him by the school gates, and so I pick up my step. I see him first and take a second to appreciate his figure, leaning against the gatepost, looking at his phone.

I slide my hand through the crook of his elbow and smile when he turns to look at me. *Hey*, I mouth.

Rhys kisses me and then holds out a small paper bag, a pleased smile on his face. **Hi**, he says. **Happy Friday.**

I take the bag and look inside it, already thrilled even if it contains nothing but cotton wool or pencil shavings or thin air. It's a chocolate cupcake adorned with an obscene amount of green icing. **Thank you**, I sign, raising myself on my tiptoes to kiss him on the cheek.

"Get a room!" a boy yells.

I blush, but Rhys is oblivious, signing something to me about girls and cupcakes. I nod as if I've understood him, then take a bite.

Do you need to be anywhere? Rhys asks me. **Want to go for a walk or something?**

I have to go to Mum's to babysit Bell, I say. **But that's not until five. A walk sounds good. How was your day?** We begin walking away from the school.

He shrugs. **Okay. You?**

I mimic the shrug. **Okay. I was thinking, we should do something together.**

Crinkles appear around his eyes as he smiles. **Something? Like what?**

Something like . . . I think about it. **An adventure. We should have an adventure.**

He nods. **Definitely. I'd love to have an adventure with you. A big one or a small one?**

Both! My mind is already alive with impossible ideas. I'm imagining the two of us in a hot air balloon, scaling Everest (Note to self: What's the British Everest?), kayaking down a river.

I could drive us somewhere? he offers. **How about somewhere on the coast? Or we could go to Brighton? We can get a train direct from Bedford.**

Maybe, I hedge. **Is that an adventure, though?**

It would be if I was with you, he says, and I immediately crack up. His face falls. **I mean it!**

I know! I try to control myself. **I'm sorry. That was just too cheesy to be real.**

He gives me a little shove. **I was being romantic. Fine, no Brighton.**

Think bigger, I say, exaggerating an excited expression.

Think a road trip around America. The Northern Lights. The beach in Goa!

He laughs. **Skydiving in New Zealand?**

Yes! A safari in South Africa. Hitchhiking across Europe! We both come to a stop at the edge of the road, waiting for the traffic lights.

I didn't know you had these kinds of dreams, Rhys says.

I know he hasn't meant it in a bad way, but the words make me sad. Do I really seem that small? To *Rhys*, who by now knows me so much better than most? How must I look to everyone else, if even he thinks this?

Of course I have dreams, I reply. **Don't you?** I want the world, I think. Even if it scares me. Doesn't everyone?

Rhys smiles instead of answering, taking my hand again as we cross the road. **I can't promise lions and tigers and bears**, he says when we've reached the other side. **But I'll think about it. I'll find an adventure for us.**

"Rhys and I are thinking of going on holiday," I say.

Mum blinks. "Really?"

I nod. "Any suggestions? Somewhere close, obviously, because we don't have that much money for travel and stuff. You can get cheap flights to basically anywhere in Europe now, right?"

"You're thinking of going abroad?" she says, her eyes widening. "Oh, Stefanie, I don't know. I don't think that's a good idea."

"Why not?" I ask, surprised. I honestly thought she'd be

pleased that I was even considering such a big step.

"The two of you are very young, for a start."

"Rhys is eighteen. He's an adult."

"And with your . . . difficulties . . ."

"Oh, thanks."

"It's probably not a good idea for you to go away without some kind of support."

"Support?" I repeat. Even though this is my mother, and we're standing in her kitchen with no one else around, I feel embarrassed. Almost ashamed that this is how she sees me.

"Why don't you go away with Tem?" she suggests, brightening.

"Because I want to go away with Rhys," I say, frowning.

"Tem could go with you," she says promptly. "And maybe some of Rhys's friends too."

"I don't need you to organize my social life for me."

"You asked me for suggestions."

"For *locations*." I try—unsuccessfully—to hide how irritated I am. "I meant, like, 'Paris or Amsterdam?' kind of thing."

"Amsterdam?" For a second, Mum looks almost panicked. "Oh no, Steffi. No, this isn't a good idea at all. Look, why don't you wait until the summer holidays? We're all going to Cornwall for a week. Rhys is welcome to come. If he doesn't mind staying in a separate room, of course."

"Mum," I groan. I can't believe she's trying to turn my first ever couple holiday into a separate-rooms family trip to a Cornish cottage. Except I can believe it, because it's Mum.

"Have a think about it," Mum says. She picks up a dishcloth and starts wiping the counter, which means she thinks the conversation is over. "But the two of you going away alone is just out of the question, love. It's just not a good idea."

I stare at her, mute with frustrated annoyance. I can't even argue, because she's being so unreasonable it's bordering on ridiculous. Finally, I manage, "Remember how you always wanted me to be more . . ." I trail off, trying to find the word. "More . . . just *more*?"

Mum pauses, her fingers stilling over the dishcloth. But then she recovers herself, scrubbing harder at an imaginary stain on the countertop. "I wanted you to be able to talk. I like Rhys. You know I like Rhys. But I don't think you want to go away because you've suddenly become braver and want to try new things and meet new people. I think it's because you think it doesn't matter anymore, because you have him."

There are a lot of things I could say to this, but none of them makes it past my lips. I swallow. "Are you telling me I can't go?"

"I'm not *telling* you," she says. She's not looking at me. "I'm giving you my advice. As your mother." There's a long pause and then she lets out a sigh that I hear from across the room, tosses the dishcloth onto the counter, and turns to face me. "Steffi, I know I can't make decisions for you. I know how exciting first love can be. But I worry that this relationship is making your world smaller, not bigger."

I frown. "Smaller? How can it be smaller, if I want to see more of it?"

She shakes her head. "Maybe you'll understand when you're older." The most frustrating sentence in the entire world of parents and teenagers. "But I've said my piece now."

I steam about this conversation for the next few hours. Have I suddenly become braver? No, but who the hell cares? Doesn't the fact that I do the things I never did before matter more than the reason why I do them? Do I think talking doesn't matter now that I have him? No, but I definitely think it matters less than I used to think it did. Of course we have our own little bubble. But it's a bloody nice bubble. Why can't she just be happy for me? Who cares how big or small my world is, so long as I'm *happy*?

21

BY FEBRUARY, RHYS AND I HAVEN'T MADE ANY PROG-
ress on our adventure-seeking. At least, not in the real world.
In fantasy land, we're well away. Rhys has drawn a series of
cartoon sketches of the two of us trekking the Inca Trail, pilot-
ing a space shuttle, discovering Atlantis, kayaking through the
Bougainville Strait. We are Bronze and Gold, intrepid explor-
ers, bound by nothing, cowed by no one. In our cartoon world,
everyone speaks BSL.

In the real world, I sit on his bed doing my homework
while he plays video games with the door open. I'm allowed
in his room now, but his mother has a habit of coming in
unannounced every twenty minutes or so. She always has a
reason for this, albeit a flimsy one: She'll bring us tea, then
collect the cups. Ask if we want snacks, come back and ask
are we sure.

Mothers, Rhys says, rolling his eyes.

But I don't mind his mother. She's taken to calling me Stefanie, which I love because no one else calls me that and it feels affectionate, and she learned how I take my tea after only being told once. I think she actually likes me, which is more than a lot of girlfriends get from their boyfriends' mothers.

Aside from me and his mother, the other girl in Rhys's life is Meg. I don't see as much of her as I'd expected I would when we were first introduced, given that they're meant to be best friends. But I quickly learned that their best friendship isn't like mine and Tem's—codependent—but far more chilled. They treat each other like family, dropping in and out of each other's lives with the easy entitlement of siblings.

We pick up where we left off, Rhys says when I ask him about this. **She's like a life friend, not a day-to-day friend.**

But still, in the handful of times we've met since Rhys and I got together, I've come to like her a lot, and being around her feels easier than it does with Rhys's male friends.

It's the second week of February, and Rhys and I have agreed to meet Meg for a drink in the pub near Rhys's house. We make it a lunchtime drink to avoid me—the only one under eighteen—getting ID-ed at the door.

She's running late, Rhys says, looking at his phone and pushing it back into his pocket. **Typical. Let's get a drink and a table.**

The guy behind the bar looks a little familiar, and I squint at him as he serves the girl in front of us. He has ginger hair and a face that is all angles. A smile that sparkles.

"Hey," he says to Rhys as the girl takes her drink and leaves. "What can I get you?"

Rhys opens his mouth to reply, but it's me that speaks, and I do it in a burst of recognition. *"Daniel?"*

The barman looks at me and his face jolts in surprise. He slaps his hand on to the bar and then points at me.

"Steffi?" he half exclaims, half asks. "Little Steffi Brons?"

"Oh my God," I say. "Hi."

It's Daniel. Daniel Carlisle, one of Clark's old friends from secondary school. He was around our house so often he called my dad by his first name. He came to the wedding when my dad married Clark's mum.

Daniel, who I haven't seen since Clark's funeral, and even then it was from across the room. Clark. Clark, who would be twenty-three.

"Hi yourself!" He puts both hands on the bar and grins. "Holy hell. Little Steffi Brons. You grew up."

"I guess I did," I say, laughing. Rhys taps my arm and looks questioningly at me. **This is Daniel**, I explain quickly. For some reason I can't quite bring myself to explain that I know him because of Clark, so I skip over it and turn back to Daniel instead. "This is Rhys," I say, gesturing. "My boyfriend."

"Cool," Daniel says, nodding. He leans over to shake Rhys's hand. "All right, mate?"

"He's deaf," I add, but to my surprise Rhys shoots me a look of annoyance. Am I not supposed to tell people this? That's new.

"You doing okay?" Daniel shifts his attention back to me. "Damn, how long's it been since I saw you last?"

"Three years? Four?" I hedge.

"Christ. And now you're in a bar," he says. "And you're *talking.*"

"Oh, that." It's true—the words are coming far more easily than I would have thought they would if I'd imagined this scenario. But I'm not going to question it. "Yeah, I talk now."

He smiles, wide and sincere. "Awesome. What do you both want to drink? It's on me."

"Aw, thanks, but you don't have to," I say automatically.

Daniel shrugs, flashing a wider grin. "Course I do. Least I can do for Clark's little sister."

My heart clenches. Am I still a little sister if the older brother is dead? For one crazy moment, I want to ask him. Instead, I force myself to smile. "Go on, then. Just a Coke for me. And . . ." I look to Rhys. **Beer?**

He nods, but his expression is unusually unreadable.

"And a pint for Rhys," I say.

Daniel pauses, his gaze flicking over to Rhys. "Is he eighteen?" he asks me.

"Yes," Rhys says.

"Oh, sorry, mate, didn't realize you could talk," Daniel says, and I wince, glancing at Rhys, wondering if I should tell

Daniel that he's being rude. Rhys looks back at me, his eyes unusually fiery, and I take the hint and say nothing. "Greene King?" Daniel's already holding the glass in front of the tap. "Hey, Steffi, how are your parents?"

"They're doing okay." This is mostly true, I think. "How is everything with you?"

"Can't complain." He gives an easy shrug. "Air in my lungs, and all that." A sad smile flickers on his face, but it's quickly swallowed by a grin. He puts two glasses in front of me.

"It was good to see you again."

"You too." He gives me a brotherly wink and I suddenly miss Clark so much I almost start to cry.

I take the two glasses and begin to turn away, taking a deep, quiet breath.

"I'll get it," Rhys says, frowning, touching my wrist. I look at him and see he's holding his debit card between two fingers.

"It's covered," Daniel says. "No worries."

Rhys looks at me, a frustrated crease in his forehead. **I don't want him to pay for your drink**, he signs.

I can't sign with the two glasses in my hand, so I just shake my head. I try and say, *Don't make a fuss*, with my eyes.

"You just look after this one," Daniel says, gesturing to me with a jovial, oblivious smile on his face.

Rhys still looks perturbed. For God's sake. Bloody boys. "Come on," I say, injecting perkiness into my voice. "Thanks, Daniel," I add, smiling as I turn away.

We get back to the table and Rhys takes his pint glass from me, taking a swig without meeting my eyes. I watch him, wondering if he's annoyed with me and, if so, exactly why. I put my Coke down on the table. **What's wrong?**

Rhys looks at me, twists his lip between his teeth, then sets his glass down beside mine and pulls me in for a hug. I settle into it, resting my head against the steadiness of his chest. I feel him press a kiss to the side of my head.

When we break apart, we both sit on the same side of the table, on the bench that's set into the wall. I curl my legs up onto the seat so I can face him. I think about telling him who Daniel is, but that would mean talking about Clark, and I just don't want to do that. Even seeing Daniel and remembering the two of them as boys has made my heart feel chafed. So I don't. **What was all that about?**

He doesn't try to pretend he doesn't know what I mean. **Sorry if I was grumpy.**

But why? I hesitate, then go ahead and ask anyway. **Do you have a problem with me talking to other boys?**

To my total relief, he laughs. An easy, genuine laugh. **No**, he says, definitive. He shakes his head, smiling. **Sorry to make you think that.** He pauses, his eyes lifting up as he thinks. I can tell he's trying to decide how to express whatever it is he's feeling. **It is difficult to watch you talk**, he signs finally.

I frown. **What?**

It makes me feel distant from you, he signs carefully. **Like we are . . . separate.**

"I don't know what you mean," I say out loud. Frustration, and something a little like guilt, is building in my chest. Like maybe my subconscious knows exactly what he means, even if the rest of me hasn't caught up yet.

When you talk to other people, you seem to forget I'm there.

I swallow. **That's not fair.**

His face scrunches. **I'm not blaming you. I'm just trying to tell you. How it feels for me. It was the same at the Halloween party.**

I find talking really hard, I sign. I can feel my face starting to redden. **You know that. How can you say this to me?**

His signing starts to become faster and more desperate as he tries to explain himself. **I know you do. That's part of the problem.**

Problem?

Not problem. That was the wrong word. But the thing is that you are getting better, Bronze. You already talk more now than you did just a couple of weeks ago. And I'm scared that . . . he stops.

Say it.

That there'll be no place for me. That you won't need me. I'll always be deaf. I can't learn to hear. We'll be . . . uneven.

My hands are shaking. I take a sip of Coke and give up trying to use BSL right now. "Are you saying you think I only like you because you can't hear and I can't talk?"

No! he signs, in a way that makes me sure he means yes. **That isn't what I mean.**

"Because that's really insulting." My voice is shaking too. "That's a really hurtful thing to say to me."

Rhys looks agonized. **Bronze.**

"And for the record my not talking is a problem, but you being deaf isn't," I continue. The words are coming out fast, way faster than if I was using BSL, and his eyes are now focused on my lips as I talk. His expression is tense and slightly panicked, and it's a face I recognize from school when anyone is talking to him, and though I feel a reflexive guilt at making him lip-read, I can't quite stop myself. "I know you can't bloody learn to hear, I'm not a moron."

I'm sorry.

"Would you rather I was properly mute so we'd be 'even'?"

No, that's not what I meant.

"I make you feel bad when I talk to people."

He tries to take my hand. **No. Bronze. No.**

"Thanks a lot." I'm too upset to stay here. I grab my bag and coat, hoping I don't start crying in front of him. "I need to go."

"Steffi," he says. He looks devastated now. **Don't go. I'm sorry.**

"And for the record," I add, pulling my bag up over my shoulder, "Daniel was Clark's friend. I talked to him because he knew my stepbrother." At the mention of Clark's name, my voice cracks and the tears spill. Damn. "He knew Clark," I repeat, and I'm not even sure why.

Rhys is standing and I can tell he's going to reach for me, so I do the worst thing I can do. I turn my back on him and walk out of the pub.

I go straight home and shut myself in my room, curling on the floor with Rita and crying into her patient furry face. I ignore my phone, which beeps every few minutes, and I ignore my dad, who puts his head around the door to ask me if I'm "feeling all right, blossom?" At some point Lucy comes into the room and tells me some long, rambling story I don't really listen to properly about how she broke up with her first boyfriend when she was sixteen.

I want to tell her that Rhys and I haven't broken up so this story is irrelevant, but my voice has deserted me (or maybe I just don't feel like talking—who knows what the difference is? Certainly not me) so I just lie there until she leaves.

At some point I move from the floor and onto the bed, pulling up my knees to my chin and resting my head on them, tracing circles on my duvet cover and thinking about Clark. I wonder what he'd think about Rhys. He'd like him, right? Except when he makes me cry.

You know how people say life goes on? Well, it does. It goes on and suddenly four years have passed and you're seventeen instead of thirteen. Clark would be twenty-three. But he's not twenty-three, and he never will be. That's how death works. I swallow, bite down on my lip, and push my chin harder against my knees.

Clark wasn't perfect—I should say that. He wasn't the best looking or the smartest or the funniest. He wasn't going to cure cancer or play for England. He probably wouldn't have changed the world. But he was good, and he was kind. He acted like a brother, as if the word "step" didn't matter at all.

I skip dinner, choosing instead to burrow my face into my pillow and ignore Dad's attempts to cajole me out of my room. I distract myself from thoughts of Clark by running over and over the argument I had with Rhys until I'm not even sure what parts are really true. I keep thinking of the way Rhys signed "uneven." How he looked at me when Daniel said he didn't need to pay.

There's another knock at my door and I groan against the pillow, not even bothering to lift my head. I hear the sliding rustle of it opening and then closing, followed by the soft thump of Rita's tail on the carpet.

"Go away, Dad," I say. "I just want to be on my own."

No response. I sigh loudly, waiting for the presence in the room to leave. After a pause, I feel the end of the bed sag a little. Rita's collar gives a jingly shake as she gets up.

I wait a little longer, then give up. I sit up with a huff, spinning round to face Dad, then let out an unglamorous shriek. It's not Dad. It's Rhys.

Christ. I bolt upright and huddle against my headboard, trying to smooth down the creases in my—*Christ*—old One Direction T-shirt. My hair is all over the place. There's makeup smudged all over my face. I look a mess and a half.

Rhys is watching me, an anxious half-smile on his face. Rita's head is resting on his knees, the traitor. He lifts the hand he's been using to stroke her neck. **Hi.**

"What are you doing here?" I demand. I feel too wrong-footed, still too raw, to use BSL.

You wouldn't answer my messages.

"Because I don't want to talk to you."

He signs one word. **Please.** There's such patient sincerity in his face. Damn him. Damn him and his constant perfection. Why can't he get flustered, just once?

It occurs to me that maybe I'm flustered enough for both of us. "Does Dad know you're here?" I ask.

He nods, the corner of his mouth twitching into a smile. **Of course. I didn't break in.**

"Rhys," I say, then stop. My voice is all crackly. "Can't you just let me be upset with you for a while?"

He frowns. **I have. That's why I waited until now. It's fine if you don't want to talk to me. But can you at least let me talk to you?**

I shrug.

Okay. He hesitates, then shifts along the bed so he's sitting in the center of it, facing me. Rita lets out an offended huff at losing his attention and sinks down onto the carpet. **Listen. I'm sorry I was weird about you talking to that guy. And I'm sorry that I obviously didn't explain why I was weird**

very well. **Of course it's great that you are getting better at talking. I want you to be happy. I just want to be part of that.**

He pauses, clearly waiting for me to respond, but I keep my hands still in my lap, watching and waiting for more.

Maybe it's my own thing that I'm worried I'm not part of it, or won't be part of it. And I shouldn't make you think it's your fault. But I just wanted to be honest with you. He inclines his head slightly so our eyes meet. **I'm sorry.** His hand moves in a slow, deliberate circle around his heart. **I'm sorry.**

I look at his sweet, gentle face. His soft brown eyes trained on me, full of hope and promises. I try to think of how to reply.

I don't ever want to let you down, he adds. **I don't want to disappoint you.**

I shake my head. **I don't understand why you'd say that. Why would you disappoint me?**

If I'm not enough. If I'm a burden.

"A *burden?*" I'm so shocked the words fall out. "What does that even mean, Rhys?"

I see him swallow. **If you have to translate for me all the time. Or push me out of the way of postal vans.**

"For God's sake," I snap, surprised at my own sudden rush of annoyance. "That was just an accident. It could have happened to anyone. Why does it bother you so much?"

Because I don't want to lose you.

You're not going to lose me. I don't know how to handle this kind of conversation. I've always been the irrational one, the one with the neuroses. Is this how Tem feels when I go off on one of my why-don't-you-get-a-better-friend-than-me ramblings? **Look.** I hesitate, trying to work out my own thoughts. **Maybe we're both still figuring things out. I don't want to lose you either. What if you get tired of me? You have to translate for me if I'm in your world. This isn't** . . . I pause, trying to find the right signs. "This isn't just a one-sided thing."

Rhys shifts a little closer to me, our hands almost touching across the space between us. **I'm sorry**, he signs again. **I'm sorry that I upset you earlier and I'm making things hard now. It's because I like you so much. It's new. I've never** . . . I see him hesitate, then take a breath. **I've never loved a girl before.**

My heart gives an almighty, chest-breaking thump. I think I actually make a little squeaking noise. We both stare at each other.

After a long, excruciating pause, he tries again. **Did you** . . . **did you get that?**

I shake my head, a small, reluctant smile tugging at my lips. **I don't think I did. Can you say it again?**

He points to himself. He puts two hands to his heart. He points to me. **I love you.**

I bridge the gap between us and kiss him, lifting myself onto his lap and winding my arms round his neck. He loves me. He loves me! We kiss until my breath runs out, and then he leans back a little and asks, **Do you feel the same?**

And of course I say, **Yes! Yes, yes, yes.** Because I do. I really, really do.

* * *

At some point during our major post-I-love-you kissing session, I realize something: My bedroom door is closed. And also: Rhys and I are kissing on my bed.

There are things you can do on a bed when the door is closed that you can't when it's left open. And once this thought has whispered through my mind, it's all I can think about. Rhys's hand is up under my T-shirt, his fingers stroking under the wire of my bra. The way he is kissing is intensifying, and it's making every single tiny nerve in my body come alive.

My T-shirt winds up on the floor and that's when his hand makes a slow, hesitant slide in the opposite direction. My skin heats up a thousand degrees. My heart starts to race. His hand reaches my hips and then stops. He breaks away, leans up on his elbow, and looks at me. **I love you**, he signs with one hand. **You're beautiful.** He hesitates, and I watch him lick his lips nervously. **Can I touch you?** he asks.

And I—shy, anxious Steffi Brons—nod. And not a tentative nod either, but a definitive one. A *yes please!* one.

Rhys moves his hand back down to my hip, pauses to look at me again for confirmation and then reaches between my legs. My jeans are still on, and he doesn't make a move for the zipper, just rests his hand there. And even that, alone, is like fire. We look at each other, both of us breathing hard, and he puts his lips to mine to kiss me again.

At first he is tentative, applying only the slightest amount of pressure (*oh my God*), and I can feel his nervousness in his kisses. I think about moving my own hand down and showing him, but I want this first time to be a moment of discovery that we share. So instead, I put my hand on him, just as tentative, just as nervous. He is hard, I can feel it, and *oh my God oh my God* this is a *penis*, this is a hard penis and I am about a millimeter of denim away from touching it for real.

And when I do—inching down his zipper, sliding my hand inside his boxers—it's nothing like I expected. Despite its "hardness," it feels oddly soft, the skin warm against my hand. I have no idea what I'm meant to do so I take it on instinct, cupping my hand round what I assume is the shaft and sort of . . . pumping it. I hear Rhys's breath catch in his throat, his hand stills between my legs. About thirty seconds later, he pushes his head into my neck to stifle the noise he makes and suddenly my hand is covered in something hot and wet. It's quite gross, to be honest. But good. That's good, right? That means he . . . well. He got there. But, oh God, my hand is still just hanging around in his boxers. Am I meant to do something else? Is that the end?

I decide the best thing to do is just to pull out my hand smooth and fast, like that magic trick where the magician removes the tablecloth without knocking over all the crockery. And of course he doesn't even notice, because now he's lying on his back with his eyes closed, breathing hard, a broad grin on his face. I grab a tissue from my bedside cabinet and surreptitiously wipe at my hand. No one ever said this kind of thing would be so messy.

Rhys's eyes open and he smiles at me, his face softer than I've ever seen it. I drop the tissue on the floor—needs must—and scooch closer to him. He cuddles me against his chest and I snuggle in, a wave of total happiness washing over me. I am in love with this boy, with his warm smile and kind eyes and his expressive hands that will one day do to me what I just did to him. And he is in love with me.

Jokes Tem made when I told her about my very first hand job:

"You're a handy girlfriend to have."

"It sounds like you handled it well."

"It must have been hard for you . . .

. . . but well done for getting a good grip on it."

"Sounds like it was a bit touch and go."

"Would you call it a seminal experience?"

"I can't think of any more. PENIS!"

22

ON TUESDAY, TEM SURPRISES ME BY TURNING UP ON my doorstep after 8 p.m., carrying a bottle of wine and a bag of mini doughnuts. The sarcastic bounce from the weekend has completely gone, and now she's doleful. It doesn't suit her, and I'm instantly worried.

"I have woe," she says. She lets out a loud sigh. "Serious woe."

I've already walked Rita, and I don't fancy the long trek to the park, so Tem and I go into my garden and sit under the crabapple tree. She opens the bottle, sips directly from the rim, and passes it to me.

"Where did you get this from?" I ask, shaking my head and passing it back.

"Oh fuck, I forgot you don't like to drink," she says. "Are you sure you don't just want a few sips? With me?"

"Wine is disgusting," I reply. "No thanks." I watch as she lifts the bottle again, then reach out to take it from her. "Okay, that'll do for now. What's up, then? Why the woe?"

"Have a doughnut." She ignores my question and waves the bag under my nose. "I got custard ones, like you like."

Obediently, I reach in and take one. I can feel the sugar, rough under my fingers in the dark. "Why do you always bring me food?"

"Because I like you," she says.

I smile. "You know I'd want to hear about your woe even if you didn't bring custard treats, right?"

I watch her face break into a smile, slightly crooked this time, as if it's being weighted on one side. It's not the full Tem smile I'm so used to, and it worries me.

"Hey," I say softly. I reach out and put my sugary fingers on her knee. "What's up?"

She's quiet for another few moments, but I let the silence stretch out between us, letting her take her time.

"I'm failing," she says finally. "At college."

"Oh," I say out loud, vocalizing my surprise. This was not at all what I'd expected her to say. In fact, I'd been so certain I'd hear the word "Karam" I don't even know what to say.

"Yeah."

"Failing . . . what exactly?" I ask carefully.

She shrugs, not looking at me. In the fading light, I can see a frown on her face. "The course. We get like a mini report thing in January so we can track our progress, and . . . well, mine's just not that great, really. A distinct *lack* of progress. Mum called Dad and everything." Tem's dad is in the Royal Navy, so he's away from home for months at a time. "Mum Called Dad" is Tem shorthand for "This Is Bad."

I still don't know what to say. "So what does that mean?"

"That I have to try harder, I guess? I don't know. It's not like I'm slacking off on purpose or anything. It's all just . . . hard. I thought that once I was studying something I was actually interested in it would be easier to concentrate. But it's not. I start looking at science-y stuff and I just zone out."

"Have you talked to Karam?"

"Oh God no." Her nose wrinkles. "He's, like, super genius. It's bad enough that I'm doing sports medicine instead of a 'real subject.' I don't want him to know what a total dunce I am."

"You're not a dunce, Tem."

"Okay, fine. I don't want him to know I have duncelike tendencies."

I can tell she's starting to steer back into jokey-Tem territory, so I try to anchor her. "Can *I* help?"

She sighs. "I don't know. Can you? You'd probably find it really easy. But it's still me that'd have to know it, at the end of the day."

"Okay, you're going to have to give me something solid here," I say, reaching over and nudging her shoulder. "A plan. It's not like you to mope."

"I know." A half-smile flickers on her face. "I just feel a bit lost." Her voice has quieted. "I thought going to college instead of sixth form would be best for me. Sports therapy sounded so perfect. I could run and actually study something cool. But the work is hard and I don't have many friends and maybe I should just've stayed at Windham. With you."

"With me?" I repeat, surprised into laughter. "What difference would I make?"

Tem looks at me, forehead still creased, eyes strained. "I'm not really sure who I am now, when I'm not one half of Steftember."

"You're Tem," I say promptly. "Do you want me to give you a list of all the reasons you're the best?"

Tem rests her head on my shoulder. "Yes, please."

"You have the best hair," I begin, reaching up and twirling one of her curls.

"Racist," she murmurs. I can hear the smile in her voice.

"You always tell me when I'm being racist," I say, "which is very helpful." I feel the breath of her laugh against my neck and I smile. "You run like the wind. You always bring me sweet treats. You brought me back that Minnie Mouse figurine from Disneyland even though it took your bag over the weight limit and you had to pay a fine at the airport."

"That's true," Tem says. "I'm basically selfless."

"Totally selfless," I agree. "And we're not even getting into the whole being-my-translator thing. Shall we talk about how I survived my childhood because of you?"

Tem curls her arm round mine and gives me a little squeeze. She doesn't answer because she doesn't need to. We sit together like that for a while, sharing the silence, until she feels ready to go home.

It's unusual for Tem to be down, and the image of her furrowed forehead lingers over the next several days, worrying me. I tell Rhys, of course, and though he makes a sympathetic face and signs something vague and reassuring, I know that the intricacies and depth of girl friendship are too beyond him for him to be much help. Tem can convey her unhappiness to me in two sentences and an expression. Explaining the context and history that cause it to Rhys would take years. Fourteen years, in fact.

But he still manages to surprise me.

At school on Wednesday, Rhys comes into math with a huge smile on his face. **I have an idea!** he says as his greeting, kissing me on the cheek.

Go on, I say, smiling in expectation. **What is it?**

I was thinking about cheering Tem up, and how I don't really know her that well, and you don't know Karam. And how you and I wanted to have a little adventure. So how about we go to Whipsnade this weekend? A double date?

My hand falls into an automatic, thrilled **YES! I love Whipsnade**. Whipsnade, the zoo on the edge of Dunstable, is my favorite place on earth. As kids, Tem and I used to go there all the time. I had my birthday there three years in a row.

Great. He looks pleased, settling against his chair as Mr. Al-Hafi comes hurrying into the classroom, looking like he just rolled out of bed. **Let me know what Tem says.**

Tem is thrilled by the idea of our first ever double date and agrees for both her and Karam, even with the short notice.

"He's said the same thing about wanting to get to know you and Rhys better," she says. "It'll be great! Brilliant! It'll be like a mini road trip! With lions! What kind of snacks does Rhys like? I'll stock up."

Her enthusiasm doesn't wane for the rest of the week, which is why I'm expecting to see Tem and Karam waiting for us both at the end of the driveway, armed with tortilla chips and sweets, when Rhys and I pull up outside her house on Saturday morning. But it's just Tem waving to us through the window. I get out to greet her.

"Good morning," she sings out.

"Hi," I say. "Where's Karam?" I don't quite mean to be so blunt, but it comes out anyway.

"Oh, he couldn't make it," she says casually, and if I were anyone else I'd have missed the way her eyes narrow slightly and then flick away from me. But I'm her best friend, so I notice.

"How come?" I ask, matching her casual tone.

"He has to work today," she says. "He was trying to swap his shifts around, which is why I couldn't tell you before today.

I only found out late last night. Is that okay?" She's anxious, her fingers circling over each other. "If you just want it to be you two, I'll understand. I don't want to be the third wheel or anything."

"Of course it's okay," I say immediately. "Let's go."

The best thing about sharing a language with Rhys is that we can have a secret conversation. **No Karam**, I say as I slide back into my seat. **He's stood us up.**

Damn, Rhys says. **Are we mad at him? Should I say something to Tem about it?**

I shake my head. **Act like it's fine.** As I sign, I say, "Karam had to work, so it's just the three of us."

Rhys gives Tem a thumbs-up in the rearview mirror. "Hey."

"Hey," she returns. "Sorry about being the third wheel."

"No way," Rhys says easily, releasing the handbrake. "You're the one we wanted anyway."

I grin. "Definitely. It would have been weirder if he'd turned up without you."

She laughs. "That's true."

As we head toward Whipsnade, I think about everything Rhys said about how I talk to other people and forget he's there, so I make a real effort with him and Tem, diligently translating everything she says, even the stuff that has nothing to do with him. I can see that Tem, too, is trying her hardest with Rhys by how normal she is acting, as if going on a day trip with her quiet best friend and her deaf boyfriend is something she does all the time. She talks at her normal volume but slightly slower than usual, facing Rhys as she speaks. She does this even as I sign.

I suggest that I buy the tickets and, because they are who they are, they don't make shocked faces, grab my arm, and remind me that this will involve talking to a complete stranger. They don't laugh and ask who I am and what I've done with the real Steffi.

And when I go to the desk and buy three tickets—I even ask for the concession price—the ceiling doesn't collapse and the floor doesn't cave in under me and the woman doesn't laugh in my face. My voice wobbles slightly at first, but it doesn't desert me. I think about how proud my therapist will be when I tell her. I almost turn cartwheels of happiness across the floor.

But I don't, obviously, because I'm still me, albeit happier and chattier than usual.

This might not sound like a big deal, and I know that for most people it wouldn't be, but for me it feels revelatory. When I am happy and relaxed, when I'm with people I absolutely trust—who love me whether I talk or not—*I can talk*. I can talk willingly and voluntarily. *To strangers.* I want to bottle this discovery and carry it with me everywhere. Lose the fear, find my voice. So simple. And, yet, so rare.

We spend the day wandering around the zoo together in the sunshine. Rhys diligently signs the names of all the animals for Tem, who scrunches her face in concentration every time and tries to mimic the movements, with varying degrees of success. When we get to the red pandas she shrieks with happiness, grabbing hold of my wrist and squeezing. They're not giant pandas—our one true love—but they're close enough. Rhys, a broad smile on his face, takes a dozen pictures of Tem and me, arms round each other, beaming like kids.

Tem insists on buying an overpriced Whispnade lollipop before we leave, even though I know for a fact she will get bored of it after ten minutes and throw it away within a week. "Don't you ever get tired of being sensible all the time?" she asks me, peeling off the plastic. "Live a little."

"I'm not sure solidified E-numbers count as living a little." The two of us are leaning against one of the picnic benches, waiting for Rhys.

"Oh my God, listen to you." Tem rolls her eyes. *Solidified E-numbers.*

"That's what they are," I say. "And, hey, remember how I have anxiety? Sensible is a coping technique."

She smiles, part of her mouth obscured by the lurid pink swirls of the lollipop. "Or a handy excuse."

The door to the shop opens and Rhys appears, a small Whispnade bag in his hand. "What did you get?" Tem calls, then remembers herself. She tries again, lowering the lollipop and speaking more clearly. "Did you buy something?"

Rhys grins and nods, settling against the bench beside me. **Look at this**, he says to me, and pulls a postcard out of the bag.

At first, I don't get it. It's a photo of two lions sitting beside one another in what looks like the lion version of a hug. It's a cute photo and I look up at Rhys, trying to guess what's he's seen in it, why he looks so pleased.

Look, he signs again. He points at the lion with the giant mane. **Gold**, he signs. And . . . he points to the lioness, whose ears are tipped with a rich reddish glow. It's probably the way the light catches them, but it looks an awful lot like . . . **Bronze**, Rhys says. He's smiling. **Bronze and Gold. It's us!**

"Let me see," Tem says, coming to stand beside me and craning her neck to get a look. "That's cute. It looks like they're hugging." I don't explain. I just smile and nod, then reach up to kiss Rhys, even though Tem is right there and I know she'll tease me about the PDA later. **You're so soppy**, I tease.

For a second he looks unsure. **Is that okay?**

I laugh. **Of course!** I reach for his hand and squeeze it, leading the way toward the car.

"God, you guys are sickening," Tem says, following. "I'm getting diabetes just looking at you."

At her request, Rhys drops Tem and me off together at my house so she can stay over. We're the kinds of friends who don't need advance notice for sleepovers—we even keep pajamas at each other's houses. By the time we are settled in my room she is quiet and contemplative, rubbing her fingers over Rita's back.

"So," I say. "Thoughts on Rhys?"

She smiles. "I've met him before. You already know my thoughts."

"Yeah, but now you've spent a whole day with him," I say. I prod her knee. "Go on."

Tem pulls one of my pillows out from under the cover and plumps it underneath her bag, then rests against the headboard. "Well," she begins. "I think he is very, very . . ."

I wait. "Very what?"

She grins. "Very awesome. I like him a lot. Why wouldn't I? He's great."

I grin back. "Yay. Isn't he, though? You see why I love him, right?"

"Obviously," she says, rolling her eyes. "You got a good one. I was thinking today, though . . . when I was watching you together. You know how your parents think he's making your world smaller?"

My heart gives a twinge of anxiety. "Yeah . . . ?"

"I don't see it."

And a whoosh of relief. "You don't?"

"No. I think he makes you bigger. In a good way, I mean. You're so open with him, you know? Your face comes alive— your whole body comes alive."

"Because I'm translating for him?"

"Maybe, but I don't know if it's just because of that. You've changed a lot these last few months. Is it just because of him?"

Tem is looking at me, her face open and unsuspicious,

waiting for me to speak. This is the perfect time to tell her about the medication, but for some reason I don't. Something about the thought of her knowing that all the good changes are down to something as mundane as medication bothers me. I'd rather she thought it was all down to a boy. Hormones over SSRIs. Love over science.

"Maybe I'm just finally growing up," I say, smiling.

To my surprise, her face falls slightly. "Just don't grow away from me, okay?"

I reach out and put both my arms round her neck, squeezing her into a hug. "Never." Life without Tem is unthinkable. "Hey, so, do you feel better?"

She frowns. "What do you mean?"

"Are you still . . ." I try to remember her exact phrasing. "Full of woe?"

"Oh, that." Her face clears. She shrugs a little. "Well, I don't think I'm suited for a career in sports therapy. I still might not pass the year. But I was talking to Ava about it, and she was really encouraging." Ava is Tem's running coach. "She said, at the end of the day, grades don't matter on the track. And I've always known that, you know? I just kind of . . . forgot it a little this year."

"Why?"

"I don't know, really. Going to college, maybe. Being with Karam. Education is so important to him, and it makes me feel a bit . . ." She hesitates. "A bit dumb."

"You're not—"

"I know, I know. It's a different kind of smart—that's it, right? Yours is animals, mine is athletics."

I nod. "Sounds about right."

"So, we're seeing how it goes," she says. "But thanks for today. It was great."

"Maybe Karam can come next time," I suggest.

She smiles and looks away, rubbing her fingers through the ruff of Rita's neck. "Yeah," she says. "Next time."

23

Sunday evening

rhysespieces: i have an idea

stefstef: what kind of idea? ☺

rhysespieces: an adventure idea

stefstef: ooh!

rhysespieces: Whipsnade was great but we can do
something bigger!

stefstef: YES! what's the idea?

rhysespieces: have you ever been to Edinburgh?

stefstef: NO!!!

rhysespieces: would you . . . want to?

stefstef: YES!! ☺☺

rhysespieces: i was thinking we could go and stay with
my brother. he's at university there. we could visit him

and he could show us round. then you could tell your
parents that you've visited and know what to expect
and stuff.

stefstef: AMAZING.

rhysespieces: fancy it?

stefstef: yes yes yes.

rhysespieces: awesome. i haven't told you this before,
but i know what you mean about your parents
worrying about you being able to do things. mine
are the same.

stefstef: really? why?

rhysespieces: . . .

stefstef: oh, the deaf thing

rhysespieces: yeah. the deaf thing. i'd like to be able to
show them too. you and me, managing together, on
our own. you know?

stefstef: I. KNOW.

rhysespieces: great. i'll speak to Aled.

stefstef: oh hey . . . you could . . . not.

rhysespieces: ?

stefstef: how about we don't tell anyone? that way they
won't all be worrying and trying to put us off. not just
an adventure, but a SECRET adventure. i won't even
tell Tem! and then we'll turn up on Aled's doorstep
like . . . HI! SURPRISE!

rhysespieces: hahaha. he would definitely be surprised.

stefstef: it's a good idea, right?

rhysespieces: yes, if we could pull it off. we'd need money and alibis.

stefstef: it's not a heist, Gold.

rhysespieces: still a mission, Bronze.

stefstef: Bronze and Gold Take On Scotland

rhysespieces: Bronze and Gold and the Mystery of the Exploding Haggis

stefstef: Bronze and Gold Play the Bagpipes

rhysespieces: ANYWAY. i meant it about the money and alibis. when would we go? a weekend?

stefstef: i'm sure there's a way. be positive. it was your idea!

rhysespieces: i'll have a think.

stefstef: we'll find a way.

rhysespieces: we will?

stefstef: we will.

Tuesday lunchtime

How about the Easter holidays? Rhys asks. **I could go away for a couple of nights if I say I'm staying with my old Ives friends. I've done that before.**

Possibly, I say, considering. **I'm at Mum's, though. So if I go away it will be more obvious.**

That's true. He makes a face. **Damn.**

Wednesday evening

stefstef: any more ideas?

rhysespieces: no ☹

stefstef: okay, if we don't think of something by the
weekend maybe we can just ask Aled? is he good
with stuff like this?

rhysespieces: yeah. but that's a last resort. i really want to
surprise him.

stefstef: MORE THINKING xxx

Friday

Mum calls just as I'm clipping the leash to Rita's collar. My
dog is panting happily, anticipating a long Friday evening walk.
"Sorry," I whisper, kissing the side of her face before dropping
the leash and answering the phone. "Hi, Mum."

"Hello, love," she says. "How are you?"

"Fine." I sit back against the wall and Rita slumps to the
floor with a huff of indignation. "How are you? How are Keir
and Bell?"

"That's what I'm calling about, actually."

"What's wrong?" My heart is instantly pounding. I sit straight
up away from the wall. If something happened to Bell . . .
"What's happened?"

"Oh, nothing," Mum says quickly. "Nothing to worry

about. Nothing immediate, anyway. I took Bell back to the dentist today to check her teeth after her fall at New Year."

"Right, okay," I say, still not ready to relax yet. "And?"

"When we went last time, the dentist was concerned about one of Bell's upper incisors and if it had been damaged by the impact. He said there was a possibility it would need to be removed, and now he's confirmed that."

"Okay," I say again. This doesn't sound so bad. "So she's having one of her teeth out?"

"Yes, but as she's so young it will need to be under general anesthetic. I thought she might be excited, but the dentist scared her by making a stupid joke about drills. She's already working herself up into a state about it. Thinks she's going to wake up with no teeth." She laughs a little. "Anyway, the surgery is scheduled for March thirty-first. That's the last Thursday of the Easter holidays."

I still have no idea where she's going with this. Rita lets out another loud huff. "Right."

"What I wanted to ask is if you'd mind reshaping our holiday plans slightly this year? As I said, Bell's in a state already, so it might be a bit of a strain around here that day. What do you think about you going back to your dad's slightly earlier? Say, Wednesday? And perhaps coming to stay with us a few days before the beginning of the holidays instead?"

I open my mouth to start complaining, then stop myself. "Have you spoken to Dad about it?"

"Oh no, I thought you could speak to him in person your-self. If it's not convenient for him—or you—that's fine. But I thought I should ask."

A slow grin has spread over my face. "No, that sounds fine. Totally fine."

We talk for a little longer and then hang up. Rita gets to her feet and gives herself a shake, her collar jingling, but I don't stand up. I open my messages and send a single text to Rhys:

Steffi:

Bronze and Gold is a go.

BEST THINGS TO DO IN EDINBURGH
(ACCORDING TO O GREAT AND MIGHTY GOOGLE):

CLIMB ARTHUR'S SEAT
VISIT EDINBURGH CASTLE SHOP ON PRINCES
    STREET
GO ON A TOUR OF THE EDINBURGH VAULTS
(NB: TOO SPOOKY FOR STEFFI?)
DRINK TEA AT THE ELEPHANT HOUSE
VISIT THE CAMERA OBSCURA
WALK AROUND GREYFRIARS KIRKYARD
STROLL DOWN THE ROYAL MILE
HAVE A SICKENINGLY ROMANTIC TIME WITH YOUR
    BOYFRIEND

24

THE PLAN, WHICH AT FIRST HAD SEEMED LIKE NOTH-
ing but a dream, begins to take shape and then solidify over
the next few days. Needless to say, I don't tell Dad about the
slight change of living arrangements over Easter. Instead, on
the Wednesday, I will leave Mum's house and go straight to the
train station, where Rhys will be waiting. Mum will think I'm
at Dad's; Dad will think I'm at Mum's. We'll go to Edinburgh,
spend a couple of days together, and then surprise Aled on
Friday. When we have met up with Aled, I'll call home to let
them know where I am, that I'm fine, that I've done something
I—and they—never thought I'd be able to do. They'll be too
proud and surprised to be angry with me.

I think.

Cost is an issue, so we decide to get a Megabus from London
to Edinburgh instead of flying or taking the train. It'll take

most of the day—over nine hours, in fact—but it's only about £20 so it's worth it. I know a nine-hour bus trip doesn't sound great, but I'm so excited my stomach keeps swooping. Nine hours on a bus with Rhys. Him and me together, squashed up close, with no distractions, no other people. We can talk and kiss and cuddle. I can fall asleep on his shoulder. It'll be unbelievably romantic and perfect.

And, after that, Edinburgh. Tartan and shortbread and bagpipes. A whole new city to explore, unhindered by agenda-setting parents or teachers. Just me and my boyfriend. And in the evening, after the inevitable hand-in-hand romantic walk, it will be just me and my boyfriend in a hotel room. A hotel room with a double bed and a door that locks.

Calm down, heart. It's not time for racing yet.

We make actual plans, like that we will climb Arthur's Seat and go and find the statue of Greyfriars Bobby, but in my head everything gets a bit fuzzy after the hotel-room bit.

I don't tell Tem any of our plans, which makes me feel guilty and a bit sad. I'm not sure when it started to be okay to keep secrets from Tem. Before my decision not to tell her about my meds, I'd never even lied to her. That seems like a long time ago now.

The only people in the world who know about the trip are me and Rhys, and that fact just makes it all the more perfect.

I arrange to work extra hours at the kennels during the first week of the Easter holidays so I can take time off for Edinburgh and also be able to afford it. The free time I have I divide between Tem, Rhys, and my mother's family. Bell is hyped about her upcoming operation, counting her teeth every night and poking her tongue out between the gap where her front teeth used to be. I tell her that the Tooth Fairy gives an extra gift when there's an operation involved, which turns out to be a mistake.

"Like another tooth?" she asks, eyes wide. She's developed a lisp since losing her teeth, plus a breathy little whistle every time she speaks.

"Er . . . no."

"Like a gold tooth?"

"What? No, Bell. Like a present."

"Is it a puppy?"

"No, Bell."

"A kitten?"

"It has to fit under your pillow, remember?"

"A hedgehog?"

"It's not alive."

"A violin?"

This goes on far longer than could possibly be considered cute.

I count the days, watching the clock on my work shifts and sharing long jackbytes conversations with Rhys in the evenings where we talk about our options as tourists (slightly limited by our lack of a car), whether we should try haggis or not (obviously), what we'll do on the bus for all those hours (KISS).

And then it's Wednesday morning. I've packed everything I

need for Edinburgh into an innocuous-looking weekend bag, just like the kind I usually take between my two houses, and glance into Bell's bedroom before I head down the stairs. She's fast asleep, so I decide not to wake her up.

"Let me know when you're back at your dad's," Mum says as I head into the hall.

"Sure," I say. I think there's still a part of me that's waiting for her to read my mind, gasp in shock, and call off the whole trip. "See you later. Love to Bell."

She gives me a quick hug. "Bye, love."

I close the door behind me and let out a breath, pulling my bag up over my shoulder and taking the left turn out of the driveway that will take me toward the train station.

When I get there, Rhys is already waiting. He's wearing a rucksack on his back and his face breaks into a huge smile as I appear.

Hi. He leans slightly down to kiss me. **Ready for an adventure?**

Ready! *Or, at least, as ready as I'll ever be*, I think. I desperately want to do this, and I'm so excited to have this time with Rhys, but I'm still me. I'm still anxious.

The train into London takes about half an hour, and then it's another twenty minutes on the Underground to Victoria Station. It's standing room only on the trains and so we are crammed together for most of the way, unable to talk. We make faces at each other instead and mouth the occasional question—Did you bring any toothpaste? and the like—and I lean into him as he rests his chin on my head. At Victoria we buy food and magazines for the journey. The magazines are totally not necessary—I have four books in my bag—but something about long journeys calls for magazines. Rhys gets a large coffee for himself and a hot chocolate for me and then we're ready. We join the line for the bus.

"Can't take that on," the driver says to Rhys. He's gruff, with a thick Scottish accent and an even thicker beard. I can see by the expression on Rhys's face that he can't lip-read through all the facial hair and my stomach clenches. The driver looks at him, waiting for a response. "Right?" he says. "Drink it all now or throw it away." He looks at me, then gestures to my cup. "You too."

Rhys, brow furrowed, turns to me. With his free hand he signs, **What?**

We can't take the drinks on the bus, I sign.

"Oh." The driver's entire face changes as he watches, realization kicking in. "Oh, shit. Uh . . ." He glances behind us at the line, then clears his throat. "You," he shouts. "Can't. Take. Hot. Drinks. On. The. Bus." He points emphatically at the cups we're holding. "Those. Throw. Away."

If I was a better person, this would be the moment that I'd probably tell him I could hear perfectly, but I don't. I put on an exaggerated confused expression and look at Rhys. **This guy thinks deaf people can hear if you shout loudly enough.**

Rhys immediately makes a gormless expression, looks at the

cup in his hand, opens his mouth in a big round O, then looks over at the trash can.

"Yes," the man bellows. "Trash."

"Come on, mate," someone behind me says. "You can't be yelling at a couple of deaf kids."

"Yeah, just let them on," another voice joins in. "It's a Megabus, not a bloody private jet."

"On a private jet you'd be allowed to take a coffee on," the first person says, and there's laughter from the line.

"It's the rules," the driver says uncertainly. He coughs, then repeats in a stronger voice, "It's the rules."

"We won't tell," private-jet man says impatiently. "Can we just all get on now?"

The driver looks back at Rhys and me just in time for us to paste identical, innocent grins on our faces. "Ach, just get on," he says, waving us toward the open door. "Don't spill anything."

We can get on, I sign quickly, pushing Rhys toward the coach before the driver can change his mind. I look back at our helpers as I go and sign a quick thank you. I know they won't be able to understand the actual sign, but there's something universal about an expression of thanks. They'll know.

It seems like a good idea to be as far away from the driver as possible, so Rhys and I choose seats at the back of the coach. He lets me have the window seat and busies himself with pushing our bags into the overhead luggage rack while I keep the two cups safe in my hands. I watch him, smiling. His T-shirt rides up and I let my eyes fall to the smooth brown skin of his stomach. It's . . . well. It's nice.

All good? He tumbles into the seat beside me, his whole face a beam, and takes his coffee from me.

All very good, I reply. I put my free hand to his collar and pull him the last few inches toward me. We kiss and it's perfect.

It's pretty goddam perfect.

We arrive in Edinburgh at half past seven—an hour late because of heavy traffic near Newcastle. I'm so happy to get off the coach I actually bounce on the pavement. This makes Rhys laugh, so it's okay that it might look weird to other people. He pulls his arms through the straps of his rucksack and then takes my hand. He gestures around, smiling, and without words he is saying, *Edinburgh.*

I squeeze his hand and look around, bubbly with happiness and stored energy. The air is cold but the sky is an almost entirely clear blue. When we left London, it was raining.

"Wow," I say quietly out loud, even though he can't hear me. "It's so much more beautiful than I was expecting."

Even though we're standing outside a bus station, which doesn't usually offer the best city views, everywhere I look the city seems beautiful. In London, if you stand in the right place and look the right way, you get a good skyline, but in Edinburgh it is everywhere. If I face left, I see old buildings shining golden against the sky, the color of the tea-stained paper we used to make in primary school so we could pretend it was ancient. A castle, a cathedral, a church. It looks like the kind of city you'd make up if you were writing a medieval fantasy.

Rhys has let go of my hand and has pulled up Maps on his phone. He has an adorable look of intense concentration on his face as he looks down to the phone and then up again, his hand absently pointing in different directions. After a minute, he puts his phone away and grins at me. **Hotel?**

I nod. Even though I didn't exactly do anything strenuous on the coach, for some reason I feel exhausted.

This is the old part of the city, Rhys tells me as we begin to walk. He is just slightly ahead of me and walking at an angle so we can still have a conversation. His excitement shows in his hands, and I love him for it. **That's the train station, there, see? Waverley. On the other side is Princes Street. That's where chain shops and things are. The newer bit. I like the old bit best.** He bumps into an older man and stumbles slightly. **Sorry!** he signs, his head clearly still in BSL mode.

"Watch it," the man grumbles, not even noticing. There's such unkindness in his tone that I'm suddenly glad that Rhys doesn't have to hear it.

Our hotel is really central, Rhys continues happily, beautifully oblivious, **considering we couldn't afford much. Maybe we should have gone for a hostel, but . . .** He pauses, embarrassed and shy. **I wanted it to be special.**

How can I not love this boy?

I reach up and kiss him on the cheek. He beams. **I'm really happy**, I tell him.

The hotel is on the corner of an old street. There are at least three pubs in sight of our window and about six within a minute's walk. When we check in, the woman at the reception desk barely blinks at my silence and Rhys's unusual voice, as if she's used to seeing young couples with communication difficulties checking in alone. She talks normally, not raising her voice or making exaggerated hand gestures. When she hands Rhys our key, my heart jumps. I think part of me had expected her to tell us we were too young to book a hotel room. Too young to . . . be in a hotel room together.

Anyway. We're here.

Rhys collapses onto the bed and lets out a happy groan, rolling onto his back like a cat. I'm filled with a sudden, ridiculous shyness and I hang back by the window, the warm metal of the radiator against my skin. Rhys and I have been alone together lots of times, of course, but there's always been someone on the other side of the door or waiting for one of us to get home. Now it really is just us. Us and a bed.

Rhys sits up a little and looks at me, a small smile on his face. Is he nervous too? Do boys get nervous about stuff like this?

Are you okay?

I nod, but I feel how hesitant it is and know there's no hiding it from him. I push myself away from the radiator with both hands and walk toward the bed, climbing up onto it beside him. The mattress and quilt sink under my knees.

He takes my hands and squeezes, nudging his nose against mine. He is saying, *It's okay. It's us. It's you and me.* He doesn't need to sign or say this for me to know that it's what he means. Maybe that sounds strange to people who use speech as naturally as breathing. Or maybe everyone has a silent language with the person they love. Either way, I relax. I nudge his nose right back.

When we kiss, it's gentle at first. He's half sitting, half lying and I'm sitting sideways on my right thigh. Only our faces touch and it's almost tentative, like we're doing it for the first time. His fingers graze my arm and land on my jaw. I can feel his thumb begin to trace circles on my neck and a shot of something hot and surprising whizzes through my entire body. It's me that opens my mouth first as we kiss and when his tongue touches mine I feel as if I've been set on fire.

In a very, very good way.

Rhys pulls me down beside him and slides his hand to my waist, his other still on my face. *We are on a bed*, I'm thinking. *We are on a bed!* I'm also thinking, *This didn't take us long*, and *Oh my God oh my God oh my God* and *I need to pee*. Shut up, no you don't. Be in the moment.

A rumble comes from somewhere between us and for a second I'm confused, before realizing it came from one of our stomachs.

It must be mine, because he hasn't reacted, and if it was his own rumble he'd have noticed it, right? So now I need to pee *and* I want to eat. Way to be passionate, Brons. And suddenly I'm laughing, slightly hysterical with panic and—yes—lust, and I break away from the kiss. **Sorry.** I try to calm down. **Sorry!**

What's wrong? he asks, looking worried. **Did I . . . ?**

No, it's me, I flail. **My stomach.**

Your stomach? He looks at me incredulously for a second, then starts to laugh. **Your stomach**, he repeats, then properly cracks up. He pulls me toward him and bear hugs me into the bed, grizzling against my neck, and by then I'm laughing so hard I really might pee there and then. I disentangle myself, punctuating my withdrawal with kisses, and go to the bathroom, locking the door behind me.

I take a second to look at my reflection; my hair is wild around my face, my eyes shiny and happy. My mascara has smudged slightly around my eyes, but I'm not sure if this happened on the coach or on the bed. This is the face of a girl on a city break with her boyfriend, I think, and I beam at myself.

When I go back into the bedroom, Rhys is sitting cross-legged on the bed with a map spread out in front of him. **Shall we go somewhere for dinner?** he asks. **The hotel has a restaurant, but it doesn't look that great.**

Okay. Where? I'm not quite sure whether he means right now or later. If he wants me to come back to the bed so we can . . . you know. Pick up where we left off. That's probably what I'm meant to do, right?

Pizza? His expression is hopeful. **I'm really hungry too. Shall we go now?**

My stomach lets out another happy rumble and I smile. **Pizza.**

By the time we get back to the hotel after dinner—Pizza Hut, because who needs luxury when you've got pizza?—I am fuzzy with happiness and sleep. So far, Edinburgh—lit up in the darkness and somehow even more beautiful—is everything I'd hoped it would be. We walk hand in hand in silence and it feels so nice I want to sink into the moment and stay there forever.

In the room, Rhys showers while I change into my pajamas. I'm so nervous I get under the covers and huddle there until he comes out. When he does, he is wearing nothing but a towel and still glistening with water droplets. Oh, hello. *Hello.*

"Um," I say.

He grins. It's the grin of a boy who knows he has abs and is very happy with them. The grin of a person who hasn't grown up watching adverts that tell him everything he should hate about his own body. Lucky him. I slide further under the covers and scrunch them around my neck.

I'm going to brush my teeth, I sign, then bolt out of bed and into the bathroom before he can get a proper look at me. Why did I choose these pajamas? They're old novelty pajamas from Canada. They have moose on them. Find me something less sexy than a moose.

I take out my nerves on my teeth, swish mouthwash for longer than is technically required, then breathe in slowly. I put my hands on the sink and meet my own gaze in the mirror. "You can do this," I whisper. "You can totally do this."

I turn off the light and walk back into the main room. I'm not sure what I should say to Rhys, how to kick-start us both into the mood we were in earlier, but my hands drop to my sides when I look at the bed. Rhys is lying on top of the covers, wearing a Yoshi T-shirt and a pair of boxers. He's on his back and his arm is splayed back against the pillows.

He's fast asleep.

Well, thank God, really. It's more of a relief than anything else. I turn off the light and slide under the covers beside him, my heart rate slowing as I relax against the pillows. Tonight, we'll sleep. Tomorrow, we'll . . . well. We'll see, won't we?

I can smell his hair, freshly shampooed, just inches away from me. I can hear his soft breath. We're sleeping together for the first time, I realize, and the thought makes me smile in the darkness. I reach over the covers and run my fingers down his arm, closing them around his hand. "I love you," I whisper into the ether, and squeeze his hand.

He squeezes back, like he's heard.

Texts from Edinburgh

To Mum:

Back at Dad's! Hope Bell is
doing okay! Xx

To Dad:

How's Rita doing? Tell her I
miss her! Xx

Um, and you and Lucy too,
obvs! xx

To Tem:

Not to boast or anything, but
my boyfriend has a very nice
face. And bum.

Tem:

STEFANIE BRONS! 😲
I'm so proud of you ilu xxxx

25

IF YOU WERE LOOKING FOR A PERFECT DAY, YOU wouldn't find much better than this.

It's early evening and the sun is just starting to dim over the city. Rhys and I are sitting on a bench looking over at Castle Rock, sharing a portion of fish and chips. It's all we can afford if we want to hit Rhys's target of spending less than £10 for the entire day—he calls it a game rather than simply being poor, and I play along because it's more fun. At lunchtime we had sandwiches from Tesco. Breakfast was the biscuits we got free from the hotel.

Everything we've done today has been free—and wonderful. In the morning we went to Greyfriars Kirkyard, and I told Rhys the story of Greyfriars Bobby, which was one of my favorite stories as a kid. We went around the cemetery together, reading the gravestones, making up lives for the people buried underneath them. My anxiety tried to interrupt, reminding me that I'd be under a gravestone one day and forever, but I pushed it away and it didn't come back.

We made up our own city walk, ignoring street signs and maps and just taking left turns for twenty minutes, then switching to right. We ended up discovering weird side streets and steep flights of cobbled stairs that would probably have been shortcuts somewhere if we'd been paying attention. Rhys bought a single Creme Egg and we shared it in tiny, nibbly bites, cuddled together on a bench in the Old Town.

As the afternoon set in we took our time on the Royal Mile, stopping in every souvenir shop and trying on tartan hats and scarves. We were the annoying English teenagers who loitered and didn't buy a single thing, and I didn't care. Nobody knew what we were saying as we signed and teased and laughed. The day, the city, the world—it was all ours.

Are you happy? Rhys asks me.

I can't stop the grin breaking over my face. **I am *so* happy.**

He grins back at me and we beam at each other like children let loose in Toys "R" Us. He leans over to kiss me and I lift my face to meet his. I taste salt and vinegar and Rhys.

What shall we do tonight? Rhys asks when we break apart.

Are we still aiming for less than £10? I ask, pondering.

He nods. **It doesn't count as a win if it's not the whole day.**

What could we do that's free? I muse, and I don't even realize what it is I've said until after my hands have finished. I flush scarlet, flail my hands a little, then look away. "God, Steffi," I groan out loud.

I hear Rhys laughing, and I look back at him, too embarrassed to speak. He kisses my nose.

You're adorable.

I cover my face with my hands and he pulls them away, pressing his lips to the tips of my fingers, his eyes on mine. God, those eyes. If I could keep just one part of Rhys, it would be his eyes. And, okay, maybe his mouth too. Basically his whole face. I'll keep his face.

Maybe we should go out for drinks, Rhys suggests, releasing my hands so we can talk.

I hold up one finger. **One, I'm seventeen.** I hold up two fingers. **Two, do we have enough left of the £10 for drinks?**

Rhys reaches into his pocket and pulls out a handful of change. He stretches out his palm and counts the coins, nibbling his bottom lip between his teeth. He looks up at me. **Do you think we could find a bottle of wine for £3.47?**

I roll my eyes. **I think you're taking the "less than £10" game a bit far with that.** "Cheapskate," I add, sticking out my tongue.

Challenge accepted! Rhys grins, eyes lighting up. **Come on.** He stands, holding out a hand to me, and I take it happily. **We'll get some cheap wine and decide what to do next.**

We walk in silence, swinging our knitted hands between us. I am squidgy with happiness, warm all over. This is love, I think, and I am in it. I have it. No wonder everyone goes on about it so much. It's really *nice*.

Rhys stops at a liquor store, and I wait outside while he goes to find an impossibly cheap bottle of wine. I dawdle, pretending to read a tour poster on the wall, trying to act like I'm not the underage girlfriend of the boy who just walked in. When he emerges again, he's beaming.

What did you get? I ask.

He twinkles. **Wait and see.**

I bet you didn't get anything, I tease, trying to grab the paper bag so I can look. **No way did you find any alcohol that cheap.**

Wrong. He waves the bag in front of my face, the weight of the bottle within unmistakeable.

I bet it's just Coke, I amend. **Or lemonade.**

He laughs, pulls me toward him, and kisses my forehead. **You'll see**, he says.

He's bought us champagne.

Okay, it's not *quite* champagne. It's sparkling wine, and it didn't cost the earth. But it has bubbles, and the cork comes off with a satisfying, heart-pinging pop. He refuses to tell me how much it cost, saying only that his £10 challenge didn't include alcohol. And, anyway, he loves me, and we deserve champagne. Or sparkling wine.

We don't even have glasses, let alone flutes, so we end up

pouring the fizz into the hotel mugs that look like they've gone through the dishwasher about five thousand times. When we toast, the mugs clunk instead of clink, but I don't mind. Everything feels perfect.

To you, Rhys says.

To *you*, I respond.

He grins. **To us. Bronze and Gold.**

Bronze and Gold, I agree, then close my eyes to take a sip. I imagine hundreds of tiny bubbles fizzing down into my stomach. When I open my eyes again, Rhys is staring at me, the softest, sweetest smile on his face.

What? I ask, bashful, even though I know what.

He says it anyway. **I love you.**

I put my mug down on the table by the bed and lean into him, resting my head against his shoulder and breathing Rhysness. He puts his arm round me and squeezes gently.

When I break away, I sign, **I love you too.**

There's a pause that stretches out into silence as we look at each other. I am giddy with happiness, light with love. Punch drunk with the freedom of being in this city, in this country, with this boy.

But mixed in with all of this is anxiety, tying my thoughts into knots, making me feel suddenly shy in a way I haven't felt around Rhys for a long time. Even though nothing has happened yet my heart is pounding, maybe in anticipation, maybe with nerves. What happens now? What happens next? Should I just lean in and kiss him?

Rhys is still watching me, his smile a little more crinkled, as if he somehow knows the confusion of feelings running through my mind. He reaches over to the bedside table, grabs hold of his iPad, and hands it to me. **Find me a song**, he signs. **A song that is exactly how you feel, right now.**

He's trying to relax me, and I love him for it because it works. The anxiety dissipates like bubbles in a glass of sparkling wine. Beaming, I open up Spotify, my mind already scrolling through the options. There's a tap on my wrist and I look over at him. **Make it a good one.** His eyes are so full. I could look at them all day.

When I make my selection and hear the first few beats, I am not sad that Rhys can't hear it too, because I understand. He doesn't need to. How had I ever thought that music was all about sound? It's not. It's about feeling.

Look, I sign, bouncing up off the bed. **I'll show you.**

The song is "You Make My Dreams (Come True)," which is a song by an old duo called Hall & Oates. It is the happiest song in existence, and it is impossible to listen to it without feeling happy. And if you listen to it while you're already deliriously happy, it will make you do this:

- play it to your deaf boyfriend when he asks you how you feel
- dance around the room to bring it to life
- sign the lyrics as you jump from one foot to the other, spinning, twirling, laughing

- sing along unselfconsciously as you do this, because you are so happy you can't believe you could ever want to be silent
- get to the line about being found, about never being the same, and burst into tears.

And it will make said boyfriend do this:

- turn the music up so loud you can feel the vibrations through your body
- jump up beside you and dance with you
- even though he can't hear the music
- even though you both look like idiots
- put his arms around you when you start to cry out of the blue
- kiss your hair
- write *I love you* onto your skin
- say it out loud
- say it with his hands
- say it with his eyes.

"I love you," I say into his ear.

The song comes to an end and then starts up again, jaunty. Rhys takes my hand and spins me, then pulls me in close. He lifts my chin with his fingers and kisses me, soft at first and then firm, opening my mouth with his, touching his tongue to mine.

We tangle around each other, his arms around me, hands at my hips and back and chest and neck. We kiss, kiss, kiss.

He pulls me down onto the bed and my heart is going, hummingbird-like, in my chest. There is no need to talk; our bodies are having a conversation of their own. Is this what it's like for everyone? Do all couples know each other's movements like this?

Rhys pulls away from me slightly to look into my eyes. His face is suddenly shy. He takes my hand, currently at his chest, squeezes it into a fist, and moves it gently in an up and down motion. **Yes?** he is asking me. **Yes?**

I nod—yes—slowly first, then faster. *Wait.* I put my hand up suddenly and he retreats immediately. I touch his wrist—*it's okay*—and then say out loud, "I am not losing my virginity to Hall and Oates."

Rhys smiles and raises his hands, palm up, rolling his eyes sweetly as he does. I scramble for the iPad and turn off Hall and Oates. I'm about to turn back to him with the music off, but then something occurs to me. We might not be able to share a musical memory, but that doesn't stop me making one for myself. I can soundtrack this, just for me, if I want to. A secret for myself.

With this thought in my mind, I glance back at Rhys. I realize I don't know the BSL for "condom," so I fingerspell the word instead.

For a second he just looks at me, then starts to laugh. **Very romantic.**

I'm suddenly worried. **Do you have one?**

He grins. **Yes.**

I flap my hands at him. **Go on, then.**

Rhys takes my hands, grips them together in a four-handed fist, then kisses my knuckles. When he lets them go, he touches his fingers to my cheek, his eyes locked on mine. There is an entire conversation in these gestures and in his eyes. When he turns to scramble in his bag for a condom, my fluttering heart has calmed. This is me and Rhys. Rhys and me.

There isn't time for a soul-searching hunt through Spotify to find the perfect losing-virginity-but-for-my-ears-only song, so I go for the first song I think of. Passenger. "Heart's On Fire." Because it is, and also because the lyrics about eyes and touch are so perfect for Rhys and me.

Everything about this moment is perfect. When he asks me if I'm ready, his eyes both nervous and excited, I mean it when I nod yes.

His touch is hesitant now, and I feel his nerves as we slide under the covers together, face to face. I kiss him to ground us both and he wraps his arms round me, pulling me close. Between kisses we shed our clothing, top to bottom, slowly at first and then faster. In no time at all we're both down to our underwear and he is starting to ease down my knickers and *oh my God* has there ever been a more perfect moment in the history of moments and I'm going to have sex and it's not going to be crap like everyone says the first time is and holy crap we're naked and he's getting on top of me and—

And then it all gets awkward very fast. Half leaning on me, Rhys pushes his hand down between us both and there's some kind of sweaty fumble, then a judder. He half thrusts, half pokes his penis at my leg. I hear him grunt, then there's another attempt at adjusting himself. I let out an involuntary "ow!" when he puts his elbow on my hair, and I'm grateful he can't hear me.

After another few awkward seconds I reach down, take hold of his penis, and guide him. He breathes into my ear, drops a kiss on my neck, then raises himself on his arm so he can kiss me as he pushes his way in. The moment itself is not exactly painful but not exactly pleasurable either, and I'm glad he's not looking at my face, because I can feel I'm screwing it up involuntarily. The whole thing is so much . . . *realer* than I was expecting, so much more physical. Maybe I'd always imagined sex as more like a dance or something, instead of this sweaty tangling of bodies and body parts that it actually is, and the reality is a sloppy, slightly anticlimactic surprise. I guess it takes time to—

And then, suddenly, it's over. Rhys's face tightens, his eyes glaze over, he lets out a noise I've never heard before, then collapses against me. He's sweaty and hot. I love him, and I'm glad we've shared this intense, sensual thing, but ew. Can I push him off? Is that allowed?

The whole thing has lasted less than two minutes. Passenger is still singing about his heart being on fire.

Rhys rolls off me and I try not to be too obvious about wiping his sweat off my chest. He beams at me, all breathless and hopeful, and oh God, I do love him.

Okay? he asks.

I nod, beaming back. He leans to kiss me, softly this time, and *I have had sex*. Suddenly, for no reason at all, I want to cry, even though the impulse makes no sense. I push my face against his chest, not caring now about the sweat, and close my eyes, listening to his heartbeat. I think, *Rhys, Rhys, Rhys*. I feel him wrap his arms round me, safe and warm and close. I think of everything that led to this moment and all that could come next for us. I think how nice it is to be part of this *us*.

Rhys pulls back a little. With one hand, he signs, **I love you**.

I look at him, trying to turn this moment into a sense memory I can keep and return to forever. **I love you too**, I sign.

26

I WAKE UP THE NEXT MORNING WITH HALF MY BODY hanging off the side of the bed. I blink, trying to figure out where I am, and then it all comes rushing in. I'm in Edinburgh! I had *sex*! (*Twice!* And the second time was *so much better*!)

I sit up and look over at Rhys, who is lying on his stomach, face buried into the pillow. It would have been more romantic to wake up in each other's arms, but oh well. Can't have everything.

I lie back down and curl up next to him, resting my cheek against the smooth slide of his shoulder blade. He makes a happy snuffling noise, but doesn't properly stir. I stay like that for a while, too awake to doze but also too relaxed to get up. Outside I can hear the soft rumble of cars through the double-glazing of the windows. Someone walks down the hallway talking loudly about the merits of croissants versus Danish pastries. I close my eyes.

Later, we go for a late brunch in a Scandinavian café on the way to Arthur's Seat. We get one full breakfast and one plate of French toast and share them across the table, tapping each other's hands out of the way to spear potatoes, dropping forks with loud clangs to speak.

I tear off a hunk of French toast and begin to chew. **So is it a mountain?** Bonus of BSL: talking with your mouth full and it not being rude.

More like a hill, he says. **Arthur's Seat is the peak. The views are amazing.**

How many times have you been up there?

Only once. I was about eight.

Is it a big climb?

He smiles. **Not really. You'll be fine. We'll be up and down in a couple of hours. Wait until you see the view. We'll get some great pictures.**

My phone gives a buzz against the table and I reach for it automatically.

Tem:

Are you at home? Can I come round?
I need to talk to you. Xxx

I hesitate, feeling my very first stab of guilt about going away in secret. Maybe I *should* have told Tem. I'm not even sure exactly why I didn't, except that I was attracted to the idea of Rhys and me being the only people in the whole world who knew.

I'm out with Rhys!
Sorry, what's up? xx

I reply finally, telling the truth but not the whole truth, nor nothing but the truth.

Tem:
Wah ☹ When can I see you today?
I REALLY need to talk to you. Xxxx

Shit.

What's wrong? Rhys asks, seeing my face.

Tem, I say, holding up my phone. **She wants to see me.** I nibble my lip, trying to figure out what to do. How can I say I can't see her until Sunday without telling her why?

Maybe you should tell her the truth?

I can't do that now. It's too late.

You were going to tell her eventually anyway. Better now than later, right?

I hesitate. He's right. But a selfish little twist in my head knows how Tem will react if I tell her where I am—what! Wow! Why! Etc. I want to be in my Bronze and Gold bubble for just a little longer. There'll be time enough for a best friend debrief.

I tap out a reply, trying to shut off the "guilt" portion of my brain.

Steffi:

I can't right now! SORRY! xx

Tem:

Steffffff ☹

Steffi:

plays the girlfriend card

I put my phone back down on the table and watch as Rhys steals the last bite of French toast. He smiles at me. **Ready to go?** I nod distractedly. My phone has lit up already.

Tem:

But I need you ☹
plays the best friend card

Steffi:

Want to phone me? I'll
answer. And talk xxx

Tem:

No! Want to talk face to faaaaace.

I feel the tiniest flicker of irritation. Since when is Tem so needy? Why can't she wait for once? I can see that there's going to be no way around telling her exactly where I am and why I can't drop everything to go and see her, at least not until I get back home on Sunday.

But I can't bear the thought of spoiling the magic of today with the reality of an argument. If she's going to be annoyed with me anyway, I can put it off for a little while. I'll phone her after I've climbed Arthur's Seat. Surely I've earned an extra hour in all our years of friendship?

Okay, I sign, smiling at Rhys. I turn off notifications from WhatsApp on my phone and push it into my pocket. **Let's go and climb a mountain.**

Rhys is right. The views are amazing.

We don't even need to be walking for very long before it's possible to turn around and look out at Edinburgh. **Wow**, I say to Rhys. **If it's like this from here, what's it like at the top?**

He laughs. **The same. But higher.**

We don't rush. For the most part he walks ahead of me and I follow his lead, turning in circles every few steps to see how the view changes each time. We stop about halfway up and sit on the grass so we can have a proper conversation as well as a breather. He tells me about the first time he visited Edinburgh as a kid, how he'd gone to see the rugby with his dad and older brother and got lost in the crowd. **Did you cry?** I ask, and he looks surprised.

No, he says. **I knew they'd find me.**

We walk for a while more hand in hand, side by side in easy silence. I am thinking about French toast and Creme Eggs, whether we'll have sex again tonight, how I haven't yet told Tem that I've lost my virginity even though I always promised I would. I wonder what Aled will say when we turn up on his doorstep. How my parents will react when I tell them where I am.

Rhys's hand drops mine and touches my wrist. **Look.** He points. **A kestrel.**

I've never seen a kestrel before. I watch it hover then swoop, disappearing from view.

Come on. Rhys taps my hand again and gestures. **Let's look for it.**

Why? I ask. **Are you going to try to catch it?**

He's already off, scampering across the grass in the general direction of the kestrel. He turns as he goes. **I need a picture!** he signs. **For my dad!**

I roll my eyes and grin at him, waving him off and turning away to look back out over the view. Edinburgh is beautiful, I think for the millionth time. I watch a plane coming in to land over the water. I can just about make out the BA logo on the side. I think of all the people inside, coming home, beginning a holiday, or going to a business meeting, perhaps. Looking out of the windows at the city growing larger beneath them.

I bounce a little on my feet, take in the air in a deep breath, then turn back round. Rhys has gone. I blink at the empty air where I'd last seen him, then do a slow 360-degree turn, scanning the hill for his familiar broad shoulders, his smiling face. No Rhys. How long does it take to photograph a bird? How far has he decided to go? I frown at his absence, waiting for him to reappear, but anxiety is already starting to scratch at me. Could he be hiding behind a bush, ready to jump out and scare me? No. We don't do that to each other.

I know I'm being stupid. Silly, overreacting, anxious Steffi. But it's *Rhys*. How can I be rational when it's Rhys?

A minute goes by, and he doesn't reappear. My heart is starting to beat faster; I can feel panic preparing itself in my chest. I look all around me, but I'm alone. Alone, on the top of a mountain in Scotland.

"Rhys!" I shout instinctively, even though it's pointless and stupid. *"Rhys?"* For the first time ever, I wish my boyfriend could hear.

I stumble over the rocky path and onto the grass where I last saw him, my anxiety now elevated to full-on alarm-bell levels. There's an incline to the grass that I hadn't noticed from where I was standing before and I follow it down, heart jack-rabbiting, and then I see him. I see him, and I swear my heart stops.

Rhys, lying on his side on the ground, not even five feet away from me. Rhys, head touching the dust. Rhys, motionless.

"Rhys!" This time the word comes out like a gasp. Who would I be shouting for? No one but myself. I close the distance between us and fall to my knees beside him, reaching out and taking hold of his arm. "Rhys. Rhys."

He lets out a groan and even though it's a noise of pain I'm so relieved I almost start crying. He turns his head so we can make eye contact and I take in that he's completely conscious, there's no blood on his face or head; he's fine. He's fine, he's fine, he's fine.

What happened? I sign, still frantic. My brain has always had a hard time letting go of the worst-case scenario, and right now it remains convinced, despite the clear evidence, that Rhys is dead.

Rhys groans again, then shakes his head.

Can you sit up? There's no response, so I try again. **Sit up. What happened? You fell?**

When he doesn't reply again—doesn't even make the most basic of acknowledging signs—I realize he's not even making eye contact. He's looking at my face, but his eyes are so screwed up with pain that he's not reading a word I'm saying.

Okay, Steffi. This is on you. Calm down. Be here for him.

I try to breathe, bite on my lip, and reach for Rhys, patting him gently, trying to find the source of his pain. Now I'm bothering to look somewhere other than his face, I can see that the ankle on his left foot has already swollen to twice its normal size. I wince and reach for it, but Rhys lets out a growl and pushes my hand away.

"Okay, okay," I say out loud. I'm trying to be soothing. "I

won't touch it." I try to take his hand. "Rhys," I say. "Rhys, look at me so I can talk to you."

As my fingers close over his wrist, he lets out a yell of agony that frightens me so much I drop his hand and stumble backward. "What?" I *am* crying now. "Rhys, what? Tell me. Talk to me. What's wrong?"

This is what everyone talks about when they say we both have communication difficulties. This exact scenario.

I would give every single one of my fingers and toes to be telepathic right now.

"Can't you sign?" I ask, realization beginning to dawn. I look back at his arms, cradled to his chest. "Did you hurt your hands?" My heart has now reached full-on thundering levels. It's so loud I can hear it inside my ears.

And then I see it. There's something wrong with his right arm; the angle is all weird. It's broken or dislocated or something. "Oh, Rhys," I try to say, my voice all mangled. My emotions are all over the place. I'm worried for him, of course, and I'm devastated that he's in pain, but I'm also starting to panic. Rhys can't walk, talk, or sign, and we're stuck at the top of Arthur's Seat.

And then the worst thing of all hits me. It really *is* all on me. No one is going to help us unless I—silent, useless Steffi—go and ask someone to help us. I am going to have to find a stranger on top of this Scottish mountain, explain that my deaf boyfriend has tripped on a rock and broken his arm and/or ankle, and ask them to . . . what? Call someone? Carry Rhys down the mountainside? While I, what, trot alongside them and make conversation?

Oh holy fuck, I can't do this. Panic sears through me, lighting my blood on fire. My hands go cold, my stomach knots like a noose. I can't breathe. I can't think.

Breathe.

Breathe, Steffi.

Now is not the time.

But panic doesn't care about stakes or context. It is loud and immediate and profoundly, all-encompassingly selfish. It has swallowed all my thoughts and my heartbeats and my breath. There is no one to rescue me; it is me who has to rescue Rhys. But I can't even rescue myself.

Breathe.

I squeeze my eyes shut. I close my mouth and breathe in slowly through my nose, counting out six beats, then let it out over eight beats. I do it again, and then again, and then again. The screaming in my ears eases, then stops. My heartbeat calms. I open my eyes.

I touch my fingers to Rhys's good shoulder and he looks at me. He's in too much pain to have noticed that I just had a panic attack, and in a weird way I'm grateful. "I'm going to find someone to help," I say slowly, enunciating. "I will be right back."

As I walk away from him, I'm thinking how unfair this is. Not just that Rhys has hurt himself, but that the fact of him hurting himself hasn't done what films and books have always promised me it would: it has not transformed me into a better version of myself. Where is the Super Steffi who is SUPPOSED to reveal herself at times of crisis? Shouldn't my love for Rhys overcome everything? Why am I still worrying about talking to a stranger when the most important thing is getting him help?

I am still me and all the crappy bits of myself are still in full attendance. When I spot a woman a few yards down the path ahead of me, my throat tightens and my palms get clammy, just as they would if I were in line at the bank. It's not fair. It's never fair.

I make my way as fast as I can down the path, ignoring my stupid tight throat and stupid clammy hands, and reach the woman. "Excuse me," I say.

It comes out, of course, like a squeak.

And she doesn't hear me.

For Christ's sake, Stefanie. Get a goddam grip.

"Excuse me." This time, I overcompensate and my voice comes out loud and harsh. The woman turns, clearly startled, and spots me. "Hello," I blurt.

"Hello," the woman says politely. It is the cautious, very-British hello that means "I am capable of assisting you" but also "I am ready to run and/or scream for help if necessary."

I look into this woman's wary face, open my mouth, and . . . nothing comes out. My words have gone. *No. No, Steffi, not now.*

I let out a choking, grunting gasp of frustration and the woman's eyes widen in alarm. She takes a step back.

No, wait, I sign automatically. **Sorry. Please don't go.**

As she watches my hands, realization dawns on her face, just as it had done with the coach driver back in London, followed by an expression I recognize: panic.

"Oh," she says. "Oh, I . . . I'm afraid I don't speak . . ."

"That's fine," I blurt out. My voice! My awful, shaky voice! There it is! "I can hear. I need help. My boyfriend needs help— he fell and he needs help." I realize I'm still signing as I talk, but it doesn't matter.

The woman's expression gets even more panicked. "Oh," she says again. "Oh dear. Where is he?"

For some reason, the fact that she seems as worried as me eases my anxiety a little. This is a situation where it is normal to be anxious.

"Over here," I say, then turn and go, hoping she'll follow.

"Loki!" the woman calls, and I glance back in confusion to see a Border collie racing up the grass toward us. The woman has a dog! A dog called Loki! A little bit more of my anxiety dissipates. "My name is Connie," she says as she catches up with me.

"I'm Steffi," I say. "Hello, Loki." The dog has raced in front of us and is prancing happily in odd little semicircles on the grass. When I speak, he darts toward me and barks. I lift my voice, encouraging and excited, "Go find Rhys!"

"He's not really—" Connie begins, but stops as Loki bounds

away from us, still barking, and disappears over the incline, where Rhys is. "Oh." She lets out a small, embarrassed laugh. "He's usually a bit dim, for a Border collie."

I don't know how to answer this so I pick up my pace and she follows my lead. Rhys is sitting up more now, leaning his weight on his uninjured thigh, his working hand rubbing tentatively on Loki's head. Loki is sitting beside him, panting proudly. When Connie and I appear, he barks.

"Good boy," I say.

"Yes, good boy," Connie echoes.

I kneel on the ground beside Rhys and smile at him. "This is Connie," I say, gesturing. "She's going to help."

Rhys grimaces, sort of like what a smile would look like if you ran over it with a Zamboni. **I love you**, I sign. **It will be fine.**

"I think he's hurt his ankle and his arm," I say to Connie. I'm still signing as I talk, and I don't look directly at her. Both these things make it easier to speak.

"Can't he tell you?" Connie asks.

"He's deaf," I say to Loki. "He can't sign because of his bad arm. And I think he's in too much pain to talk. Usually, he can talk if he needs to."

"Hello," Connie says, squatting down beside us both. "I'm Connie."

This is Connie, I sign.

"Hi," Rhys manages, and I have to stop myself throwing my arms around him.

"His name is Rhys," I add.

"Did you see what happened?" Connie asks me, and I shake my head. She swallows and smiles uncertainly at Rhys. "Well, we'll need to get him down to ground level," she says to me. "I don't think an air ambulance will come for a broken ankle. Between the two of us, do you think we could help him down?"

I look at Rhys and then at her. Another jolt of panic, which I try to squash as far down as it will go. I nod, because my voice has deserted me again.

"We can go straight to my car," Connie continues. I'm not sure who out of the three of us she's talking to. It seems to be mostly herself. "And I'll drive you both to the ER. Is that . . ." She hesitates, then looks at me. "Does that sound right?"

I nod again, because it's not like I have any better ideas.

"Right," Connie says briskly. "Rhys," she begins, her voice suddenly much louder. "I'm going to help you up now. Do you think you can manage?"

Rhys looks at me, his face twisted in pain and frustration. When he says my name, it is a hoarse breath, barely a whisper. "Steffi."

We're going to help you, I sign. **It'll be fine.** I make myself smile encouragingly.

He moves his uninjured hand to his chest and circles his fist around his heart. **Sorry.**

You don't need to be sorry. Get ready, okay? This might hurt.

It's awkward not only because a total stranger is helping me lift up my 150-pound boyfriend, but also on a practical level: Rhys's left leg and right arm are hurt, which means it is not as simple as acting like a crutch.

We struggle for about three minutes before Connie stops, shaking her head. "This isn't going to work," she says, panting slightly. "We need someone else."

Before I can say anything in response she is jogging off toward a person further down the path. I spin round to face Rhys and look carefully at him, scanning his face, trying to read him. He manages a smile, and I smile back, lean up, and kiss him on the cheek.

Connie comes back with a man who must be around my dad's age. "He's a doctor!" she tells me, almost glowing with relief.

"Hello," the man says, looking almost amused. "Not experienced climbers, then, are we?"

This strikes me as a bit of a jerk thing to say, all things considered, but I'm too me to say so, so I just shake my head like an idiot.

"All right, chap," the man says to Rhys. "I'm Stuart. Let's take a look at you before we try moving you any more."

"He's deaf," I say.

"Are you his interpreter?" he asks me.

"No," I say. "I'm his girlfriend."

Stuart looks right past me and makes a long-suffering face at Connie, who smiles uncertainly back. "Do you speak sign language?" he says to me, his voice an exasperated sigh.

"Yes."

"Fantastic," he says pointedly. "That'll make things a bit easier." He turns back to Rhys. "Now, chap. What happened?"

"His name is Rhys," I say.

Rhys waves, gets my attention, and then makes a series of gestures with his working hand, his face moving through a variety of expressions. He points at his foot, then moves his hand in a circular motion.

"He tripped," I say to Stuart. Rhys coughs. "On a rock," I add.

"Fell awkwardly, did you?" Stuart says gamely. As annoying as he's being, at least he doesn't raise his voice when he talks to Rhys. "Let's take a look." With gentle hands, he takes Rhys's injured arm. "It looks like you've dislocated your elbow," he says. "The ankle could be broken or just sprained—you'll need an X-ray to know for sure. Did you hit your head?"

Rhys looks to me and I sign a quick translation. He shakes his head.

"No," I say.

"That's lucky, then. Let's get you down to the ground, shall we?"

27

WITH STUART'S HELP, IT'S DEFINITELY EASIER TO maneuver Rhys down the green slopes of Holyrood Park, but it still takes a while. Rhys gives up trying to be stoic and groans pretty much the whole way down. After the first few sympathetic winces and worried signs, I stop bothering and instead listen in on Stuart and Connie, who are bonding over the fact that they're both wearing North Face jackets. Loki is lolloping along beside me, and I tell him in soft whispers about Rhys and me, our Edinburgh adventure. Like all dogs, he's a good listener.

Connie's car is a small olive Golf. Books cover the back seat and she apologizes as she hastily sweeps the lot into one corner. One slips out of her grip and bounces onto the concrete. "I'm a school librarian," she says. "I read a lot."

Stuart laughs and says something about how she should see his own car; it's full of medical journals and issues of *New*

Scientist. I'm already imagining how they'll tell this story on their wedding day—"And then she opened her car door . . ." ". . . And all the books fell out!" *Pause for laughter*—and I quirk an eyebrow at Rhys, grinning, but he just looks at me in confusion. Of course, he's missed the entire thing.

I wonder how the two of us will feature in the retelling of this story. The Deaf boy with the busted ankle. The girl who couldn't speak. But then, I *have* spoken. So who am I? Just the girlfriend?

Stuart helps to ease Rhys into the front seat of the car, having pushed it as far back as it will go so Rhys has room if he needs it. I sit in the back seat and tap Rhys's shoulder. **How are you?**

He wiggles his hand. *So-so.*

Does it hurt a lot?

Yes.

When Connie slides into the front seat and starts the car, I realize Stuart isn't coming with us. He gives us a friendly wave as Connie reverses out of the space. I want to ask her if she got his number, but I don't know how. What would Tem say? She'd make a joke out of it. She'd be so funny and charming that Connie would be laughing all the way to the hospital.

Rhys leans his head against the rest and I see him close his eyes. There are pain wrinkles in his forehead.

"He'll be fine," Connie says, and I realize she's looking at me in the rearview mirror.

Have I even said thank you to this woman?

"Thanks for . . . um. Doing this."

"Oh, it's no trouble," Connie replies easily. "Nothing like a spot of mountain rescue on a Saturday afternoon!"

"I don't really . . ." I stop, embarrassed, but then the silence is so expectant and awkward I have to finish. "I don't really know what I'm doing."

There's a pause as Connie slows for traffic. She glances at her rearview mirror again and smiles at me. "What did you say your name was? Steffi?"

I nod.

"No one does, Steffi. No one knows what they're doing."

"Stuart seemed like he did," I say, and Connie laughs. I made a joke! And she laughed!

"Some people pretend better than others," she concedes. "It must be tough for you, having a deaf boyfriend?"

"No," I say, defensive on his behalf. "He's brilliant."

She smiles again, fond and a little wistful, even though she doesn't know either of us. "I'm sure he is."

"He takes care of me," I add.

"It seems like you take good care of him too."

This is a nice thing to say, so I don't contradict her. I try to think of something else to say, because it's kind of nice having a conversation instead of sitting in awkward silence, but I can't think of anything.

"Is there anyone you should call?" Connie asks.

"Call?" I echo, instantly anxious again. The word alone is Pavlovian to me. I hear that one syllable and start sweating.

"Your boyfriend's parents?" she prompts. "So they can come and get you both?"

Nausea rises, hot and thick in my throat. I will have to *call* people. I will have to call Rhys's parents and explain that we took off without telling anyone and now Rhys has broken at least one bone on the top of a mountain in Scotland. They are going to *yell* at me.

Oh *shit*.

I suddenly want, more than anything else, to be back on top of that stupid mountain. Preferably by myself.

"Do you have a phone?" Connie asks when I don't say anything.

I nod wordlessly. I have a sudden, insane urge to ask her to make the calls for me. But how crazy would that look?

"We're just a few minutes away from the hospital, so you should wait until you've spoken to a doctor," Connie says. "You have some time." She gives me another smile, like she knows. Like she understands.

The hospital is loud, chaotic, and full of people. Three things I *hate*. Connie waits until Rhys and I have spoken to the woman at reception before she says her good-byes. I'd hoped she would stay, but I know there's no reason for her to do that.

"We don't have anyone who speaks sign language here." The receptionist has come over to where we've sat down to tell me this. "So you'll need to make sure you're always around to translate for your friend, okay?"

I nod, because what else can I do, and sign a quick explanation to Rhys, who gives us both a tired thumbs-up.

"It may be a while," the woman adds, standing up. "We've had a few messy ones today."

I don't ask what she means by this, even though I really want to know. When she leaves, Rhys fumbles with his pocket, trying to pull out his phone.

No phones, I sign, pointing at the written sign on the wall.

He shakes me off, letting out an irritated huff.

No phones, I sign again, reaching over and taking it from him.

"Hey," Rhys barks, so loudly people turn to stare at us.

"Hey yourself," I hiss back, flushing. Then add, for good measure, **Shhh**.

Rhys raises both eyebrows and makes a face at me, which I'm pretty sure is his equivalent of a sarcastic comment about Silent Steffi telling someone else to shhh, but I decide to give him the benefit of the doubt and let it go.

The frustration is coming off him in waves and I both love and hate him for it. This isn't easy for me either, I want to tell him. You think I'm enjoying this?

We sit in silence for the next half an hour, which is how long it takes for Rhys's name to be called. He's given a wheelchair so he doesn't have to hobble, but he doesn't seem very grateful.

The doctor directs all his questions at me and barely looks at

338

Rhys, right down to "How much pain is he in?" and "Did he hit his head?" I have flashes of my mute childhood when people would talk about me instead of to me, using my name but never looking at me. I hated it just as much then as I do now.

I want to share this feeling of annoyed understanding with Rhys, but he's unusually crotchety, so I can't. He keeps turning his head so I'm barely in his peripheral vision, let alone visible enough for him to read, and I know he's doing it on purpose. His whole energy bristles.

In between the X-rays and the results, when the two of us are left alone for a while behind a hastily pulled paper curtain, we still don't talk. I recognize there's something ironic about either of us giving anyone the silent treatment, but that is undoubtedly what is happening right now. I wonder if he blames me for what happened, but that doesn't feel like it. He's been given plenty of painkillers, so the creases have gone from his forehead and the crinkles from around his eyes. But still he scowls.

My sweet, warm boyfriend has somehow been replaced by this sullen grump of a teenage boy. I don't like this version so much.

How old do you think that doctor is? I ask.

Shrug.

He seems young, right?

Shrug.

Have you ever broken any bones before?

Yes.

Which one?

He points to his collarbone.

When? How?

A shake of the head.

Talk to me.

Rhys looks directly at me, his eyes meeting mine. He looks about ready to boil over. *How?* he mouths deliberately. The sign for **How** requires both his hands, and with one be-slinged he can't say it. But his eyes are saying, *Stop trying.*

So I do.

We're at the hospital for several hours while Rhys gets fixed up, and it's all just about as fun as it sounds. I get sick of playing interpreter but I do it anyway, of course. They realign Rhys's elbow and set it, telling him—through me—about recovery times and early motion exercises. His ankle is sprained rather than broken, which is something at least. The only time I leave him is for the few minutes it takes for me to call Aled, and even then it's only after I've put it off for as long as I can.

It takes me seven minutes to work up the courage to press call on the phone I have borrowed from Rhys. I do it sitting on a garden wall opposite the hospital, biting my thumbnail until it splits and bleeds.

"Hello!" Aled reveals himself as the kind of person who answers the phone with an exclamation instead of a question.

"Um, hi," I say. I clutch my hand around my wrist and

squeeze until my nails dig into my skin. I imagine the half-moon marks appearing. I try to remember to breathe.

"Hello," Aled repeats, sounding amused. "Who's this?"

"Um," I say again. I dig my nails in tighter. "My name is Steffi."

"Steffi who?" And then, before I can reply, he answers his own question. "Rhys's Steffi?"

"Um." STOP UMMING, STEFFI. "Yeah."

There's a pause, and then suddenly Aled's voice is urgent and serious. "Has something happened to my brother?"

"Yes," I say. "Well, I mean, no, nothing, like, really bad. You don't need to worry."

"Okay, stop. You're rambling." There's a control and authority to the way he speaks that I find both impressive and intimidating. "Just give me the facts."

I give myself a moment to get my nerves under control, and the fact that he allows me this makes me think that Rhys has told him more than just a little about my issues. "We're in Edinburgh," I begin. "We went up Arthur's Seat. And Rhys kind of . . . fell."

"Shit." There's a catch in his voice, and something about it makes me think of Clark.

"It's just broken bones," I say hastily. I probably should have opened with that. "He's fine. It's just, he can't sign because . . . well, you know. So . . ."

"Where are you now?"

"The hospital. Can you . . ."

"Yes. I'll come right now, okay? I'm on my way."

Seven hours later and I am in bed at Dad's house, staring at the ceiling, trying to figure out exactly how I got here.

It just seems so, overwhelmingly, *unfair*. Rhys stumbles slightly on a pebble and by a trick of misfortune he falls awkwardly instead of righting himself, as he would have done ninety-nine other times out of a hundred. And that tiny accident—the step he took to right himself being off by a couple of degrees—has ruined everything.

After Aled arrived at the hospital, everything seemed to happen really fast. I was suddenly no longer necessary now that a functioning male adult was present and, worst of all, I found myself out of reasons to put off calling my parents. Any hope I might have had of Rhys and I being able to continue our mini holiday were well and truly dashed. Aled was friendly, but he had a no-nonsense way about him and it was clear that secret fun time was over.

I called Dad and explained what had happened, which was not the most enjoyable conversation of my life, especially when I had to ask him for money so I could buy a ticket home.

"I'll do one better," he said. "I'm coming to get you."

And he did. He went straight to the airport and got on a flight to Edinburgh so fast he actually made it there before I'd even left the hospital.

"Are you angry with me?" I ventured, ten minutes after take-off. He'd barely said three words to me up to that point.

Dad took off his glasses and rubbed his eyes. "No," he said finally. "Surprised. Disappointed, maybe." He blinked a little, then slid his glasses back up his nose before looking directly at me. "And a little proud."

I felt my face jerk in surprise. "Proud?"

"Just a little." I saw a small smile spread on his face before he looked away from me and out of the window at the darkening sky.

I'm staring at the dark ceiling, letting this memory wind its way lazily through my mind, when my heart gives an almighty, sickening lurch.

Tem.

I have forgotten Tem.

I grab for my phone, tapping on to WhatsApp, hearing my panicked breath in my ears. Why did I turn the notifications off? *Why?!* There are seventeen unread messages from her and seven missed calls. Oh God.

Tem:

Why can't I come over?
It's okay if you're with Rhys!
I can come over later ☺ Steeeefffffffffiiiiiiii
Stef?

[Missed call x 3]

Why have you stopped replying? ☹

343

Please call me. I need you.
STEFFI

[Missed call]

My heart is broken. I need my best friend.
Where.
Are.
You.
K I'm starting to get mad now.

[Missed call x 2]

Are you seriously ignoring me for a boy?
FOR GOD'S SAKE STEF I'M CRYING HERE
My heart hurts

[Missed call]

Fine. Have fun with your boyfriend.
I hate you.

My hands are shaking as I send the quickest replies I can.

Steffi:

I'm here. I'm SO sorry. Rhys

344

had an accident, have been in
the hospital. Turned off phone.

I know it's not enough. It's almost ten hours since I stopped replying to her first messages. There's no excuse for ignoring her for that long.

I'm too wired with nerves to wait for her to reply, so I carry on.

I was in Edinburgh. It was a
secret trip for me and Rhys. I
was going to tell you.

I end up sending her five messages in my panic, too full of adrenaline to stop and think about whether or not this is a good idea. Trying to explain myself is suddenly all that's important in the entire world.

It's in the silence after my frantic typing that I realize what I've just done, which is to pour out my guilt with no context or accompanying apology-face. I've made a giant, colossal mistake. I should have apologized briefly but sincerely, then waited until tomorrow morning to go and speak to her in person. Sending her a stream of consciousness ramble is the worst thing I could have done.

I can't take the messages back. They sit there, taunting me, just waiting for Tem's eyes to take them in and narrow in fury.

It's midnight. I'm lying alone in the dark of my bedroom. And I have ruined everything.

28

I'M PREPARED FOR THE FALLOUT TO LAST ALL WEEK.

I try to avoid it for as long as I can, burying myself into my pillow and hoping everyone will think I'm sleeping. But eventually Lucy knocks on my door and pokes her head round.

"Good morning, sunshine," she says. There's a smile in her voice, which surprises me. "Stop hiding."

I poke my head out from under the covers. "Not hiding."

"It looks quite a bit like hiding to me," Lucy says. "I'll make you some breakfast if you get up now. Your dad's at work, and your mother is coming over this evening so we can all have a chat about what happened."

Oh, *great*. Not only do I get to have the "we're so disappointed" speech from three of my parents, I also get an entire day of anticipation.

"Hmph," I mutter.

"Your dad gave Rhys's parents a ring before he left this morning," Lucy adds. I sit up immediately and brush my hair out of my eyes. "He stayed in Edinburgh last night with his brother, and he's getting the train back this morning. In fact"—she glances at her watch—"he's most likely well on the way. So if you wanted to go and see him, go this afternoon. Give his parents a little time to grill him first, though." She smiles at me. "Now. Breakfast?"

I stare at her, a little thrown. To be honest, this isn't what I was expecting. Why is she being so friendly? Is she trying to lull me into a false sense of security? Is she getting me to Rhys's house so they can all ambush us together?

But as worried as I am about that, it's nothing compared to how I feel about seeing Rhys again. I haven't heard a word from him since I last saw him in the hospital—no jackbytes, not even a text. I keep thinking about his grumpy face, how he barely touched me when we said good-bye. What if what happened has ruined things between us? Has he realized that I'm too much of a liability to have around? Panicking in times of turmoil instead of taking control, losing my voice when I'm the one who should speak for us both. Does he think he'd be better off with someone who speaks his language properly? Or, at the very least, someone who can speak for herself?

I want desperately to see my boyfriend. I ache with needing to see him. But what if he doesn't want to be my boyfriend anymore? What do I do then?

And then there's Tem. Tem, who hasn't replied to any of my messages even though I can tell by the blue WhatsApp check marks that she's seen them. Tem, who feels so deeply. Tem, who depends on me. Could I just stay here in bed all day and pretend that none of this is happening? I burrow down into my pillow and seriously consider it. I'm just wondering if I could get food delivered directly to my bedroom if I ordered online and asked very nicely, when something warm, heavy, and furry lands directly on me. A nose snuffles into my ear. I groan. "Get off, Rita."

Rita flops down beside me, head on my pillow, one plaintive eye trained on me.

"Okay, okay." I throw back my covers and she leaps up happily, jumping onto the floor and spinning in a circle.

Maybe I could pretend to myself. I could even pretend to my family. But Rita would never be fooled.

I go to the Gold house sometime after lunch, taking Rita for moral support. She's thrilled by the unusually long walk, happy, as ever, just to be with me. This might sound stupid, but that helps. When I walk down the street, I wrap the leash round my hand, concentrating on the sensation of tightness on my fingers, anchoring myself in the moment to stop myself spiralling.

This is Rhys. It's stupid to be so nervous. But . . . it's *Rhys*.

"Oh." It's his mother who opens the door. "Hello, Stefanie."

God, I didn't even think about being scared of seeing his

mother. She's looking at me like I just trampled her chrysanthe-mums. I have a sudden flash of how she used to check on us in Rhys's room, how we always had to keep the door open. *Ah.* She knows why we were in Edinburgh.

"Hi," I squeak. "Um. Can I see Rhys?"

I half expect her to make some comment about me having seen quite enough of him over the weekend, but she doesn't. She nods, tells me to wait in the garden with Rita, then disap-pears back into the house.

It takes a few minutes for Rhys to come and join me in the garden. He's not using a crutch, which I take to be a good sign. I stand to greet him, my heart already pounding.

I swallow. **Hi.**

His eyes meet mine. **Hi.**

Rhys. There's a cut by his right eye, a sling around his injured arm. His expression isn't angry or disappointed. It's just blank.

We look at each other for a moment, neither of us speaking in any language. I have no idea what to say. I want to ask him if he's angry with me, but I can't bear to hear the answer if it's yes. **Can you sign?** I ask eventually.

He nods and shrugs at the same time. **If I take it slow.**

Another silence. I open with the only thing I can think of. **I'm sorry.**

He frowns. **Why?**

My heart tightens. Is he really so angry with me he's going to make me go through it all? **That you got hurt.**

That wasn't your fault.

For not looking after you.

You did.

I take in his set jaw and feel my own start to quiver. *Don't cry.*

Why didn't you message me? I ask.

I didn't know what to say.

You could have said anything.

You didn't message me, either.

I was waiting for you!

Is this an argument? It's so hard to tell. I don't understand what he means by what he's saying. BSL depends just as much on body language and facial expressions as it does on individual signs, and he's giving me absolutely nothing in this area.

Are you angry with me? A last resort. A pathetic thing to say. But I have to ask.

Now he makes an expression. It's like his whole face crumples. **No, Bronze**, he says. **I'm angry with me.**

I'm startled. **Why?!**

Now he looks angry. **Because I screwed everything up. I ruined our trip. I made you panic. You had to look after me. I'm supposed to look after you.**

I shake my head. I'm about to say that we look after each other, but his hands are already moving again.

I had to depend on you. I don't want to do that.

My heart hurts. **You don't want to depend on me?**

350

No.

Why not? But I know why. Because I'm not strong enough. Because I am the last person who can carry the weight of another. Didn't I prove that on Arthur's Seat? If he has to depend on someone, it needs to be someone better than me.

Because I want to be able to look after you.

You can do that too!

But I didn't. I finally understand what the expression on his face is. Frustration. He's buzzing with it. **I didn't look after you. I just made things harder. I can't take that. It's too hard.**

I can feel tears pressing behind my eyes. "What are you saying?" I ask out loud.

"I don't know," he replies. His unslinged arm drops to his side. "That's the problem."

I don't want to go home. Not yet, anyway.

I take Rita to the park and let her off the leash, watching her fly joyfully across the grass as if her owner isn't currently trying to hold off a breakdown. Rhys and I haven't broken up, but we don't exactly feel together right now, either. I'm so confused by what he said and what he didn't say, what I'm feeling and what I want.

I'm trying to understand what he meant, but I keep coming back to that moment on Arthur's Seat when I had the panic attack. That was right in front of him. He saw me do that. I feel so ashamed of my stupid, weak self that I want to claw my hands into my skin and rip it into pieces. Of course he doesn't want to depend on me. Who would? *I* don't even want to depend on me. I just don't get a choice.

I stop at home to drop Rita off and then head straight back out again. The need to see Tem is suddenly so strong it almost hurts. I decide to get the bus, but when I step up to pay the driver I find my voice has deserted me. God, I'm falling apart. I'd come so far and now I've slunk right back down again.

"Where you going, love?" the driver asks, brusque and impatient, into the awkward silence.

I look at him. *Speak, Steffi. Your voice is yours. This choice is yours.* I could hold up two fingers to indicate that I want a £2 ticket. He will understand this—I know from experience that they always do—but, God, I have to be able to do this.

I focus on a small cut on the corner of his jaw. I imagine this man shaving in front of the mirror, in the home he probably shares with his family, when he is an ordinary person with ordinary worries and not anyone remotely scary.

"Bourne Street," I say, my eyes on the cut. My voice comes out funny, kind of flattened and deep, but I don't care. I have done what I thought was impossible. I have spoken when my voice had disappeared; I have found it again.

I rip out the ticket when it appears and stumble to the nearest free seat, slightly dazed, replaying the moment in my head. I hear myself saying *Bourne Street, Bourne Street, Bourne Street* over and over until the words lose all meaning.

I get off at the Bourne Street bus stop and walk the five minutes to Tem's house, suddenly wishing I had Rita back by my side. My bus confusion has disappeared, replaced by the all-encompassing terror of facing an angry friend.

It's Ebla who answers the door. As soon as she sees me I know that she knows, and I almost turn and run away.

"Ah," she says. "Hello, Steffi." The faint accent that is all that remains from her life before England is always clearer on the syllables of my name. Tem used to say my name that way, back when she was still learning to talk and her entire world was her mother, her father, and me.

"Hi," I say. "I've . . . I've come to see Tem?"

Ebla hesitates and my heart gives an almighty lurch. I am as welcome in this house as I am in both of my own. Tem and I are Steftember. There is no hesitation when it comes to us.

"I don't think . . ." Ebla pauses again. I see her bite her lip. "I don't think Tem really wants to see you."

My voice comes out in a high-pitched, garbled mess. "Oh God, it's not—I'm here to—I tried to—I got the bus here and I need to see her and she does want to see me."

Ebla blinks.

I swallow. "Please can I see her?" I say. "Please."

She lets me in, of course. When I get upstairs, Tem's door is closed and for a moment I actually stand outside it, trying to figure out what to do. I can't remember ever seeing Tem's door closed. At least, not without me on the right side of it.

353

So I do the thing that simultaneously makes sense and no sense at all. I knock.

I'm greeted with this: a pajama-clad September, hair wild and free, face scowling. She stares at me for a moment, saying nothing.

"Hi," I squeak.

She doesn't reply. Her eyes flicker from my face to my shoes and back again.

"Can we . . . can I come in? Can we talk?"

Tem's eyes narrow further. She doesn't reply but steps aside so I can walk into her bedroom. It's messier than usual, the bed-covers crumpled and strewn, clothes scattered over the floor.

"Are you sorting?" I ask inanely.

Silence. Oh God. Is this what it's like for other people, when they try to talk to me?

"I like this top," I say, poking a long-sleeved dragonfly shirt with my foot. "Don't get rid of this one."

"I'm not sorting my clothes," Tem says, her voice low, more like a growl than anything else.

"Okay," I say. "Do you want me to help you tidy up?" When she says nothing, I start picking up clothes. "Is this knitted thing machine-washable?"

"For God's sake!" Tem explodes. "Just say you're sorry!"

I freeze, an inside-out T-shirt that I'd been about to pull the right way around dangling from my fingertips.

"Say, I'm sorry, September," Tem continues, her eyes fierce

and blazing. She advances on me. "Say, I'm so sorry I ignored you, Tem. So sorry I waited *ten freaking hours* before replying to your *very frantic* messages. So sorry I wasn't there when you needed me. So sorry I turned into the most *boring cliché ever* and chose my boyfriend over you at the first opportunity."

She is standing right in front of me now, her face inches from mine. Tem is utterly fearless, and it's one of the things I love most about her, but now that it's turned on me I'm cowed rather than impressed. And very guilty.

"So?" she prompts.

"I'm sorry," I mumble.

"What?"

"I'm sorry!" It comes out like a shout.

"Good!" she shouts back. "You *should* be sorry! Ten hours, Stef. I was waiting for you."

"Rhys had an—"

"Accident, yeah. I read your messages. A couple of broken bones, right? That sucks, but it doesn't take ten hours, and it's not a reason to ignore me. And that's not even starting on you being in freaking *Edinburgh* and not telling me. Why wouldn't you tell me that? *Why?*" Her expression has moved from anger to bafflement. On balance, it's preferable, but it doesn't make me feel any less guilty.

"I don't have to tell you everything," I say, and immediately regret it. Her face crumples, right in on itself, tissuelike and surprisingly fragile.

"But you *do* tell me everything," she says, and her voice is all crackly, and my heart is pounding guiltily and anxiously, and my head is still going *RhysRhysRhysRhys*, and I just don't know what to say.

"I'm *sorry*," I say again, because what else can I say? "You know I would have been here if I could. I'm always there for you. Always."

She lets out a noise that is half snort, half laugh. "Sure, Stef. Always. Always, because you don't have anywhere else to be."

Her words sock me right in the stomach. I'm almost winded. "That's . . ." My voice dies. *That's not fair*, I want to say. *That's not true.*

"I know you think I take you for granted, because I'm the sociable one or whatever, but I don't. It's you—*you* take *me* for granted. And I don't like it."

I lick my lips, then swallow, playing for time. *Speak, Steffi. Speak, speak, speak. Defend yourself.* "I . . ." I begin, and my voice is shaky, but it's there. "I let you down once." I squeeze my hands into fists at my sides, trying to anchor myself. *"Once."*

Tem looks at me for a long moment, the silence stretching between us, then seems to make a decision. "Oh yeah?" she says, finally. "How are things with me and Karam?"

The question throws me. "Uh," I say. This must be a trick question, right? This is clearly linked to whatever she was upset about. "Not . . . good?"

Her eyes blaze. "No. Not good."

I wait for more. When she offers nothing, I say, tentatively, "I thought things were going so great for you both."

"Well, they weren't," she snaps.

"What went wrong?"

"Nothing went wrong, it was just never right," she says. "And you'd know that if you'd ever asked."

My heart drops. "What?"

"You could have asked me, Stef," she says. Her face is tense. "How's it going with Karam, Tem? Hey, how's you and Karam?"

"I just . . . I just thought it was going well. . . ."

"So what? You thought that was boring or something? You should have wanted to hear about it if it was going well or not."

"That's not fair," I protest, but weakly, because I'm worried she's got a point. "I always listen when you talk about boys you like."

"No, you don't," she says bluntly. "You think you know what I'm going to say, so you don't listen. God, Steffi, just because I talk more than you, that doesn't mean the extra words don't mean anything."

"I know that! You know I know that!"

"Do you? Then where were you? Why didn't you find out why I wanted to talk to you? It was important, and I needed you, and you weren't there." Her hands have clenched into tight little fists, the strained skin around her joints turning white.

Tem and I have never been the fighting kind. Not since we were kids, when it was clear that she was capable of walking all over me if she wanted to, so we both made a kind of unspoken agreement to not get ourselves into the kind of situation where that could happen. Plus, we've never really had anything to argue about. I'm too grateful for her to get mad at her, and I'm too easygoing and pliable for her to get mad at me.

At least, that's what I thought. But maybe I just never gave her a reason before.

"I'm here now," I say. "So why don't you tell me?"

"Because I don't want to tell you now," Tem says.

A wave of frustration is starting to build in my stomach. I can feel it burning up into my throat. "For God's sake, Tem," I say, even though I know it won't help the situation, because I can't help myself.

"Oh for God's sake yourself," she snaps. "Look, why don't you just go? I'm sure Rhys needs you, or something."

I think of the way Rhys looked at me on his doorstep. Like I'm the last person in the world he needs.

"Tem," I try. My voice is all thin and pathetic. I open my mouth to tell her this, to tell her that Rhys and I might have broken up, that I might have ruined everything. But her face has closed, and even though Tem is standing right there, my best friend has gone.

"Go," she says again. Her voice is hard.

So I do.

29

I WALK HOME IN TEARS.

I should really get the bus, but I can't bear the thought of having to speak to anyone, even—especially—strangers/bus drivers. It takes me forty-five minutes to get from Tem's house to my dad's house, but even in that time I'm not done crying, so I circle back round, looping through the streets until I'm done.

I could say I don't understand what happened or where I went wrong, but that wouldn't really be true, would it? I do know. I came out of my comfort zone and it was just as uncomfortable as I'd always known it would be. This is what happens when you come out of your shell. You get rocks thrown at you by the universe. I tried to be brave and bold, but fortune didn't favor me—it laughed in my face. It waved a boyfriend in front of me then snatched him away, taking my best friend as an extra-mean bonus.

I should never have tried to prove myself this year. I should have just stayed how I was. Being quiet isn't the worst thing in the world. It might not make my life exciting, but at least it makes it less scary.

Except, that's not quite true either, is it? I still found everything scary. Oh God, what's the point in anything? Why do I even bother?

I kick a pebble off the curb and watch it skitter across the road. I'm all cried out and now I just feel desolate. If I can't even handle something as ordinary as a trip away with my boyfriend, how am I ever going to manage a huge life change like university? Maybe my parents have been right all along. Maybe it really is too much for me.

I shove my hands into my pockets and take the turn onto my dad's street. I see almost immediately that Mum is already there from the sight of her car parked outside. When I let myself into the house, I can hear her clattering around the kitchen—she tends to do this when she visits my dad's house, as if her mind regresses to the point when they were living together—while she lets out random exclamations of . . . what? Shock? Anger? I can't tell from the hall.

But when I walk into the kitchen, I'm faced not with shock or anger. Instead, Mum is all smiles, sitting across the table from Dad, her hands around a steaming mug.

"Oh, there you are," she says. "We were just talking about you." Her smile fades a little when she sees my face. "Oh, love. Have you been crying?"

I pause in the doorway, confused. Where's the outburst of rage and disappointment? I shake my head at the question, even though I clearly have been crying, and hover in the doorway, trying to think of what to say.

"Come and sit down," Dad says. He points to a cup of tea. "That's for you. Excellent timing—your mother just made it, so it's hot." I sink into the chair and look from Mum to Dad to Lucy, who is sitting beside Dad, searching for clues. "You're not . . ." I hesitate, then say it anyway. "Mad?"

They all laugh. "No," Mum says. "We're not mad."

"We tried to be," Dad says.

"We tried really hard," Mum agrees. They look at each other and start to laugh again.

I'm so confused.

"Do you want us to be angry?" Mum continues. She looks amused. "Was that what you were hoping for?"

I frown. "What's that supposed to mean?"

"A big, bold gesture?" Mum offers, raising her eyebrows. She's still smiling. "Weren't you trying to prove something to us?"

Well, yes. "Of course not!" I can't quite think of how to follow this, so I take a glug of tea instead. No one says anything, so finally I add, "You're not upset that I lied?"

"Yes, I am upset that you lied," Mum allows with a slow nod. "But, love . . . you could have lied about hitchhiking to a drug-crazed rave in a field in Scotland. You could have lied about eloping to Amsterdam."

"Or cooking meth," Lucy adds.

"Or covering up a murder," Dad says.

"Or planning one!" Mum says.

They're *enjoying* this, aren't they?

"What we're saying," Dad says, seeing my face and smiling gently, "is that we know that teenagers lie to their parents all the time."

"And the fact that you did it in order to go to spend a weekend in Edinburgh with your lovely and trustworthy boyfriend . . ." Mum's mouth twitches. "Well, that's quite sweet, really. If this is you being bad . . . I think that's quite good."

I'm not sure how to take all of this. On one hand—yay! I'm not in trouble! On the other—this is quite patronizing and offensive, isn't it? Aren't they basically calling me a sad excuse for a teenager?

"I think I'd rather you were angry," I say, frowning.

"You still should have told us," Lucy says and, despite the conversation, part of my mind registers how she includes herself so naturally in the "us."

"You're not *that* off the hook."

"I thought you wouldn't let me go," I say.

"Why wouldn't we?" Dad asks, confused. "The two of you are seventeen and eighteen. Of course you can go away for the weekend if you want to. Why wouldn't you?"

"Mum said she didn't think I could go away without support," I say.

"*Oh.*" Mum's face clears. "That's what this is about." She closes her eyes for a moment and rubs her forehead. "Steffi, that was just concern. It wasn't an order. It wasn't me trying to restrict you."

"Sounded like it," I mumble grumpily.

"Why *didn't* you tell anyone?" Lucy asks gently. "Is it just because you thought we'd stop you?"

I shrug. "We wanted it to be ours."

"It would have been," Mum says, "but you still could have left a note."

"I was going to call you from there," I say. "After we'd met up with his brother. We just wanted some time alone first."

"If you were going to call while you were there, why not tell us before you went?" Mum asks.

"This is going round in circles," Dad says. "Who wants some more tea?"

"I wanted to surprise you," I say. "I wanted to show you that I could do it without support, okay?"

"Well, you succeeded," Mum says.

"No, I didn't." Here we go: my voice cracks and tears spring to my eyes. "I completely failed, actually."

There's a pause. I keep my eyes on the tablecloth, but I know they're all looking at each other.

"What do you mean?" It's Lucy who asks. "Why do you think you failed?"

"I messed everything up," I say. So much for being out of tears. "I couldn't help Rhys. And Tem's mad at me."

Mum gets up from her seat and comes to sit beside me, putting her hand on my back and rubbing gently. "What makes you say that you couldn't help Rhys?" she asks. "It sounds like you *did* help him. You went to get help, and you got him down from that hill. That's what help is, love."

I shake my head. Tears start sliding down my cheeks. "I had a panic attack. I was all by myself and I freaked out. You were right. I can't look after myself."

"It must have been frightening," Lucy says softly. "Rhys being hurt like that, and it just being the two of you."

"What happened after the panic attack?" Dad asks.

I take a deep breath, trying to swallow back more tears. "Well, I had to go and find someone. And there was a woman with her dog nearby, so I got her."

"You got her?" Mum repeats. "You went to speak to her?"

I nod. "She came to help us."

"You spoke to her?" Mum says again.

"Yeah. Sort of. I kind of gabbled a bit. But she was so nice. And she went and got another man to help us because we couldn't get Rhys down by ourselves. And Connie—that's the woman—took us to the hospital and then left. And all the nurses and doctors and stuff were just, like, ignoring Rhys and just talking to me. And he was really grumpy and all cross because he couldn't communicate. And then I had to call his brother because I knew I had to, because I couldn't look after us."

I look up to see that they're all staring at me.

"You spoke to this woman—Connie—" Dad says carefully. "And then, this other man . . . did you speak to him?"

I nod. "Stuart. He was a doctor and a bit smug, but he really helped."

"And then you spoke at the hospital? And called Rhys's brother?"

I nod again. "I was all shaky and I just . . . I just wanted to run away. It was pathetic."

"Steffi," Mum says. It sounds like she's struggling not to laugh, but when I look at her I see there are tears in her eyes. "Steffi. Can't you hear everything you're saying? Don't you see what you did?"

I shake my head. "I couldn't handle it."

"But you did handle it," Lucy says. "You spoke to all those people, Steffi. You found it hard, yes, but you still did it. That's all anyone can ask of anyone else."

"You even used the phone," Mum says, squeezing my hand. "Oh, Steffi. I'm so, so proud."

"But I had a panic attack," I say. "Right there. In front of Rhys."

"And then you got up and went to get help," Dad says.

"I wanted to run away," I say again.

"But you didn't," Mum says.

"I upset Tem," I say, abruptly changing tack as I remember the other thing I had to cry about. "She's mad at me."

"So?" Mum says, so frankly I actually smile.

"She's not speaking to me anymore."

Dad gets up and starts bustling with the kettle, filling it under the tap and then putting it on to boil. He starts gathering mugs, asking a quiet, "Tea? Tea?" to each of us.

"I give that a day, at most," Mum says. "Friends fight, Steffi. Even best ones."

"Especially best ones," Lucy puts in, smiling.

"I let her down," I say. "I lied to her."

"So tell her you're sorry and let her be angry for a while," Mum says. "Storms pass, love. They always pass."

Lucy nods and the two of them smile encouragingly, but also slightly condescendingly, at me from across the table. "If you've done something wrong, often the best thing to do is let her be angry for a while," Lucy says.

"She told me to leave," I say.

"I don't imagine she meant forever," Mum says, her mouth twitching. "Tem can be very stormy herself, but she loves you, Steffi. Being angry for a while won't change that."

Dad passes around fresh cups of tea and then sits down again. "I think it's a good sign if you've had a bit of a falling out," he says. "Mistakes are an unfortunate side effect of actually doing things, but they're usually worth it in the end."

I look at the three of them, all patient and pleased with themselves. I can't quite get my head round the fact that they seem proud of me for screwing up.

"Why are you being so nice to me? This is what you always said. That me and Rhys weren't good for each other. That not being able to communicate would lead to trouble. Well, it did."

"That's not what we said," Dad says, frowning. "Or, at least—" he gives Mum a look—"*I* didn't. It was never about 'trouble.' I was worried that you might come to rely too much on Rhys, yes, that's true. I was worried you wouldn't try to push yourself. But I was clearly worried about nothing. When you had to, you did, Steffi. That's incredibly reassuring to hear, as your dad."

"It is?"

"Of course it is. We worry because we love you. We know you find the world quite hard, and we know we can't make it easier for you, or make decisions for you. But you're growing up and you're learning how to navigate it in your own way. That's fantastic."

"Is it?"

"Yes!"

I look at the three of them in turn, trying to believe them. But I'm so used to feeling like I'm disappointing them that I'm not quite sure what to do with this level of support.

"I want to go to university," I say, surprising myself as much as all of them. "You're right—you can't make decisions for me. But that's what you're trying to do with university."

"This is quite a tangent—" Mum starts to say, but I interrupt, my voice suddenly strong.

"No, it's not." Out of the corner of my eye, I swear I see Lucy smile. "It's all the same thing. If you want me to be more confident, you have to let me learn how. So I'm not going to try to prove anything to you anymore." My heart is starting to pound, but it's with energy now instead of anxiety. To be honest, it feels pretty much the same. "Me going to university has nothing to do with you letting me go or not. It's my choice."

There's a long silence. Finally, Dad says, "We worry because we love you."

"I know." I think I really do know, now. "And I love you too." I swallow. "So, can I go?"

They all look at each other. Dad takes a sip of tea and then puts the cup back down, a wry smile on his face. "Now, Steffi," he says. "I don't think that's up to us, is it?"

I eat dinner and go to my bedroom early, tired of the world and everyone in it. I get into bed fully clothed and curl up with my phone, opening my inbox to check my emails so I can do something mind-numbing like delete spam or look at luxury holidays in far-off countries I won't ever visit.

But what I see is the opposite of mind-numbing. An email from Rhys. He's never emailed me before. The subject line is "You and me." I hesitate, my finger hovering over it. Do I want to read it? I can guess what it will be. We're over, aren't we? He can't see a future for us. Do I really want to read that before I go to sleep?

No, but I don't have much of a choice now. If I don't read it, I'll never sleep.

From: Rhys
To: Steffi
Subject: You and me

Steffi,

I'm sorry about earlier. That's not how I wanted it all to go. There's so much I wanted to say, but I couldn't. It would all come out wrong. And I can't talk properly right now. But I want to try to explain myself, because this is important, and I need to know you understand.

Stef, I love you. You know I love you. I'm sorry I couldn't give you the perfect weekend away. I'm sorry I ruined it. Everything was going so great, wasn't it? And then I did the worst thing I could ever do to you.

You did an amazing job taking care of me. Thank you. I'm sorry I didn't say that at the time—it was all just so monumentally crap, and I was so mad at myself, and I couldn't talk properly anyway. That's a shitty excuse. I'm sorry about that too.

God, there's so much I want to say and even now I can't say it.

Stef, are our parents right? Maybe we really are too different. Do we have a future together? If I can't even give you a weekend in Scotland, how can I give you all the things I want to?

Be honest with me. I can take it. Tell me if you want better than me. I'll understand.

Love,
Rhys xxx

I tap out a hundred different replies. I call him an idiot. I tell him I love him. I tell him I don't give the tiniest of fucks about how well he can or can't hear or whether he can take care of me. I tell him that's boy bullshit. I tell him my communication problems are way worse than his anyway, and he's being a self-involved twat. I remind him that he slipped on a rock—it's not like he stabbed me in the neck or pushed me off a cliff. I tell him that maybe we're not right together at all.

And then I delete every attempt and send him one line.

Meet me tomorrow at St. Swithun's Church. 1:30 p.m.

And then I go to sleep.

30

THE NEXT DAY, THE FIRST THING I DO IS GO TO SEE
Tem. This time, it's her that opens the front door, and she's clearly not expecting to see me.

"Oh," she says.

I know why she's surprised. I am not the kind of person to actively seek potential conflict. What I'd usually do in this scenario is send multiple apology texts and wait at home until she decides to come and talk to me. But, no, here I am.

"I'm sorry," I say. It seems like the sensible thing to open with this time.

Tem blinks at me. She looks torn, as if she might be angry but can't quite decide if she can be bothered to work up the energy.

"You lied to me," she says eventually. "You *lied*."

"So very sorry."

"To *me*!"

I hold out the bouquet of carnations I've brought with me. I had planned to get something more impressive, but it turns out flowers are expensive, so I'd just picked the nicest ones I could afford. "Extremely and inexpressibly sorry."

She reaches out and pokes my shoulder. "Frogspawn."

"Very sorry frogspawn," I say. I wave the flowers. "Frogspawn with flowers."

Tem reaches out and takes the flowers in one disagreeable grab. "I can't forgive you until you tell me why you did it," she says. "Why didn't you tell me about Edinburgh?"

"Because . . ." I suddenly can't think of a single reason why. "Because I'm frogspawn."

A reluctant smile flickers on her face, but she bites it back. "Okay, you can come in," she says, stepping back.

Victory.

We go up to her bedroom, which is looking far tidier than yesterday, and sit on her bed. "It was a stupid secret couple thing," I say. "You know how sometimes you keep things a secret because it's more exciting?"

"I didn't know *you* did that," Tem says. "And you're not meant to keep secrets from the best friend. I'm meant to be like the alibi!"

"I tell you most things," I say. I have no idea why I'm pushing this instead of just apologizing for the omission and promising never to keep her in the dark again. But somehow I find myself talking, spilling thoughts I hadn't even known I had. "But I can keep some things to myself, right? A lot's changed this year. Sixth form and stuff."

"Because of Rhys?"

"Well, yeah, but not just because of him." I take a deep breath, then bite down on my lip. "Look, there's something I haven't told you, but don't freak out, okay?"

She looks worried. "Oh God, what?"

"I've been taking medication," I say in a rush. "Since last summer. For my anxiety."

Her eyes go wide in an instant. "Oh my God!" she lets out in a burst. I've genuinely shocked her. "Are you kidding?"

I shake my head.

"Steffi!" Her mouth is hanging open. "Wow . . ."

"I know," I say.

"That really explains a lot."

"Does it?" I realize how desperately I want her view on this. On me.

"Yeah. I mean, I guess I'd put it down to you going to sixth form and getting a boyfriend."

"Put what down to that?"

"Just . . . you. You being more confident and—no, not confident, exactly. Like, more comfortable? Does that make sense? Talking more and doing more things."

"I don't think it's just because of the meds," I say. "They help, but they're not everything. Going to sixth form without you and getting together with Rhys have a lot to do with it too. It's all the things working together."

She nods. "Why didn't you tell me, though?" There's a sudden sadness in her face. "Didn't you want to?"

"I did, but . . . I also didn't. I didn't want you to be . . . *looking* for it, you know? Like, if you saw me talking more, I didn't want you to immediately be, like, 'Oh, Steffi, the meds are working!' You know?"

She lifts her shoulders. "I guess. Still feels huge, though. Does it for you?"

"It did. Not so much anymore, though. I'm used to it now. Anyway, what did you want to talk to *me* about?" I ask. I pull my legs up under me and cross them. "I am all ears. You have my attention. Undivided and . . . attentive."

"Oh, that," Tem says. She looks away from me, picks up her toy lemur, and starts walking him across her pillow. "I've calmed down a bit now."

"Well, if you want to get worked up again, that's fine too."

She smiles. "Don't encourage me. Unless you want me to start yelling at you again?"

"Nah, you're all right, thanks." There's a pause. I watch Tem lean back against the wall, her eyes not meeting mine. "So what happened?" I ask gently.

"Karam," she says simply. "Karam happened."

I make a face. "Oh dear. What did he do?"

"Oh, just . . ." She gives a careless shrug. "Just got a girlfriend, you know. A girlfriend who isn't me."

"Oh, Tem," I say, agonized for her. I get up and move over to her, reaching out my arms to pull her in for a hug. "I'm sorry. How did you find out?"

"He told me. Said she wanted to make it Facebook official, so he wanted me to know first."

I hesitate. "Well, I guess that's nice of him."

"He must have been seeing her for ages," she says, ignoring this comment. "I don't even know how long. I can't believe he was stringing me along. That's such a cliché dick move. He hasn't just dicked me over, he's *clichéd* dicked me over. I feel so stupid."

"You're not stupid."

"Oh no, I am. I really, really am." She takes a breath. I see her press her lips together. "I mean . . . really stupid, Stef. Really. Stupid."

My heart rate starts to pick up. Is she saying . . . "Tem," I say, like she's standing on a ledge. "Tem . . . you haven't . . . you didn't . . . sleep with him?"

She doesn't say anything. Her eyes flicker up to me and the answer is in them.

"Tem," I say again. I'm so shocked I don't even know what to do with my face. "When?"

She says something, but it's too quiet for me to hear.

"What?" I ask.

"New Year," she says.

Oh. That's a long time ago. A lot of lies by omission.

"And . . . well, and quite a few times. Since, I mean."

My fingers feel all tingly.

"Oh," I say in a very small voice. What am I supposed to say to this? Am I angry? A little. Sad? Yes. But I don't understand anything I'm feeling or what I should say. I manage, "I think you owe me some carnations."

Tem looks up and our eyes meet. There's a moment of silence that feels taut as a tightrope, the two of us hovering between okay and not okay. There's so much between us that we could fight about. A decision that feels almost tangible: mountain or molehill?

And then we're laughing so hard the bed creaks. There are tears on Tem's face. She leans over and picks up the carnations she'd put on her desk, then ostentatiously hands them to me. I take a big, overstated sniff, then hand them back.

We stay like that for a while, passing carnations back and forth and hiccupping, until we calm down. And then, finally, we talk. I tell her about Edinburgh and Rhys and sex—at which point she shrieks so loudly it actually hurts my ears—and how perfect it all was until he fell over his own feet. She tells me about Karam, how she'd believed all his reasons for not wanting a girlfriend but still thought that he'd change his mind. How New Year had seemed so perfect—"It *was* perfect"—until the morning after, when she'd asked him—"in *bed*!"—if he'd be her boyfriend, and he'd said no.

We talk, at length, about sex. She says that the only good

376

thing she has to say about Karam is that he made her first time nice—"Not orgasm-nice, but . . . you know. Nice."—and that the times since had never been anything but good. That she really hadn't regretted it until he'd told her about the girlfriend.

"I was saving it," she says, her brow scrunched. "I was meant to be saving it."

I think hard about the best thing to say to this. "What were you saving it for?" I ask finally.

She gives me a funny look. "Marriage?"

"Okay, yes, but why?"

"Because I wanted it to be special."

"Don't you think the marriage bit is the bit that will be special?" I see her pause.

"Well. Yes, I guess."

"I don't see why the state of your hymen has anything to do with how special it will be."

She snorts out a laugh. "I guess I always kind of thought I was saving it for him. Whoever my husband will be, I mean."

"Well, you weren't," I say robustly. "You were saving it for *you*. And *you* decided when, and *you* said it was nice. That's more than a lot of people get. You still made the choice."

Tem looks at me, her head slightly tilted, eyes squinting a little. "Oh my *God*," she says, surprising me. "I'm lucky to have you."

I laugh. "Obviously."

She presses her hands into the bed and lifts herself slightly so she's leaning against me. "I know that was probably best-friend-bullshit, but it actually helps."

"Good, that's what I'm here for."

"Helpful bullshit?"

"Any day of the week."

I go home for lunch and then set off for the church with Rita. I end up getting there not long after one o'clock. It's a cool day, but not so cold that I mind waiting on the bench outside the church and listening to the silence by myself.

I'm not religious, but I like churches. I like how I feel when I'm in and around them, like I'm standing in the past. I even like St. Swithun's, however sad its connotations are for me now.

Rhys arrives early too. He spots me from some distance away and waves automatically. I wave back and let Rita bound ahead of me to greet him. When he comes to sit next to me, I can see that some, if not all, of the frustrated tension has left him. His shoulders are looser and his face has lifted.

I lean over and kiss his cheek, allowing myself a second to rest my head against his shoulder and breathe him in.

Nice church, Rhys says when I lift my head back up. I smile.

Yeah, it's okay, isn't it?

We look at each other. I can see his eyes scanning my face, searching for clues.

I want to show you something, I say, standing. **Come on.**

We walk through the churchyard together, following the

path round to the back of the church. **Is it okay for her to be in here?** Rhys asks nervously, pointing at Rita.

I nod. **We've been here lots of times.** This isn't quite true—I haven't been here for ages, let alone with Rita. But still.

My heart is starting to pound harder as I lead us off the path and toward the newer section of the graveyard. The gravestones become less and less shabby. The flowers get fresher. We pass photos not yet faded by the sun.

Rita gets there first. She sits down next to the grave, my well-trained, beautiful dog, and turns her head to look at me.

"Good girl," I murmur. Her tail thumps.

I feel Rhys's hand take hold of mine and squeeze. I look at him.

"This is Clark," I say. I drop Rhys's hand and take the pansies I'd collected from Lucy's garden, sinking to my knees on the grass to rest them by the gravestone. "Hey," I whisper. "It's me."

Rhys puts a hand on my shoulder and eases himself down to sit beside me, settling his sling against his chest.

"There's a lot I want to say," I begin. I sign as I talk, taking things slow so I can get both right. "And I felt like I wanted to come here to do it."

He nods, but I can tell he doesn't understand.

"Your email annoyed me," I say. "But after I stopped being annoyed I thought a lot. And I think we have the same problem."

Rhys's eyebrows lift a little. **You do?**

Yes. "I mean, we look like we have different problems.

Really simply, you can't hear and I can't speak. But it causes the same thing, and that's that we don't talk to each other." I gesture to the gravestone and the small picture of Clark still leaning against it, curling a little at the edges. It was taken on his eighteenth birthday and he's grinning that wide, unself-conscious Clark-grin that I miss so much. "Clark was a big talker. He wasn't into keeping secrets or not saying how he felt. I used to find it annoying." I find myself smiling a little. "That's why I wanted to meet you here. Just to have a bit of a memory of that."

As I talk, I watch Rhys's face. His eyes are slightly squinted, all of his concentration on my face and my lips, reading what I am saying to him. **Am I talking too fast?** I ask.

A smile creases his face and he shakes his head. **No**, he signs. **It's perfect.**

"Okay, great. So. I forgot what I was saying." We look at each other for a moment, and then out of nowhere we're both laughing.

Clark liked to talk, Rhys prompts.

"Oh, right. Yeah. So I was thinking about Clark, and how he used to tell me that it was okay if I wasn't a big talker like him. And that made me think about how I haven't really talked about him much with you, and why that is, and how my parents don't really like to talk about him much, and how that's because it's hard, and painful, still. And all *that* made me think about talking in general, and how there are actually loads of different reasons why someone might not talk.

"Like, me not talking about Clark much to you isn't the same as me not talking to the receptionist at the Edinburgh hotel. And you not talking on Arthur's Seat isn't the same as either of those things." I can see I've confused him, but I carry on. "I think I've been thinking of them all as the same thing. Because talking or not talking is such a big part of my life. Or it was, until you. But now I see the differences. So you see—our problems don't make us different, they make us the same. It's all about communication."

So . . . we're the same because we can't communicate?

"Because we *can*," I insist. "Just differently. And so long as we know that about each other it's not a problem. Rhys, all relationships have barriers. All people have problems. These are just ours. What if you could hear but you couldn't walk? Or if I wasn't anxious but I had . . . I don't know . . . chronic asthma? Imagine us trying to climb Arthur's Seat like that! Do you see what I'm saying?"

He laughs. **Yes, I literally see what you're saying.** He points from my face to his eyes and grins hopefully at me.

"You don't have to depend on me," I say. "And I don't have to depend on you. But we can still lean on each other when we need to. That's still okay." I have never spoken this much in one go in my entire life. My mouth actually feels dry from talking. But there's still more. "It's not up to you to make my world smaller or bigger," I say. "That's up to me. But I want you to be in it. And I want to be in yours." I reach out and touch his hand. "Is that what you want too?"

Rhys takes my hand, lifts it to his lips, and kisses my fingers. He releases it to speak. **Yes. That's what I want. But I'm worried.**

Worried about what?

That I'll let you down.

Why?

He doesn't answer, just shakes his head a little.

"No," I say, signing as I go. "No, don't just clam up on me. Tell me what you're thinking." I realize in this instant that this is exactly what my therapist meant when she told me about dialogue being a two-way street. "I can't read your mind, Rhys. You need to tell me."

You need someone who can look after you, he begins.

I stop him, one hand up. "No. That's not true. I have my own problems, but they're not for you to fix. Just like I'm not here to fix you being deaf. That would be stupid. So don't make this about that. If you think you need to take care of me, that's on you, not me."

My God, my therapist would be so proud of me right now. I should have brought a Dictaphone.

"Try again," I say. "This time without the 'need' bit."

He smiles a little. **Okay. You want me to be honest. I'm scared to be honest.**

Why?

382

Because I might say something you don't want to hear.

I almost laugh. **Story of my life, Gold. Story of my selective mutism.**

A lot of the time I don't say what I'm thinking, he admits. **It's really easy not to, because I get to think about everything before I say it. And so I just . . .** he hesitates. **It's like I censor myself. I don't say the bad stuff.**

I think about this. I try to remember a time Rhys said a single bad thing about anyone, or to me. Has he ever told me he's annoyed with me? Or anyone? No. Did I think that, just because he never said it, he didn't feel it?

But most of all I'm thinking about how it could be *me* saying all this. We really do share the same problem.

And so when things get really bad, like they did in Scotland, it's like there's so much to say I can't say anything. I feel like I can't talk at all.

And then you get grumpy, I say, nodding. **Grumpy like other people get when they're hungry.**

He laughs. **Is that what it's like?**

I nod. "Totally."

Well, that's no good, is it?

Maybe you just need practice, I say, chancing a smile. **Maybe we both do.**

Maybe. His eyes meet mine and he smiles. **Maybe we can practice together.**

I smile back. **Maybe we can.** I take another breath. **You**

383

can say anything to me. **Even the bad stuff. It doesn't matter how you tell me. Sign it, or write it down, or say it out loud. I'm here for all of it.**

Sometimes, he signs, then stops. He makes a face.

Go on, I urge. **Tell me.**

He bites his lip. **Sometimes I don't feel strong enough for this world.**

"Oh God," I say, smiling. **Neither do I. But we can be soft together. Anyway, soft is more . . .** "huggable."

He grins. **You are very . . .** "huggable." **Among other things.**

I like that. Among other things. I can be more than one thing.

Sometimes I feel like I'm in two worlds, he continues. **The hearing world and the Deaf world. But I'm not sure which one I belong in.**

Does that bother you a lot?

Sometimes, yeah.

Maybe you're still figuring it out, I say. **And maybe that's okay? So long as there's room for me?**

A smile, wide and genuine, blooms on his face. **I'm sure I can make room for you. If you'll have me.**

I lift myself up and move toward him and he opens his arms to me, pulling me in for a hug. I settle against him, curling my head against his chest, closing my eyes. No one needs to be able to hear or speak to hug. We could be any couple, with any problems, making up after a fight about anything.

Maybe we won't be together forever. Maybe we won't even make it to next year. And, if that happens, maybe it'll be because of these problems or new problems we haven't even imagined yet. But I love him, and he loves me.

And that, among other things, is enough.

Author's Note

If, like Steffi, you're struggling with a form of anxiety, you're not alone. Understanding and awareness are getting better every year, and there is help available. You are not making it up, or overreacting, or making a fuss out of nothing. You deserve to feel confident and safe and happy. If you think you might have anxiety, speak to your doctor or try a service like the Anxiety and Depression Association of America (adaa.org) for help and advice.

You can find more information, support, and advice about selective mutism specifically at the SMart Center (selectivemutismcenter.org).

A Quiet Kind of Thunder is set in the UK, which is why the form of sign language that is used between Rhys and Steffi is British Sign Language (BSL) rather than American Sign Language (ASL). You'll notice that throughout the book, the word "deaf" is spelled either with a capital *D* or a lowercase *d*.

In very simple terms, "deaf" is used to signify the physical condition of hearing loss, while "Deaf" is used in relation to Deaf culture, identity, and community. However, the linguistic use of "deaf" versus "Deaf" is an ongoing and complex conversation within the Deaf community that deserves far more space and insight than I can give here. I encourage you to visit the National Association of the Deaf website (www.nad.org) for more information and resources.

If you'd like to find out more about BSL or ASL, or perhaps even learn it yourself, there are plenty of online and in-person courses available, offering accredited qualifications from beginner level through expert.

BSL and ASL are fascinating and beautiful visual languages, with their own grammar structure and syntax. I've tried to represent BSL as accurately and authentically as possible, but if there are any errors in the descriptions of certain signs, they're my fault, and I'm very sorry!

Even if you have just a passing interest in sign language, I urge you to watch some ASL or BSL songs on YouTube—they are *amazing*.

Acknowledgments

First and foremost, thanks, as ever, to Claire Wilson, best agent and excellent human, and everyone at RCW.

Thank you to Liesa Abrams and all at Simon Pulse in the United States for championing my little British book with such enthusiasm.

And thank you to . . .

Rachael Veazey and Claire Sloan, who gave their insight and expertise on Deaf culture and BSL with generosity, patience, and warmth.

The amazing UKYA community for your unfailing encouragement, enthusiasm, and support. You all know who you are, but a special shout out to Katie, George, Lucy, Arianne, Non, Holly, Lexi, Christie, Anna, Lauren, Harriet, Eleanor, Cat, and anyone else I've inevitably missed. Sharing this with all of you is an absolute joy.

Holly Bourne, for being the kind of writer-buddy who understands that the process is 40 percent tea, 40 percent cake, and 20 percent actual writing.

Mel Salisbury, for so many things, but especially for all the handy puns. Those handy, handy puns.

My lovely family, especially Dad, who taught me that "quieter people make the most noise."

Lora, my template for everything a best friend can be.

And finally, Tom—thank you for sharing this love story with me.

Read on for a glimpse at a powerful novel from Sara Barnard about the drastic fallout that comes from the pressure to be perfect.

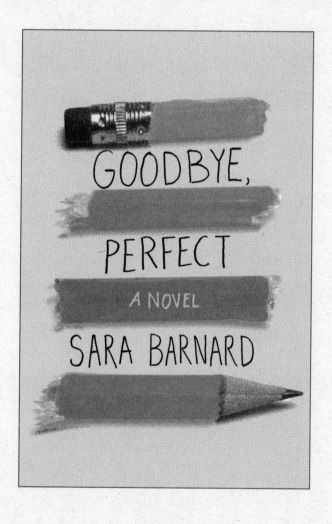

THE POLICE ARRIVE WHEN I'M IN THE SHOWER.

I don't realize straight away, of course, because when I shower on a Saturday afternoon I make the most of it. So around the time they're walking over our threshold, I'm covered in a tea-tree-and-minty lather, eyes closed against the bubbles, singing a medley from *The Lion King* at the top of my voice.

The singing might be why I don't hear my adoptive mother, Carolyn, knocking on the bathroom door. And *that* might be why she chooses to break the most sacred of McKinley household rules: she walks right in and bangs her fist on the glass of the shower door.

I scream, obviously.

"Eden!" she yells, which is pretty unnecessary considering (a) she's already got my attention, and (b) it's not like there's anyone else in the shower she could be talking to but me.

I should say here that this is very un-Carolyn-like behavior, and it's that weirdness, more than the actual request, that makes me turn off the shower, open the door just enough to poke my dripping head out and demand, *"What?!"*

"Can you finish up and come downstairs, please?" she asks, back to her usual calm self, like this is just a normal, reasonable request.

"Why?"

"The police are here," she says. "They want to talk to you."

I feel my entire face drop, my eyes go wide. *"Why?"* I say again, more panicked this time.

"I think you know why," she says, which is terrifying. "I need you downstairs in five minutes, okay?"

I go to close the shower door again—partly out of obedience, but mostly so she can't see my face and whatever might be written across it—but Carolyn puts out a hand to stop me.

"Bonnie's mother is here too," she says, then lets the door slide closed, right in my stunned, guilty face.

I do know why. That's true.

Not because I was expecting them, or because I've done anything wrong, but because this morning I got this message from my best friend, Bonnie: **I'm doing it. I'm running away with**

Jack. EEEEEEKKK!!!!! Don't tell anyone! Talk later! Xxx And by "this morning," I mean at 4:17 a.m.

Okay, I realize this might sound a bit alarming out of context. Especially with the whole police-at-the-door thing. But when I read it a few hours after it was sent—bleary-eyed, still half asleep—I was just a bit confused, maybe a little annoyed, mostly because Bonnie and I had made plans to go to Canterbury today, and her unexpected bailing meant I was suddenly planless on a Saturday. She'd agreed that this would be our free day from studying, our chill-out day, practically the only time she's allowed in the ridiculously strict study schedule she's been sticking to since April. Our first exam of our GCSEs, the exams we've been working toward for the last five years, the exams that—apparently—will decide our futures, is on Wednesday. Four days away.

I replied just the way you might expect me to. **Huh?**

Can't talk right now, but I'll call later! Just say you haven't heard from me if anyone asks! I'm on an ADVENTURE! <3 xx

I didn't think for a minute that she really was running away, because that's just not something Bonnie would do, and even if it was, she's got no reason to leave. So I chalked her messages up to exaggeration—*maybe* she's staying out for the night with her secret boyfriend (more on him later) without telling her mother, at most—and put my energy into salvaging my Saturday.

I carried right on thinking that all morning, which is why, when her mother called Carolyn to ask if I'd heard from Bonnie, I said no, as promised.

"I thought the two of you had plans?" Carolyn asked, her hand cupping the phone to her chest.

"We did," I said. "But she changed them last night. Didn't say why."

"Last night?" Carolyn repeated.

"Yeah," I said.

"And you haven't heard from her since?"

"Nope," I said. I didn't think twice about lying for Bonnie. As far as I was concerned, she'd asked, and I'd agreed, and that was that. I didn't need any more details or context. A promise is a promise, and a best friend is a best friend. But I had to try to make it believable, and also get the attention away from me, so I added, "I wouldn't worry about it, though. She's probably with Jack."

Carolyn's eyebrows went up. "Who's Jack?"

"Her boyfriend," I said, telling myself that Bonnie could hardly expect Jack to stay a secret if she'd "run away" with him. "That's probably where she is," I added. "I'm sure she'll be back soon."

That's literally all I know about her secret boyfriend, by the way: his name, and the fact that he's a secret. I'd actually been sure "secret" was just Bonnie-speak for "imaginary," especially as I was never allowed to meet him, or even see a picture. But apparently not.

Thinking that made me a little uneasy, so I tried to call Bonnie to ask for more details on the whole running-away thing, but she didn't answer. I sent her a message—**You're okay, right?**—and it took her a few minutes but she finally replied: **More than okay. Don't worry! xx**

I relaxed, because there's no one I trust more than Bonnie, and if she says she's okay, then I know it's true.

So, I knew from this that Bonnie's absence had been noticed by her parents, which I thought was a bit weird, even then, because how could they know so quickly—and know enough to be so worried that they'd call Carolyn—that she'd even gone anywhere? But I didn't think about it for very long because, like I said, it's Bonnie, and Bonnie doesn't get into trouble. Not real trouble. And that's not an opinion—it's a fact.

Here are a few things about Bonnie Wiston-Stanley, aged fifteen and three-quarters:

- She likes to break candy bars into little pieces and stir them through vanilla ice cream.
- She's head prefect and everyone expects her to be head girl when she's eligible next year.
- She plays the flute, and not just in a has-to-because-her-parents-make-her way, but actually properly plays it, like with grades and everything.
- She wears glasses with thin brown frames.
- She has freckles, which she hates even though I think they suit her.

- She never used to wear makeup, not until a couple of months ago.
- She's the best, most steady, most reliable friend in the world.

I guess you'll want to know about me, too. What are a few things about me? Well, my name is Eden. Eden Rose McKinley, in full. I like plants and flowers and things I can grow with my hands. I was adopted when I was nine years old. I live in Kent. I have a boyfriend called Connor. I once got suspended for drawing mustaches on the portraits of the senior staff in the main entrance hall during a fire drill. My teachers call me "spirited" when they're trying to be nice, and "disruptive" when they're not. One day I'm going to get a tattoo of a dandelion on my shoulder. I used to have a recurring dream that I was being flown around in the beak of a pelican. I like cannoli better than anything else in the world. I'm not always as nice as I'd like to be.

There. Now you know about us both.

Anyway, so yes, I do know why the police have turned up at my doorstep, but I know it in a very basic, process-of-elimination way, not in a proper knowing way. For one thing, I've got no idea why the police are involved at all, and even less why they'd want to speak to me. Why would the police be involved in a teenage girl going off with her boyfriend for a bit without telling her mother? Since when is that a crime?

Shit, maybe I shouldn't have mentioned Jack. Maybe that's what this is all about. But I'd got so used to thinking of him as not real that even saying his name out loud hadn't quite felt real. She'd never told me anything concrete about him, never shown me a picture, even. Just given me tidbits vague enough that I'd assumed they were lies; *bad* lies, at that. How old is he? *Older.* How did you meet him? *A flute thing.* I'd figured she was jealous of Connor and me and had made up her own imaginary equivalent, and who was I to spoil that for her?

I know that might sound a bit unlikely, but Bonnie has been known to have a pretty wild imagination when it comes to things like boyfriends. It's like a combination of wish-fulfillment and too much fan fiction. When we were fourteen, she returned from summer camp full of stories about her new boyfriend, Freddie. I believed her, because why wouldn't I, and it took almost six months for me to finally catch on that the whole thing was basically a fantasy. Freddie was just a boy she'd had a crush on and then kissed on the last night of camp. Not exactly a love story.

So as far as I'd been concerned, "Jack" was either entirely imaginary or just a friend from orchestra or something that she *wanted* to be her boyfriend. Otherwise, why wouldn't I have met him?

I get out of the shower and head for my room, trying to get my head straight. It's not long after four, which means it's about twelve hours since Bonnie sent me her first message, and six since her mother started making calls. It doesn't seem like long enough to get so freaked out you'd get the police involved, but then, what do I know about parenthood?

I towel off in a kind of fast/slow hybrid, because I'm not sure whether I want to hurry up and get downstairs, as instructed, or put it off for as long as possible. I take my time toweling my hair, thinking back to everything I've done over the last twelve hours, just in case they ask.

The answer is, not much. I made French toast for my little sister, Daisy, because she's grounded at the moment for getting into trouble at school, and I felt sorry for her. It wasn't long after that when Carolyn started asking her questions about when I'd last spoken to Bonnie, and I'd figured it was a good idea to get out of the house, so I did. And by that, I mean I went to see my boyfriend. My lovely, non-secret boyfriend, Connor.

I tried to call him before I left, but he didn't answer, so I just sent him a text to let him know I was about to turn up on his doorstep. We have the kind of relationship where that kind of thing is okay, so I knew he wouldn't mind.

It took me about fifteen minutes to walk to Connor's house—we both live in Larking, which is a boring little market town in Kent—and he was already waiting in the doorway when I started walking up the drive. He was half dressed, his jeans hanging low, revealing a strip of blue boxers. He was shirtless, his hair sticking up at all angles, his eyes morning-blinky. But still he was grinning, his face lit up, like every time he sees me. When I took the step up to walk through the door, he leaned down and dropped a kiss on my lips. He tasted of peanut butter.

"Hey," I said. "You just got up?" This is unusual for Connor, who's usually up before seven a.m. every day of the week.

He shrugged. "I was up most of the night."

"Oh shit," I said. "Sorry."

"It's okay; everything's fine now."

"Um, what happened?" I wasn't sure how to ask this—or whether I even should—but he didn't seem annoyed.

"Mum had a fall," he said.

"Shit," I said again. Connor's mother has rheumatoid arthritis, and he's been her carer since he was eight. His gran lives with them and helps look after them both, even though she's in her seventies and probably needs more care than Connor does, nowadays.

"She's fine," he added. "I mean, not fine. But, you know, fine enough. We had to go to hospital, but it's nothing major, just a couple of fractures."

"A couple?" I repeated, horrified. I tried to remind myself that in Connor's house this qualifies as "nothing major." But I couldn't help but think of how *completely major* it would be if Carolyn had to spend half the night in hospital. I wouldn't shut up about it for weeks. But this didn't even warrant a text.

Connor smiled at me. "Just a couple," he said. "She's sleeping now. So's Gran."

"You can go back to sleep too," I said quickly. "I can go."

He shook his head. "No way. Stay, obviously." He leaned down to kiss me again—he's just taller enough than me that he has to lean when we kiss, which I love—and we stayed like that for a while, broken bones and runaway friends skittered from my mind.

Connor and I shouldn't be a perfect match. Him, the shy ginger kid, and me, the wild(ish), difficult one. But the thing about Connor is he isn't actually that shy at all. And I'm not wild or difficult, not really. Sometimes it just takes that one person to see beyond what everyone tells them they're meant to see.

Here are a few things about Connor Elliott, aged sixteen years and six months:

- He was bullied from Year 7 to Year 9, but he doesn't ever talk about it, even now.
- He loves birds and wants to be an ornithologist, and he's proud of this, not even slightly embarrassed, even though the other kids have always tried to make him be.
- He can tell what bird it is just by the sound it makes.
- He knows how to cook.
- He's dyslexic, like me, but he tries harder and he actually likes to read.
- He has blue eyes and hair the color of paprika.

- He broke his nose when he was nine and now it has a bump on it.
- His mum and gran say he's the best boy on the planet.
- I agree.

No one thought we would work, let alone last. But here we are, more than a year on, happy. We're like veterans of a teenage love story.

I didn't stay at Connor's long, because even though he tried to hide it he was clearly knackered. We spent a lazy couple of hours in his bedroom, watching TV, kissing and playing Portal, which is the only video game I ever agree to play with him, even though he insists it's old now and I should give some newer games a chance. Every now and then, he left to go check on his mother and gran—both still sleeping off the previous night's stresses—and to replenish our bowl of tortilla chips.

"I should go," I said finally, after he'd literally fallen asleep on my shoulder twice.

"Nah, stay," he started to say, but he broke into yet another massive yawn instead. When he was done he laughed, sheepish. "Okay, maybe I'm a bit tired. Don't go, though."

"I'll see you tomorrow," I suggested. "When you're a bit more awake."

He made a face like a little boy refusing a nap. "But you're here," he said. "It's a waste of Eden-time."

I rolled my eyes. "Go to sleep."

"Cuddle first?" he suggested, pulling back the covers and burrowing under them.

"You're so macho, Connor," I said. "I can't handle what a manly man you are."

He laughed, pulling me under the covers toward him. His skinny frame was warm and cozy, impossible to resist. Connor is comfortable with himself like no other boy our age I've ever met. Not in a loves-himself way, either. More like he has his priorities, and he knows what matters, and what matters isn't wasting energy on worrying that he isn't the model of masculinity. It's basically the thing that made me fall in love with him in the first place. That and the fact that warmth comes off him like a radiator in winter.

Anyway, that was it with Connor today. I didn't even tell him about Bonnie. I must have left his house sometime after two, come home, mooched for a bit, and then decided to have the proper long shower that Carolyn ended up interrupting.

And now here I am, in my room with the police downstairs waiting for me, stepping into my jeans and deciding that, yes, I'll carry on telling the small lie, as promised. I can't see what difference Bonnie's message from earlier would really make to anything, anyway, and I don't want Carolyn getting mad at me for lying to her this morning.

Carolyn's head appears around my bedroom door and I jump, almost tripping over my own feet.

"Are you nearly ready?" she asks.

"Let me just do my hair," I say.

"Eden," Carolyn says warningly.

The tone in her voice, together with the situation, makes me feel suddenly panicky. "Why do the police want to talk to me?" I demand. "I don't know where Bonnie is. I really don't!"

"They're not expecting you to know," Carolyn replies. "They just want to talk to you. And anyway, if you ask me, Bonnie's mother is the one you should be more concerned about. The woman's practically hysterical."

"Why do they think I'll know *anything*, though?"

"Because you're her best friend. God knows, if you disappeared, Bonnie is the first person I'd want to speak to."

"No, I mean, why are they freaking out like this? Why are the police even involved? She's probably just off with her boyfriend somewhere."

Carolyn lets out a little noise I can't interpret, and I frown at her, trying to get a reading. What is going on? None of this feels right.

"I know Bonnie's usually Miss Responsible, or whatever," I add. "So yeah, maybe it's a bit unusual. But not police-unusual."

Carolyn doesn't answer this, just glances behind her at the empty corridor and then back at me, raising her eyebrows in a silent *hurry up*. "The police are going to ask you why Bonnie has run away with Jack," she says.

"Why would I know—"

"There's no point in wasting your breath telling me," Carolyn breaks in. "You're just going to have to repeat yourself. So let's go downstairs and speak to the police, okay? I'll be right there, and you don't need to be nervous."

"I'm not nervous," I say, surprised.

Carolyn mutters something, which I think for a second might be *I am*, but she's already turning away and heading down the hall, so I follow.

There are two police officers waiting for me when we get downstairs. One is a man, gray and gruff, who does all the talking. The other is a woman, younger than Carolyn, who takes notes in almost total silence.

"There's no need to be nervous," the man says, after we're done with the introductions and preamble. His name is DC Delmonte, and it's making me think of peaches. "All we need from you is the truth."

"I don't know anything," I say. Actually, I've already said this four times. No one seems to be listening.

Matilda, Bonnie's mother—who's never liked me, by the way—let's out a loud "hmm."

"I don't!" I insist.

"Just tell us what you *do* know," DC Delmonte says. "Even the things that may seem . . . insignificant. When did Bonnie meet Jack?"

"I don't know," I say.

"Well, how long have they been in a relationship?"

"I don't know," I say.

"Did Bonnie ask for your assistance in keeping their relationship a secret?"

"What? No. Why would she?"

"Have you spoken to her today?"

"No." WhatsApp messages don't count as speaking, do they?

"Did you speak to her yesterday?"

"Yes. But just to talk about studying."

"Did you talk about Jack?"

"No." Why are they so obsessed with Jack? Is this all because I mentioned his name to Carolyn this morning?

They're all looking at me like they're waiting for me to say something very specific, but I have no idea what it is. It's like having an inside joke described to me by the group of people it involves in painstaking detail, and everyone's waiting for my reaction to the punch line.

"What the hell is going on?" I ask finally.

"Eden," Carolyn says, her voice straining with the clear effort of staying calm. "Do you know who Jack *is*?"

There's a tense, potent silence. I can hear Bonnie's mother's labored breathing, her eyes brimming and rage-filled. The policewoman has her head tilted slightly, concentration in the lines of her face, and I get the unnerving sense that she's profiling me, or something.

"No," I say, and I hear how small my voice is in the room,

shrunken by adult voices, strident and loud. And, suddenly, I'm scared.

"It's Jack Cohn," Carolyn says.

"Who?" I ask. My brain is too frazzled, too anxious to process the information. I don't know anyone called Jack Cohn.

"For God's sake!" Bonnie's mother shrieks in a sudden burst of frustration, so unexpectedly that I actually jump. She takes a step toward me and I shrink back. Why is she so angry at *me*? I'm not the one who's disappeared. "Just tell us where they are, Eden!"

And that's the moment that Carolyn says it, and everything I thought I knew shatters. "*Mr.* Cohn, Eden," she says. "Jack is Mr. Cohn."

An image pops into my head, then. Waiting in the music block for Bonnie to finish her flute lesson. Leaning against the whitewashed wall, my head resting underneath a nameplate. MR. J. COHN: HEAD OF MUSIC.

Mr. Cohn, music teacher. Mr. Cohn, full-grown adult man.

Mr. Cohn, my best friend's secret boyfriend.

Holy. Shit.

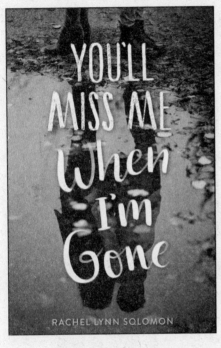